LEAVING
Patrick

LEAVING
Patrick

PRUE LEITH

THOMAS DUNNE BOOKS
ST. MARTIN'S GRIFFIN ⚏ NEW YORK

THOMAS DUNNE BOOKS.
An imprint of St. Martin's Press.

LEAVING PATRICK. Copyright © 1999 by Prue Leith. All rights reserved.
Printed in the United States of America. No part of this book may be
used or reproduced in any manner whatsoever without written permission except in the case of brief quotations embodied in critical arti-
cles or reviews. For information, address St. Martin's Press, 175 Fifth
Avenue, New York, N.Y. 10010.

www.stmartins.com

Library of Congress Cataloging-in-Publication Data

ISBN 0-312-28258-3 (hc)
ISBN 0-312-31118-4 (pbk)

First published in Great Britain by Penguin Books,
an imprint of the Penguin Group

First U.S. Edition: November 2001
First St. Martin's Griffin Edition: March 2003

10 9 8 7 6 5 4 3 2 1

For Rayne

ACKNOWLEDGMENTS

When I determined to write this book, I expected friends and professionals alike to tell me to stick to writing cookbooks, but no one did. I have been astonished at the encouragement from all quarters, so I have a host of people to thank.

Top of the list is my husband, whose only reservation was his fear that our son and daughter would be embarrassed by the sexy bits. Meanwhile said son and daughter feared their father would be embarrassed by the sexy bits.

Then there is the Arvon Foundation whose four-day novel-writing course started me off, and particularly my tutor Denise Neuhaus. Then my agent Pat Kavanagh from Peters, Fraser and Dunlop, who told me firmly that the first draft would not do—she was right—and Julia Bell from The Literary Consultancy, who made great suggestions for getting it right.

On the nitty-gritty side I must thank Gilli Shaw, Claire Maurice and Sydney Kentridge QC for advice on legal offices and cases; Ram Gidoomal for checking the manuscript for boo-boos in the Indian part of the story; Peter Verstappen and Penny Colston for help with Stella's American slang; Nick Tarayan for his wine expertise; Dr. Jill Barling for warning me that an early medical plot would not wash, and Kate Wiggins, Lucy Ellerington and Toppy Wharton, who were my twenty-something test readers, and who fixed my typos.

And finally Louise Moore, my editor at Penguin, who was unequivocally enthusiastic and constructive, made me sign a two-book deal and came up with the title.

PROLOGUE

Jane stood in the bleak gray of Terminal One, her brief-case and computer hanging from her slight shoulders as she rummaged in her handbag for her telephone. Her long hair, shiny and dark, slithered forward as she bent her head, covering her face and impeding her search. Her thin fingers scrabbled blind for the cellphone's familiar shape. Bingo. Extracting it care-fully, she shook back her hair, revealing an oval face with a high forehead over far-apart brows and deep green eyes. Her nose was straight and a little bony, but was compensated for by a sensuous mouth, and a clear Celtic complexion. A good-looking thirty-something face, but right now lacking animation or beauty.

Holding the telephone in her right palm she pressed the but-tons with the practiced thumb of the same hand. *No signal*. She walked to the smeary plate glass, and faced the wet tarmac. *Net-work busy*. She kept trying as her gaze swung back to the Arrivals Hall. The luggage carousel was unmoving and empty, the wait-ing passengers stoical, like refugees.

God, this place is soulless, she thought, and I spend half my life here.

Her shoulders ached, and she lowered her laptop and brief-case to the floor, trapping them upright between her calves. Then she dumped her handbag, heavy with her survival kit of make-up, Filofax, calculator, spare tights and purse, next to them and flexed her shoulders, luxuriating in a kind of tired pain. Her new shoes hurt. She slipped one foot out for a moment of blissful relief, knowing it would hurt even more when she pushed it back.

1

Retrying. Calling. Connecting. "Jane's Restaurant. Good evening."

"Oh, Silvino. It's Jane. Is Patrick still there?"

"No, he's left. But he told me to tell you he's gone to have supper at Theodora's. He said he'll expect you there."

"But it's only 10 p.m. And it's Friday. Aren't you busy?"

"Sadly, no. It's been very quiet."

"OK. Thanks, Silvino. See you soon."

At last the six-inch-thick brown-wrapped parcel of legal papers wobbled into sight in the middle of the carousel, teetered on the cusp, and bumped down to join the circling bags and cases. She had difficulty in getting hold of it. There was nothing to grab on to. No one helped her, and she had to let it go.

But on its second circuit, she managed it. Then she had to sling her laptop carrier and her bulging briefcase over her shoulder again, pick up her handbag and clutch the documents against her chest. Between them all, she felt like an undersized packhorse. I give in, she thought. From now on, stuff looking good. I'll get one of those old ladies' bags on wheels.

It took twenty minutes in the line to get a taxi.

"Primrose Hill Studios, NW1," she said. Until she gave the driver her address, she had intended to go to Theodora's. But suddenly she wasn't in the mood for restaurateurs' talk. She didn't want to see Patrick putting on a brave face about falling covers, or hear anyone raving about anyone else's new place.

And the fact was, she realized, she wanted to have the house to herself. To get back before Patrick did. To get these bloody shoes off, pour a large whiskey and have Benedicat sitting on the edge of her bath, sticking a curious paw into the bubbles and purring like a steam train. Then she thought, God, how middle-aged. Have I got to the stage when a hot bath, a drink and the company of a cat beckon louder than dinner with my husband?

She excused herself with the thought that the legal papers were confidential, and she'd probably forget them at Theodora's. She'd taken enough of a risk checking them in for the flight. And

2

besides, when she was tired she got ratty, and Patrick had enough troubles without a snappy wife. She was going home for his sake as much as hers.

And it had been one hell of a week. She'd spent Monday briefing Counsel about the Hong Kong case. It was a nightmare. It involved shipping agents, carriers and insurers in Shanghai, Hong Kong and London. Then because Junior Counsel had been ill on Monday, she'd had to do it all again for him on Tuesday.

Then on Wednesday she'd flown to Glasgow about another case, and not got back until midnight. On Thursday she'd left the house at 6:30, while Patrick was still asleep. At 10 p.m. she was about to leave her desk, now satisfyingly cleared of paperwork, when her New York client came on the line about a possible appeal in the tanker insurance case.

Patrick had been asleep when she got home, and there was a note on her pillow. "What do you look like? Please leave photo."

And today had been just awful.

She didn't much like Giles Charteris, her clever but pompous senior partner, and she'd had the whole day with him. It had started badly when her heel came off on the escalator. Giles was irritated.

"You can't buy another pair of shoes now. The flight's been called."

"Of course I can. I've got ten minutes. I can't hobble into the client's boardroom on this." She held up a trim black shoe, the high heel hanging off the sole.

"God. Women. Why do you wear such ridiculous things anyway?"

"Because, dear Giles, you guys like them. And *you* made the rule about no women in trousers at Chalkers. I could have worn boots with trousers."

She'd given him her wide smile and said, "I'll catch up with you. Can you grab me a *Financial Times*?"

She'd bought the first pair of shoes she tried. They were

3

navy suede with leather piping around the edge, and were high enough to make her thin legs look longer and more shapely than they were. She looked more than a skinny 5'4". She'd done a quick twirl in front of the mirror, noticing with satisfaction that the red and navy hound's-tooth suit with its short skirt and long jacket gave her both a businesslike and a feminine air. Pleased with herself for being so decisive, and looking forward to proving to Giles that shopping for shoes could be done in five minutes, she tendered her Amex card and dumped the old shoes in the shop's bin, an action she now regretted. They had been expensive, and comfortable, and they could have been fixed. But there wasn't space for them in her briefcase, and she hadn't wanted to cart a carrier bag all over Paris.

She imagined Patrick saying, only half teasing, "Can't a beautiful, clever, top lady lawyer be seen with a carrier bag? Even a designer one? Don't Bally have elegant bags with rope handles that would go with your pinstripes?" His tone would be affectionate, and he'd probably kiss her as he said it, but the criticism would be there.

The new shoes were torture. Another reason not to go to Theodora's.

Patrick watched Theodora's around chins crease together as she concentrated on ladling out the cassoulet. A warm wave of affection for his friend and the rich smell of pork and beans enfolded him like a blessing.

When everyone was served, Theodora lifted her apron carefully over her head to avoid any further depredations to her hairdo. Half a dozen hairpins had already been lost in the rush of the service, and her gray chignon was now in danger of collapse. Theodora's barely lined sixty-year-old face was flushed from an evening of fast and hot work, and she sat down heavily next to Patrick. She looked at him intently for a moment, thinking that he had a country-boy look about him for all his, what, forty years. More like a big Somerset farmer than an ex-army officer and a businessman. His hair was cut conventionally, but it was unruly, flopping over his forehead in thick, light brown curls. He had a square, open face which spoke of intelligence and integrity, and hazel-green eyes, lined at the corners.

She said, "Well, I'm glad you're smiling now. You looked worried to death when you came in. What's up?"

"Oh, nothing. Or nothing that a few hundred more customers wouldn't cure." He smiled to lighten the admission, turn it into a joke.

She smiled back, and said, "Snap. It's been slow here too." He knew she was lying, but was grateful. She stretched her large plump arm across the table to pat his hand with a stroking motion.

"And where is the lovely Jane?" she asked.

"Last seen heading for Paris. But she should come on here. I left a message for her."

"Good. She needs feeding. She's very thin, Patrick."

Patrick smiled and nodded. But he was thinking that, though his beautiful wife certainly needed something, it wasn't feeding. He was suddenly tempted to tell Theodora that she, like everyone else, had it all wrong; that he and Jane were not a model couple; that the present rocky patch showed signs of turning into an unclimbable mountain. That Jane had become a drivingly ambitious woman with no time left for him.

As Theodora turned to hurry the waiter slicing ficelles on the servery guillotine, he closed his eyes and substituted Jane for Theodora, a brood of children for the tableful of friends and restaurateurs, and a country kitchen for the Soho restaurant. It was a familiar fantasy, but silly. Jane did not want children. Or to live in the country.

But Serge and Theodora have something Jane and I lack, he thought. They know what's important. Theodora's was closed on Sundays and Mondays, because they wanted time to themselves. They took last orders at 10 p.m., because they thought two sittings uncivilized, and they liked to eat after the service.

5

Like most restaurateurs, Serge fed his staff at 6 p.m. to forestall hungry waiters nicking the petits fours, but he and Theodora always ate late. They had the same supper the staff had eaten earlier, usually something like spaghetti bolognaise or chicken stew made with the giblets and legs (the breasts having gone to the customers) or sausage hot-pot. And anyone was welcome.

So from 11 p.m. on week nights, later on Fridays and Saturdays, Theodora and Serge's friends in the business would drift in for a nightcap or for something to eat. If the restaurant was still full, Theodora would shoo them upstairs to their flat, with a bottle to be getting on with. As often as not, Serge's old mother, or their daughter and son-in-law, or a friend from abroad, would be there.

As soon as the service was over, they would all clatter down to the restaurant, where every inch told of indifference to fashion but a care for comfort. The curtains were heavy and velvet and had faded from red to rusty brown. The padded mahogany chairs were graceless, solid and comfortable. The walls, once cream, had aged to a yellow born of crêpes Suzette made at the table and cigar smoke. But little of their paint was visible. From dado to picture rail, the walls were covered in dark oil paintings, family photographs and framed certificates testifying to the qualifications of some long-gone chef or sommelier.

An old, noisy Gaggia machine hissed on the bar, and thick dark green octagonal cups were stacked upside down upon it, keeping warm. The heavy old-fashioned knives and forks were honorably scarred, but buffed to a deep shine; the linen was white, the napkins enormous. They came from France. Theodora said no English supplier knew what a proper table napkin was for—they thought they were making hankies.

Patrick watched Theodora's napkin ritual with admiration. She snapped open the starched cloth with a jerk, then tucked one corner deeply into her garnet necklace. She spread the cloth across her chest, tucking the sides under her arms and carefully covering her lap. She was preparing for pleasure, and pleasure was a serious business.

"Serge, come *tout de suite*. We are drinking the Volnay, and the cassoulet will be cold."

Patrick looked around the table, at the great white soup plates of cassoulet, the gleaming amalgam of beans, duck, sausage and pork commanding the concentrated attention of the diners. Even Lou, a garrulous wine-merchant who seemed to live on alcohol and cigarettes, fell silent and reached for a fork as Theodora pushed a plateful at him.

In the middle of the table was a stainless-steel kitchen bowl of lamb's lettuce. Two curled fists of leaves bounced out of the bowl as Serge plunged his cook's spoons, doing duty for salad servers, in at the sides. He tossed them back with his fingers and deftly turned the salad—enough to give a shine to every leaf but not to bruise them. The ceiling spotlight caught the sheen and doubled it to a glowing radiating green.

The lengths of french bread, flaking and crusty, deposited their crumbs on the white tablecloth. Two open bottles of Burgundy stood in the middle of a clutch of classic wine glasses: 12 oz long-stemmed, round-bellied goblets made of thin rimless clear glass, polished to perfection.

It's a painting by Chardin, thought Patrick, or at least a photo-shoot for a *Sunday Times* mag. And yet it was entirely artless. The appeal lay in its wholesomeness, its lack of pretension.

"Theodora. When I eat with you, I remember why I wanted to be a restaurateur. It was to give people this sort of pleasure. You are Earth Mother, and Serge is a great chef."

Serge, his mouth full of bread, shook his head. "*Ça, non,*" he said. "I learned cooking from my mother and my grandmother. Great chefs start in hotel school. They do *haute cuisine*. I only know low cuisine."

"Was your father in the restaurant business? Did he cook?"

"No, he was a *garagiste*, and he taught me to fix cars and to play chess. But he died, and the women couldn't fix cars, so they turned the garage into a restaurant. *Et voilà.*"

Patrick thought of the chessboard upstairs, and the ongoing match that engaged Serge and his eleven-year-old grandson. And Theodora's passion for antique silver, shared with her daughter. He'd heard them planning to trawl the Kempton Park stalls tomorrow at dawn and to do Bermondsey market on Friday.

He thought, they have a life, that's what.

When Patrick got home, he undressed without switching on the light, settling his clothes on the Edwardian valet-stand Jane had given him years ago: he put his tan wool jacket around the smooth shoulders of polished elm, folded his fawn twill trousers neatly at the crease then hung them over the straight bar at the top, and put his shoes side by side on the rack underneath. He told himself that he couldn't be too drunk if he could perform this routine with such economy of movement and in absolute silence. But then he thought, the very fact that I'm trying so hard means I am distinctly drunk. Must have had a bottle and a half of that Volnay. But Theodora does that to you. She's so warm and welcoming and relaxing. Restorative, like a whiskey toddy.

In the bathroom he saw his note about the photo lying on Jane's make-up tray. For a second he wanted to wake her up and say, "Look, lady. This note required an answer. Even a scribbled kiss would have done." But then he thought of the bulging briefcase and the laptop left recharging in the hall, and forgave her. She works harder than I do, he thought. But how long can we go on like this? It's crazy.

He cleaned his teeth with his old toothbrush—the electric one would wake Jane—and returned to the bedroom. He slipped into the bed beside her, and leaned over her to kiss her cheek. She murmured a contented mmmm, and snuggled further into the bed. Away from him, he noted. She pulled the duvet round her as she burrowed. Preventive wrapping, thought Patrick.

Patrick had been drinking double espressos with Theodora, and now he could not sleep. He tried to tell himself that night thoughts, black thoughts, were not to be trusted. In the morning both he and Jane would be cheerful and loving.

But in his heart he knew they'd failed. Sooner or later it would be over.

ONE

Jane eyed the short length of threadbare rug covering two concrete steps, both cracked, into Delhi station, and said, "Red Carpet Welcome indeed." She read aloud from the leaflet in her hand: " 'An unforgettable train-journey into the Orient, cushioned by the luxury of the Rajahs.' "

"Oh, I don't know," replied Sally. "In a country where most of the population is starving, luxury is bound to be relative. I think it's rather quaint." And she took a photograph of the sign above the door. Hanging off its hinges and with a pane missing, its neon tube illuminated the words:

RECEPTION
Maharajah Express

I've made a serious mistake, thought Jane, doubts clutching at her like indigestion.

Would she and Sally survive each other's company for a fortnight? What if Sally snored? Worse, what if *she* snored? Could they peaceably share a sleeper each night and a table each evening, sit amicably side by side in tour coaches, in rickshaws and, for all she knew, on camels and elephants?

She liked and admired her sister-in-law. The attraction of opposites perhaps. Big-boned, healthy, sensible Sally was *solid,* and free of surprises. She voted Tory, read the *Telegraph,* shopped at Jaeger and repeatedly prevented Tom, her husband (Jane's brother and Member of Parliament for Stratford), from writing letters to *The Times* about bleeding hearts and woolly liberalism.

But two weeks of Sally? Of her bossiness, of her mothering, of her brisk cheerfulness? She knew Sally thought her flighty, extravagant, willful. She knew too that Sally saw this holiday as medicine for Jane's emotional woes, and believed it her job to see that Jane took, and enjoyed, the medicine. Sally might use the enforced intimacy to try and "make her see sense" and go back to Patrick. Jane both wanted Sally's re-assuring good sense and feared it would drive her mad.

By the time the eighty-odd passengers, pressed together in the comparative warmth of the waiting room, or toughing it out on the chilly platform, were summoned for "Welcome Check-In," Sally had worked out how matters could be better handled.

"What they should do," she said, "is make a proper fuss of us on arrival. They should have handsome fellows in British Raj uniforms bowing us out of our taxis and into our carriages, don't you think? Or maybe hostesses in saris putting those marigold garlands around our necks."

Jane did not agree, and didn't answer. She looked at their fellow travelers with apprehension. Big confident-looking Germans wearing Berghaus jackets and hiking boots. Loud Americans. Japanese with more cameras than luggage. She thought, every one a national stereotype. I don't want anything to do with any of them—which I suppose makes me a stereotypical Brit.

Sally was still reordering matters. "Honestly, Jane, we should not have to hang around like this. The proper place to meet one's fellow travelers is in the bar-car over a gin and tonic. First impressions count, and they could do so much better, so easily. We should write to Cox and Kings."

Jane's thoughts were less constructive. She was mourning her Donna Karan jacket, which was now smeared with axle grease or engine oil from sitting on a station trolley of some sort. The brochure had given her the idea that the Maharajah Express was India's answer to the Orient Express, requiring casual under-stated elegance. So she'd bought the light cream coat and had her hair cut by Nicky Clarke, Mayfair's most fashionable, and expensive, hairdresser.

Now such personal polishing made her uneasy. Even in London she'd felt uncomfortable dropping 50 pence into a homeless youth's hat before stepping into the perfumed air of Nicky's salon. But with a mixture of flattery and bullying, Nicky had talked her into a cut that, shorter at the back than the front, exposed her thin nape, while letting the sides fall forward to frame her face. It made her look both vulnerable and sophisticated. She'd loved it.

Now she was cross with herself over both coat and hairdo. It wasn't so much the expense. Nicky's bill had been astronomical, but she could afford it, and God knows she worked hard enough. But she suspected she was play-acting, aspiring to belong to some jet set. How *could* she have been so daft as to have her hair (which up to now she'd managed with a bottle of shampoo and an occasional rubber band) cut so as to require a hair-drier, curling brush, mousse and frequent visits to the crimper?

And she'd known as she bought it that the coat wasn't practical. The combination of cashmere and silk, heavy but soft, hung with the swirl of a cape from her slight shoulders. In the fitting room at Black's she'd felt like a model in a commercial. But now the silent, staring semi-circle of Indian travelers, wrapped in blankets and holding string-tied bundles, unnerved her. They don't know this coat cost enough to feed a family for a year, thought Jane. But I wish I'd come in an anorak, like the Germans. No, I don't, but I should have brought my old riding jacket.

A female voice, high-pitched and monotone, obtruded. "I always get them down to ten percent of their first price—I got ten of these bracelets for a hundred rupees, and the fellow started off at a thousand, didn't he, Elmer?" The young American woman raised her voice in an attempt to include Sally and Jane, and pushing up the sleeve of her Day-Glo pink tracksuit, displayed a suntanned arm festooned with inlaid brass bracelets, all identical.

Sally smiled and looked away. Jane pretended she hadn't heard. For the first time in her life, she was embarrassed to be white, and embarrassed to be a tourist. She did not like feeling lumped together with the American woman and the timid Elmer; with the heavy German videoing the Indians with their bundles as though filming animals in a wildlife park; with the bearded Scot tormenting the young Indian in the Cox and Kings uniform.

"Laddie, I distinctly asked for a non-smoking carriage. A non-smoking compartment is no' the same thing." He stabbed the ticket with his finger.

"Please, sir. The salon at the end of the carriage is also non-smoking. You will most certainly not be at all inconvenienced by the smoking of tobacco. Not a bit of it."

"Och, but we will be. The other compartments are smoking compartments, are they no'? This ticket says 'Carriage: Non-smoking,' does it no'? The reek o' smoke will be all through the corridors, everywhere. Laddie, we want a non-smoking carriage."

The unhappy travel rep tried again. "The ill-advised misuse of the word carriage will be brought to the attention of Head Office. And I will make immediate amends. I will ask the other passengers in the carriage to be so obliging as not to indulge in tobacco in the corridors, but to confine their fumigation to the compartments."

The Scot would not be amused, and would not be mollified. I don't believe this man, thought Jane, and lit a Marlboro from the pack that was never to have been opened, the one that was to prove she'd given up.

At last they were in the train, and in the care of Umesh. Umesh, short, very dark, thick-bearded and with a turban boasting a tail down his back to his knees, announced himself, with a bow and a *namaste*, as their personal boy, their servant. Jane

13

didn't like either word, but told herself that if you pay £2,000 for a trip on the Maharajah Express, you cannot object to mem-sahib treatment. And Umesh was wonderful: unobsequious and dignified, but reassuringly efficient. He supervised their luggage, requested orders for tea ("or whiskey, or what-you-like"), informed them they would like the train very much, and told them to summon him any time, day or night.

He should give us a lamp to rub, thought Jane.

Jane was feeling better, soothed by the nannying of Umesh and aided by the Indian "claret" at dinner and the pleasant rocking of the bar-car. Dinner had been surprisingly good despite an ominous menu that offered a choice of "Imperial English Cuisine" and "The Maharajah's Table of Delights." It had proved fruitless asking for the Indian menu, because the stewards brought all the dishes, English or Indian, as the cooks produced them, and did their best to get a spoonful of everything onto everyone's plate. But their determination was no match for Sally's and, on behalf of them both, she had managed to refuse the greasy roast chicken, frozen vegetables in thick white sauce and leathery potatoes, and they had dined very well on a succession of mild curries and excellent pilau.

Feeling mellow, the two women were now in the bar-car. Jane, in an ornate armchair, faced Sally across a Benares brass table, the top a around shiny tray.

"Would you mind if we joined you? I'm Lucy."

Sally looked up, apprehensive. Then, relieved at Lucy's middle-class Englishness, she made room on the little brocade sofa. Lucy, tall and thin, fortyish, with pale freckled skin and prematurely gray hair pinned back with two tortoiseshell combs, sat down. She was wearing a black cotton jersey dress, its scoop neck underlining a heavy silver necklace. Her sun-tanned feet were in rope-soled espadrilles. Jane liked her immediately.

"And that's my husband John getting the drinks. I think we four are the only Brits on this train, at least the only four who can talk to each other. We tried talking to the bearded Scot and his wife, but he doesn't talk to smokers, and John smokes. And I'm not up to international relations just yet."

John steered his rounded bulk with surprising grace between the tables, leaning first one way, then the other to counteract the train's lurching, and put a tray of four beers on the coffee table.

"I hope you like Kingfisher," he said. "Beer is the only booze that's affordable in this country."

"Beer's perfect," said Jane. "And so deftly served! You must be a tightrope walker."

"Worked as a guard on South African Railways once." He beamed from Jane to Sally and back. "But I was younger and thinner then." He patted his sloping diaphragm without embarrassment. "I love trains. All trains. Even Hornby train sets and the Bluebell line. Isn't this fun?" And he swung a gilt-edged armchair around from an adjoining table and sat on it.

Jane, catching his mood, thought with some surprise, yes, it is. It is fun.

Sally made the introductions, clearly and fast, as if addressing an audience, "I'm a boring housewife, mother and Tory wife. We live in Tom's constituency in Warwickshire, and I do all the Tory wife things—fundraisers, fêtes, Pony Club, the garden and sewing on name-tapes. This is Jane, my high-flying sister-in-law. She's a partner in a fancy London firm of solicitors, and is the world authority on shipping insurance, or how not to pay out for skulduggery, piracy, scuttling and dumping at sea."

"Heavens," said John. "If you produce information at that lick, we'll have nothing left to tell each other by tomorrow."

"Oh, Lord," said Lucy, "two solicitors, what bad luck. John's a lawyer too, for all he wants to pass himself off as a train buff."

With relief they settled into a comfortable exploratory conversation, carefully weighing each other up, and admitting to themselves, though not to each other, that they might stick together, and so avoid the necessity of mixing with anyone else.

"I think the truth is that we took this package because we

were frightened of India, of the poverty or of getting food poisoning. We wanted insulating. But now I think a fortnight with this lot might be worse," said Jane.

"Oh, I don't agree," replied John. "That cantankerous Scottish professor might be interesting once he relaxes, and his wife looks a good soul. I wonder what he's professor of?"

Sally answered, "Sociology, I bet. Probably ethnic studies or gender issues. And it will be an ex-poly, not a proper university. Real profs aren't called prof very often, and if they are, they don't stick it on their compartment door."

"Oh, Sally." Jane laughed. "You are becoming as stuffy as my brother. Poor fellow, just because he objects to the dreaded weed and has got a beard. But his wife is terrified of the whole adventure. She's brought two suitcases of bottled water from Strathclyde. They must feel absolute fools. You can get bottled water anywhere."

"What you say is correct." The sudden interruption came from the thickset suntanned German who had been filming the Indians on the platform. He leaned across the aisle from the table where he sat with a youngish, safari-suited man. His English was only slightly accented but he spoke, Jane thought, too loud, as if he expected to be challenged. "But you are not able to guarantee the food, not even on this train. I have inspected the kitchen. It is not hygienic. There is nothing wrapped up or covered over. Johann and I, we have brought all our food with us, for two weeks. We will not be foolish. Why pay so much money for your holiday, and spend all night with your head in the toilet bowl?"

Jane, offended by the image, rose to the bait. "That's mad. Why come to India at all . . ."

John interrupted, rising to his feet, and extending a hand to the speaker with a wide smile that included Johann.

"How nice to meet you. I'm John. Lucy, my wife. Sally. Jane. And you are?"

"He's Hans. Hans Engleman." Johann said quickly. His relief

16

at John's intervention was obvious. "We are from Frankfurt."

His English was unaccented, his voice soft. Looking with affection at Hans he continued, "Hans is very cautious, but I have hopes that we will graduate from dried food reconstituted in boiling water to something comparatively safe. Like hot vegetarian curries, *ja?*" He smiled the question at Hans. Hans did not return the look.

"Not a chance," he said.

The conversation continued, John steering the talk to safe topics like how badly English football fans behave in Germany. Jane slowly sipped her Kingfisher and watched the Germans over her glass. Hans was attractive in a rather obvious way. His bulk was more muscle than fat, and his skin had a ski-slope tan. He was probably only forty but his blond hair was beginning to thin, giving him a deep forehead. He wore metal square-framed specs behind which his pale blue eyes seemed, perhaps, larger than they were. He wore an immaculately ironed light blue shirt, open at the neck, a gold signet ring and a Rolex. He looked, thought Jane, European and expensive without appearing flashy. A confident, powerful man.

Johann was very different. He was slight, and wore an olive green cardigan over a white silk polo. He had short curly black hair, a thin good-looking face with deep-set brown eyes and a full mouth. But his chin was weak. And he seemed nervous. His hands darted to light John's cigarette or to top up Hans's drink like a waiter on his first job, thought Jane. It's obvious who is master here. Hans is a bully. I wonder if they are out of the closet?

The men talked first football and then work—Johann was in advertising, Hans in machine-tool manufacturing. Lucy and Sally talked children, Sally boasting of her three daughters' horsey and hockey achievements, Lucy wryly deprecating her eleven-year-old twin boys: "One is a young fogey, determined to get me to dress properly and his father to swap our battered old Suzuki for a Range Rover or something that will raise his status at school. The other is so dreamy he wouldn't notice if I arrived wearing a nightie and driving a truck." Jane, who sensed both women were missing their children already, felt smugly child-free. They moved on to houses, gardens and holidays. Jane, who so seldom had time for "woman-talk," was enjoying herself.

Lucy said, "This trip is my fortieth birthday present, and I'm going to blow a heap of money on entirely frivolous things. Like rugs or bedspreads or junky jewelry. John is into culture and history and will spend forever in the museums and palaces. But I'm for the bazaar."

"And I'm for bed," said Sally. "Tomorrow it's Jaipur, and we have to have breakfast at eight. And Jane, you wanted to wash your hair. Shall we go?"

Jane, like a bossed-about child, was about to protest, then thought, she's right. If I have another beer I'll get a hangover and a reputation as a boozer. So they said their goodbyes, real smiles for Lucy and John, more hesitant ones for Hans and Johann, and made their lurching way to their compartment.

At the end of each carriage, and at the start of the next, they had to negotiate the train servants' sleeping areas: narrow bunks had been let down in unlikely spaces, and on each one was a young man asleep, reading or just smoking. Without their uniforms and turbans they looked scruffy and a little frightening. But those who were still awake, leapt up as Sally and Jane passed, put their hands together with a bow, and said a polite "Goodnight, madam" without a hint of resentment at having their privacy so invaded. At the start of their carriage Umesh sat on his bunk with another young man, smoking, Jane was sure, marijuana.

Umesh leapt up at once, and in one movement passed his cigarette to his friend and swung his turban onto his head. He followed them to their door.

"A nightcap, madam? Some tea perhaps?"

As they assured him, no, no, they were fine, so sorry to have disturbed you, Jane wondered, with a suppressed giggle, what he'd say if they asked for a couple of ganja joints.

She tried to explain to Sally what was amusing her, but it was hopeless. Sally had never smoked marijuana in her life, hadn't recognized the smell, didn't believe the young men could possibly have been doing so, and thought Jane's interest in the matter dangerous.

In the bathroom, Jane concentrated on the "facilities." She abandoned an attempt to put her washbag or its contents on the already crowded little shelf over the basin, and put it on the floor. The cupboard, a cheap wall-mounted medicine chest, was already full of toilet-paper rolls—at least ten of them. A precaution for fragile Western guts, she supposed. The paper-holder on the wall was a bit of bent wire, and threaded on to it were two further rolls. The lavatory had a plastic seat, rather loose. The antiquated geyser above the sit-down shower reminded her of her bedsit days. The tiles, with their crude decorative border, were unevenly stuck on three walls, the fourth being covered in beige formica. The floor was tiled too, with large rough tiles, sloping towards the shower end.

Jane studied it all with amused satisfaction. She was glad the train was not glamorous and international, with deep-pile toweling bathrobes, Roger & Gallet soap and a decorator's color scheme. The bathroom was, after all, as clean as a whistle. There was soap (unwrapped and unbranded) in the soapdish, the loo flushed with enthusiasm and the geyser produced, with a lot of noise, spluttering hot water.

She sat, naked, on the little plastic stool, a four-gallon bucket of hot water between her knees, and soaped herself and shampooed her hair. She then used the two-pint plastic jug to sloosh great streams of water over her. I prefer this to an English shower, she thought. No chilly edges or sudden changes of temperature. And the rocking of the train made the whole thing an adventure. It was exciting to be doing something as ordinary as washing her hair as the train roared through the countryside.

Later, when Sally emerged from her turn in the bathroom,

Jane found herself giving Sally's shoulders, solid under the quilted dressing-gown, a hug as she said, "It's all right, you know. I won't go off the rails and run away with Umesh or anything." Sally looked serious.

"I know you won't do that," she said. "But you might do something just as irresponsible. The fact is, whether you admit it or not, you are in a classically vulnerable, unstable state. Separation is quite as traumatic as divorce. More so sometimes, because it doesn't have the clarity of decision."

"Oh, Sally, I love you. You are such a solid citizen," said Jane, laughing.

Neither of them could sleep. The train rocked and rattled at what seemed like breakneck speed. So much so that their bodies, thrown from side to side, built up a momentum that had them bumping into the compartment walls on one side and in danger of falling out of bed the other.

Sally lay in bed working out that if the beds had been intelligently installed at right angles to the track, like they are in a British sleeper, the side-to-side lurching of the train would have little or no effect. She determined to get Umesh to move the beds in the morning, if they were not built-in. She felt around the edge and discovered that her bed, anyway, was free-standing. She then applied her mind to the concurrent problems of bedside table and reading lights that such rearrangement would bring in its wake.

Jane didn't mind that she couldn't sleep. She loved the movement of the train. It was both comforting, like being a child in a rocking cradle, and exciting. She snuggled under the bedclothes, which were light and warm with a soft, clean-smelling cotton sheet against her bare legs and under her cheek and chin. I do believe, she thought, that I am, at this moment anyway, *happy*. When was I last happy? Certainly not since leaving Patrick. Not in the months, maybe years, before. Always guilty about leaving work in time to catch Patrick before he left for the restaurant, or guilty at sneaking out my briefcase at weekends. Well, I don't feel guilty now. I feel free, excited, maybe reckless. Six hours ago I was sure this trip would be a disaster. Now I'm sure it will be wonderful. Sally's right. I must be unstable.

TWO

For four months, ever since the night he'd come home to find her gone, Patrick had been trying not to think about Jane, and had mostly succeeded. But now the knowledge that she was miles away, and on holiday, plagued him.

Their holidays together, probably two a year for fifteen years, had all been blissful, even the recent ones. The insulation from work and worry and the isolation from other people reliably worked its healing magic. They would arrive somewhere beautiful and sun-soaked and Patrick would be conscious of Jane's separateness, and feel her long silences as a reproach. But within a few days her silences would be peaceful and companionable, and sex would once more be deep and loving. They'd planned India for after Christmas.

Patrick was unhappy, and irritated with himself for being so. Slumping on the office sofa and picking over "relationships" was unmanly. Any more of this and he'd need *counseling*, for Christ's sake.

But he couldn't shed his mood. It clung to him like a shroud. A sporadic but frequent gnawed-gut feeling assailed him every time the thought of Jane entered his mind. Which it did almost hourly. It was ridiculous, she'd left last October. Three months, two weeks and four days ago, to be exact.

Patrick sat up with a jolt. He should shake himself out of this, settle next week's party menus. He swung himself out of the chesterfield and crossed the two feet of rush matting to his desk. He leaned over to open the door between his office and his secretary's, so that Sandra would know he was no longer brooding. With luck she'd believe he'd been thinking.

Sandra's office was smaller and shabbier than his, her desk a muddle of invoices and letters, tasting notes and orders. Her walls, except where there were ledgers and files, were covered in pin boards, with scrawled messages on yellow stickers, holiday postcards, Employees' Liability Insurance Certificate, suppliers' price lists and newspaper cuttings overlapping crookedly.

Even the glassed door to the yard and the little window were covered in stickers for American Express, Visa, Eurocard and a dozen others. Patrick refused to have these on the restaurant's elegant front door, reckoning that any customer who could afford Jane's would know without being told that they took every kind of plastic. But Sandra couldn't bear to throw the stickers away and had used them to obliterate what little daylight might have found its way into her office.

Patrick's office was in need of redecoration, but it was very neat. The ox-blood leather sofa was comfortably worn and the old roll-top desk was solid oak—a gift from Jane when they opened twelve years ago. There was nothing on it but his computer and a buff folder. The top book shelves held orderly collections of food guides, wine books and cookbooks and the bottom shelf a neat row of wine bottles with stickers over their labels: "Returned as corked/Table 7/Jan 2" in his sommelier's writing, underneath which Patrick had written, "Bollocks. It's perfect." Other stickers read, "Secondary fermentation. Return whole order"; "Taste for Corby dinner (Oxtail and Mash)"; "Sell? Sotheby's?"; "Oxidized. Jan 11/Credit 1 bott/Roger account."

The sash window, like Sandra's, gave on to the yard, but was clear except for an art nouveau flower pot, now empty. It had contained a white azalea put there by Jane a year ago, but the thing had died.

Patrick picked up the telephone and buzzed the kitchen.

"Alastair? Can you give me ten minutes? The Collier secretary says the boss is tired of ravioli, tired of olive oil, and heartily sick of coriander. We'll have to think again."

He put the phone down quickly, before his volatile Scottish chef could deliver the usual tirade about ignorant customers with more money than tastebuds.

Patrick took some solace from the knowledge that he was, at least publicly, behaving well. He had not made any scenes. He had not cried on anyone's shoulder. He had defended Jane's decision to bossy Sally, who was all for wading in and acting Chief Marriage Counselor. He had even continued to feed and stroke Jane's Abyssinian cat, Benedicat—who *definitely* needed a counselor. The beast had peed on his shoes and on his briefcase.

He was working harder than ever, driving his kitchen and waiting staff with the blend of toughness, sympathy and enthusiasm that made the rough respect him and the gentle worship him. Ten years of leading troops as they leapt from army planes or dived backward off inflatables had served him well as a restaurateur. He was good at his job and proud of his staff. He even liked his customers, which was more than most of his rivals did, and certainly more than Alastair did.

Jane's had got a Michelin star two years ago, and Patrick knew they deserved it. The food was contemporary and fashionable without appearing to strive too hard, and the wine list regularly scooped the awards. Patrick was passionate about wine— more so than about food, and spent at least six weeks of every year visiting growers from the Bekaa Valley to New Zealand. His big burly frame and open face were as familiar on the terraces of Bordeaux châteaux as in the tasting rooms of London auction houses. The wine trade liked him because he was knowledgeable without a hint of pretension, and because he paid his bills on time.

He was probably better known as a wine buff than a restaurateur, but it was the restaurant that paid his wages—dealing in wine was a chancy business and Patrick confined his passion to buying for the restaurant and for a few friends and customers who wanted to drink the stuff, not sit on it and then flog it at a profit.

Alastair, small, skinny, thirty years old but with the look of an undernourished kid, stuck his head around the door. He was wearing chef's whites and a butcher's apron down to his knees. His freckled face was red and sweating from the heat of the charcoal grill on which he'd been branding rounds of butternut squash. His short red hair was dark with sweat where it showed beneath his tight chef's skullcap.

"So that silly bitch at Collier's doesn't want crab cakes with coriander. Why on earth do they leave it to some dumb girl in the office to order their dinner? What does she know about it?"

"It's not her. It's the boss. He says that everywhere he goes he's given ravioli of something or other, and his wife hates coriander, and what about cod with polenta? He had that at the new Conran place and it was wonderful."

"Christ, Patrick, how can you stand these people?" Alastair was getting angry, yanking his torchon out of his apron and using it to wipe his forehead.

"Alastair, calm down. Why can't the man have cod? You like cod. You put it on the *plat du jour* last week."

"I've nothing against cod. Cod is an OK fish. But it has become so bloody fashionable you have to pay more for it than for sea bass. These people can't be seen eating anything that isn't the flavor of the fucking month."

"Alastair. You're being childish. The man just rejected pumpkin ravioli, and nothing could be more flavor-of-the-month than that. Is it the mention of Conran's that's got to you?"

Alastair ignored the question. "And *polenta*, for God's sake. Polenta with cod is a crap idea. Polenta needs something powerful with it, with a bit of bloody flavor, like garlic and tomato, or wild boar, or bacon. Not *cod*. Cod will never—"

Patrick interrupted him equably but firmly, "Alastair, stop. What is it with you young chefs? Can't you produce a single sentence without a fuck or a bloody in it? Let's have a bit of professionalism around here. Make up any menu you like, but stay off ravioli, coriander and olive oil. OK?" Alastair's expression changed from indignation to sulkiness. He sighed audibly, but said nothing. Patrick continued, "Collier is not being unreasonable. And we need the man's money. This joint is not actually turning people away night after night, you know. If Collier wants to put vanilla ice-cream in his Château d'Yquem, we'll just take his money and smile at him as if he's a hero. Understood?"

Alastair looked chastened. "OK. Sorry. I'll think of something." He picked up the Collier file.

"And let's have less swearing from now on. Right?"

"Right, boss."

Alastair returned to the kitchen. As he passed Sonia deftly lifting scallops from their shells, he said, "Patrick is getting edgy. The competition must be getting to him. Tomorrow we'd better dream up some menus that give us a better gross profit than these things."

He fingered the plump shiny scallops with the mixture of admiration and possessiveness with which Midas might have handled gold. He'd serve them tender and raw in the middle, charred on the outside. With a timbale of couscous and a mild curry sauce. Maybe a bit of lemongrass.

Patrick had spent an hour on next year's budgets when Alastair buzzed through to say the Environmental Health Officer was in the kitchen.

That's all I need, thought Patrick. I've still not bought that blast chiller. And the new lid for the ice-cream freezer hasn't arrived either.

Jane's kitchen had been state-of-the-art once, but twelve years of success had taken its toll. Alastair's brigade kept the quarry-tiled floor, stainless-steel tables, even the inside of the ovens, spotless, but somehow the impression was dingy. The only natural light was from narrow windows above the shelves, and an attempt to brighten things up by painting the ceiling, ventilation ducts and upper walls bright orange had been a mistake. Patrick knew the kitchen needed refurbishment and he also knew he couldn't afford it.

He braced himself for battle, and walked into the kitchen.

"Good morning, Mr. Neem," he said, forcing cheerfulness. "I see you are dressed for the part."

Mr. Neem was small, dapper, had a salt-and-pepper mustache, and was wearing a white coat over his suit and a plastic-straw hat over a thick blue hairnet. He looked, thought Patrick, like a pantomime dame.

"Good morning, Mr. Chambers," responded Mr. Neem equably. "Yes, since we recommend that all visitors entering a kitchen should wear protective covering and headwear, we have to practice what we preach. Though I do dislike the blue hairnets. I wouldn't be seen by Mrs. Neem in one." He smiled, trying to be friends.

"I wouldn't be seen dead in one," responded Patrick.

Mr. Neem pretended he had not heard, and went on, "And since we are supposed to set a good example, we'll just wash our hands, shall we?" He put his fingers under the bacteriological soap dispenser and pulled the lever. Nothing came out.

He looked meaningfully at Patrick, who said, "Alastair, get someone to fill the soap dispenser, will you?" While Alastair hurried to the store, got a plastic bag of soap, and fitted it himself, Mr. Neem made a note on his clipboard, then turned to Alastair.

"Chef, could I ask you if you got this soap from the chemical store?"

"Sure. Yes. It's only a cupboard, not a proper storeroom. We keep all the cleaning gear in there, not just the poisonous stuff. Bleach, soap, stuff for the ovens . . ."

"Do you keep it locked, Chef?"

"Yes, normally, but we were just stocking it when . . ."

"It should be locked."

He made another note on the clipboard, and then put it on the shelf above the basin and made a thorough job of hand-washing, rubbing between his fingers and washing carefully up to his wrists.

As he dried his hands on a disposable towel with similar thoroughness, he made way at the basin for Patrick. Patrick, feeling bullied, swished his hands quickly under the tap, and dried them perfunctorily.

"Do you have a coat?" asked Mr. Neem. Patrick knew perfectly well that Neem was inviting him to don a white jacket, but decided to pretend he thought Neem was offering him one.

"No, thanks," he said. "As I'm not intending to cook anything, or touch anything, I'll not bother." Neem said nothing, but made another note on his clipboard, which goaded Patrick into protest. "And you know I do not follow the logic of the white-coat business. Presumably that coat you are wearing did not come in a sterile bag, and was not donned in a sterile ante chamber, so you might, for all I know, be importing germs on it into my kitchen, mightn't you?"

As he spoke, Patrick regretted it. Putting the guy's back up before he'd even started his inspection was stupid. So he tried again. "But anyway I don't come into the kitchen much, and you know Alastair runs a very clean ship. Would you like a cup of coffee?"

"No, thank you," said Mr. Neem.

"Are you sure? It's made."

"Mr. Chambers, I don't want to seem rude when you are being hospitable, but I am afraid I must tell you that eating and drinking in the kitchen is not good hygiene practice."

"Good Lord, man, it may not be good hygiene practice, but eating is essential. How do you cook if you can't taste, for God's sake? And any chef working for four hours between the oven and the charcoal grill would faint from dehydration if he didn't drink. The temperature must be in the nineties."

"I was going to mention that," replied Mr. Neem. "We discussed the heat of the kitchen on my last visit, I am sure you recall."

28

He waited for a response, but Patrick just closed his eyes and sighed in exasperation. Mr. Neem continued, "It is true that upper limits on working temperatures are not set under the Safety at Work Act, but we do recommend that the temperature of a work room should not exceed eighty-four degrees."

Patrick opened his mouth, then shut it.

Neem did not pursue it, and Patrick followed him around the kitchen. While he pried apart the folds of the gaskets in the fridge doors, knelt to peer under the oven, and checked the sell-by dates on the *crème fraîche*, Patrick was conscious of Alastair quietly preceding him and surreptitiously removing offending objects (wooden-handled knife; cardboard vegetable box; grubby oven cloth).

The Health Officer made no further comment until he opened the vegetable fridge and saw forty-eight small pots of peach-colored flowering geraniums in two trays on the floor.

"Mr. Chambers. I am afraid this is unacceptable." Mr. Neem spoke mildly, and Alastair looked baffled. But Patrick understood and found his anger rising.

"For God's sake, Neem. No one is going to get listeriosis because we are storing the table flowers in the fridge for a couple of hours. I want them as fresh as possible for tonight, and with the central heating on in the dining rooms, they're better off in here."

"Mr. Chambers, you really should not put those geraniums in their pots on the dining tables."

Anger made Patrick articulate.

"Why on earth not? And are you really telling me, Mr. Neem, that if I do, some very old lady, or pregnant and sickly woman, or some new-born infant is going to come into my restaurant and contract listeriosis? Do you think, at fifty quid a head, we appeal to the geriatric, the sick and the new-born? Who, as you very well know, are the only *remotely* likely victims of an almost unheard-of disease."

In an adrenalin-assisted burst of fluency, he continued, "And are you telling me that this unlikely customer is going to stick her fingers into the soil of the geranium pot, and the soil is going to be thick with listeria bugs, and she is then going to lick her fingers? And then she is going to get listeriosis and die of it? That's the general scenario, isn't it?"

Alastair and Sonia watched open-mouthed as Patrick's voice hardened into sarcasm. Mr. Neem looked taken aback, even a little nervous. But he stood his ground.

He said, "You will be able to consider the matter when you get my report. Shall we proceed?"

They did, and the matter of the blast chiller resurfaced.

Patrick protested. "Mr. Neem. We've been cooling pots for twelve years by the simple method of standing the pots in a sinkful of cold water and letting the cold tap trickle into the water. The water must keep them as cold as a fridge, if not colder. Why don't you come one morning at eight and take a swab and see if we've grown any bugs? I bet we haven't. But if we have, I promise you I will buy a blast chiller."

"You may be right, Mr. Chambers, but I am afraid that is not the point. You know as well as I do that the regulations require cooked food to be refrigerated after four hours. From midnight, when I assume the chefs leave, to eight a.m. is eight hours."

"So if I put the food away, blazing hot, in the fridges, I'll be satisfying you, even though it's a crazy thing to do?" Patrick's voice was on the rise again.

"Mr. Chambers, I am sure you know, and certainly your chef knows, that if you refrigerate hot food in an ordinary fridge you will raise the temperature of the fridge above the regulation limit. The only answer is a blast chiller."

Neem's careful manner, his air of talking to a fractious child, infuriated Patrick. With a feeling of relief, he gave up on self-control, advanced on Neem, and said very loudly, "Neem, I am not buying a blast chiller. Take me to court if you like. You are only hounding Jane's because if you bully me into a blast chiller you win brownie points back at the sodding council." Neem stepped back as Patrick, waving his arms in mounting fury, continued, "I bet you're not asking that greasy spoon at the end of the road to buy a blast chiller, because you *know* they can't afford it. They cool their pots by standing them out on the back step where any passing dog can piss in them. Rats probably *drown* in them . . ."

Neem raised his clipboard and free hand in protest but Patrick, now shouting, was not to be stopped.

"Well, I can't afford one either. We'll be lucky if Jane's clears £20,000 this year and I'm not spending it all to appease some illogical, power-mad, bunch of bloody bureaucrats."

He stopped. No one said anything. Regaining control of his voice, he said, "I'll be in my office." He pushed past Neem and the astonished Alastair.

At his desk, anger and humiliation took turns. His hands were shaking, and he thought with horror how very nearly he had come to hitting the little inspector. How could he have lost his temper like that? He'd never done so in all his years in the army or in twelve years here. How could he have let Neem rattle him so? Poor bastard was only doing his job. But what a wretched little bureaucrat. Anger resurfaced as he remembered how Neem had insisted Alastair throw out all the wooden spoons, chopping boards and the butcher's block just before new evidence emerged that wood harbored bugs rather less than plastic did.

But all the time Patrick was castigating himself and Neem in turns, he knew he was doing so to avoid thinking of something worse. But he couldn't keep the thought out, and finally he shut his eyes and faced it: he'd let the cat out of the bag about Jane's profits. He'd as good as told the kitchen they were only just breaking even. The cooks weren't fools. They knew two and two added up to redundancy. By this evening every member of staff would believe Jane's was on the edge, that their jobs were on the line. Oh, Christ, I'll have to reassure them, he thought.

But how can I? And they won't believe me, and they'll be right.

And I'll have to give in to Neem. Patrick pushed the fingers of both hands up through his thick hair, then dragged them down again, pressing his palms into his eyes and pulling down his cheeks. I need to redo the whole kitchen, not just buy a chiller. Alastair has to have new kit, and we should replace the old angle-iron dry-goods shelves with stainless-steel ones. And new ventilation quiet enough to stop the neighbors bitching will cost a mint.

Patrick turned to his computer:

Ventilation	£20,000
Soufflé oven	£2,000
Combi steamer	£12,000
Blast chiller	£12,000
Ice-cream fridge	£2,000
Benches with refrigeration drawers × 2	£16,000
New compressors (cold room and freezer)	£10,000
Misc kit, say	£20,000
Shelving units	£8,000
Fitting/painting	£12,000

Patrick totaled it up and thought, if I redo the bar, even just re-cover the sofas and paint the walls, it will be another forty grand. I'll be into £150,000 in no time. Christ, and I still have 30K to pay off on the dining-room redecoration loan, so no one's going to lend to me anymore. Not on current earnings, that's for sure. And I can hardly dip into Jane's (the wife's) account to finance Jane's (the restaurant's) face-lift now, can I?

Patrick suddenly ached for Jane. He needed her sense of humor, her irreverent stance to all things official, her casualness about money, her ability to see things in proportion. Well, she's gone, he told himself, swallowing against the familiar twist of misery. Time you got used to it. And you've got more pressing problems than a lost wife. The restaurant could be going down the tubes.

He stood up, and mentally shook himself. It will be all right. Nothing is ever as bad as it seems. It just needs logical, careful thought. Followed by decisive action. But not right now. I can't face even Alastair right now. He pulled on his jacket and stuck his head through Sandra's door.

"I'm off to the Restaurateurs' Association junket. The combination of Alastair the temperamental star and Neem the tight-assed bureaucrat has done it for me. If either need me, or anyone else does for that matter, invent something, will you? I need a drink, that's what. Expect me when you see me, OK?"

Sandra looked at her departing boss in astonishment. For the first time she'd heard him shouting. And he never used words like tight-arsed. And he didn't drink at lunchtime.

He'd gone before she had recovered sufficiently to reply. She shrugged, dismissing a matronly concern for him. Anyway, she thought, it's just as well he's not in this afternoon. He's not going to like last month's figures. And this month's are going to be worse.

THREE

It was cold when they stepped down from the train at Jaipur. The cleaners sluiced the platform with buckets of water, sweeping water, dirt and debris off the platform edge onto the tracks. They wore blankets over their shoulders and heads, and it was hard to tell if the bent figures were men or women. They did not look up as the bright gaggle of tourists crossed the platform into the glare of the station forecourt.

Jane was uneasy at the sight that met them. Oh, God, she thought, as she bent her head for the proffered marigold garland. Why can't we just melt quietly into the scene? Why all this fuss? The fuss was indeed quite something. Two elephants formed a guard of honor, their heads, trunks and ears elaborately painted with entwined pink, yellow and blue flowers. On their backs they bore great silk-draped howdahs with multi-colored hangings reaching almost to the ground. Half-sunk in each elephant's cushioned headdress perched a mahout, looking bored. Beyond the elephants was a motley band of musicians, mostly very old men, playing beribboned drums. The sling of meager flesh under the leader's upper arms trembled as he played, and his knees, protruding from the dismal swag of his dhoti, were knobbly as Gandhi's.

The tourists, with shyness or bravado, walked between the elephants, and then stood around in little groups, waiting for something to happen. Not much did, except that the elephants proved adept at gripping 5- or 10-rupee notes in their trunks, and swinging them up to their mahouts, who, unsmiling, pocketed them.

"It's a photo-opportunity," said John, coming up and kissing both Sally and Jane on both cheeks with the casualness of a brother. "Haven't you brought a camera?"

"I have," replied Sally, "but Jane takes the lofty view that looking through a lens robs the scene of reality. Don't you, Jane?"

"Well, I do think that chap over there might as well stay in his living room and watch an Indian travel movie. Last night at supper, didn't you see? He was videoing his food. But the real reason I don't have a camera is they put me into such a temper. Either they jam, or the battery is drained, or I have the wrong film, or no film or I forget to bring the thing at all."

John said, "Cheer up. Lucy is worse. She sent our wedding film off to be processed, and when it came back, we'd got someone else's. Some old codger's Day Out in Skegness, all deserted seafront, mournful seagulls and the backs of pensioners climbing into a coach."

Lucy joined in. "It was a sad little film, but he (or she?) must have got a good laugh out of our wedding. I was nine months pregnant, and could hardly get up the registry office stairs. And when we reached the top, the registrar said, 'Don't worry, dearie, I'm a midwife.' "

They all laughed, but Sally was a little shocked. She wasn't used to such quick intimacy. But she was pleased to see Jane really laughing, relaxed and happy, with no trace of her forced London cheerfulness. She thought on the whole the Applebys would be good for them.

By the time they got to the castle-fort of Amber and trooped out of the "luxury air-conditioned coach"—in fact a superannuated bus—it was hot enough to have nettled Hans, and he directed his irritation at their guide, Rajiv. "Why is the air-cool not working? This bus is no good. In the brochure it says 'Luxury Coach.' Is this luxury? With air-cool kaput? *Hein*?"

Hans was several inches shorter than Rajiv, but he thrust out his chin and glared up into Rajiv's face, demanding a reply. He stood with his feet slightly apart, his strong buttocks and thighs visibly flexed under his pale khaki chinos.

Rajiv listened attentively, his hands in his pockets, his lean frame stooping slightly toward Hans. He was nodding, but not attempting to speak until Hans had had his say. Then he said, in perfect English, "I do apologize. And I agree. This coach is dreadful. And the air-conditioning is a joke." He smiled, shaking his head in rueful apology.

There was a pause. Hans was momentarily thrown by Rajiv's assumption of equality and air of composure. But Hans rallied and, resuming his aggressive stance, said, "I do not consider it a joke. It is a disgrace. What are you going to do about it?"

"Nothing right now, I am afraid," replied Rajiv. "This being India, there is no chance of a better coach today. But I will complain tonight so perhaps we will get a better one tomorrow."

The guide's classical good looks and lack of obsequiousness combined to provoke Hans further. "That is not good enough. This trip, which is very expensive, advertises itself as *grand luxe*. I demand . . ."

Oh, do shut up, thought Jane, walking away. Why don't you open your eyes and just *look* at that castle? As she gazed across the lake to the hill opposite, the banality of the argument ceased to impinge, and the castle claimed her whole attention. It was enormous, even from below, and they were way below. It occupied the whole of the top of the hill, sheer stone walls rising straight and unadorned from the ground for five or six stories before breaking out in a double row of arched windows, with, every few hundred feet, a rounded dome on an octagonal turret. The sky behind was postcard blue, and the pale palace was, thought Jane, perfect. Quite perfect. For all its size, she thought, it has a delicacy and lightness you never see in European castles. Perhaps it's the sun. It's hard to be forbidding in the sun.

Further musing was cut short by the arrival of a crowd of hawkers. They had been caught unawares by the coach's arrival and came running along the edge of the lake, in a straggly pack, the teenage boys and young men to the fore, children behind. Within seconds, every tourist had a determined seller at his or her elbow.

Those who had been in India before, or even for a few days in Delhi, took no notice, and, talking firmly to each other but without a glance at their followers, walked the few hundred meters to the yard at the bottom of the path to the castle. Sally instinctively did the same, only the determined set of her jaw betraying her consciousness of a youth tugging at her sleeve, pushing a silk-dressed puppet at her face and repeating, like a mantra, "Only ten dollars. Very beautiful. You buy. Only ten dollars. Very beautiful. You buy."

But Jane could not pretend people were not there when they were. She looked at her pursuer's proffered scarves, shook her head, met his entreating eyes, smiled, and said, "No thank you." Instantly she was surrounded by half a dozen other hawkers, who left their stony-faced targets for this softer possibility. One thrust a turban at her. "Five hundred rupees. Real silk. Very cheap. You buy." Another held up a clutch of miniature picture frames, studded in glass mosaic, pretty and well made. "Ten, ten, only ten," he said. A small girl, of six or seven, was the most insistent, tugging her jacket and pushing a crudely made ektari at her with, "You rich. Me very poor. You buy. You rich. Me very poor. You buy." She plucked at the instrument's single string and danced in front of Jane.

Jane tried to walk on, but she was surrounded. She began to feel trapped, and a little panicky, and thought the way out might be to buy something. She turned to the picture-frame seller, a boy of perhaps fourteen, with soft imploring eyes, clear skin and a University of Michigan baseball cap, worn backward, covering his thick hair. She took one of his frames, a round silver-backed one with blue and white mosaic, in her hand. Instantly he turned on the other sellers, said something low and threatening, and they fell back. Jane walked on, still looking at the picture frame, her importuner at her side.

"It is very beautiful. Where are they made?"

As soon as he replied, "In my village," she remembered Giles's advice, delivered in the Chalker and Day lift: "Just remember one thing about the Indians. They seldom tell the truth, but they always tell you what you want to hear." Rajiv, the guide, did not tell Hans what he wanted to hear, she thought inconsequentially, and Hans did not like the truth. For an instant she wondered about Rajiv, so relaxed, well spoken and good-looking. He seemed too well educated to be a tour-guide. Then her trinket-seller's "Very cheap. Very beautiful" brought her back to the matter in hand.

Fascinated by the minute workmanship and pretty, traditional patterning of the tiny frames, she examined her seller's stock, dithering between the round blue one and an octagonal brass one set with a minuscule mosaic of green and gold. Her vendor, walking backwards in front of her, never let up his sales talk, now adding the spurious provenance "Traditional handicraft from my village" to his former "Very cheap. Only ten. Very beautiful."

She caught up with Sally waiting in a crush of tourists to mount a short flight of stone steps to a platform from where the guides were settling them on to elephants, two to a side, four to an elephant. Once loaded, the great beasts made a lurching turn toward the steep ascent to the castle. The line moved slowly, bottlenecking as the path narrowed.

Sally said at once, "You don't want that picture frame, Jane. You can get them in the Oxfam shop for half the price."

"It's only ten rupees," said Jane. "And it's pretty. I'll hang it on the Christmas tree. And anyway, if I buy it, maybe I'll get some peace."

She pulled out 10 rupees and offered it to the hawker.

His face registered insult and outrage.

Jane said, almost apologetic, "You said ten."

"Ten dollar. Not rupee. Ten dollar," he said.

The next fifteen minutes were very unpleasant. Sally would not let her pay 10 dollars for something worth, at most, two, and which she didn't want anyway. Jane was feeling a fool, and a little ashamed of offering only 10 rupees. She was too English and polite (or feeble, thought Jane) to drive the hawker away. And he, a veteran of much more abuse in an average day than Jane had heard in her whole life, knew a soft touch when he saw one. He never for one minute let up the soft continuous pleading, though the price came steadily down. Jane would have paid him to go away, but feared he'd take the money and keep up the sleeve-tugging.

Suddenly their neighbor in the line, the confident American woman, she of the bangles on Delhi station, took charge.

"I'll get that cute little frame for you at ten rupees, you see if I don't. Now you do just as I tell you. You must not buy it until you are just about to get on your elephant. He'll be mighty desperate by then. He'll have wasted his entire time on you, and he'll have to take whatever you give him. You just keep telling him it's way too much."

She spoke as if the hawker did not understand a word of English, which Jane thought rude, but she was nonetheless relieved to have the matter taken out of her hands. She did as instructed. At intervals she glanced at the trinket and shook her head.

Gradually, oh so gradually, the line to the elephant platform shortened, and they moved first to the bottom, then step by step up the stairs.

The crush was oppressive, and a little frightening. The steps had no rail, and Jane, on the outside, had to press close to her tormentor to avoid being pushed over the edge. He bent his knees and twisted his head to look up into her face as she stared miserably at her feet. To avoid his gaze she would then stare fixedly over his shoulder, at the crush of tourists on the top of the platform. Suddenly she was aware that she was looking into the face of Rajiv, the guide. He was on the platform, looking down. He smiled and she noticed the curious streaky topaz of his eyes. For a second she thought she might appeal to him to relieve her of the attentions of the hawker. But then her spirit kicked in and she thought how ridiculously feeble she was. She turned her head back to the vendor without acknowledging Rajiv, and shook her head once more in answer to the boy's whine. He responded with renewed effort, and a lower price.

The tourists were mostly silent now, bored by the waiting and stonily enduring the whining pleas of the hawkers. Most had succumbed, and were carrying their purchases.

At last they were at the top of the steps. Jane's mentor, who had by now announced herself as Cindy, took over.

"OK, kid. He's down to thirty rupees. Offer him ten, and I bet you anything you like he takes it."

Jane did so, again tentatively proffering her 10-rupee note. She was aware that Rajiv was quietly watching the transaction. She wished he wasn't, because she felt a fool. She disliked doing what Cindy told her, and she disliked beating down the boy. But suddenly he shrugged and took the money. He handed her the picture frame without looking at her, his mind and eyes already on the next prospect.

"There, what did I tell you?" crowed Cindy. "They're all crooks and conmen. You just gotta play their game. It's expected."

Rajiv helped Cindy and Elmer onto one side of an elephant. As Cindy, beaming with triumph, settled herself next to Elmer on the howdah's cushioned seat, Jane suddenly thrust the picture frame into her hand.

"You have it," she said. "I don't want it."

The mahout prodded the elephant and it swung heavily around to present its other side to the mounting platform, and the assistant indicated to Jane and Sally to climb on, their backs to Cindy and Elmer. Jane pulled Sally by the elbow.

"No," she said. Then, to the Japanese couple behind them in the line, a hint of desperation in her voice: "You go. Please."

"Is there a problem?" asked Rajiv. "Can I help?"

"No, no. It's fine. I just don't want that elephant." She knew she sounded capricious and idiotic.

Sally said, "Are you OK, Jane? We needn't go . . ."

Jane again said to the Japanese, "Please. You go. Honestly. We'll wait."

Shrugging, the assistant settled in the substitute pair, slotting the guard rail across their laps. He clicked at the elephant, who plodded majestically off, his mahout flapping his legs in encouragement.

"You no want elephant?"

"Yes, yes, we do, please. Just not that one. Can we have the next one?"

Rajiv intervened, saying something in Hindi to the man, who responded with another shrug and, "OK. OK. Memsahib have what elephant you want. This good elephant. Very nice elephant."

As their beast wheeled away from the platform, Jane caught Rajiv's eye and smiled her apology. He grinned at her, shaking his head slightly. "I'm sorry," she called. "Take no notice. I'm nuts."

"What was all that about?" asked Sally, as their elephant dipped and swayed up the hill, Jane and Sally on one side, their backs to two strangers on the other.

"I just couldn't bear that woman's jubilation over beating down the trinket seller. What possible difference can it make to any of us if we pay twenty pence or a hundred and twenty pence for something?" Jane spoke with more passion than she meant to show.

Sally didn't agree, but she was too wise to take Jane on. She's very emotional for a supposedly hard-bitten City solicitor, she thought. I *do* think she's slightly unstable.

So she changed the subject, and pointed out the formal garden below them, apparently floating in the lake. It was an enormous, flat rectangular island, covered by a repetitive lacework

41

of low stone walls dividing the ground into small plots, now all grassed uniformly. The garden was connected to the bank by a walled path.

Sally consulted her guidebook. "The little walled compartments used to have aromatic herbs or flowers in them. The garden was designed to be seen, like a carpet, from the windows and terraces of the palace. Or you could walk along that central path, which sprouted fountains, and smell the flowers. It must have cost an absolute mint."

Jane loved the sheer extravagance and folly of it. How wonderful to care so much about design, and beauty, and pleasure, that you build a garden in a lake just to look at from above, or to walk through in the cool of the evening.

Once at the top, they split up, Sally sticking obediently with the guide, Jane glad of the chance to escape the group. There was blessed relief from the hawkers, who were barred from the castle. The warm morning sun felt like a blessing on her back. She pulled off her cotton sweater and tied it around her waist. The breeze stirred the extravagant trusses of purple bougainvillea against the yellow walls, and rippled the long silky coats of the monkeys stalking the terraces and steps. Jane stopped to watch them as she climbed from the wide forecourt into the castle proper. With their little black faces framed in a gray-blond ruff, their long encompassing arms protecting the tiniest of babies, they concentrated comically on grooming each other or eating marigold garlands, presumably filched from some castle shrine.

The pleasurable mood that had taken hold of her on first seeing the castle, and which had been so thoroughly swept away by the arrival of the hawkers, returned.

She wandered from courtyard to terrace, through inner garden and colonnaded arcade, through long-deserted living quarters and public rooms. The palace, now the property of the impoverished state, had an air of neglect. The gardens were only half-planted and some walls were black-streaked and crumbling. But Jane felt extraordinarily peaceful.

Even the thought of Patrick failed to produce the usual guilt-ridden angst. London, and Patrick, and Chalkers seemed a world away. For the first time in months she felt free. Free of her marriage and its three-month aftermath of doubts and wavering, free of her mother's solicitude and ill-hidden disapproval.

Everything delighted her. The ancient but still bright fresco of the elephant god Ganesh reminded her of Celeste in her childhood Babar books. Ganesh sat on a plump cushioned stool, his crown jauntily tipped to the back of his head.

She began to regret eschewing Rajiv's tour. She wanted to know who had built this palace, whose instinct for beauty ensured that the frilly-edged marble arches, which repeated themselves in all directions, at last perfectly framed the view of sky and mountains. She imagined herself as concubine or wife, with a life devoted to pleasuring her lord, walking with him in jasmine-scented gardens, making love in the little domed room whose walls and ceiling, inlaid with tiny mirror pieces, turned the light of a single candle into that of a thousand stars. What a simple life. With time for indulgence, for music, for dreaming. No women's rights, no guilt, no treadmill of getting and spending, no ambition beyond pleasure and beauty.

Is it all fantasy? she thought. Or is it time to change my life? Jump off the City ladder? Buy a farm and make goats cheese and babies?

At this last preposterous thought, she gave a fractional shake of her head, frowning at the distant hills. What an idiotic idea. If you wanted that, she told herself, you should have listened to Patrick. It's what he wanted. Pine-scrubbed tables, fresh bread in the Aga, football with five-year-olds on the lawn.

Well, she didn't believe in the country-kitchen dream. She'd seen the dulling, withering effect of home and hearth on her friends; once bright lawyers or literary agents turned fraught or mushy by domesticity; once interesting couples reduced to talk of school fees and mortgages.

"For God's sake, Jane, where the hell have you been?" Sally came striding, almost running, across the wide roof terrace to where Jane was sitting on a parapet.

Jane turned from her contemplation of the ancient wall across the valley which, like a junior Great Wall of China, climbed up and down the surrounding hills, and replied, "Oh, Sally, don't be cross. It's heaven up here. That wall must completely encircle this palace . . ."

"Jane, will you listen? The bus should have left ages ago. They're all waiting for us at the bottom. We only noticed you were missing halfway down, and they thought you must have walked ahead of us, but I knew you'd be daydreaming somewhere, so I came back. It really is too bad. Actually, it's selfish. You need a nanny, that's what." And she turned on her heel and marched back the way she'd come.

Jane stamped out her cigarette and hurried after her, chastened. "You're right, of course. I am sorry, and I will grovel suitably, especially to Hans, who is probably apoplectic. Is he?"

Mollified, Sally laughed. "He was all for going without you, but Rajiv said he wasn't allowed to lose any passengers. Hans consults that itinerary he has all the time. I don't think he's going to have much of a holiday. His happiness seems to depend on everything happening to schedule. He's probably bullied poor Rajiv into leaving without us both by now."

"I doubt it. Rajiv doesn't look easily bullied. He got the better of Hans this morning. But still, I do feel bad, especially as the bus has 'no air-cool'."

When the two women mounted the steps into the bus they were greeted with an ironic cheer, good-natured on the part of most of the passengers, but followed by Hans's immediate "Do you not have a watch?" He tapped his own watch vigorously with his right hand to make his point. "It is not right to be so late, so we have to sit in the bus with no air-cool."

The only empty seats were right opposite Johann and Hans, and Hans sat on the aisle.

"You go in," muttered Jane in an undertone, ushering Sally into the window seat. "I'll fix him, I promise."

She sat down, leaned across the aisle to Hans and looked into his offended face. She noticed the hostile eyes and fine sheen of sweat. But her own face registered only contrition.

"Hans. I'm so sorry. It was disgraceful of me. I was so enchanted with the place, I just lost track of time, and it's true, I don't have a watch, which is stupid. You are right to be cross. I won't do it again, I promise. Will you forgive me?" There was no hint of mockery in her voice. The passengers within ear-shot took her apology as genuine, if a bit over the top.

Hans believed her too. Jane thought, it's like taking candy from a baby. He's too self-important to wonder why I should so extravagantly woo his forgiveness. He must think he's God's gift.

Hans's expression softened, then he sat back and laughed, showing even teeth, two of them gold. "*Ja,* I forgive you! And Johann will give you his watch, eh, Johann? Then there will be no next time, *hein*? Johann, your watch." He tapped his partner's knee in command.

"No, no, Hans, I don't want . . ." Jane protested, alarmed.

Hans, now expansive and jovial, said, "I insist. Johann has a Rolex also. Like mine. So you can wear this one. It is only a Sekonda."

Johann, eager to please both Hans and Jane, undid his watch, and leaning past Hans, tried to give it to Jane.

"No, Johann. Please. You can't give it to me." Jane shrank away from the proffered watch, shaking both head and hands in defense.

Johann hesitated, and, still smiling, withdrew the watch reluctantly. But Hans said, "I insist. Do what I tell you, Johann." It was an order. The smile disappeared from Johann's face, and for a second he looked like a small boy, as if he might cry.

Jane said, "Hans. I don't want Johann's watch. I really don't. Why should he—"

Hans interrupted, a tinge of impatience in his voice. "He does not mind. You do not mind, eh, Johann?"

"No, of course I do not mind. Here, Jane. Please. Take it." Jane caught the subtext of anxiety, and feeling sorry for him and angry with Hans, gave in. She took the watch, a thin gold one with a white face and brown crocodile strap.

She started to buckle the strap around her wrist, but Hans leaned over with proprietorial authority, and took over. Jane, not liking the inevitable touch of their competing fingers, let him do it. The watch face covered her whole wrist, and even on the tightest hole, the strap was loose. Hans encircled her wrist, watch and all, with his large, freckled and slightly damp hand and said, too quietly for the others to hear, "An elegant wrist. You make even Johann's Sekonda look fashionable."

Jane pulled her hand away, and Hans sat back, content. Jane looked across him at Johann and saw his face clouded and anxious. She realized that Hans's pleasure had been in hurting Johann, not flirting with her. What a bastard.

She smiled across at Johann, signaling, I don't want him, I promise. He's yours.

"Serves you right," muttered Sally. "You shouldn't play games."

FOUR

In Sally's opinion Jane was becoming obsessed with India. It was fine to read the Raj Quartet and even *Midnight's Children* (if you could finish it, and she'd never met anyone who had) before you got here, but Jane had had her nose in a book every minute that she wasn't looking at India, eating India or talking India—mostly to Rajiv or Umesh. Rajiv was paid to talk to the guests of course but Sally suspected Umesh would prefer his charges to stay their side of an invisible boundary, to behave like proper memsahibs, but was too polite, too Indian, to rebuff Jane's constant questioning.

Sally was sitting with John and Lucy in the bar-car, tired after a day of sightseeing. It was dark outside, and you needed to press your face to the window to see anything on the station. Sally did so, then pulled down the blind, dismissing the bleak sight of sleeping families on the platform. She turned to the brightly lit warmth of brocade, brass and comforting whiskey, and said, "Jane would have gone native in no time if she'd been a British Raj wife. She said she'd join us for a drink, but she's bought some book on Hinduism, and I left her drawing Krishna's family tree in her notebook, and complaining that she couldn't get the hang of it because the gods change their names with every reincarnation or something. Someone will have to fetch her or she'll never turn up."

"She's great," replied Lucy. "Beautiful brainy people are supposed to be vain and rude. But she's funny and friendly. Everyone likes her, from the waiters to the horrible Huns."

"Racist," said John. "There is nothing wrong with Johann,

other than he's a mite wet, and his taste in lovers is bizarre. Hans, I agree, does not improve on acquaintance. But you are right that everyone loves Jane. Even Hans does, God help her."

Sally laughed. "He certainly does, and she's paying through the nose for charming him when we were late for the bus. This morning he cornered her in the museum and stuck to her all morning, reading from the guidebook."

Sally's voice, though low, had carrying power born of disciplining horses, dogs and children from across a field. She was as unaware of the approach of Hans and Johann as she was of John's eyebrow signals. She continued. "I don't think he really knows anymore about India than we do, but being efficient and German, he gets up at six in the morning and mugs it all up so he can drive us mad contradicting the guides."

"It is of me you speak, is it not?" Hans's voice was hard and accusing.

John, rising, said, "Oh, Hans, take no notice . . ."

But Hans was not to be pacified. Indeed his irritation was turning into anger. "I do not contradict the guides to drive you mad. I do not care at all about you. And I do not contradict them when they are accurate—I do not contradict Rajiv. I contradict the others because they are ignorant and make history up."

"Oh, Hans, don't be so po-faced. What does it matter?" demanded Sally, too loudly.

"Of course it matters. We were promised historians as guides, not out of work taxi drivers whose one idea is to lead you to their brother's jewelry store or carpet shop. How can you British be so weak? You will put up with anything and never complain."

Pushing his reddening face into Sally's, he spun Johann's restraining hand from his shoulder with an angry jerk.

Sally shrank from Hans's anger, but there was nowhere to go. She was trapped between his face and the window. She tried to stand up, but his looming bulk prevented that too. Indignation at his rudeness combined with guilt at her own stung her into

48

attack. "And how can you Germans be so demanding and intolerant? At least we have some degree of tolerance and sense of humor and only rise when it's bloody necessary. Why the hell can't you just enjoy India, and stop trying to improve it all the time? You are ruining everyone else's holiday with your constant gripes about beggars and dirt and 'no air-cool' and being ten minutes behind schedule."

Hans straightened up. No one risked word or gesture. Then Hans, with a stiffness more suitable to the stage, clicked his heels, jerked his head in a bow, spun on his heel and marched down the bar-car. Johann hurried after him.

At that moment, the train gave a sudden jerk, then stopped, propelling Hans into a young steward carrying a tray of beers. One of the bottles rose in an arc, trailing a fountain of beer. The steward tried to catch it, and the remaining bottles catapulted into a table of Japanese women. They rose in panic as a shower of beer and bottles descended upon them.

The train again lurched forward, this time successfully gathering speed. The steward tried to retrieve the rolling bottles and to apologize to Hans and the drenched women, who stood in silent freeze-frame. Johann's hands fluttered like frightened birds, and his voice, rising in panic, could be heard. "No, Hans. No, please."

At this moment Jane entered the bar-car and stopped dead. Hans caught a glimpse of her open mouth and wide eyes.

Humiliation at Sally's lecture, fury at his own clumsiness, exasperation at Johann's fussing had stretched Hans's self-control, but the appearance of Jane snapped it.

Whirling with animal agility, he grabbed two handfuls of the steward's buttoned coat, each fist clutching sufficient cloth to lift the man bodily, and slammed him against the train window.

"You clumsy bastard." He swung his right fist into the man's stomach and kneed his prisoner in the groin.

The young man, released by Hans, fell to the train floor,

doubling up with his hands between his legs. His turban rolled off his head to reveal a boyishly thin neck, and short curly hair, thick and glossy. His eyes starting with tears, his mouth distorted as he drew uneven jerks of breath, he looked like a child.

Instantly Jane was kneeling on the train floor, her own head bent over his, one arm around his shoulders, one hand holding his head against her bosom. "It's OK, Ram. Ram, you'll be OK." Ram struggled for breath, groaned, and as Jane sank to a sitting position, buried his head in her lap.

Sally pulled the emergency cord. The train slowed fast and all those standing staggered forward, then backward as the last jolt brought them to a complete halt. Then Hans stepped over Jane's legs and the steward's still-curled body, and left. Johann, with an anguished look toward Sally, followed.

The bar customers, regaining normality, had mixed feelings. Outrage at Hans, yes. Admiration too for the quick sympathy of Jane. But also something of disapproval. Why did she know Ram's name? Should she be sitting on the floor of the carriage, hugging the steward like a mother?

Certainly the guide, Rajiv, didn't think so. Entering the bar-car, he snaked his way through the passengers and, putting an arm under Jane's elbow, said, "You must get up now, Mrs. Chambers." As soon as she was standing, he knelt beside Ram and said something to him in Hindi, then helped him to his feet, and out of the carriage. With rounded back, one hand over his genitals and one holding his stomach, Ram shuffled to the door, not looking at Jane. Indeed looking ashamed, as if the whole episode had been his fault.

Picking up Ram's turban, Jane said, her voice shaking, "How could he? Ram's only a boy. Why did he do it? Why?"

John shepherded the two women back to their table and ordered whiskies. Jane lit a Marlboro with unsteady hands. After a few minutes the train resumed its journey and the passengers settled down to discuss the incident, and to wonder whether dinner would be delayed.

• • •

Jane, in bed with *The Story of Krishna*, could not concentrate. She read whole pages without taking in a word. The image of Hans's departing back as he strode from the carriage, his bottom rolling tightly in his pale blue trousers, his heavy shoulders defiant, kept invading her mind, each time offending her anew. She felt again hot indignation at the injustice of the incident, and her question "How could he?" came back and back, an unwanted refrain, almost a torment.

Sally looked up from the latest Joanna Trollope.

"You're fretting about that boy, aren't you?" she said.

"It is so unfair . . ."

"Jane. You are a solicitor. You know that life is unfair."

Jane, feeling accused of lack of professional distance, replied hotly, "But that doesn't mean I don't care about it. Maybe I'm a solicitor *because* I care about fairness. And anyway, since I'm not in criminal law, I seldom see villains and victims."

"You should just forget it. The fact is that bullies bully, and the meek get hurt. It's sad, but you can't do anything about it."

Jane said, "But I hate letting that pig get away with it. In England we could have helped Ram. He could have had Hans for assault. And gone for damages in the civil courts."

"In England you'd be too busy for philanthropy," said Sally dryly. "And neither of us will be any more help here. We aren't going to offer to be witnesses in some Delhi court in two years' time, are we? None of us is."

Jane, chastened, had to agree, but she was still indignant and angry. "If that oaf has made Ram sterile or impotent for life, Mother India will probably consider it a blessing, not a case for damages. On top of that, Ram would have no chance against Hans's international lawyers and pocketful of bribes. And anyway, there's no Legal Aid in India, so he's screwed before he begins."

They both went back to their books, but presently Sally said,

51

"If you really want to fix Hans, and compensate Ram, it would be quite easy, you know."

Next morning, Jane was still excited by the audacity of Sally's plan. But she felt uneasy too, taking the moral high ground and dispensing justice without judge or jury.

It reminded her of the time at boarding school when the prefects had drawn lots, and she had ended up the sixth-form emissary telling the headmistress that they didn't like the way she made the girls cry and then comforted them, fondling their bums and their half-grown breasts as she did so. Full of prudish self-righteousness as she started her indictment, she had ended feeling anguish and sympathy for the plump middle-aged woman, who listened in absolute silence as purple shame rose from her white collar to engulf her neck and face.

Sally had no such qualms. "Don't be daft, Jane. The man is a monster, and what can he do? What we are doing is legal, isn't it?"

"Well, it comes pretty close to blackmail," said Jane, "but it's legal, and I'm game. Let's do it before my courage collapses." They set off for the dining-car.

Jane kept an eye on the progress of Hans and Johann's breakfast. When Hans had dispatched, with concentration and in silence, a loaded plate of bacon, sausages, eggs and fried bread, and Johann had eaten stewed fruit and yogurt, and they were both on coffee and toast, Jane said, "So much for the ersatz food they were going to live on in India. I wonder what conquered Hans's scruples, Johann's persuasion or plain greed?"

"Must be greed. He takes too much pleasure in hurting Johann to do something to please him. Come on. Let's do it."

The two women rose and walked down the swaying train, steadying themselves on the backs of the dining chairs. As they passed the Germans' table, Sally dropped a note on Johann's side-plate. Both women walked on, and out of the carriage.

Hans, peremptory, put his hand out, and Johann obediently handed the paper to him.

Dear Passenger,
You will have heard about, or seen, the unfortunate incident last evening when one of our fellow passengers assaulted Ram Dasani, the eighteen-year-old bar steward, by viciously knee-ing him in the groin and punching him in the belly. It is not yet known if Ram has suffered permanent damage, but even if he hasn't, I am sure you will understand the humiliation and distress such an incident must cause him.

To show Ram that he has our sympathy, and that we Maharajah Express passengers would like to apologize for the behavior of one of us, we are organizing a collection for Ram, who has returned to his mother in Jaipur.

If everyone gives 250 rupees, Ram will have R20,000, enough to be off work for months if he has to, or to marry his fiancée if he recovers quickly.

If you would like to make a donation, please do so to Jane Chambers or Sally Finlay in Compartment 4, Carriage H.

Hans sat very still. He read the note through twice. As he did so his jaw tightened and his face paled. Johann, watching intently, felt the familiar twist of fear. But Hans said nothing. Johann stared at Hans's damp forehead, to which a fine film of sweat gave an unhealthy sheen, then at his strong, thick neck—blotchy now with uneven patches of color, like bad sunburn. Hans's stillness, while his face underwent such rapid and invol-untary changes, touched him. Very gently, he asked, "Can I do anything, Hans?"

"Yes, you can," said Hans, looking up. His eyes had a beaten look. "Get me out of this mess." It was a plea, not an order, and Johann felt a clutch of love. Hans handed him the note, and with an obvious effort at control, picked up the *Times of India* and stared at it.

Johann took the note and read it. He wanted to say something gentle, but Hans would not look up from his paper. Johann said, "I'll be back."

He found the women in their carriage.

"Can I talk to you?"

"Oh, lord. Johann, I'm so glad it's you," burst out Jane. "I was scared stiff it would be Hans. Where is he?"

"I left him in the dining-car. He's reading the *Times of India*. Or trying to."

"Sit down," said Jane, shifting to make room for him on the bed.

There was a short pause, then he handed the note to Jane and said, with a rush, "You can't do this. Have you distributed this to everyone? It's not fair on Hans. He just lost his temper, that's all. He doesn't mean to. He's not like that really. I promise you, he is really kind. I know he doesn't always—"

"Johann, stop," said Sally firmly. "I'm sure Hans isn't all bad, or he wouldn't have you in tow. But he behaved like a—"

"But he didn't mean it. But when you said all that about us, about the Germans, he lost control. He's very patriotic."

"Kneeing people in the groin isn't patriotic. It is criminal. And it's nothing to do with being German. You're German and you would never hurt anyone. Hans is a brute in any language."

Jane, seeing the pain on Johann's face, said, "Sally, stop. It's not Johann's fault."

Sally's face softened and she said, "True. I'm sorry, Johann. And I did provoke him, I agree. And no, we haven't distributed the note."

Jane smiled at him, trying to lighten his anxiety, and interjected, "Mainly because we haven't got a photocopier, and we're not writing that out eighty times."

But Johann could not be distracted. He kept his eyes on Sally. "Please. There must be some way. I'd do anything to stop Hans being humiliated. And he is genuinely sorry about last night. I know he is."

"Has he said so?" asked Sally.

"Well, no, but I know he is. He's always sorry when his temper gets the better of him. And he's soft really. Sometimes he cries . . ."

"Sentimentality is as bad as brutality," said Sally. Too crushingly, Jane thought.

Johann, earnest and pleading now, said, "If Hans pays the whole 20,000 rupees to the steward, will that satisfy you? Will you give up the collection?"

Sally shifted to face Johann full on and said, "Yes. But only if he apologizes to Ram too. Tell him that if he pays Ram 20,000 rupees, and writes Ram a note to go with it, and I see the note and the money, we'll get Rajiv to deliver it. But Johann, this is non-negotiable. We don't want Hans muttering about blackmail or trying to bargain. We didn't ask him to come up with the money. We're just organizing a whip-round, that's all. Do you understand?"

Johann nodded. "Yes, yes, I understand. And there won't be any trouble, I promise. Thank you. Thank you both."

Jane, included in Johann's gratitude, felt a fraud. She'd taken no part in laying down the conditions, and she was in fact taken aback by Sally's commanding confidence. She was sorry for Johann. She reached across to the bedside table, picked up the Sekonda and handed it to him.

"Here. I'm sorry Hans made you give me this. I didn't want it, but he's such a bully. I don't know how you bear it. You'll get hurt one day, you know. Though I suppose it's none of my business." She spoke gently, looking into Johann's face.

He avoided her eyes, stood abruptly, and said, "No, it's not your business." He took the watch and put it in his pocket. "I'll see you get the money." He left the compartment in haste, fumbling the handle the wrong way, stumbling over the sill, failing to close the door completely.

"Poor sod," said Jane.

FIVE

That evening, at 5:30, Johann delivered the 20,000 rupees, and a note:

For the attention of Mr. Ram Dasani. I trust you will accept this R20,000 as a token of apology and as full compensation for any injury I may have caused you. Please sign this note to confirm that you agree you have no further claim on me, and return it to me. Hans Engleman.

Jane did not think much of the apology, but lacked the stomach for any further exchange. She found Rajiv in the bar, a mess of paperwork before him on the little brass table.

"Can I disturb you?" she asked.

"Of course." Rajiv stood up and smiled. "Can I get you a drink?"

What nice old-fashioned manners, thought Jane. "A Diet Coke would be nice," she said.

She watched him walk to the bar, tucking his cotton shirt into his trousers as he went. Tall and lanky, he moved with an easy grace. She again wondered what his background was. He looked too confident, too upper-class, to be a tour guide.

Rajiv put her Coke and a Kingfisher for himself on the table. Scooping his papers into his briefcase, he said, "What can I do for you?"

"I wondered if you could get some money we've collected to Ram, the steward. You know, the one that Hans assaulted. He's gone to his mother in Jaipur, hasn't he?"

"Collected? You had a collection for him?" He was clearly impressed. "You English! You'd find a lame duck cause to campaign for on the Arctic."

Jane was tempted to let him believe it had been a whip-round. His admiration was very pleasant. But she replied, "Well, we did threaten to, but then Hans did the decent thing. Here, I'll show you." She pulled the note addressed to the passengers out of her handbag, and handed it to him.

She looked at his thick black hair and his thin fingers with their clean oval nails, as he bent over the paper. She waited expectantly for his laugh. But when he looked up at her, his peculiar topaz eyes were puzzled.

"So, you did not send this?"

"No, but we showed it to Hans. And he paid up the 20,000 rupees himself."

"Isn't that blackmail?" He looked more stern than admiring, thought Jane, and she regretted telling him.

But she answered with spirit, "Absolutely not. We did not demand money by force. We just agreed, at Hans's request, to abandon the whip-round. And since he was to be so generous, there was no longer any need."

Jane had the satisfaction of seeing the admiration return to his gaze. Half laughing, Rajiv shook his head and said, "You women. You take my breath away. You should be a lawyer."

Jane burst out laughing. "I am a lawyer."

Once Jane had Rajiv's agreement to get the money to Ram, they sat in silence for a minute or two. Jane looked through the window as scenes skittered past—children and goats on the track-side, women stooped over, ramshackle houses. She shifted her gaze to the horizon, and at once the view became peaceful: a little-changing panorama of dun-colored landscape, distant wash of hills, faded sky behind a dinner-plate orange sun.

Jane was aware that Rajiv was looking at her, and she turned her eyes to him. She liked the open frankness of his gaze. But she was taken aback by his question.

"Are you married, Mrs. Chambers?"

"Yes . . . I mean, no." She laughed, embarrassed. "What I mean is, we're separated."

"Oh, God. How clumsy of me. I'm sorry." He looked into her eyes, his apology more formal than earnest.

"It's OK. I'm getting used to it. It's been four months. And it's fine. No dramas, no recriminations. He's a great chap."

"What is his name?"

"Patrick. Patrick Chambers. He's a restaurateur. In London. His restaurant is called Jane's." She smiled again, a little rueful. "Not many women can boast of a restaurant named after them, can they? Not quite as impressive as a rose, but still . . ."

"I'm impressed."

"Good."

They talked on, and the bar-car began to fill with pre-dinner drinkers. Jane swapped from Diet Coke to beer, and found herself telling Rajiv about Patrick.

"My mother thinks I'm wicked to have left him. But I think I've done him a favor. Made way for the sort of wife who'd suit him."

"And what sort of wife is that?"

"Oh, the motherly type. Keen on children, happy to be at home in the country."

"Don't you like children?"

"No, I don't think I do. Well, I quite like other people's in small doses. But kids aren't the point. Surely the only reason to spend every night of your life with the same person is because he's more important to you than anything else. It used to be like that for us. Well, somewhere we lost it. Patrick spends all his time in Jane's, and I spend all mine in the City." She paused, thoughtful. "And then, I'm much more ambitious than Patrick. I want to be a top lawyer. The best."

Jane realized with surprise that she was discussing things with this comparative stranger that she never discussed with anyone, not even Sally. And for the first time she was talking about her split from Patrick without her voice cracking or her throat tightening. She ended firmly. "So you can see it was hopeless."

It was clear that Rajiv did not understand. She'd have liked him to understand, to declare himself on her side. But he wouldn't, would he? He's a man for a start. And on top of that he's Indian. Probably thinks baby-farming is what women are for.

But later that evening, when Sally had put out the light and the train was hurtling through the blackness, Jane stared at the invisible ceiling and asked herself Rajiv's unspoken question, the question everyone asked her, and to which she had no answer. Why had she left Patrick?

The truth was she did not know. She did not have one big decent reason. There were bits of answers, that's all.

For one thing, they'd both been living a half-life. And for another, she did not love Patrick enough. If she had, she would surely have taken a job that left her with the energy to join him after Jane's closed. Been a company lawyer and knocked off at six. But there was no question of that. Her job was vital to her. She was good at it, and it made heaps of money.

And then, she'd stopped taking an interest in Patrick's life. The restaurant was great, but she seldom went there. She no longer asked how it was doing, what Patrick's ambitions were. She feared, indeed she knew, they were diverging from hers. On the rare evenings when they were both free, he preferred poached eggs and the telly to a concert or the theater. He was obliging, of course: did what she wanted; did not press her to fall in line with his desires.

He didn't even press her much about children. Although she knew that, more than anything, he wanted a family. But children would mean the end for her. A descent into baby-talk, boring clothes, saggy breasts and middle age.

She'd *had* to make the break when she did. If she'd stayed, neither of them would have had another chance. One of them

59

would have had to compromise and end up disappointed: Patrick, childless and stoical. Or her, unfulfilled and bitter.

Her mind went, as it did so often, back to the weekend that decided it for her.

Even now, the memory fanned small flames of indignation. Patrick had planned a weekend in Scotland, to celebrate her thirty-sixth birthday. He'd been good about her putting it off once because a case had kept her in Rotterdam. And when, the next weekend, they'd finally arrived at the mini-castle overlooking the River Tweed, it had been travel-brochure heaven. The air was balmy and clear, the trees tinged with russet and yellow, the river flashing as it scurried down stony slopes and eddied around big flat rocks.

They'd had a drink on the terrace, and felt work and London slough away as the peace and whiskey seeped into them. When it got too cold and murky to sit out, they had gone in to dinner, and had a perfectly disgusting meal, and a perfectly nice time. Neither had complained about the indifferent service and horrible cooking, and they'd gone to bed early. Jane was too tired to make love, and had gone to sleep with Patrick reading a Scottish Borders travel guide by her side.

She should have realized he was up to something sooner than she did. Glenshiel Castle was hardly the five-star escape they usually went for. But it wasn't until their last day at breakfast, when the owner offered Patrick a free rod for the Glenshiel beat, that it all came out. Patrick refused the fishing, saying he and Jane had planned a drive.

When the man had gone Jane exclaimed, "How extraordinary!"

"What?" asked Patrick.

"Owners of prime beats don't give away lucrative salmon fishing to complete strangers. Or offer to lend them expensive kit. Does he know you?"

Then Patrick had told her. Yes, they did know each other. Talking steadily and earnestly, holding on to both Jane's hands, he'd explained that he'd been working on this plan for months, but hadn't wanted to discuss it with her until he knew the scheme was possible, and until they had time to do so properly, away from her job, and his.

He said he'd made two previous visits to Glenshiel, and had taken an option on the hotel. He'd brought her here to show her, to make her see how wonderful it would be. They could sell Jane's, sell the Normandy farmhouse, sell the Primrose Hill house. Turn this failing set-up into a top-class fishing hotel.

Jane had pulled her hands out of his, leaned back in disbelief, started to protest. But he'd begged her to hear him out. He'd done his homework. There was a shortage of good hotel beds in the area; the place was under-marketed; the restaurant, if only it sold decent food, could have a trade independent of the hotel; they could probably rent the stables to a riding school and offer riding to the guests; restore the tennis court. He didn't think they could afford to buy the fishing beat, but the owner, if a hopeless hotelier, was a great fisherman, and was happy to keep the beat and let the hotel guests buy rods.

He went on and on, seemingly oblivious of Jane's mounting anger. But finally she exploded.

"But what about *me*, Patrick? Have you thought for one minute about what *I'd* like? How could you just assume I'd want to give up my career to live in bloody *Scotland?*" She spat the word out, as if it was poisonous.

"Darling, I'm not asking you to give up your career. We are only an hour from Edinburgh; if you want to join a law firm, there are half a dozen good ones that would kill to get Jane Chambers."

Jane shook her head, anger flushing her cheeks. "I don't believe I'm hearing this. I'm a marine insurance specialist, not some poxy domestics lawyer who can go anywhere, knowing there's always a market in divorce."

Patrick closed his eyes for a second, making a visible effort to stay calm. He said, "Darling, at least consider what I am sug-

61

gesting. I will never do something that you don't want. You know that. So stop being angry, and start being rational. I think we could have a most wonderful life here. I want you to think about it before you junk the idea. OK?"

Jane did not answer. She stared at him, her face closed and hostile.

He tried again. "Or we could run the place together. Why not? You have a genius for making places comfortable without looking done up by expensive designers. And you would be a brilliant business manager, much better, I guess, than me. And I could do the Mine Host stuff. We'd be a terrific team."

He tried to touch her cheek, but she reared back, saying, "How *could* you go making plans without even mentioning it? Sneaking off without saying a word?" Her voice was rising and neighboring breakfasters were studying their porridge while straining their ears.

He said, "I didn't, darling. It is not a done deal. That's why I brought you here . . ."

He tried to regain her hands. But she whisked them away.

Patrick stood up and said, his voice controlled and low, "OK, darling. I should have told you before. But let's discuss it on our own, shall we? Not with an audience. I'll be down by the fishing hut." He leaned over and kissed her indignant cheek, and left.

She hadn't joined him by the river, and her anger and the feeling of being left out, taken for granted, had stayed with her, even after their return to London. Patrick, tired of explaining, had given up his Glenshiel dream with a stoical cheerfulness that upset Jane further.

But now the fact that he'd not consulted her in advance didn't seem so terrible: he'd hoped the place would bewitch her. But the more she brooded on the episode, the clearer it was that he wanted a different life. He'd always loved Scotland and fishing. When they were first married they'd vacationed in Highland B and Bs, fishing or walking. When she had got her partnership and a raise, she'd bought him a week's fishing on the Spey, and she'd been content to read and dream on the bank all day while he stood waist deep in the water. But once they'd bought La Prairie, or rather once *she'd* bought La Prairie, they went there instead, or to some hot glamorous jet-set spot. The fact was, they were living the life that she wanted to live, but it wasn't enough.

God, I'm a selfish bitch, she thought, punching the pillow against the cabin wall, and flinging her head into it. Did I leave Patrick because I couldn't give him what he wanted? Or because he always gave me what I wanted?

Rajiv arranged to have the money delivered to Ram at Jaipur when the train passed through again on their way to Agra. Jane rather hoped Ram would take the money, but not sign the note, leaving Hans to nightmares of later prosecution. John said Ram would surely sign it, as all Indians had an exaggerated respect for that legacy of British rule, the chitty.

Hans avoided the English party, refusing to acknowledge even Lucy and John. As Hans ignored her "Nice morning," she turned to Jane. "That's your fault. But I'm honored to be judged guilty by association."

Only Johann seemed unhappy at the cold war, smiling at them, then hurrying past. Sally suspected that Hans allowed him few friends, and that he'd enjoyed the simple pleasure of someone other than Hans to talk to.

Umesh had warned them it would be hotter in Jaisalmer, but still the heat was an assault, buffeting them rudely as they stepped down from the train.

John lifted his wide-brimmed cricket hat that had served him well twenty-five years ago at school and every summer since on the village cricket ground, wiped his forehead with a red spotted handkerchief and said, "I don't believe we are going bargain-hunting in the bazaar. Today is for a cool museum with ample benches, or mint juleps by a hotel pool."

The four friends stood at the station entrance, where half a dozen drummers beat their instruments with more energy than musicality, at least to Jane's ears, and where a mournful snake charmer set his snake to earn its keep.

The snake waited for a maximum audience before weaving swiftly up from the basket and gazing, stony eyed, at the crowd. He stayed up just long enough for his owner's assistant, a ragged girl of perhaps ten, to make her rounds with a collecting bowl, then sank back without ceremony into a neat coil. A half-hearted spatter of clapping signaled an abrupt stop to the drumming. Jane, listless with heat, felt relief at the silence, mixed with uneasiness at European indifference to all this Eastern effort.

Lucy, dropping a few rupees into the drummers' basket, said, "Let's bunk off once we get into the center. I refuse to look around one more Rajput palace or Hindu temple. I want a shady corner to sketch."

Lucy was carrying nothing but a sketchbook and her box of pencils, charcoals and chalks. As she swung her willowy frame into the waiting bus, she looked, thought Jane, cool and graceful without being the least conscious of fashion. She was wearing sandals with wide straps of black elastic on wooden soles, a thin gray and white cotton dress with long loose sleeves, and a single strand of gray and black beads, like glass marbles, around her neck. This muted ensemble was brought alive by a brilliant orange scarf of thin Indian cotton, loosely tied around her hips. Jane watched her with admiration, tinged with envy. No make-up, no effort, and she looks so good.

Once on the edge of the town, Rajiv let them off the coach, and mercifully off the leash as well, but with firm instructions to be back at the bus by one o'clock.

Though hot, it was exhilarating to be away from their fellow tourists. Now confident enough to ignore the beggar-children who trailed after them, repetitively playing "Frère Jacques" on bamboo bansuris, the four friends wandered through the streets.

The children soon gave up to pursue more likely pickings. The four strolled slowly, stopping to watch the daily routines of street life. The Jaisalmer market traders took little notice of the

Westerners, and seemed unresentful of their open stares. Although a strikingly beautiful woman, ironing with a foot-high iron that took both arms to lift, knew her picturesque worth and demanded 10 rupees per photograph.

A fat balding man squatted easily on his hunkers, a great stone mortar full of some yellow paste between his knees. He swung a giant wooden pestle up and down with ease, his arm muscles tensing and relaxing in time to the wobbling of his belly. He seemed tireless, lost in the rhythm of his pounding.

"I wish Patrick could see this," said Jane. "You know his principal bugbear is the health inspector." She waved an arm to encompass sweetmeats being deep-fried on a rickety gas ring (its gas lead connecting it to a cylinder several yards away at just the right height to trip the unwary) and the betel-leaf seller whose wares were spread on the pavement, his customers squatting around him, chewing and spitting in silence.

Sally shuddered. "They must have iron guts. Look at that."

Jane followed Sally's gaze to a cow conscientiously licking the nozzle of the electric juice extractor belonging to the mango-juice seller.

The thought of Patrick suddenly clouded Jane's spirits. Damn it, she thought, I miss him.

Lucy said, "You go on. I'm going to sit here for a bit and sketch."

John protested. "Darling, you'll be plagued by beggars."

"I'll be fine." She sat down on the steps of a barber shop and opened her sketchbook.

As Sally, Jane and John left the market, a flat bullock cart bearing a dead cow pushed its way through the narrow street, four young men running along the flanks, like escorts or pall-bearers. The friends flattened themselves against the wall to let it pass.

They walked up the twists and turns of the sloping stone ramp to the wide square of the old castle fort. John, red and sweating, said he'd get the agony over while he could still breathe, and, followed by Sally, set off to climb to an ancient cannon emplacement from where the guidebook promised views over fort, town and desert.

Jane declined the further climb. She wanted to see the Jain temples, and was glad to be on her own, briefly out of Sally's bossy care.

But she didn't like them. They were mostly dark, and slightly sinister. She felt oppressed by the attendants, not knowing whether they were official priests, or opportunistic vendors. And she studiously had to ignore the proffered plates anyway, as she'd foolishly left her purse with one of the young boys outside.

She was uneasy about that. The lad had promised to guard her handbag. It seemed the Jains' reverence for the cow extended to banning anything made of leather. She'd noticed most tourists removed their purses from their bags and their cameras from their cases before handing them over, but she'd felt embarrassed to do this—it implied an insulting lack of trust. Now she regretted being such an ass.

And then she felt awkward gawping at carvings and shrines when so many Indians were obviously genuine pilgrims, here on legitimate religious business. And she wanted to distance herself from a group of loutish Englishmen, in their late twenties or early thirties. One had, she saw with distaste, a beer bottle in his hand. They were talking loudly, deaf to centuries of worship.

Once again Jane felt a sharp longing for Patrick. She wasn't supposed to need male protection, but Patrick had always had comforting army-officer manners. She felt his authoritative arm shepherding her firmly away from these yobs. If he'd been here, she'd not have been intimidated by the saffron-robed priests with their mysterious offerings, or by the pushing pilgrims.

She returned to the welcome glare of the steps, retrieved her bag (with contents intact, of course) and sat down to wait for Sally and John.

She watched an American couple outside the tourist shop

opposite. They were bickering in that almost ritual manner that meant they'd been quarrelling for so many years they did it on auto-pilot. She thought of poor Emily married to the testy prof. What a nightmare marriage. And of Johann, doomed to misery with Hans. Even Sally's marriage to her brother Tom was more to do with convenience than love. Only Lucy and John seemed really happy, easy with each other, relaxed and fond.

She thought, but is that enough? Oh, Patrick, I'm easy with you. And fond. Maybe I even love you. But is that *it?* Is that our lot? Are child-begetting and middle-aged comfort all that are left?

Suddenly she was angry with Patrick. Why didn't he mind things more? Why was he so stoical and solid? Why did he just let her go? He'd not telephoned her once since she'd left. Not once. She'd had her hand on the phone a dozen times, longing to just give in, capitulate into the warmth of him. But she'd always pulled back in time, knowing she was being weak and stupid.

Once she'd seen him in Vivat Flora, buying armloads of roses, and she'd felt a wash of jealousy, until she'd heard him give the restaurant address for delivery. Must be for a customer's party. She'd hidden behind a bay tree, heart banging. Ridiculous.

Oh, Patrick, she thought, why do you always have to be so bloody *supportive*? Why didn't he rant and rave, shake her and hug her? Lock her in or lock her out? But no, he behaved like a bloody army officer under fire. Polite. Stiff upper lip. Civilized. Treated her as a grown-up independent woman who could make her own decisions.

Jane pressed the heels of her hands into her cheeks at the memory, eyes wide open to stop them spilling.

Maybe he just didn't care that much. He'd been happy, he said. No complaints. But *why* hadn't he complained? Didn't he want something more than a descent into domesticity? Before middle age claimed them? Couldn't he feel time was running out? She felt the tears of self-pity prick her eyes and overflow as she rummaged angrily in her bag for a tissue.

When Sally turned the corner and saw Jane on the steps, she stopped. She waited until Jane had blown her nose, taken her sunglasses off, wiped her eyes, and put them back. Then she advanced, saying, "Come along, Jane. We'll be late for the bus."

SIX

The annual Restaurateurs' Association meeting and lunch was being held in one of the new mega-restaurants in Soho. The place was a converted cinema, and the restaurant was on two levels, each serving close on 300 people. The Association lunch was in the lower, more fashionable level. Tables downstairs were in more demand partly because, being cheaper, they were closer together, and there was a consequent buzz from a generally younger media crowd. But also because the enormous bar, made of thick frosted greenish glass and stretching almost the length of the room, was ruled by Rick, London's most highly paid barman. He was Australian, with dyed yellow hair, friendly eyes, a sun-lamp tan and a surfer's physique. He managed to be attractive to both men and women, and to appear interested in every one of the thirty-odd people on and around his bar stools. And he mixed the best margaritas in town.

But today Rick was behind the upstairs bar, comforting his downstairs regulars miffed at a private party keeping them out. Upstairs had been fully booked for three weeks, but Rick was dispensing drinks and chatting to the super-egos who drifted in expecting someone to magic a table out of nowhere for them. He could make the most self-obsessed feel that waiting for a bar stool was a privilege.

Patrick waved to Rick over the heads of the bar crowd, and made his way down the wide curved staircase. The noise increased as he descended. At the bottom he needed to shout his name into the ear of the seater and greeter checking names on her list. He thought, in mixed envy and amazement, this joint must be clearing three million, maybe four, a year.

In spite of a canny decision to allow only fizzy water on the tables while the AGM proceeded, the organizers had difficulty in obtaining anything like silence so the proceedings could begin. The minimally decorated walls, deliberately smooth to create "buzz" by amplifying noise, were not designed for speeches. These were delivered from a raised platform more often used for a jazz group, and were quite as boring as Patrick had expected. Very soon he couldn't hear anyway. Most of the 250 restaurateurs who had turned up were more interested in checking out this newest flavor-of-the-month restaurant, and in seeing their mates, than in the chairman's Annual Statement.

Four young men at his table were talking, none too quietly, about a new South African restaurant, which served, if Patrick was overhearing right, fried caterpillars called mopane worms. They talked with enthusiasm. They made Patrick feel very old.

But not quite as old, he thought, as those old farts conducting this meeting. Why are they determined to argue the unarguable? No one will ever get restaurateurs to agree on anything, let alone on whether service charges should be included in the bill, or whether there should be a Code of Practice to stop cowboys ripping off tourists.

But finally clapping at the front signaled the end, and Patrick swung his chair back to face the table and take an interest in mopane worms.

He found himself looking at an astonishingly pretty young woman, slipping into the chair at his side. She was wearing extraordinary clothes. Dungarees made of some soft blue suede-like material worn over a scoop-necked white T-shirt gave her a kookie clown-like air. And yet she looked expensive. Designer dungarees, he supposed. She had what Jane scornfully called "big hair" but hers was not fluffed up or moussed or teased. It erupted from her head in zigzag curls, shiny and untidy, and there was a prodigious amount of it. It was somewhere between blond and red. Under the hair hung modern silver earrings, spi-

70

raling down to swing just clear of her shoulders. Behind oval steel-rimmed specs, enormous blue, almost aquamarine, eyes, wide open and friendly, looked straight into his. Is she real? thought Patrick, staring like an adolescent at her mouth, unmade-up but plum-red as if from rubbing or biting.

"Hi," she said. "I'm Stella. On the *Dispatch*." She had a model's smile—teeth white and even, gums pink and pearly.

"I don't believe it," said Patrick, taking her outstretched hand, cool and small. "You cannot be Stella."

Her smile broadened to a grin. "Why not?"

"Well, you are too young for a start. To have got that knowledgeable, not to say crusty and picky, you'd need to be at least sixty."

She broadened her slight American accent to a stage Southern one. "Well, gee, thanks, mister, you sure know how to make a gal feel appreciated."

Patrick said, "Besides no one who looks as edible as you could be so vitriolic."

Stella laughed. "Jeezus. Just my luck. Now I've got to have lunch sitting next to some poor guy whose joint I didn't like. You have to be a restaurateur, I guess?" Her voice was light and teasing. "But thanks for the edible bit. From a restaurateur I guess that's a compliment. Or are you a chef?"

"No, I'm Patrick Chambers. I own Jane's. That's the one you said was stuck in a seventies time warp, and whose customers all looked like bank managers and accountants, and whose wine waiter shook the Château Palmer like castanets."

She looked hard at him for a moment, then helped herself to mineral water before she said, "And wasn't any of it true? I've yet to meet a goddam restaurateur or chef who didn't think that all praise is deserved and all criticism unjustified. So I'm ready for it. Go on. Zap me." She was still smiling, confident, unfazed.

"OK. I'll tell you. The time-warp thing hurt because I'd just spent a bundle redecorating the dining rooms, which were never seventies anyway. And you managed to come the week before we closed to do it, and your piece came out the week we reopened."

"Maybe if you'd sent me a press release saying you were scrapping the decor, I could have said so."

"All right. But is it my fault you don't like the look of my customers? Sure we get businessmen at lunchtime. We're an expensive Michelin-star restaurant and not too many ladies who lunch or media trendies want the bill that comes with Michelin stars. Maybe I should introduce a house rule: no suits or ties allowed—"

Stella cut in, "Journalists can only write as they find."

Patrick ignored the interruption. "At night, Jane's is not gray suits at all. It's good for lovers, who want to hear and not be overheard, and for the fashionable rich celebrating high days and holidays. You might even like it."

He smiled at her, determined to keep his tone light and inconsequential. But Stella caught the bitter undertow and said, "Hey, loosen up. Aren't you over-reacting a bit here? Why take it so personally?"

"Because it is personal. Like having your darling child described as stupid and ugly. It's bad enough if it's true, but you made that bit up about the Château Palmer. Wine's my big thing, you see. And I'd have served that wine. Only I didn't because nobody did. After your review came out, I checked the wine sales, and we didn't serve any Château Palmer at all that week."

Her eyes flicked away from his for a second. "I don't remember the wine thing," she said quickly. "But I did say I liked the food. I know I did, because the food was great."

Her eyes, huge and blue, returned to his, challenging. Patrick smiled, relaxing, thinking, she's right, why take it personally? "Sure you did, and I'm grateful. But would you go to a time-warp restaurant full of accountants to eat good food?"

Let it go, he said to himself. She was only doing her job. And if the restaurant is doing badly, it's because of places like this, bloody great barns serving good food, not-so-cheap but cheerful, and that's what people want these days. Few Michelin-star restaurants made any money at all. Most of them were flag-ships for hotels or restaurant groups, or belonged to multi-millionaires who footed the losses because they liked to show off.

He was relieved when the waiter brought the first course, a carefully constructed tower of warm new potatoes, caramelized red onions, and air-dried ham topped with an explosion of exotic leaves. Patrick mentally conceded that the chef had more de-signer pizazz than the classic Alastair.

One of the young men across the table button-holed Stella, trying to persuade her to visit his wine bar in Chester. She was polite, and took his card, and soon she was talking to the others, laughing and throwing back her head so that her great messy mane of hair covered the straps of her dungarees, and the back of her chair. When she laughed, Patrick could see into her mouth. She had the pink tongue of a child and not a single filling. She's as clean and healthy as a puppy, he thought, mo-mentarily imagining her lips and teeth nuzzling his hand, her tumbling hair caressing his forearm. God, I feel quite drunk, he thought. Get a grip.

When the main course came, Patrick burst out laughing.

"What's the matter?" Stella asked quickly.

"Oh, it's nothing," said Patrick, "but this morning a mighty powerful customer asked us to do cod and polenta for a posh dinner, and Alastair, my chef, had a tantrum because he said both cod and polenta are overpriced, overrated, and overdone in every brasserie in town. And look!" He pointed to their plates, on which pieces of cod, their skin charred to crispness, sat on a fat plinth of grilled polenta.

"Well, he's right there," said Stella. "I guess I've personally depleted the cod stocks by enough to endanger the fishing trade."

Patrick asked her how she'd got the job on the *Dispatch*,

imagining she'd talk to him of journalism school, or working her way up from cub reporter, but he said, "I won a competition."

"What?"

"Yeah, I did. I was working on the arts pages of a magazine owned by the same bunch of sharks as the *Dispatch*. But I've always liked food as much as art, so I entered their competition for gourmet writing. The prize was a secondment to the London office. But then the old fart who used to do the restaurant crits croaked on the job. So here I am."

The combination of Stella's perfect beauty and her irreverence was unnerving. Patrick had never met anyone like her.

She went on talking to Patrick, but he was having trouble following her. He wished she'd talk to the others so he could just watch her without the demand, the pressure, of her eyes. When she stretched forward to reach the water or the wine the bib of her dungarees fell forward, leaving a gap, and Patrick imagined his hand slipping in under the bib. This is crazy, he thought. I'm as randy as a teenager. And I've only just met the woman.

Discomforted by his thoughts, Patrick responded to a shout from a neighboring table, and went to say hello to Theodora. She and Serge had recently opened a second Soho restaurant, called Chez Serge, this time a converted pub. They swapped turnover stories, Patrick lying about the number of bums on his restaurant seats, Theodora brushing aside congratulations on the *succès fou* of the new one.

"Oh, Patrick. It's a complete fiasco. No one knows what they are doing. We are far too full too soon. If we don't get it right soon, the *Dispatch* will eat us alive."

Patrick thought of telling her that Stella was here. But he thought he might betray the effect she'd had on him, and said instead, "Theodora, Chez Serge is good. Really good. I went there for lunch, and the sausage and mash was so good I bought more for supper. I spent my night off scoffing it while watching the rugby."

Patrick endured Theodora's friendly inquiries after Jane and whether separation might turn into divorce. But he didn't want to think of his wife, and he resumed his table-hopping. But Jane obtruded, as she so often did. She had always teased him about the professional way he "worked a room," exchanging pleasantries with everyone he knew and quite a few he didn't. She'd said it was a hangover from his time in the officers' mess. And that he'd have made a perfect equerry to a royal. She also said it was what made him a great restaurateur—the ability to find boring people interesting, to give them three minutes' undivided attention and somehow move on without offending them.

Patrick, remembering this, thought bitterly that what she'd probably meant was that he'd have made a great air hostess, whereas *she* valued the higher things of life, and would spend three hours at a party talking to the same person, male or female, if they had something interesting to say. As he clapped backs, kissed cheeks and shook hands, his mind was half on Jane, mentally quarrelling with her to justify his desire for Stella. After twenty minutes away from his table, deliberately staying out of Stella's unsettling orbit, the sudden thought that she might leave, that he might not see her again, had him hurrying back.

"I'm sorry," he said as he sat down.

She looked up, open-faced, friendly.

"No sweat. I kept a piece of pie for you."

She smiled her dazzling smile. Here I go again, thought Patrick. No one has dazzling smiles except in movie magazines. You expect her teeth to send out pinging little stars like a toothpaste commercial.

"Sticky stuff?" She held a half bottle of Beaumes-de-Venise over his glass, and looked at him for confirmation to pour. Their eyes met, and held. He failed to answer her question, and she tipped the bottle to fill the glass without looking at it. He said "Thanks," also without taking his eyes off hers. They both knew they were signing a pact.

She blinked, closing her eyes a fraction too slowly, for a second too long, opening them again, still on his: a message of raw sex.

He looked down at his glass. "I hate Beaumes-de-Venise."

"You should have said no."

"How could I say no?"

She smiled, pleased with herself, confident of capture.

Halfway through the lemon curd tart Patrick arrested her hand as she pushed the crème fraîche toward him. Gripping her narrow wrist in his fingers, he said, "Let's get out of here. Three hours is long enough to be in a basement."

She hardly paused. "Sure," she said. "Why not?"

She stood at once, scooping up her handbag, a soft leather cross between a satchel and a backpack, slung it over her shoulder, and with a "Bye, you guys," headed for the door.

They came out into bright sunshine, and Patrick had a moment of panic. God, what am I doing? It's years since I picked up a girl. I'm mad. It's the drink. Or reaction after months of no-Jane. It's cradle snatching. I'm twice her age. Maybe we can just walk through Soho and then I'll send her off in a cab and escape.

Stella put her arm through his. She felt tiny next to him. They window-shopped, Stella leading him into almost every shop and gallery, chattering knowledgeably and unselfconsciously about modern painting and sculpture, food and restaurants. Patrick was conscious of little except her arm through his. He wanted her to stop talking and let him push her up against a wall, any wall. They walked through Neal's Yard, and Stella bought some Somerset goats cheese and an expensive loaf of stoneground bread, stuffing them into her bag.

They wandered into a wine shop and she picked out a bottle of Mumm champagne.

"Why Mumm?" asked Patrick.

"It's the cheapest. And we've got to have real champagne. The champagne is for before, and the bread and cheese is for after. I'm always starving after sex."

She turned to face him. He stood stock still. She came up very close, lowered her bag to the floor, and put her arms, the champagne bottle still in one hand, around his neck, and lifted her face so that he had no option but to kiss her.

Jesus, she is delicious. What the hell am I doing—a middle-aged bloke kissing a young woman in a wine shop? But he couldn't stop. He was floating in the smell of her.

He pulled back, and lifted his head to see the youth at the till gazing at them with a would-be sardonic air. He took the bottle of Mumm from Stella, and returned it to the shelf.

"We'll have a bottle of Veuve Clicquot La Grande Dame, chilled for three minutes please."

The young man dropped his smirk at Patrick's brisk command.

He said, "Certainly, sir," And put the bottle in the Insta-Chill.

Waiting for the lad to return his Amex card, and for the machine to do its miracle cooling, seemed an eternity. Patrick wanted to get back to kissing Stella, who was pressing her tits against his back, and had one arm around his chest under his jacket, her fingers trying to find a way in between his shirt buttons. He took her hand in his, firmly lowering it to her side. When the assistant turned away to wrap the icy bottle, he whispered, so close to her ear it was almost a kiss, "Control yourself, woman. All things come to those who wait."

They hailed a cab. Patrick barely had time to say "Claridges" over the cabbie's shoulder before Stella was on him, her tongue in his mouth, her hands feeling for him, her hair enveloping him. She was a live thing, all youth and demand and urgency, careless that it was 4 p.m. on a working day and they were in a London taxi.

Patrick leaned over her, pulled down the dicky seat behind the driver and said, "Stella, you are going to sit demurely over there, or we'll both be arrested for public indecency."

He pushed her roughly onto the seat, and sat back, looking

at her, longing for her, but also enjoying denying her, controlling her. She was enjoying the game too, and contented herself with pushing her sneaker-clad foot gently between his legs, clumsily rubbing. Patrick gripped her foot, and slid his hand up her dungarees, registering with a further stab of lust, that she didn't shave her legs. Her calves were smooth and cool as silk, but he could feel the tiny hairs on her shins resisting his upward stroke.

At the hotel, Patrick booked a room, staring down the raised eyebrow of Michael, the duty manager, whom he knew. In the old-fashioned lift, plush as a boudoir, Stella was mercifully well behaved. She sat on the tiny upholstered sofa and stared at the youth operating the controls. Patrick felt a second of intense jealousy at the thought that she was nearer to the lift-boy's age than to his.

"How old are you, Stella?" he asked as he shut the bedroom door.

"Twenty-four. Why?"

"I just want to know that what we are about to do is legal," he said. He slid the straps of her dungarees down over her shoulders, pushed her backward onto the double bed, and yanked at her trouser legs. They jammed on her sneakers, and she squirmed over, out of his grip, saying, "But what about the champagne?"

"Too late, darling," he said, his voice gravelly. "All that cock-teasing in the taxi is your undoing. Champagne is now for afters."

He reached for her, pulled her back and rolled her over again with ease. He carefully took off her glasses, then held first one foot and then the other as he twisted off her sneakers. He pulled off her dungarees and knickers together, and was in her at once, without preamble. Not even a kiss.

Christ, he thought, she's magic. This is going to be all over any second. He looked down at her tangled hair, her open mouth, young firm tits bouncing upward as she arched her back.

He shut his eyes, trying to hold back by shutting out the

sight of her, but with his eyes closed, the smell of her took over: the heady mix of her breath, ardent and animal, and her healthy faintly perfumed hair was worse. He gave up, gave in. Just did it. He fucked her, missionary style, hard and fast, no frills.

When he collapsed, her head was under his neck, her body completely submerged by his. She couldn't breathe, and he rolled off her.

"I know. I know." Patrick's voice was deep, half groan, half sigh. "I won't ask How Was It For You?" He leaned on one elbow, then kissed her belly. "My only excuses are no sex for months, and the mitigating circumstances of your strumpet behavior. 'She drove me to it m'lud.' "

They drank the champagne out of the bathroom toothmugs. Presently Patrick said, kissing her deeply as desire returned, "OK. This one is for you."

He ran his hands up under her T-shirt. She wore no bra, and her nipples rose to the touch of his fingers. He caressed her shoulders, armpits and her stomach, then pulled her T-shirt over her head, and removed one sock that had somehow survived his previous onslaught.

He looked down at her body, marveling at its perfection. With his fingers he traced the contours of her hips and belly, down one smooth brown thigh, and up the other. At first she lay still, but soon small sighs, then moans, escaped her. Then suddenly she was frantic, writhing and arching her back and trying to pull him down to her. Her uninhibited randiness overcame his efforts to keep her waiting, and this time he made love to her slowly, delaying his climax until she was there too. Her moans became deep-throated cries, then faded as the waves of orgasm weakened.

He looked into her face, so young and flawlessly beautiful. He felt transported and euphoric. For a minute she returned his gaze, contented as a cat. Then she said, "Get off me, you great oaf. I can't see a thing without my glasses. And I'm starving. Where's the bread and cheese?"

79

SEVEN

The ceremonial receptions on station platforms were becoming less extravagant as the journey progressed. At Jaipur there had been the elephant guard of honor. At Jodhpur the platform had been painted in colored chalks, like a giant carpet, and a row of women in red saris had touched each tourist's forehead with a talik of yellow or red, and garlanded their necks with long thick necklaces of double marigolds, tasselled with colored silks at the join. The passengers, by now used to the garlands which were offered at every lunchtime hotel and as they stepped from the tour bus at almost every fort or palace, accepted them without embarrassment, but with little grace. Jane had learned to return the hands-together greeting with bowed head. Sally thought such Indian antics affected, and just said, "Thank you."

At Jaisalmer they were down to the ragged drummers and snake charmer. At Sawai Madhopur a pair of mounted spear carriers flanked the station entrance, both horses and riders malnourished and half asleep.

And now, at Chittorgarh, a single banner had been slung crookedly across the iron gates of the station. Hanging back to front, it wasn't legible from the station side, but you could look back and read:

Chittorgarh
and the Indian Tourism Development Corp
WELCOMES
most heartily
Maharajah Express

Jane was relieved. It meant less hanging around for the Japanese to smile into each other's cameras, and for the video enthusiasts to record enough footage to bore their friends to death.

Jane and John sat in the front of the coach, with Sally and Lucy immediately behind them. As the bus bullied its way through villages and hamlets, they gazed down on preparations for parades and celebrations. A local festival, the driver said, shrugging. Everyone seemed to be going somewhere else, by bike or donkey or bus. The women and girls wore bright Rajasthani skirts and blouses, their headdresses edged with gold or silver thread, their arms bangled from wrist to elbow. The men's turbans were of every shape and shade, but hot colors predominated—reds and oranges, or bright sulfur yellow.

Trapped inside the air-conditioned coach, Jane longed to be down on the street and part of the scene, and wished the whole oversized, intruding busload of them were not there at all.

"Look how proud that dad is," she said, her eyes on the driver of the donkey cart ahead of them. He turned constantly to check on his passengers, a pair of nine- or ten-year-old schoolgirls, hair in bright blue ribbons, white blouses blinding in the sun. "You can almost feel the effort those girls are making not to get dirty." Excitement had the girls wriggling and grinning, until they looked up and caught Jane's eye. Embarrassed, they bent their heads and giggled behind their hands.

Something almost wistful in Jane's voice prompted John to say, "Would you have wanted children?"

The past tense dismayed her. She didn't answer for a moment, then said, "I suppose I still do. But not yet. Which probably means never."

"Explain," said John.

Jane looked out of the window, marshalling her thoughts. "I guess I always thought I could have everything. Successful career, nice life, husband, children. But you can't. Anyway it's too late now. Unless I make a mad dash for instant divorce, a new fella and children—all before my biological clock goes into ter-

81

minal decline." She turned and smiled weakly at him.

He said, "Oh come on, Jane, you must have years of possible baby-making ahead of you. And why *can't* you have it all? We have a woman partner with children, and she's the mainstay of the firm. We don't *like* it when she's off for three months on another breeding bat, but we'd be up a gum tree without her." He held the upright pole next to his seat as the bus swayed and bumped over the rutted road.

"She'd never make it at Chalker and Day, that's for sure," said Jane. "I'm the first female partner they've let into the fold at all. And they didn't have much option really, because I'm the best marine specialist they've got, and they can't claim I don't pull my weight. But I'm still a woman, and we all know, don't we chaps, that women aren't really *committed*." She ran her fingers through her hair from forehead to crown, raking it off her face.

Watching her, John said, "You don't think there's a bit of feminist paranoia in all this, do you?"

"Absolutely not." Jane's riposte had more heat in it than John's mild question deserved. "The only reason they gave me a partnership at all was because Ince and Co., who are *the* marine legal firm, offered me a better deal. They couldn't match the money so they made me a partner."

John put his hand on her knee and gave it a little shake, saying, "Well, there you are then. The next step will be an equity partnership."

Jane snapped back, smiling but brittle. "Not a chance. Chalker and Day has been owned entirely by blokes since ever, and they are not about to change. I guess a female would lower the tone of the annual equity partners' dinner. She might pass the port to the right or something."

Jane stopped. Though she spoke with self-mocking banter, she was raw on the subject. She was in danger of sounding too shrill, too emotional. John, seeing her face tighten as she looked quickly out of the window, let the matter drop.

What's the matter with me? thought Jane. I'm falling to bits here. For a moment then I was tempted to blub on this guy's shoulder. Which is crazy, since I've nothing whatever to cry about.

John chatted amiably about nothing much, giving Jane recovery time as he would for one of his eleven-year-olds.

Presently she said, "Look at that little shrine. I think what I like most about India is the way the supernatural and the natural are so mixed up. If a rock is even faintly rounded or phallic-looking, it'll wake up one day and find itself a fertility symbol, covered in red paint, doused in honey and decorated with flowers."

They talked companionably until they reached the mountain-top fort, negotiating hairpin bends and the fort's seven gates, one with fearsome elephant-repelling spikes on its massive wooden doors, one so narrow the bus got through with no more than an inch each side to spare.

Once on top of the mountain, and within castle walls that rose sheer from the precipice of rock, Jane felt easy again. The area was wide, flat and open, with room for scattered temples, palaces, towers, gardens, even for rough fields. It was surprisingly green.

On climbing down from the bus, the four friends set off in the opposite direction to that taken by everyone else.

After an hour of diligent exploration they sat on a rocky outcrop, surrounded by monkeys, drinking Coke.

"Can I join you?" It was the guide, Rajiv.

"Of course." John moved up and Rajiv sat down, removing his Maharajah Express waistcoat and laying it carefully on the smooth rock at his side.

"Oh, I love all this," said Jane. She stretched out her arms to encompass the valley below, the scattered buildings of the fort, the monkeys, the sun, her friends.

"What particularly?" asked Rajiv.

"Well, you will think me silly, especially since you are Indian. But for me it's just the very Indian-ness, the strangeness of it all. And the romance."

"Romance? It's more blood than romance," said Sally. "This place alone seems to have seen enough war and widowhood—"

Jane interrupted. "I know, but it is still romantic. All those Chittorgarh women—jumping into fires in their *thousands* rather than be taken as spoils of war. That's romantic, isn't it?"

Rajiv said, "You're both right. India's history is full of blood and we've been weaving romance out of it for centuries. If you lot hadn't wandered off on your own, you would have heard me expound the romantic tale of Princess Padmini. I hope you renegades at least visited her palace?"

Jane thought, for the umpteenth time, that his tone was odd for a guide. I bet his employers don't know he calls his customers "you lot" and "renegades." But the tone carried no rudeness. Rather she felt complimented by the familiarity. She liked him. She offered him a cigarette and took one herself. He produced a lighter and lit them both as Lucy said, "We did visit her palace. But Jane hogged the guidebook. So tell us about Padmini."

"OK," said Rajiv. "But I shall expect to be bought a drink tonight. Making the guide do his stuff twice is not on."

He sat forward, his long arms around his knees, his eyes looking over the valley below. For half a minute he didn't speak, as though giving Padmini and her ghosts time to assemble in his mind.

"So. The story of Padmini. Here is a princess, famed for her beauty and grace, and beloved by her family and their people. She is the pride of her father, the jewel of the princedom. But a ruthless Moghul warlord has heard tell of her, and he wants her, partly because of her beauty, but mostly because she is the most precious thing her father owns, and he is at war with her father. He besieges the fort, surrounding the mountain, and starving everyone up here. They have water, and what food they can raise, but they are trapped by their own fortifications. Their enemies cannot get in, but neither can any supplies. They will not surrender their precious princess, but they are in a terrible trap.

"But down in the valley the besieging forces are not doing much better. They cannot scale the cliffs. They cannot break through the mighty gates. They are easy targets on the steep paths. They fear Padmini's father will never give in, and the lovely Padmini will be starved into ugliness. So the Moghul warlord compromises: he agrees that he will settle for a glimpse of her face. Padmini's father agrees, but, to save his daughter's modesty, the Moghul is only allowed to see her reflection in a mirror as she strolls in her water garden. You saw the little room, I hope, with the mirror high up on the wall?"

Rajiv turned to look at Jane for confirmation. Jane, her eyes distant and unfocused, nodded.

Rajiv continued, "But that single glimpse of Princess Padmini inflames the warrior. Before he wanted her as a prize. Now he is enthralled, enslaved, by her loveliness. He *must* have her. Compromise is now unthinkable. So he returns to his army below, and attacks the fort again. Inspired by love and lust, he wins the battle. He enters the fort in triumph. Only to find the beautiful Padmini, and all her ladies, dead on a suicide pyre."

He stopped, still looking over the valley, eyes narrowed as if seeing the scenes he described. Jane, moved by the extravagance of the story, sighed and said, "Oh, it is a beautiful tale. If that was part of your history, you'd be bound to believe in miracles, I think. It makes King Arthur's exploits very tame stuff, don't you think?"

Presently Rajiv went to around up the scattered tourists. Jane left the others to inspect the grim monuments to three waves of female suicide in the Mahasati ground, and walked back to Padmini's Palace. How can I make sure I remember this place? she thought. It will become overlaid with other Indian sights, or be squeezed out by Chalker and Day.

She bought a home-made postcard from a child. It was a crayon drawing of a lop-sided green and blue bird, with orange

85

legs and red bill and feet. It cost 5 rupees—less than half the price of the faded photographic postcards sold by the adult vendors. As she put it between the pages of her book, she willed herself to remember this empty fort, a ghost-town monument to the valor and history of centuries, and the pleasure, the real pleasure, it gave her.

The next day at noon they were sitting in the bar of the Lake Palace Hotel of Udaipur. The room was blissfully cool, if a little gloomy, distanced from the glare of the courtyard by the deep covered terrace. Jane was drinking fresh mango juice flavored with lime and mint, and the others had tall glasses of beer, so cold the glasses were icy and wet on the outside.

Jane was working on her companions to leave the train, to go off on their own.

"But," protested Sally, "we've still got nearly a week of the tour, and we can't get our money back just because you've had enough of Hans and the rest of our merry gang. It'd be such a waste of money."

"But being on the train is becoming a waste of my life, of our lives, which is much worse," pleaded Jane. "If I have to watch Cindy bargaining for tourist tat one more time. I shall go mad. She's determined to buy up every horrible artifact produced in Rajasthan. I don't care if we have to pay twice to see the same places. We'll enjoy it a million times more if we do it on our own."

"I wouldn't mind missing the bus ride back to the train," said Lucy. "That new guide is hell-bent on organizing a singsong."

"He is," said John. "His ambition is to own a karaoke bar. He told me. Which is another reason to abandon ship. What's happened to Rajiv, by the way?"

Lucy replied, "He went back home after Chittorgarh yesterday. He's a guide for the same company in Khajuraho and he was just filling in for this chap, who's been sick."

Jane felt suddenly hurt. She hadn't realized Rajiv had gone for good. She'd have thought he would say goodbye, at least to her. Her mind flipped to their shared pleasure over the defeat of Hans, and yesterday's magical tale of Padmini. I thought he was a friend, she thought.

Sally was leaning forward and fixing John with a determined eye. "But John, be sensible. You don't want to get off, do you? You're the one mad about trains. You don't want to miss the rest of the trip."

"It's the bus rides and group tours we are aiming to miss," interjected Jane, shaking off thoughts of Rajiv's disappearance.

"And think how nice it would be to have another round of drinks in the cool while we watch the others gird themselves for the bus ride back," said John. "And we could have a dip in the Residents Only pool, by dint of becoming residents."

"I'm game," said Lucy. "While John drags you around the City Palace tomorrow, I shall have a happy time with my paint-box."

"More like help the local economy with your Visa card," said John. Lucy screwed up her face at him.

Sally gave it one last go. "Be serious, you two. We cannot get off here. Our luggage is still on the train, and this evening it will trundle off somewhere else. Even if we ever recover it, it won't be in time for tonight."

"Oh, Sally." Jane let out an exasperated moan. "Don't be so maddeningly sensible. We'll sleep in the buff, and we'll swim in our knickers. The only things we couldn't manage without are money and Lucy's paints. And we've got both. So, let's agree. We jump ship."

In fact, it was easy to do. The long-suffering Maharajah Express rep, perhaps used to privileged passengers' curious demands, agreed to have all their belongings packed up and delivered by taxi the next morning. His only real anxiety was that the absconding party would somehow evade paying their bar-car bills, but John's credit card number and a fat tip resolved that too.

The hotel receptionist's frostiness thawed as the foursome translated themselves from day-trippers on a package lunch to high-rollers wanting the best rooms with a view of the town across the lake.

Jane admired John's cheerful confidence as he explained they had no luggage, would all need tooth-brushes and wanted their clothes washed and ironed overnight. That's what public school does for you, she thought. If he asked for condoms or a packet of ganja, no one would blink. Patrick has that confidence too. He gives orders as if he expects to be obeyed, and people obey. I don't dare give orders, and expect to be found out—a jumped up grammar-school kid living above her station. I quite expected to be told, "Madam, we do not have luggage-less persons in this establishment."

They agreed not to tell the other passengers of their defection. During lunch, Jane regarded her soon-to-be-erstwhile companions with something akin to affection. She looked at Hans's tight roll of sunburned neck with equanimity, watched the Professor harrying the dithering Emily to make up her mind at the buffet with some sympathy. Even the thought of Cindy's bargaining prowess seemed more amusing than embarrassing now her exposure to it was over. She was tempted to say goodbye, at least to Emily and to Johann. But she didn't. John was right: it would have led to exclamations and explanations.

Watching their fellow travelers wearily gathering themselves, John said, "Right. Let's order some more coffee, then kip till it's cooler. Then how about a boat trip around the lake and a stroll through the gardens of Saheliyon ki Bari?"

Jane headed for the hotel shop. She bought a plain blue swimsuit, baggy blue cotton trousers and Nehru-style shirt, and put them on. She also bought suncream and a paperback copy of *A*

Princess Remembers, the story of the Maharani of Jaipur.

Feeling cool and free, and carrying her sandals, she made for the pool. Ignoring the comfortable loungers, she spread her towel on the newly mown grass.

The sharp herby-green smell of the still-bruised lawn, and the sound of the hand mower (squeaky clatter as the gardener pulled it toward him, growly purr as he pushed it forward) at once filled her mind with an image of her father. Strong and lithe at forty, he had pushed just such an ancient machine over the grass of their garden. She would watch from Tom's old tree house, built years before when Tom had been her age.

Suddenly she remembered, as if it was yesterday, the morning her father bought an electric mower, a Flymo, and how, as soon as the excitement of watching it leave the ground and hover in circles had worn off, she resented it. "You can't be jealous of a lawn mower," her mother had said. But she was: it took all her father's attention to operate. And it made a noise all the time. With the old one, which Tom said should have been in a museum, there was a silence between push and pull, or when he stopped to turn, and then she could call out, "Daddy!" And he would smile and lift her down from the tree, and let her have a go. Hands above her head, she would hold the mower's handles just below his big brown hands, and walk safe and important between his arms. She wasn't allowed near the Flymo. Too dangerous, darling. It could take your little toes off.

Jane opened her book, but found it poorly written and obviously ghosted, and it didn't hold her attention. She lay on her stomach and thought about herself—something her father would *not* have approved of. He'd had a Scotsman's distaste for self-absorption, just as he'd had a Scotsman's distaste for lying in bed in the morning. I suppose I owe my success to Dad, she thought. The Protestant work ethic. I wish he'd lived to see me made a partner, albeit not an equity one. She imagined his look, proud as the day Tom was elected MP by the constituents of Stratford. He'd not have said much. Maybe only "Good work, lass." But that would have been reward enough.

This thought was followed immediately by another—that at least he hadn't lived to see his darling daughter walk out on a good man. Her father had loved Patrick, particularly at the end, when Patrick had been much better for him than either she or her mother.

What Jane felt, as her father lay gaunt, his breath coming in uneven gasping rasps, was anger. He'd never before let her down, and now he was doing it in spades. She needed him. She wanted him there to discuss cases with, to argue politics with, to help her make the big decisions, to bring her back to first principles. But most of all she wanted him there as audience. To admire her, to approve of her and to be proud of her.

He had absolutely no bloody right to die. She wasn't ready for him to die. She told herself that at seventy-two he'd had more than his three score years and ten, so death should somehow be OK. But it wasn't OK. Her father had not been *old*, or not until he got sick, when old age fell on him like a vulture—stripping him of himself. Turning him into a sunken, depleted, strange-smelling *other person*.

She and Patrick dutifully went down at weekends, but she avoided her father's sickroom as much as possible, leaving the nursing to the others.

She'd been no help to her mother either, who was wounded that her husband of nearly fifty years had ended by shutting her out. He had no energy other than for breathing. He didn't want her to hold his hand and look into his eyes, because this required response. He didn't want her in their bed, because he was in pain, and had enough to do without considering her. He preferred the nurse to feed him, because she did it with less sympathy and no love. He hadn't the strength for love.

Her mother understood all this, but wanted some solace from Jane. But Jane could not give it. She acted sympathetic, but she didn't feel it, and her efforts did not comfort her mother. Jane could feel only anger and misery.

Patrick, of course, had been wonderful, which had made Jane angrier, though she could not explain why. Even now, two years later, and lying by a swimming pool in India, she felt a little flash of resentment. At weekends Patrick did everything the nurse did in the week, including cope with the colostomy bag. He shrugged such things off with a quip about there being worse things in the army. If there was nothing practical that needed doing, he'd put Haydn on the deck, and settle down peaceably with a book, as though the heave and wheeze of laboring lungs was a normal accompaniment. Her father seemed more peaceful if he was there, perhaps because Patrick behaved to him as he might to a sick stranger on an airplane—he was helpful, but he didn't fuss.

Patrick was marvelous with her mother too, holding her in his arms and stroking her gray head when she broke into undignified, wailing grief.

Jane remembered this scene, and how, to hide her resentment, she'd had to get up and leave the room. What a cow I was, she thought. I was jealous of Mother for claiming Patrick's comfort, jealous of Patrick for doing my duty by Dad, and angry at Patrick for not realizing how desperate I was. He thought, poor sod, that because I had him, I wouldn't miss Dad.

And now I've got neither. Jane pushed her face into the grass, breathing in its familiar smell with a jerky intake of breath. She knew she would miss her father for the rest of her life. She missed him now. Or maybe she missed Patrick. It was hard to tell.

EIGHT

Two days later, at 8 a.m. on the terrace of the Taj Mahal, Jane decided not to go home with Sally.

She'd been working up to it for days. In the gardens of Saheliyon ki Bari they had watched a bridal couple being photographed, and Jane had realized she was no nearer "real India" than on the day they'd arrived. It frustrated her that the only Indians they met were desk clerks, waiters and taxi drivers. The bride, very young, wore a red and gold sari and delicate shiny sandals. She kept her eyes down and was only with difficulty persuaded to drop the veil from her face. Her bridegroom was plump and sleek in Western suit, dark glasses and heavy gold jewelry. He stared with confidence, even arrogance, at the camera. Jane longed to know: was this an arranged marriage? Was the young man as rich as he looked, or was he in borrowed finery? What did he do? Where would they live?

And then yesterday they had spent two hours in the deserted palace-town of Fatehpur Sikri. It was fascinating, but nothing to do with real life.

Jane had wanted to stop at the little hamlet outside the walls, where they caught glimpses of a bicycle repairer tending his row of upside-down cycles and a dancing bear on the end of a lead made of electric cable. But the taxi driver had been against it, and they hadn't insisted.

Jane's vague discontent with the tourist trail was hardening into resolve, yet it was the tourist Mecca of all time, the Taj Mahal, that did it. She had been told, many times, that the Taj Mahal had never disappointed anyone, but she had seen it on film and heard its story so often she feared its potency would have leaked away. And anyway, the presence of a thousand other tourists would, she thought, kill any remaining pulse of magic.

But she was wrong. They'd come late yesterday, and Jane had stood quite still for ten minutes staring, staring at the mausoleum. Such a dark, ugly word for something so light and sublime. Her throat felt tight as if she might weep, and she could feel her heartbeating. It was, as all the guidebooks said, exquisite. Unimaginable, unimprovable, and not of this earth.

Now she was back, alone, to see it in the early morning light. Last night the dome and minarets had been bright white, softening to yellow as the sun went down. Now as the mist cleared, they were a warm pink. The mist left the river last, and as Jane watched trees, buildings and a pylon on the farther bank gain substance, and felt the first sun's rays through her shirt, she thought, why should I go back? Chalker and Day won't fall apart if I'm away for another week. I'm not ready for that dismal apartment, for sleet and gray skies.

And I'm thirty-six, quite old enough to manage on my own.

Before John and Lucy had left Delhi for Goa, they'd all exchanged addresses, Jane wondering if they really would stay friends or if the entry in her Filofax—"Appleby, John and Lucy"—would one day puzzle her.

She hoped not. She liked them both and admired Lucy. She wanted to see her paintings and meet the boys. And she wanted new friends who were nothing to do with work or with Patrick.

Waving goodbye as their taxi bumped away from the Oberoi Hotel, coughing black exhaust fumes, Jane wished her sister-in-law was leaving with them. But Sally wasn't going until tomorrow, and that meant she had twenty-four hours to badger Jane to go with her. Exhausted from constant sightseeing, they had agreed on a day to recover before flying home. But then Jane had made her announcement.

Sally returned to the fray from a cushioned lounger in the

hotel gardens. "Jane," she said, keeping her voice level. "Staying on alone is not a sensible idea. You are being irresponsible."

Jane looked up from her book with reluctance. "No, I'm not. What's irresponsible about it?"

"You don't even know where you are going. You haven't a plan at all."

"No, but I will have by this evening." She drew on her cigarette and tapped the pile of guides and maps beside her on the grass.

"You haven't any hotel bookings. You cannot just bum off like a sixteen-year-old and bunk up in a hippie hostel." Sally waved a hand in exasperation, as though shooing flies.

"I don't intend to. I'll stay in exactly the same sort of posh hotels, called Taj this and Taj that, that we've been in this week."

"You'll never get in. It's high season."

"We managed fine with John and Lucy, and there were four of us."

Sally said nothing more, and Jane went back to her Cadogan Guide. She knew Sally wasn't defeated, just regrouping. Sure enough: "Jane, I'm sorry to say this but this is a symptom of your not being quite OK yet. It is not a rational or sensible thing to do, and you *are* a bit fragile . . ."

Jane sighed with exaggerated patience and once more lowered her book.

"I am not fragile. I'm absolutely fine, and it's because I'm fine, and happy here, that I want to stay."

"Well, I shall stay too then," said Sally, martyrdom evident. "I expect Tom will understand."

Jane's voice rose. "Sally, I don't *want* you to stay." Then, relenting: " '*I vant to be alone.*' " Her Garbo imitation didn't come off and Sally didn't smile.

"You don't know what you want, that's the truth, Jane. You seem to have no idea of what is important and what isn't. I shouldn't say this but—"

"Then don't." Jane stubbed her cigarette out on the grass and tossed the butt into the bushes.

"I've got to. You have a perfectly good husband in Patrick . . ."

Jane gripped her book hard. "This is nothing to do with Patrick . . ."

"It has everything to do with Patrick. You are suffering from classic seven-year itch, or twelve-year itch or whatever it is." Sally sat up, the better to confront Jane squarely. "You don't want to make the transition from Young Love to Real Life. So you think you'll just change everything. Off with the Old, on with the New."

"Oh, rot!" Jane sat up too and faced Sally. "I just want to stay in India, by myself. I like it here. That's all."

"It's not all. What you are doing is waving some sort of Jane Chambers independence flag, showing that you are above what the rest of us need—which is other people. The truth is you should give in and have a baby. That's what Patrick wants, and I bet what you really want too."

Jane opened her mouth, amazement and indignation combined. Then she said, "I don't believe this. Did Patrick tell you he wanted us to have a baby? He'd no right . . ."

Sally waved a dismissive arm. "Jane. It's obvious what went wrong between you and Patrick. You earn a pile of money and spend it as fast as you get it on designer gear and the good life, and Patrick, who doesn't earn much, could hardly object. But he's a *man* and men are easily de-balled. Even one as uncomplicated as Patrick likes being in the driving seat sometimes."

Jane picked up her books and maps, fumbled, dropped a book, retrieved it. She clutched them close, to stop her hands shaking. She said, "I'm not discussing this. You've got it wrong, that's all. I'm off."

Lying in the bath, cooling bubbles prickling her ears and chin, Jane was still indignant, but she was beginning to feel uneasy too. Sally, damn her, was always right. Or nearly right.

Patrick *had* been disquieted by the way she spent money. He'd never minded that she made more than he did. And he'd never tried to stop her buying the Normandy farmhouse, filling it with Provençal fabrics at ludicrous prices, buying their groceries at Harvey Nicks, or her clothes at Black's. But he'd teased her, saying she was a label victim. He wore M & S from his socks to his overcoat, and had needed bullying to buy anything new, ever.

And Patrick *had* wanted children. He'd said they should have them now, two or three close together, while they had the energy to enjoy them. And soon so they'd be out of the nest in time for Jane and him to spend their late fifties unhampered by school fees and chickenpox.

Damn him, she thought. I might have stayed with him if only he wasn't so bloody sensible. He'd have been the perfect dad too—good at nappies, night feeds, cricket on the lawn, Saturdays on the freezing touchline.

Her mother had been baffled. "But he's such a good man, darling." Then: "He doesn't hit you dear, does he?" And later: "He's not unfaithful, is he?"

The only person who seemed to understand was Patrick. And that drove her mad. He'd said, leaning against the kitchen wall, his voice flat with exhaustion and despair, "I want you here because I love you. If you don't want to be here, then you don't love me, and you are right to leave. It's that simple."

She hadn't explained to him that turning thirty-six frightened her, because she despised herself for minding. She scorned women who worried about their age, who spent hours getting their faces on. But being thirty-six gnawed at her. A newspaper report described a woman who had stabbed her ex-lover as "thirty-six and childless," as if that explained all. An article about an actress was subtitled, "Thirty-six, and still playing the romantic lead."

Up to now she'd felt carefree. Blessed even. She'd liked her thirty-five-year-old self: clever, good-looking, successful, civilized.

At thirty-five it hadn't mattered that she did not have an equity partnership at Chalkers. She was a junior partner, and that was great.

But she *had* to be an equity partner by forty.

"Why?" Patrick had asked. "You can't have everything. Something has to go."

She'd snapped, "Easy for you to say. It's not you that has to have the kids. You won't have to give anything up."

"Don't you think the pleasure of having and rearing children might be worth giving up a few rungs of the ladder for?"

"How do I know? It might be hell on earth. I might have horrible pregnancies, hate my babies, get fat and washed out. I might find I've given up a great career to fret about nappy rash and projectile vomiting."

Patrick burst into his barking laugh. "Oh, Jane. What the hell is projectile vomiting?"

Bear-hugging her shoulders, and speaking into her hair, he continued, "And why do you know about it if you are so uninterested in babies? Anyway you'd be a wonderful mum. And still be beautiful and bright and funny. You just might have to take your dash to the top of the legal profession a bit slower, that's all."

But she'd not been persuaded. A cruel little ditty she'd read somewhere and could not dismiss plagued her:

> See the mothers in the park,
> Ugly creatures chiefly,
> Someone must have loved them once,
> In the dark, and briefly.

She'd left Patrick because she couldn't be Superwoman. She'd had to choose, and she'd chosen to be a bloody good lawyer. It was too late for babies, and too late for her and Patrick.

Now she wondered, was that really it? Or did I just run away?

She drew her knees up, put her head back and slid down to sink under the water. As she rubbed her face with both hands, to wash away dust, tears and black thoughts, she resolved to be nice to Sally.

Sally was talking slowly and clearly, and trying to fix the young clerk's gaze. But he was looking at the reception desk.

"But since I did not get any sleep in the room, I do not think you should charge me for it."

"But you most kindly made reservation for room, madam. One double with twin beds. We have provided room, as specified." The clerk smiled and bowed.

"Yes, but I booked it to *sleep* in. I was awake the whole night, listening to banging and hammering."

"I understand most perfectly, madam. But there was a major emergency of great proportions. Builders are obliged to refurbish water pipe which is unexpectedly exploded. Cannot wait till morning. Act of God."

"Acts of God are your problem, not mine."

"No problem, madam. Not a problem. All pipes mended now."

Sally tried another tack. "Is it my fault that you had a burst pipe in the night?"

"Oh, no, madam. You are not at fault. It is we who have goofed up completely. I am most sympathetic."

"Well then, why not show your sympathy by cancelling the bill?"

The clerk smiled, shaking his head and looking at his feet. "I am unfortunately not in position to cancel bill." Then, cheering up, he added, "And your friend, she sleep. No waking by builders."

"Yes, she did sleep. With the help of a sleeping pill and

earplugs. But *I* booked the room. It is in *my* name, and *I* got no sleep at all. I got up four times, and each time the night porter said he would stop the banging. Which he did, just until I fell asleep again." Sally was losing her patient tone.

"Madam is perhaps a very light sleeper."

"I sleep like a log. Are you saying I should be able to sleep through builders banging the pipes all night?"

"Oh, no, madam. But your friend, she sleep dead to the world with almighty noise of builders mending pipes."

"Do you admit that I did not get what you want me to pay for—a quiet hotel room in which I could sleep?"

"Willingly, willingly, madam. I admit. You did not get a top-notch experience."

"Well, why are you insisting I pay top-notch prices then?"

"Madam. I cannot forgive the bill. It is customary for clients to pay their bills before departure."

"Look, this is ridiculous. I have traveled all over the world, and stayed in all the best hotels. I am not a difficult customer. Are you saying that I am being unreasonable?"

"Oh, no, madam. I have great respect for you. In India we have much respect for women, and also for old people. You are much seasoned traveler, with infinitely more experience than me. I am yet young, and I bow before your venerable age and great experience."

Ordinarily Sally would have laughed. But frazzled by a combination of Jane's obduracy and her own lack of sleep, she lost her temper.

"Well, just bloody do as this venerable old woman tells you and tear up the bill."

"Oh, madam, I cannot do this. I am not authorized."

"Christ almighty, this is crazy. Who is authorized?"

"It is Sunday, madam. Everyone off. Too early also. Office closed."

Jane appeared at Sally's side. She said, "Sally, this conversation is going absolutely nowhere. I've paid the bill."

"What?" Sally rounded on Jane. "Jane, you couldn't. How could you? Anyway, I've got the bill here."

"I got the cashier to print out another."

The clerk bowed to Jane. "I congratulate you, madam. You have most skillfully resolved all our little difficulties." He beamed at them both, delighted, pleased as if he'd given them a present.

Jane took Sally's arm. "Poor Sally. Lost two battles in a row. It's not like you. But you'll miss your plane if you insist on battling for British fair play any longer. The trick in India, I'm rapidly deciding, is to go with the flow."

NINE

Jane arrived at Khajuraho airport feeling anxious but excited. She collected her case and emerged into the blinding glare of the airport forecourt. For a moment she was dismayed. The place seemed to be a building site, with dust, lorries and wire mesh fences all around. But then she spotted the familiar yellow-topped black taxi, and secured it just ahead of a trio of Japanese.

The driver spoke passable English, but refused to find her an ordinary Indian hotel, as requested. Maybe he didn't understand. Or maybe Western women traveling alone should not, or could not, stay in one. Or maybe there wasn't one. But most likely, thought Jane, he got a big fat tip from the Taj Chandella. But how did he know I could afford the most expensive hotel in town? Maybe he can tell real Ray-Bans from street-market rip-offs, or maybe it was the soft leather case from Gucci. Whatever the reason, Jane found herself once more in the familiar surroundings of Western luxury only faintly touched by Indian influence—the smell of mild Westernized curry from the buffet, the traditionally sari'd women staff.

The hotel pool, surrounded by shady trees and massed dahlias, their glaring heads the size of soup plates, proved too much of a temptation. Jane spent the heat of the day in swimsuit and suncream alternately dozing in a deckchair and mugging up on the temples she should have been visiting.

The pool and garden were deserted. She spoke to no one except the waiter, who kept her supplied with Diet Coke, and at lunchtime brought her a toasted sandwich. Her fellow residents

101

were all lunching, sleeping in air-conditioned rooms or dutifully sightseeing.

The fact that no one had any idea where she was pleased her. No one—not Sally, nor her mother, nor Patrick nor her partners at Chalkers—could get hold of her. She felt free and light-headed.

At 3:30 she stretched with an abandon born of knowing she was alone, and dived in. She swam four lengths, luxuriating in sole occupation of the pool. Then, wrapped in a toweling robe, but still dripping, she went up to her room for a shower. Her skin was goose-bumpy from the cold water, but pink and hot to the touch from the sun. There was a sharp line at the top of her thighs and in a scoop around her neck. As she smoothed after-sun onto legs and arms, she told herself she'd end up with skin cancer. But she knew she looked good: the warm tones of sun-burn suited her, went well with her straight dark hair, made her eyes look greener.

She pulled on a cream cotton shift-dress, belted it with a multi-colored plaited belt, and pushed her feet into red leather sandals. She crammed her straw hat onto her wet head, and grabbed her sunglasses, guidebook and canvas bag. She picked up her cigarette pack, checking the contents. One cigarette left. Damn.

Then on an impulse she crumpled the pack, crushing the lone cigarette, and threw it in the waste-basket. That's it. She grinned. I'm an ex-smoker.

As she swung out of the room, she blew herself a kiss in the mirror, then smiled at the childish gesture. No make-up, she thought, but you'll do.

Her mood of narcissistic self-confidence did not last. She had wanted to tour the western temples unaided, by herself, not in a group. But she didn't know what to look at, where to begin. It was all too much. There was not an inch of temple surface not covered in statues. There were row upon row of them, and Jane felt out-faced, abashed by so much detail, so many sculptures, so much to take in.

And though she wanted to see the famous erotic figures, she didn't know where to look for them, and she was embarrassed to ask. She was sure that if she offered a few rupees to any of the guards, they'd show her. But some idiotic pride, a desire not to be thought a likely candidate for "dirty postcards," stopped her asking. So she wandered about, trying to make sense of the different temples, but finding them (with the exception of the one with the great bull Nandi) curiously alike. Large or small, they were all cool, dark and claustrophobic inside, encrusted and unintelligible outside.

At sunset the temples closed, and Jane, tired and deflated, took a taxi back to the Chandella. At the hotel desk she arranged for a private guide, an English-speaking one, for the following afternoon. She'd again spend the morning by the pool, then have another stab at culture once the heat had gone out of the day.

At three the next afternoon her telephone rang. "Mrs. Chambers. I'm Rajiv, your guide for the afternoon."

She recognized his voice immediately. But it couldn't be. There are nearly a billion people in India. Thousands of people called Rajiv probably sound like that. The voice said, "Mrs. Chambers? Are you there?"

"Rajiv? Not Rajiv from the Maharajah Express?"

He said, "Who is this?" She knew it was him.

She wondered fleetingly if she could reject him and ask the hotel for someone else. Rajiv was too confident, too good-looking, too *male*. And then she thought, oh, my God, he'll think I asked for him.

He asked, "Do I know you, Mrs. Chambers?"

A flick of hurt licked her. She had recognized his voice. Why didn't he know hers? And then she thought that was unfair, since he'd announced himself as Rajiv. And then she thought, why am I concerned? He's only the guide, damn it.

She said, "It's Jane. I'll be down."

103

As she went down in the lift her mind whirled about, a jumble of conflicting thoughts. He'll think I followed him here. So what? It's none of his business. Do I look all right? I should have at least worn some lipstick. Why? You don't want to seduce a tour guide, do you?

He was standing in the lobby, thin and lanky in light khaki chinos, bare feet in brown leather sandals, and a short-sleeved white cotton shirt, open at the neck. As soon as the lift doors parted he stepped toward her, smiling widely.

"What a pleasure! Is Sally with you?"

"No, she's gone back to England. And John and Lucy are in Goa. So it's just me."

"How did you find me?"

She laughed, embarrassment replaced by the pleasure of teasing him. "I knew you'd think I'd asked for you. Oh, the vanity of the male!"

"And you didn't?" He was smiling, but disbelieving.

"Nope. I had even forgotten that you lived in Khajuraho. Pure fluke."

"Not such a fluke really. India may be vast, but the first-class tourist track is pretty narrow. There are only about a dozen private guides accredited to this hotel, and most of us work for the company that supplies guides for the Maharajah Express. I hope you don't mind?"

She did rather mind, but she could hardly say so. Especially as her objection seemed to be that he was sexually attractive.

"Of course not. You are a very good guide."

She was immediately slightly embarrassed by the primness of her reply, and they walked in silence to the white Ambassador. Its doors were open in an attempt to keep it cool, the driver lounging beside it.

"The air-conditioning has broken down. I'm sorry," said Rajiv.

Suddenly they both remembered Hans, and said, simultaneously, "No air-cool!"

Laughing, Rajiv said, "Poor fellow. I wonder if he stuck the rest of the tour. He didn't seem to enjoy it much, and you and Sally were not very nice to him." His topaz eyes were amused, and Jane noticed how dark his lids and lashes were. His eyes were deep set, the lids darker than the surrounding skin, the lashes short and thick, as if they'd been curled. Their upward bent added to the merriment of his expression.

"No, we weren't. I'm a little ashamed of that. But I don't know if he stuck it. We jumped ship with the Applebys the day after you left."

As soon as she said it, she wanted to qualify it—to explain their leaving was nothing to do with losing him, but everything to do with the discomfort of the bus. But she couldn't without making too much of it.

But once they were on the road, and he was telling her the history of the Chandella dynasty, descendants of the moon god Chandra, and how Khajuraho had survived Muslim destruction because it was in the middle of nowhere, she relaxed and started to listen.

This time the temples made more sense. Rajiv's obvious love of his subject was catching. He talked of the tenth and eleventh centuries as if they were yesterday, of the dancing figures and lines of women doing housewifely tasks like drawing water as if they were real.

"Come and look at this," he said, showing her a row of near identical statues of the elephant god Ganesh, a little above eye level.

"They are wonderful," said Jane, marveling at the detailed carving, and the sheer number of the sculptures.

"Look at the one toward the end."

Jane looked, and saw that the head of one of the elephants was turned, looking to his side. The others all faced forward, trunks hanging down. She went up close, to see what the elephant was looking at, and burst out laughing. The panel beside the peering Ganesh was pornographic, a man taking a woman

105

from behind. She was bent double, and his cock was half in and half out of her.

"I love that, don't you?" said Rajiv. "The sculptor must have had such fun making one Ganesh a voyeur, while all the others face forward, unaware of what is happening in the corner."

"It's marvelous," said Jane. "It's so funny. And also beautiful." She didn't mention that she found it erotic too. The little figures stirred her as, she was sure, the sculptor meant them to.

Rajiv said, "I love the way the erotic statues are in among the others, dotted about in a casual way, because sex is just part of life."

"You wouldn't believe that if you saw the tourist postcards in Delhi. You'd think Khajuraho was the capital of pornography."

"I know. It's a pity. But it brings the tourists, so . . ."

He shrugged, unconcerned, his thin shirt, pulling briefly at his belt, clinging to the muscles of his diaphragm as he did so. Why did I notice that? thought Jane. All this erotica is getting to me.

They wandered from temple to temple, sometimes sitting on low walls or stone steps so Rajiv could explain something, sometimes entering temples where he pointed out interesting carvings or explained what the occasional devotee was up to.

"The lingam, this phallic stone, is a manifestation of the god Shiva, who concerns himself with both destruction and creation. That woman painting oil and honey on it and scattering petals is probably praying for a boy."

Jane was enjoying herself. There was, she realized, an added pleasure in seeing all these erotic sculptures and rituals of procreation in the company of such a good-looking man, of having him tell her of sexual rituals and religious practices. It was intimate, but safe. She hadn't fancied anyone for a long time, not even her husband, and it felt good. Like lusting clandestinely after the lifeguard as a teenager. She felt close to him, and both intellectually and physically interested. A safe, one-sided, little thrill.

The carved processions, especially on the great Kandariya Mahadev temple, were full of energy and movement. Like the Notting Hill Carnival, she thought. She loved the way the female figures were idealized, with swaying hips and high, round breasts.

Rajiv had no well-rehearsed patter. Often he didn't speak at all. He was relaxed and companionable.

Jane said, "You know, yesterday I walked all around these temples and felt depressed. I thought maybe I could only appreciate Indian art in the Muslim tradition, like the Taj Mahal."

"That's because the Taj Mahal is basically simple. Its simplicity allows anyone and everyone to understand and love it. It's 'accessible.' Hindu art is *in*accessible. But stick with it. It's worth the effort."

Two hours later, strolling back to the road across the mowed and manicured gardens, green lawns brilliant in the sun, Jane said, "I wanted to see the Jain temples too. But I'm too tired. Must be the heat."

"That and the culture clash. I remember visiting the Palace of Versailles and thinking that one more gilt mirror would finish me off."

Jane was surprised. "You've been to France?"

"Sure. I worked in the Louvre for a while, studying Sanskrit texts. Or rather doing the boring bit of sorting them out so that my boss could study them. I'm a historian."

"Really?" Jane was embarrassed to ask, but then asked anyway, "Then why are you working as a guide?"

"Simple. There aren't any jobs for Sanskrit scholars. Or rather, not enough. And this pays well."

Rajiv produced a packet of Gauloises, and offered Jane one. Jane started to accept, then jerked back her hand.

"No thanks, I've given up."

"Since how long?"

"Since yesterday."

They both laughed, and Rajiv said, "I'm impressed. I can't stand women who smoke."

"How very chauvinist of you," she said, not really minding, but thinking she must have made no impression on him at all. She'd been smoking on the train. Indeed they'd smoked together once or twice.

"I know. I apologize. All Indians are chauvinists. Do you mind if I do?"

"No, of course not, go ahead." She watched as he bent his head over the lighter, his hands, well manicured with long slim fingers, cupping the flame. His arms, visible below the short sleeves, were pale brown and smooth, the fine brown hairs all growing evenly the same way. His trousers hung low on bony hips, held up by a plain brown leather belt. His bent head, hair black and thick, glistened in the sun. His face was aquiline, even severe. And when he looked up, his eyes were strange. Quite different from the dark merriment she'd noticed in the taxi. They were deep-set and large, with finely defined lids, and those thick short lashes. But what gave them their peculiarly compelling gaze was the curious topaz color, slightly streaky, like a cat's.

"How about a cup of tea?" he asked, dropping the cigarette packet and lighter into his breast pocket.

"Isn't my time up? We've been statue-gazing for two hours."

"I know, but I'm now off duty." He grinned. "And I'd rather you bought me a cup of tea, than dismissed me with a tip."

Jane laughed. "What makes you think I was going to tip you?"

"All the upper-class English tip. Especially the ladies."

"I'm not upper class."

"Oh, you must be. You are a very posh lady." He gave her a mock bow.

"No, I'm definitely middle class. OK. I'll buy you tea and

108

explain the English class system. And you can explain the Indian caste system."

They walked to the Raja Café Restaurant, and sat outside in the rather dingy courtyard, made pleasant by overhanging trees and floral plastic tablecloths.

"Indian tea is my only disappointment with your country," said Jane. "I thought tea would be the one thing I'd feel at home with, but you seem to cook the tea with the milk and sugar in it, and I can't bear it. Even on that posh train it was undrinkable."

Rajiv smiled. "When I was in England I longed for Indian tea cooked just as you describe. I found your version thin and flavorless."

"When were you in England?" Jane tried to hide her surprise that a temple guide should be so well traveled. "That explains your perfect English."

"I went to school in London. My father was an accountant, tipped out of Uganda by Idi Amin, and we ended up in England. But we originally came from Madhya Pradesh, so when my father retired, we came back here." Rajiv stood up. "I shall now oversee the making of the perfect English cuppa. Would you like that?"

"Yes. But don't bother, really. It's not important."

"Ah, but it is." Rajiv disappeared through a curtain of multicolored plastic strips.

When the waiter arrived, followed by Rajiv, the tea was made, the tea bags floating in two glasses of boiled water, the milk in a jug. The waiter looked doubtful. Rajiv spoke to him, causing a smile and a shrug.

"He thinks you are nuts. But there we are. *Thé à l'anglaise.*"

They talked, easily and pleasurably, until the sun had gone and the air was cold. By that time Jane had told Rajiv of her secret pleasure at the departure of Sally, of her hopes of visiting Varanasi, of her desire to try to see something of the real India, of her struggles to begin to understand Hinduism.

He said, "That's a tall order for a week. Hinduism is such a rag-bag. It is all superstition, myth and magic—as much about storytelling as anything. And it's a mishmash of half a dozen religions and dozens of cultures, and varies with every village."

"Will you teach me? Can I hire you as guru as well as guide?" The idea had come to her out of the blue, and she'd expressed it before she had time to censor the thought.

He looked disappointed. "Oh, dear. Not another lost Westerner in search of enlightenment."

She laughed. "Not in the religious sense. I'm not religious, and never will be. I'm not joining the hippie trail. But I would like to understand India a bit better than I do, and Hinduism might be a good place to start. I bought a book on the subject and it's incomprehensible."

He did not answer at once. He seemed to be weighing the matter up. Then he said, "You're on. I shall collect you in the morning at 8, when it's still cool, and we will visit the Jain temples. Then when the sun's at its worst we will retreat to the Chandella and I will enchant you with epic tales from the Mahabharata."

He said it semi-seriously. Jane was pleased, but also a little nonplussed by the way he had so quickly taken command. He was assuming, with his role of teacher, an authority that she thought lay with her, the employer. And she both liked and resented the confidence of his gaze. He thinks he can handle women, she thought. Well, not this woman, he can't.

She said, "We could try. If I still can't make head nor tail of it, or I don't enjoy it, we will stop."

"Yes, madam." He was smiling, and his topaz eyes teased her for being pompous. "It shall be as the memsahib desires. I shall give you a test run, free of charge, right now. Think of a Hindu god, any god."

"Ganesh."

"Why Ganesh?"

"I liked his sculptures today, and in Amber I loved that fresco of him. You know, over the door into the inner palace. You'll think it's irreverent, but he reminds me of a book I had as a child. *Babar the Elephant*. Only he looks more like Celeste, Babar's wife."

Rajiv smiled, delighted. "How amazing. When I was in London I had Babar books too. And Celeste reminded me of Ganesh."

"Really? I don't believe it."

"It's true. Now I shall tell you a story of Ganesh, god of good luck."

TEN

The large round table, usually used for parties of ten, had only six chairs. Before each place there was a stack of three plates, and beside each place, a water tumbler, half a dozen spoons and as many forks but no knives. There were no flowers, no side-plates, no napkins, no wineglasses. There was a jug of water in the middle of the table, and to the left of each place was a note pad and pencil.

It was 3:30 in the afternoon and the quarterly menu tasting for Jane's was about to take place.

Patrick buzzed through to the kitchen. He could hear from the clatter and buzz that Alastair had the telephone on "hands free." He had a mental picture of Alastair whirling round, working with proficiency and speed. He asked, "Chef, how close are you?"

"Ten minutes, boss." Alastair's shouted reply sounded confident. Good, thought Patrick, maybe we'll get through this tasting without histrionics. Maybe.

"Fine, I'll call the others."

He walked to the top of the cellar steps, called "Silvino. Ten minutes," waited for an answering *"Si, signor,"* then went into the main dining room, a large square room with two sets of french windows opening onto a Regency balcony. Tony, his head waiter, was up a stepladder unscrewing a spotlight.

"Tony, Alastair will be ready in ten minutes. OK?"

"No sweat."

"What are you doing up there? Don't tell me another of those damn things has blown?"

"Yup. 'Fraid so. And that is the second last spare." He pointed to a box lying open on the table. "Can you pass it to me?"

Patrick lifted the heavy new fitting, and handed it to Tony, who gave him the old one, which was dusty and felt greasy. Tony clipped the new one into place, expertly connecting the wires.

"Thank God for a head waiter who is also an electrician," said Patrick, stuffing the dirty lamp into the box. "The trouble is these things are obsolete. I can't get anything that looks even vaguely like them. New ones, which are much smaller and completely different, cost £100 or more each."

"A hundred pounds *each*? We should get ordinary spots."

Patrick shook his head. "I like the light the halogen ones give. They concentrate the beam to light the food without showing up anyone's bald patches or wrinkles."

"Well, you've only got one left now."

"When the next one goes you'll have to cannibalize the ones in the bar. There are only six in there, and it won't matter if they are different from the ones in the dining rooms."

There were thirty-six spots in the rooms, Patrick knew. He shook his head in weary disbelief. Using the bar ones would stave off the evil hour for a few months, but sooner or later he'd need to find £4,000 just for new light fittings. Plus an electrician to fit them. He could hardly expect Tony to wire up forty-two ceiling lights.

They entered the smaller dining room as Alastair and Sonia were pushing through the swing doors from the kitchen, Sonia carrying a loaded waiter's tray on which were two stacks of plates, stainless-steel collars separating each plate and protecting its contents. There were three plates to a stack and the top plate on each had a flat aluminium canteen cloche on it. Sonia rested the corner of the tray on the table and everyone helped to disassemble the plate stacks, laying the uncovered plates in the center of the table.

As six fish dishes, all different, were revealed, Patrick said, "Bravo, Chef. They look good." Alastair had obviously taken to heart his lectures on the need for a bit of showmanship in presentation. Maybe some of the expensive trips to eat in his rivals' restaurants were paying off.

As they took their places, Silvino said, "Tony, you can't count. You've laid for six."

Tony said, "Ask the boss," without looking at Patrick. Instead, he lifted the water jug and busied himself with filling the tumblers.

"I asked Stella to join us," said Patrick. "She might write a fly-on-the-wall piece about the tasting."

Alastair, who was in the process of lowering himself into his chair, shot upright. "Christ, Patrick, I'm not having a sodding journalist sitting in on this. These dishes are not for picking over by . . ."

"Alastair, relax. She knows this is a working session. It will make good copy, and we could do with the publicity."

Alastair muttered, "Jesus, I don't believe this."

Patrick pretended he had not heard and said nothing. There was a short silence, broken by Alastair, who said, "OK. Fine. But where is she then? I'm not having everything collapse while we hang about."

"We will not wait. She knows that. And anyway she needn't be here for the whole session to get a story. She can join us any time." Patrick picked up his fork and pulled one of the central dishes toward him.

They started with the black inkfish risotto with a piece of perfectly poached turbot, glistening white, on top of it. The only decoration was a pair of thin chive leaves laid parallel across the top. Patrick resisted Tony's plea for more color, and backed up his chef when Alastair said the whole point about turbot was its perfect flavor and absolute whiteness and that it shouldn't be messed about with. Alastair also successfully fought off Silvino's suggestions for Parmesan in the risotto, claiming it would be too rich and powerful. "It's perfect as it is," he said. Patrick agreed, knowing that half his customers would demand Parmesan anyway. Still, Alastair wouldn't see it.

"Will you be able to get the turbot?" he asked.

"Well, if I can't, I'll not do it." Alastair sat back with finality.

Tony protested that it was the waiters who had to bear the customers' displeasure about dishes being off the menu. But Patrick silenced him with: "Oh, Tony, you can charm the birds from the trees. You know you will just tell them that the chef has been lucky enough to get halibut or whatever instead, and they'll love it."

They proceeded through the six dishes, each digging into the central plate, sometimes transferring bits to their own, but more often tasting straight from the plate. Good thing Mr. Neem isn't here, thought Patrick. Whatever germs the five of us have, are now communal ones.

The trouble started when they got to the sea bass. There was a thick chunk of fillet, sitting on top of a neat coil of Chinese noodles. The fish skin was finely scored on the diagonal, bubbled and crisp from a furious grill, the charred slashes revealing white flesh beneath. The noodles and the plate were covered with a white wine sauce in which the flavors of good fish stock, Gewurztraminer, whisked-in butter and rosemary coexisted in melting harmony. A few tiny diamonds of skinless raw tomato flesh studded the plate. Patrick's overriding thought was a wish that Stella were there to taste it. He'd defy her to say she'd ever, anywhere, had anything better. Even Silvino was awed into praise.

"That is truly something, isn't it? I'd never have said rosemary could go with fish." Silvino stuck his finger into the sauce, sweeping it around to scoop up a fingerful, and transferred it, dripping, to his mouth.

"Silvino. Use a spoon," said Patrick, tapping the pile of spoons next to Silvino.

Looking surprised and slightly resentful, Silvino said, "OK, boss. But it tastes better off the finger."

Patrick turned to Alastair. "This is a masterpiece, Chef. But how much is the sea bass? This is wild fish, isn't it?"

"It is. If you want sea bass on the menu, it's got to be wild, and a decent size. I'm not cooking that farmed rubbish." Alastair pulled a crumpled packet of Camels out of his trouser pocket and fished for a cigarette.

"But how much are you paying for it?"

"Patrick, you've got to pay for quality. Sure it costs a bit more, but those farmed fish are too small, they've no texture—they are mushy as brill, and they . . ."

Patrick leaned over and confiscated Alastair's ashtray, swinging around to deposit it on the table behind him. "Alastair. Do me a favor and don't smoke until we've done justice to your creations."

Alastair shrugged and put the cigarette packet down, his unlit cigarette on top of it.

Once again, Patrick said, "How much?" He tapped the plate-rim of the half-eaten sea bass with his fork.

Unable to avoid the question any longer, Alastair answered, "Eight pounds twenty per pound."

"Eight pounds twenty? God, Alastair. Be reasonable. To make the margin we'd have to price it beyond the point when anyone would buy it." He reached for his calculator, lying on the table beside his pad. "That's with head and tail and guts, I presume?"

"Yes. It's easier to tell the quality with whole fish, and I need the bones for stock."

Patrick tapped the keys. "That's £32.80 per portion. Plus VAT."

Tony laughed. "That's more than most customers want to pay for a three-course dinner including booze."

"You'll have to think again, Chef," said Patrick. "Either you halve the portion, bump it up with something cheaper, use farmed fish, or forget it."

"Jesus, Patrick. It is the best dish here. You know it is. We can sell it a bit under seventy-five percent GP. I'll make it up on something else. And the price will come down. Last month it was £5.40."

"OK," said Patrick, relenting. "Let's come back to it when we've tasted everything else."

Agreement was more easily reached with Alastair's trademark salmon, fashioned into fat noisettes, painted on both sides in melted butter, pressed into his home-made mix of Cajun spices, and dry-fried in a blazing pan—so hot the spices charred to black while the middle of the salmon was still sticky and barely cooked. He served it with a warm new potato salad and a brilliant-hued coriander and mango salsa. It was the best seller on the current menu, and, though Patrick and Silvino agreed there wasn't a wine in the world that went with it, it was too good to scrap.

Alastair himself rejected the red mullet in a roasted garlic broth, saying the dish had not come out as planned and was crude and boring. And Patrick dug his heels in over the soft-shell crabs, adding the unreliability of supply to his objections on the grounds of cost. Alastair, perhaps sensing that winning on the sea bass was enough victory for the day, agreed to do something with mussels on which they could get a whacking good margin—maybe 90 percent gross profit—to make up for the enforced underpricing of the sea bass.

Sonia had just brought in the second tray load of dishes, this time all meat and poultry, when Stella swung through the kitchen doors. She was eating a lacy almond tuile, holding it delicately between finger and thumb.

"Hi, guys," she said as she hoisted her bag onto a neighboring table and fluttered the fingers of her free hand briefly across the table at Patrick. She flopped into the empty chair and broke

117

her biscuit into two over her plate. She offered Tony, sitting to the right of her, a piece, saying, "Want some? It's delicious." He shook his head. Then she said, to no one in particular, "I'd kill for a glass of Chardonnay."

"Stella, love, this is a working session." Patrick's tone was affectionate but admonitory.

"Oh, honey. Don't be such a wet blanket. I'm sure Silvino won't mind getting me a glass." She turned her full open-eyed gaze on Silvino, who got up, saying, "No problem."

"Let's get on," said Patrick. "What have we got here, Chef?" Alastair did not answer and Patrick turned to him. Alastair's cheeks were flushed and his mouth set in anger. Oh, lord, thought Patrick, what's up now? I thought he was reconciled to Stella's presence. Deciding to tackle it head-on he asked, "What's the matter, Alastair? You look cross."

"I don't think you want to know." Alastair was speaking through clenched teeth, and looking at the tablecloth.

Patrick, surprised and concerned at his chef's stolid angry face, said, "Come on, Alastair. We're all friends here. Out with it."

"OK, boss. You asked for it, remember." Alastair swung around to face Stella squarely and said, "For one thing, I object to you walking through my kitchen. Even Patrick, who owns the place, doesn't just barge in. Second, no one, not even the food critic of the bloody *Dispatch*, helps themselves to my almond tuiles. It's stealing, and if you were a waiter, I'd have your guts. Christ, who do you think you are?" Alastair had started angry but controlled, but now his freckled face was crimson and he stood up, rocking the table in his urgency. "And I object to your being here at all. This is not a sodding public relations exercise— it's a serious business to set my spring menu. And you can't even bloody well turn up in time. I know you're used to every chef in town licking your feet, but here's one that won't."

Patrick jumped up. "Alastair, how dare you . . ."

But Alastair picked up his Camels and said, "I'll leave you

to settle the main courses." He slammed through the swing doors with a mix of dignity and bluster.

The reappearance of Silvino with Stella's glass of white wine was a merciful distraction, and Patrick said, "OK. Let's get on with it. I know Alastair is happy with everything here so it is just a matter of keeping two dishes from the current menu, and picking four more. OK?" With businesslike briskness which belied his internal confusion, Patrick conducted the rest of the tasting. They settled on a hot ox-cheek terrine, a guinea-fowl breast in a mustard sauce, lamb shanks with beetroot, and a poached poussin for the new main courses. They kept the classic rib eye steak with béarnaise and the pastry-latticed veal kidneys from the winter menu.

By the time the pastry chef arrived with six possible puddings and deserts, Patrick was having trouble concentrating. Stella, however, was enjoying herself, oohing and aahing and taking copious notes. The others seemed not to notice Patrick's distraction, for which he was grateful.

At 5 p.m. they were finally through and Stella, standing up to leave, said with breezy good humor, "Tell Alastair I apologize for violating his space and stealing his cookies. Who would have thought he'd be so uptight? Maybe he'll forgive me if I say he makes the best tuiles in town?"

Patrick held her shoulders. "Darling Stella, you are wonderful. How can you be so forgiving? He behaved abominably."

Stella backed out of his hold, smiling her shining smile. "Oh, Patrick. Who cares? Life's too short. See you." And she was gone.

But Patrick did care. And he was too much an army officer to ignore bad behavior. Though tempted to do nothing, and fearing he would like the coming interview even less than Alastair would, he buzzed the kitchen. Sonia answered.

"Tell Chef I'd like to see him, please."

When Alastair arrived, Patrick motioned him to sit on the chesterfield, and himself sat on one padded arm. He said, "OK. So what was all that about?"

Alastair was calm now, and had obviously rehearsed the speech he now delivered. "Look, Patrick. I don't think you and I should discuss Stella. I don't like her. You two are an item. You are my boss. It could all get very nasty."

"But I insist. What exactly have you got against her? It cannot be just that she came through your kitchen and pinched a tuile. For both of which, by the way, she was good enough to ask me to apologize to you."

"Did she, then?" Alastair's tone was mocking. "Well, that's all right, then." He made to get up, but Patrick waved him back.

"What did you mean by saying that every chef in town licked her feet?"

"Nothing. Or nothing that matters." Alastair shrugged without conviction.

"It matters to me."

"What's the point, boss? You wouldn't believe me anyway." Alastair's reluctance translated into sulkiness.

Patrick, feeling the indignity of this conversation with his chef, nevertheless could not put a stop to it. He wanted to know. He said, "Try me." He spoke quietly, but his eyes were determined.

Alastair felt cornered by Patrick's gaze. He shifted in the sofa, pushing his small frame back against the leather. "Patrick, you must know about Stella. Everyone knows about Stella."

Patrick felt his solar plexus cramp. He said, very evenly, "No, I don't. Why don't you tell me?" He folded his arms across his chest, partly to still his banging heart, partly to look relaxed.

"Because you will likely shoot the messenger." Alastair smiled, his nervousness showing.

"I won't. If there is something other people know about Stella, and I don't, then I'd better hear it."

Alastair was incapable of tact. Once beaten, he launched on his revelations, pumping them out at full speed, careless of the effect on Patrick.

"Patrick, Stella is a chef groupie. She's been shagged by half

120

the Circle Culinaire. Head chefs only, mind, from the best restaurants. Fuck knows why she's got her hooks into you, boss. You are not her type. She usually likes them young with tattoos. And maybe two or three at a time. The reason she thought she could walk through my kitchen is because she once tried it on with me, only I was too drunk to take her up on it."

Patrick jumped up. "I don't believe it . . ."

"I told you you wouldn't. But it's true. Ask her. She's not the sort to deny it. John Reilly's wife packed her bags and left him because of her. She's dynamite."

"She had an affair with John Reilly? Alastair, this is invention." Patrick swung around in a circle, like an animal trying to get out of a cage. Alastair continued, remorseless. "It is not. Ask him. How else do you think that wanker got a double-page spread in the *Dispatch* and his face on the cover of *Chef*? That's what led to his TV series."

Patrick's face had drained of all color. A part of his mind told him he should reprove Alastair for the word "wanker" but he said nothing.

Alastair went on. "She's using you, boss. Getting you to squire her everywhere, and tagging along on your wine trips."

Patrick wanted to stop Alastair now. With a visible effort, he said, "OK, Alastair. Thank you. I don't want to discuss it anymore, but if that is the kitchen gossip about Stella, then I guess I should be grateful to you for letting me know."

He patted Alastair's shoulder in a forced show of friendly dismissal, and Alastair stood up and made for the door. As he was closing it behind him, he hesitated, made up his mind, yanked it open again and pushed his head back into the office.

He said loudly and firmly, "Patrick, it is not gossip." He pulled the door closed behind him and turned to see Sandra, about to enter.

"What's not gossip?" she said.

Alastair dropped his voice and replied, "I just told the boss that Stella is turned on by all the lads in white, and that she's got him well and truly by the balls. But he doesn't believe me, poor sod."

Sandra opened her mouth in surprise, but Alastair pushed past her, saying, "I wouldn't go in there for a bit if I was you."

But Sandra went in, and found Patrick slumped on the sofa, his head back and eyes closed. He opened them and looked dully up at her. He said, "I didn't even know the staff knew about me and Stella. God, it's undignified." He rubbed his face with both hands, as though washing it.

Sandra said, "The trouble is, Tony's getting fed up with having to do so many of your shifts so you can go to other restaurants with Stella, and he complains to the others."

"He gets paid for the extra shifts."

"I don't think that's the point. The real point is that everyone is worried sick about the future of Jane's. Seeing you unconcerned is unsettling."

"Don't you think I'm concerned?"

"Not recently. Oh, Patrick, somehow when we all knew you were driving this ship, we just thought it was rough water. A bad patch. But now you don't seem to be steering, I think we'll sink."

Patrick was touched by this sustained naval metaphor. Sandra was a good woman, and she was right, his mind was not one hundred percent on the job. He smiled at her.

Sandra looked at Patrick as at an erring child, exasperation and devotion mixed. She went on, her eyes pleading, "You've hardly looked at the profit and loss for the last month. The average spend has been static for a year. Costs are up eight percent. Covers are down twelve percent. Don't you care?"

ELEVEN

Four days after her arrival in Khajuraho, Jane was sick with lust. She wanted Rajiv. She thought of nothing else, though she tried. She knew this was ridiculous. Undignified. Trite beyond belief, like a Mills and Boon novel. Falling in love with a tourist guide was on a par with falling for the ski instructor. Understandable in a calf-sick teenager, but idiotic in a grown-up.

But no amount of lecturing herself made any difference. She studied stories from the Mahabharata to impress him. She shaved her legs every morning just in case this was the day he might run his hand up her calf. Twenty times a day she thought, I don't care. There is no one here to see. Why shouldn't I fall for him? Why shouldn't I want to sleep with him? But something in his manner, something controlled and austere, made making a move impossible.

She had never felt like this. Even in the heady days at Oxford, when she had first met Patrick, she hadn't been so invaded and overturned by her own desire. She thought now that she had probably fallen in love with Patrick because she was programmed to by her middle-class upbringing. She'd been in love with the *idea* of being in love. Patrick was in the army by then, and had returned to Magdalen for the Commem Ball—partly to oblige his tutor, and partly for old time's sake. Somehow the combination of his dress uniform, too much champagne, punting on the Cherwell as the dawn broke and the fact that she was twenty years old and a virgin made their union inevitable.

She had been determined to shed her virginity. It had been

123

a cause of anxiety ever since the lower sixth, when she'd realized she was the only girl in her gang that hadn't "done it." She had gone to Patrick's hotel, allegedly for breakfast, but they both knew they'd end up in bed. Jane was relieved that, however embarrassing, this wouldn't be a squalid scramble in a car back seat with some fumbling boy.

Jane had explained, earnest now that she was sobering up, and talking fast while studying her scrambled eggs and sausages, that this would be the first time for her. She'd understand if he wanted to duck out. She didn't expect any kind of ongoing relationship, but, well, she'd really like to get it over with.

He hadn't laughed. He'd said, "Come on then. Let's see what we can do." And they'd left the breakfast half eaten, and he'd led her upstairs by the hand, kissed her deeply in the lift, and made expert love to her on the Randolph Hotel's candlewick bedspread.

After this, she'd fallen in love, gradually and naturally. Each time he left her to go back to his regiment, she missed him a bit more, until they needed each other all the time. They married four years later.

But this thing with Rajiv was different. The whole adventure was unsuitable, as Sally would have said. Rajiv was engaged to be married. He was Indian. He lived in Khajuraho. And anyway he didn't return her desire.

Jane only sometimes thought this last was true. Sometimes Rajiv showed a sympathy and warmth that she was sure was more than friendship. And there was an excitement, a tension, a palpable happiness that he must surely feel?

She had wanted him since that first evening at the Raja Café, when he'd told her the first of his Hindu myths, about the God Shiva chopping off his son's head because he'd stopped him from visiting his wife Parvati while she was bathing. Repenting, Shiva gave him a new head—an elephant's—and Ganesh was born.

When Rajiv was in his teacher role, recounting legends or

telling her stories of Rajput battles, he lost his coolness, his austerity, and became, like an actor, whatever he described. He was sad, merry, intense by turn.

Jane was enchanted by Rajiv's myths, but also obsessed by his body. She watched his long-fingered hands, slim and cool, like a pianist's, as he gestured. She found herself staring at the little hollow of his neck, below his Adam's apple. She longed to stroke the smoothness of his neck, kiss the hollow, slip her fingers into the gap of his shirt.

Sometimes his eyes would meet hers, and she'd have to look away, ashamed, convinced he could read her thoughts. But he would just smile, and continue.

In the mornings, from 10 till noon, they would visit the temples or a museum. Then Jane would return for a swim and lunch at the hotel, and Rajiv would turn up again at three. They had taken to spending the hot afternoons in her bedroom. It was too hot by the pool, and Rajiv was irritated by the piped music in the lobby. And he liked to get up and walk about as he talked, which drew attention to them. Hotel guests had stopped and stared at the curious pair—earnest Indian and rapt young Westerner. After the first session, Rajiv said, "Tomorrow I suggest we use your room. We can spread the books about, and there'll be no one to wonder what's going on."

Jane had a fleeting thought that what might go on would not be all scholarly education, but there was no hint of sexual intent in Rajiv's manner. Neither then, nor in the three days that followed.

Their afternoon sessions were precisely three hours, and Rajiv divided them into an hour of Hindu story-telling, and two hours of history. History, according to him, included social customs, Moghul garden design, vegetarian cooking, Independence and Mahatma Gandhi, even today's political corruption—anything that interested him. He brought books of Hindu art, plans of Rajasthan castles, copies of the *Times of India*, and video tapes of episodes of the Ramayana, which had been on television for two years. They watched these with the sound turned low, Rajiv narrating and speaking all the parts.

If Rajiv wanted her to look at a picture or a map, he'd get up from the chair, and spread the book between them on the bed. At such times his proximity, and the connotations of the large double bed, would sweep Jane's mind of all but animal longing. Her eyes would be bewitched by his arm protruding from the untidily rolled-up sleeve, and run down to his bent-back wrist, creased and dark at the angle of his hand. Her mind would taste the saltiness of his wrist while she let the sound of his voice caress her. She would not hear one word that he said.

On the third day of her lessons, Jane proposed that Rajiv ask her to supper with his mother and father, so that, she said, she could have a real Indian experience, not an academic, secondhand one.

"The thing is, Rajiv, I'm still living in the Taj Chandella, eating hotel food toned down for Western palates. I'd give anything to go into a real Indian home, meet a family, eat home-cooking. You can charge me double your hourly rate."

Jane did not know if she'd offended him or not, and she said, "It doesn't have to be your family. Maybe you know some people who would like . . ." Her voice trailed off. The truth was she did not want any family. She wanted to see Rajiv at home. Or rather she wanted him to see *her* in his home.

He said, "I'll speak to my mother. But if you are our guest, you will not pay."

That evening he telephoned the hotel while she was having dinner and left a message. "Supper arranged for tomorrow evening. My mother and Meera delighted."

Jane knew about Meera. She was Rajiv's fiancée, and they had been engaged since she was fifteen. Jane knew that Meera's existence should have put a brake on her ambition to seduce Rajiv, but all moral scruples seemed to have left her. She had no conscience about lusting after another woman's fiancé. It was as if Meera did not count. She did not form part of her story, which,

Jane recognized, was an ignoble one of sexual desire. I should be ashamed, thought Jane, but I simply do not care.

She felt no jealousy or resentment toward the beautiful Meera. Rajiv had told her she was seventeen and very lovely. Maybe it would be different once she'd seen her. But at the moment, she didn't altogether believe in Meera.

But now Jane wondered what the significance of including her name in the message was. To warn her that Meera would be there? To warn her off by a timely reminder of his engagement? Both, she suspected.

Jane took care getting dressed. She washed and blow-dried her hair, rolling the brush to curve her short bob around her face.

Rajiv had said "something casual," and she decided on just-below-the-knee cream culottes, her black leather sandals and a black T-shirt. Then a flat silver collar and matching clip-on earrings. On her brown arm she wore a heavy Thai bangle of black polished wood inlaid with silver hoops and white bone.

She used no foundation or blusher, knowing her tanned skin looked good, smooth and rosy. But she made her eyes up carefully: a mixture of brown and smoky green eyeshadow to darken her lids and accentuate the greenness of her eyes; two lots of mascara, then a dry brush to separate every lash; and finally, orange-brown lip-gloss.

She carried nothing—she meant to impress Rajiv with a disdain for encumbrances like handbags and make-up, and she wanted to feel free of them. And she knew her tan meant she looked good enough not to need repairs halfway through the evening.

When he buzzed her from the lobby, her insides jumped like a teenager's. She forced herself to look cool and casual. And he declared himself impressed, saying, "You look wonderful. Like a Calvin Klein commercial."

When they got to the Kumars', Jane felt she'd misjudged her clothes. Mrs. Kumar was in an embroidered glittery sari, with silver bangles from wrist to elbow. She greeted Jane with a garland of white jasmine, and pressed a talik to her forehead.

And then Jane felt wrong-footed by Meera. Though she'd known Meera was young and beautiful, she hadn't expected her to be exquisite: small but willowy, with fine, large dark eyes, a pale flawless complexion and full dark mouth. She wore red oleander flowers in her thick glossy hair, filigree gold earrings, and a deep green sari with a red-and-gold border.

Meera's English was hesitant, and she was shy. She seemed to take refuge in helping the servant to bring in the drinks. She poured whiskey for Mr. Kumar and for Jane, and Coca-Cola for Rajiv, then handed around spiced nuts. Her every gesture was graceful, like a dancer's. Jane noticed she slipped off her sandals to enter the kitchen, and her feet were perfect: small, delicate and smooth as marble.

No wonder he's not interested in me, thought Jane. That girl has to be any man's dream. Beautiful, modest and useful. She had a sudden recollection of the bride and groom that she'd seen being photographed in Rajasthan, and she thought what a handsome picture Rajiv and Meera would make in the family album: Meera dutiful and shy, Rajiv relaxed and dignified.

Rajiv's father was dressed in traditional long well-tailored jacket, buttoned Nehru-style to the neck, cotton trousers and sandals. His manner was warm and cheerful, his eyes merry behind steel-rimmed spectacles. His English was as good as Rajiv's, but he spoke with a pronounced Indian accent.

"I wish I spoke your Queen's English like my son," he said. "Whereas, in fact, I speak it like Peter Sellers, don't you think?"

Jane was embarrassed, because that was exactly how he did speak it. But she said, "That's only because Peter Sellers was a good mimic, not because you shouldn't have an Indian accent."

"Well, I suppose so. But I had many years in London, and did not improve my accent one jot."

Jane liked the old man, and for the moment managed to put her desire for Rajiv out of her mind, while she questioned him about life in Southall and the family's return to Khajuraho.

Soon, to Jane's consternation, Meera stooped before her, proffering a large brass bowl of water with petals floating in it. For a split second she was nonplussed, but Rajiv said, "You are honored, Jane. We are usually expected to wash our hands in the bathroom, without any frills like rose petals and scented water."

Jane dipped her fingers in the water, and dried them on the cotton towel Meera offered.

"Thank you," she said to Meera, hoping she'd performed the ritual correctly. Meera smiled but would not meet her eye.

Jane had expected pot-luck with the family, but it was obvious that enormous care had been taken. The table was decorated with petals and colored sweets, and the amount and variety of dishes astonished her.

She had never eaten any of them before and didn't know how to begin. She helped herself to a spoonful of everything and asked Mrs. Kumar what they were.

"They are all specialities of this region," she said. "And since my son has lately become a good vegetarian, we don't have meat when he's here. I hope you don't mind?"

"Of course not." She looked across at Rajiv. "I thought all Hindus were vegetarian."

"No," said Rajiv. "But many are. And all the Jains. Some of them are vegan. Mostly it is a question of habit and economics as much as religion. Meat is expensive."

"Why are you vegetarian, if your family aren't?" Jane asked, and at once felt it was crass to ask so personal a question.

His answer confirmed the feeling. "I'm trying to eat a diet that cools the blood and stills desire."

He smiled as he said this and looked at Meera. Jane didn't know if he was joking, or if the remark was truly aimed at Meera. She suspected it might be a dig at herself. Was her lust so obvious? Pretending she hadn't heard, she asked Mrs. Kumar to tell her how the dishes were made.

Mrs. Kumar set off on a detailed and, to Jane, incomprehensible description of their preparation, and of the spices that went into them. When she realized that Jane was lost, she sent Meera for paper and pencil, and wrote down the names: bharva tinda (stuffed cucumbers); kathal (Jackfruit); sufaid moolee ke kofte (white radishes in spicy sauce); kudhi (fritters in yoghurt); baingan (stuffed aubergines) and dal pakori (dal fritters). She talked on tirelessly, unaware of Jane's flagging attention. She would have added the recipes too if Rajiv hadn't stopped her.

"Mother, stop. The poor woman will never absorb in one go what has taken you a lifetime to learn. Why don't you show her how to make a biryani or something tomorrow? That will be more use to her than lists of spices."

Mrs. Kumar looked up at Jane, delighted. "Oh, I would like that very much. Would you? Meera, we will do it. Shall we show our guest some real Indian cooking? Better than all those curry take-aways the English think is Indian cooking."

And so it was agreed. Jane would give up her morning's guided tour from the son for two hours of cooking lessons from the mother. But her ready agreement did not let her off the hook of second helpings. Mrs. Kumar pressed her relentlessly. Jane knew Mrs. Kumar would find her refusal hurtful, so she gingerly helped herself to tiny amounts of the least fiery dishes. The food was hotter than she could have imagined, and as sweat burst out on her forehead, she felt ugly and embarrassed.

And then, just as she'd managed to clear her plate by swallowing a piece of pickled lemon so bitter only a determined effort mastered the urge to spit it out, Rajiv said, "Mother, Jane is eager for Indian experiences. Let us have second helpings in the Indian way." Turning to Jane, he explained, "When it is just the family we eat Eastern-style, with our fingers. We'll show you."

Jane, dismayed but unable to protest, watched as Meera and Mrs. Kumar quickly cleared the plates and brought large cut squares of banana leaf, putting one before each of them. Rajiv explained she must use only her left hand for spooning the food

130

onto her leaf, and her right one for eating. He demonstrated, spooning neat piles of the different foods onto his leaf, then deftly rolling mouthfuls of them in small bread pieces torn from his roti.

Jane longed to be excused more food. But she could not refuse, and tried gamely to do as instructed. But her unpracticed left hand spilt an orange splotch of sauce on the table, and her clumsiness in using one hand for such a complicated maneuver as breaking the roti, scooping up the food with it and rolling it into an elegant mouthful was beyond her. She abandoned the attempt, but Rajiv insisted, "Come on, Jane. It is not like you to give up at the first try. Watch Meera. She is a very elegant eater."

Indeed she was. She smiled shyly, showing perfect bright white teeth. Small neat rolls of roti were lifted without haste or mess into her perfect mouth. As they watched her, she looked at Rajiv with the adoration, thought Jane, of a pet dog.

At last dinner was over, the banana leaves folded so as not to give offense (Rajiv had to fold Jane's for her). Meera and Mrs. Kumar helped clear the table while Jane and the two men returned to the sitting room.

They talked about Jane's plans to visit Varanasi and about her job at Chalker and Day.

Then Mr. Kumar, lighting a thin cheroot, quite suddenly said, "Jane, do you think Rajiv is a good teacher?"

"He's an excellent teacher." Jane glanced at Rajiv, whose eyes met hers, friendly and intimate.

Mr. Kumar said, "He has a British passport, you know, because of our refugee status after Uganda."

"What has that got to do with my teaching?" inquired Rajiv. Jane watched him stretch lazily in his chair, with the satisfaction of the well fed. His mind seemed only marginally engaged by the conversation.

Mr. Kumar replied, "You should marry Meera and go to England and get a job. Maybe as a school teacher. Then your children will get British passports too."

"I'm not a school teacher. But one day I will return to England. With luck to work in the British Library or British Museum, Asia section."

"You are thirty years old, my son. One day is too late. You should be settling down now. How long are you going to wait before you get married and find a proper job? Do you not agree, Jane? This tour-guide business is unworthy."

Jane did not know what to say. She felt trapped between agreement with the father and disloyalty to the son. And she could not bring herself to recommend his marriage. Happily, before she could find an answer, Rajiv said, "Meera is too young to marry, father." He said it without heat, a statement of fact.

"Nonsense, boy. Your mother was sixteen and I was twenty-two when we married."

Rajiv did not answer. He smiled, shrugged and stood up, putting out a hand to pull Jane out of the deep armchair. He addressed her, not his father. "As you see, this is a well-honed family argument. We all know our parts by heart, and indeed we know each other's too." He turned to his father, laying an affectionate hand on his shoulder and said, "I'll walk Jane to a taxi and see her home."

Meera and Mrs. Kumar reappeared and Jane said her good-byes, trying to make up for her social blunders with repeated thanks.

At last they were out in the cool fresh air.

"Doesn't Meera need escorting home too?"

"She lives in the house immediately behind ours. There's a path between the gardens." He looked back toward the house, gesturing.

Jane asked, "Is that how you met, over the garden wall?" She both wanted to know about Meera and didn't.

"No. She's my second cousin. Our families have been close for generations. She's not just the girl next door. She's also the personification of my family's hopes for me." He spoke matter-of-factly, as if such considerations were normal.

132

"Tell me about her. How long have you been engaged?" Jane kept her voice light and her eyes on the pavement before her.

"Officially for a year. In fact, ever since she was born."

"I thought arranged marriages didn't happen much anymore."

Rajiv shepherded her across the road, guiding her with his hand on her back. She felt the warmth of his fingers, and the loss of them when he dropped his arm. He said, "Oh, they do. But parents are more subtle about it now. I do not have to marry Meera, and she does not have to marry me."

"So it's love then?" It took an effort to ask the question, and she dreaded the answer. She got what she dreaded.

"Certainly I love her. Who would not? She's everything a man should want in a wife. She's beautiful, is she not? Her family is rich, or at least richer than we are. And she's longing to be a good and dutiful wife and mother."

"Then why not let her? As your father says, why wait?"

"Because she is a child. She can't possibly know if I'm the right man for her. She's practically never met any others. She's seventeen. She's just doing what her father wants. I've got to wait until she's old enough to judge for herself."

"She won't change her mind. I've seen the way she looks at you. She adores you."

"That's because I don't pursue her. She may be young but she's woman enough to want what seems unattainable."

"Why don't you pursue her? It's obvious you want to." Jane hoped he would deny the desire, but he didn't.

He said, "Because if I'm right and she grows up to think better of it, I'll have ruined her life. Virginity in our society still matters more than it does in yours."

Jane felt there was a righteousness in his tone, a hint of criticism. But she dismissed it and asked, "Hence the vegetarian diet?"

"Yes."

"You are not serious?"

"I am." They walked on a few paces and Jane thought he'd dropped the subject, but then he said, "Though avoiding meat on its own isn't enough. If you really want a celibate life, you have to give up very hot spices and garlic and onions and almost anything with any flavor. I'm trying, but not very successfully."

"And you really believe that? That desire can be dimmed by diet? If true, the Jains would be extinct by now."

"No, it's a combination of diet, and meditation, and self-control. Very Indian. You wouldn't understand."

She was about to protest that she did understand, but thought better of it. The truth was, she didn't. They walked on in silence, Jane conscious of a widening cultural gap. The closer she got to Rajiv, the less she seemed to know him. But the more desirable he became.

They came to the taxi rank, with one lone taxi waiting under the street lamp. Rajiv opened the door for her. She stood for a moment before getting in, unsure whether she should shake his hand as she would her guide or kiss his cheek as she would a friend.

In the event she did neither, but climbed into the back seat and closed the door. Rajiv leaned through the window and kissed her lightly on the cheek. "See you tomorrow. You'll find cooking Indian food less of an ordeal than eating it."

She protested, without conviction, "No, Rajiv, I loved it. And your family were wonderful. Thank you." As she drove away she could still feel the brush of his lips on her cheek.

The following afternoon Rajiv and Jane were lying in deckchairs on the terrace of the Taj Chandella, by the pool. Rajiv had brought Jane back after her cooking lesson with Meera and his mother.

"You know, I cannot cook in English, so you can imagine how I got on in Hindi," she said. "Your mother must have thought I was completely useless."

"My mother thinks you are altogether charming."

Jane had been amazed at the sheer competence of the two women. With hardly a word of communication, they would each tackle their separate tasks with quick practiced fingers, sorting, pressing, rolling, folding, turning, kneading. Apart from a sharp knife and a kind of cleaver used for fine slicing and finer chopping, they had few tools.

It had not really been a cooking lesson, and Jane had enjoyed it. She'd expected Mrs. Kumar to teach her the vegetarian dishes her son liked, but Rajiv had decreed that meat dishes familiar in the West would be more use to her. They had made a vegetable pilau, a biryani, rogan josh and a lamb korma. Jane had been given the jobs she could handle, like shaking a pan over the flame, or picking through the rice. She even enjoyed the latter, quickly acquiring the technique of pushing the good grains of rice, in clumps of two or three, to one side of the tray, flicking any tiny stones or black grains to the other.

And then they had eaten the products of the teach-in, sitting on the shady Kumar verandah, and Jane had for the first time experienced the satisfaction of watching someone she cared for eating food she had taken pains to prepare. It pleased her to see Rajiv helping himself to food she had mixed and stirred, chopped and tasted.

Jane could feel her face aflame from the fiery kitchen and her mouth burning from the heat of the spices. Her lips felt swollen and hot from tasting fresh chili. She held her frosty Coca-Cola glass against her mouth, revelling in its cold kiss. It made her lips tingle and accentuated the heightened feeling in them.

Her mind was full of the experiences and images of the morning: the brilliant reds and yellows of chilli and spices, the powerful smells, the sizzling sounds of frying, the crack and the pop as turgid peppers were split, the rhythmical thwack of cleaver on board. Even the silky feel of raw meat. She had not realized that cooking could be so sensual.

And then the scene of sun filtering through the creeper, brightly colored dishes and glowing food had made her feel languorous and sexy. Almost drunk.

She had watched Rajiv's long fingers fold, tenderly but firmly, around a small clump of pilau and lift it to his mouth. As he ate, she imagined *her* fingers, rather than his, at his mouth. She could feel his lips, dry and firm at first touch, then warm and soft.

She'd made a half-hearted effort to shake off such thoughts, and listen to the conversation, but within minutes she was reversing the fantasy, imagining *his* fingers at *her* mouth. They would feel smooth and cool, and she would swallow their offering quickly, so she could kiss his fingers and keep them there. He would perhaps push a forefinger between her teeth, and she would close her teeth on it, hard enough to prevent escape.

Now, an hour later by the pool, she again felt the stirring of desire, and thought, God, I'm a raving nymphomaniac. She jumped out of her deckchair and said, "I'm for a swim. What about you?"

Without opening his eyes he replied, "No, thanks. But you go ahead."

She persisted, "The hotel will lend you swimming trunks, I'm sure."

"No. It's not hot enough." He opened his eyes and smiled at her. "February is early spring, you know. If it was July or August, I might join you."

Jane dived into the pool with scarcely a splash, and struck out with a confident crawl for the far end. There she sat on the pool steps, half in and half out of the water, thinking about Rajiv. The cool water had its effect, and she felt a little ashamed of herself. She would have thought that meeting Meera, and hearing Rajiv say unequivocally that he loved her, would have been the no-go sign she needed. But it wasn't like that. The more she reflected on their conversation about Meera, the more he became not just an object of desire but a challenge. She wanted to conquer him, to seduce him despite all his defenses: despite the lovely Meera; despite his self-control, his ascetism, his meditation and his anti-inflammatory diet.

She told herself she'd be doing him a favor. It wasn't natural, at thirty, to be celibate. And anyway his protestations about protecting Meera were probably self-delusion. More likely he was protecting himself from a conventional marriage that would bore him stiff.

Jane could feel his eyes on her as she swam back toward him, then did a length underwater. She came up for air at the far end and turned, she knew, with the sleek grace of the competent swimmer. This is a mating display, she thought. Perhaps porpoises do it. Pushing herself off again she did the return length in a few strokes of lazy crawl, hoping he'd notice how little she disturbed the water, her body rolling gently, her knees almost straight, feet beating fast and rhythmically. She hauled herself neatly out of the pool, and tossed her head to flick her wet hair off her face.

She said, "Rajiv. I have a proposition for you. Could we continue my immersion in Indian culture in Varanasi, do you think?"

He looked at her steadily without answering. Disconcerted by his gaze, she crouched beside his chair, reaching behind him for her towel. She knew her hair was stuck flat to her head, and she could feel the water running down her face and neck in rivulets, and into the channel between her breasts. As she looked up at him she was conscious of her nipples hard as little beads under her costume, and of her skin, tingling between the cool of the water and the heat of the sun on her back.

Oh, Jesus, I want you, she thought. But what she said, in a surprisingly steady, almost off-hand, voice was, "I'll never find another guide like you. No one who will lecture me on polo or pig-sticking one minute and funeral pyres the next."

With water running into her eyes she could not clearly read his expression. She buried her face briefly in the towel, then looking up again, she hurried on, trying to forestall his refusal. "Go on, Rajiv. I know you'll get all male and proud about the money, but the fact is that I'm a respectable tourist and you are a brilliant guide. Why can't I hire you for a few more days?"

At last he spoke.

"You can," he said, "but this time it will be different."

"Why?"

"You know why," he said, looking into her face. Then he dropped his gaze to her breasts and with his finger traced the scoop of her swimsuit neckline. Then with the back of his knuckles he lightly brushed one nipple. She looked down and saw both nipples swell and rise under the wet costume.

Rajiv slowly slipped his hand under her swimsuit and held one cold wet breast. With the other arm he pulled her to him and kissed her. Her lips, still tingling from the chili, seemed to burn and swell, all sensation and desire concentrated in them. She sank into the kiss, offering her mouth to him, hot, swollen, open. She wanted a river of this. Of this soft long time kissing.

But he pulled away and put three fingers over her mouth, both caressing her lips and restraining her mouth seeking to regain his.

He said, "I'm going now. I will collect you at six and we'll eat together, somewhere else, not here. This hotel is your territory, and if we are to make love, I want it on mine."

Jane's heart was pounding, and she was shaking. Triumph, desire, anxiety and relief took turns. She laughed out loud.

"Rajiv, you are soaking wet. I'm sorry."

He looked down at his shirt, wet from hugging her, and said, "No, you are not. And it will dry. I'll see you at six." And he was gone.

TWELVE

Jane faxed the office: "Delhi Belly I'm afraid. Back Monday week. Really sorry."

How interesting, she thought. I'm a supposedly truthful lawyer and I've no qualms about lying to my partners. She told herself her senior partner would not waste any sympathy on her. He'd believe her, but think getting sick was irresponsible and weak, something women tended to do. She also knew she would pay for her absence more dearly than her partners. An extra week in India would probably mean years more hard graft on the cases no one else wanted.

But she didn't care. For the first time since she'd joined the firm, straight after Oxford, she hardly gave the office a thought. She was drunk on her new life. It wasn't just the sex and Rajiv. It was India. And particularly Varanasi.

She and Rajiv had been in the city for three days and were staying with Dharam, a friend of Rajiv's from his Delhi University days. Dharam was a headmaster of a primary school, and lived in a two room bungalow at the edge of the bare patch of earth that passed for a playground. He had given up his bedroom for Rajiv and Jane, and slept on a charpoy on the verandah.

Dharam was seldom at home. He taught all day at the school, and in his spare time he supplemented his salary by taking tourists on early-morning tours of the ghats or leading them through the ancient city's tangle of alleys and passages.

Dharam, though polite, smiled little and never laughed. Jane suspected disapproval. "Does Dharam regard me as a wicked woman?" she asked Rajiv. They were sitting on the verandah

139

steps, his hand between hers. By rubbing her thumb across the back of it she could feel the bones and sinews under the skin.

He watched her kneading his hand and replied, "Dharam is very religious. He's worried for my soul, or rather for my rebirth."

She looked up. "Am I jeopardizing your reincarnation prospects?"

He nodded. "I guess so. Dharam would think so. He's a good man."

She resumed her fondling of his hand. "Are you not a good man?"

"Well, I'm not a good Hindu, that's for sure. Dharam is. He sticks to his moral code. His dharma."

"Don't you?"

"Not like Dharam." Rajiv smiled. "His dharma wouldn't allow him to pretend to his parents and fiancée that he is away working when he's dallying with a wicked woman."

"*Do you* think I'm a wicked woman?"

"Very wicked. And delicious." He kissed her forehead.

Jane did not pursue it. But she felt a twist of unease. Rajiv was ducking the question.

Dharam rose before five, either to collect tourists from the hotels and take them to the river or to meditate, which he did facing the rising sun under an ancient banyan tree at the school gates.

Once he was gone, Rajiv and Jane would make love. Jane would wake to find her dreams sliding into wakeful desire. She would try to stay asleep as long as possible, to hold onto the dream, to pretend that she was unaware of Rajiv's hands caressing her back, his breath on the nape of her neck. Wordlessly and carefully he would roll her onto her back and stroke her breasts, her belly, her thighs. Jane would keep her eyes shut, her mouth relaxed, her breathing deep and steady. She would feign sleep, letting the dream happen.

But she couldn't keep it up. She would not be able to contain the sounds of love.

She felt that Rajiv played her like an instrument. He seemed to envelop them both in a wave of sex, like nothing she had ever known. Each time it was the same: first mounting arousal, then headlong flying desire, followed by a climax so intense she felt obliterated by it. She lost her separateness, became his creature, his possession. Whatever he wanted, her need leapt to meet his. She would have done anything he asked her at that moment, let him kill her if he'd wanted to.

But what he wanted, was more of her. Over and over again her body would respond, until at last, he would be satisfied. He would curl around her, his arms imprisoning her as he slept.

It took ages to come round. She wallowed in the closeness, the feeling of him. She bathed in it. It lapped around her and flowed into her. She stayed enveloped in the magic while they got up. Only gradually did she drift to the surface, and talk to him. It was like a religious experience, she thought.

Once, distanced by a shower and breakfast from just such heady sex, she said, "I can't get over the *power* you have over me, and my utter subjugation. I begin to think there is nothing in the Kama Sutra that I won't want."

Rajiv smiled, warm and deep. As he left the kitchen he kissed her shoulder and said, "Maybe you never had a good lover before."

Jane thought about it. Maybe he was right. Patrick had been her only lover, and she'd thought he was wonderful. He'd been good at it, had taught her, and they'd had some great sex, especially at the beginning, and latterly on holiday. But this with Rajiv was on another plane. A mystical, transcendental one. Even putting on a condom was an erotic rite, a prelude, a privilege. She began to understand why women fell so completely in the power of men. It was like a drug, she could not get enough of it, and she thought about it night and day.

141

Rajiv and Jane spent the cool of the morning exploring the town on foot—rickshaws and taxis could only make it down the widest of the streets. And even those were so potholed and rutted, and so choked with bicycles, cows, carts and people that better progress could be made walking.

Jane revelled in Rajiv's presence. She tried to keep the pride of possession out of her gaze, but she felt smug watching Western tourists trailing after their guides, heads averted as beggars tugged their sleeves or pushed handless arms or ragged children under their noses. The same beggars ignored her as Rajiv dropped a few rupees into a begging bowl or outstretched hand.

When Rajiv worshipped in a Shiva temple, she would watch him ring the bell, or pray, or walk clock-wise around and around the idol. He did this casually, and it seemed to her haphazardly. She watched without embarrassment, happy to feel somehow part of it. She could not make head nor tail of the rituals, but she loved the strangeness of it—the smell of incense and camphor, the sound of the bell, the devotees waving candles.

And she was enjoying living in an Indian house, shopping with Rajiv for vegetables and rice, and cooking, in the bungalow's far-from-hygienic kitchen, the few dishes Rajiv's mother had taught her. It was like playing house: not real, not forever, but exciting.

Rajiv helped her buy presents—Indian cotton table cloths, a cashmere shawl, silver earrings and neon-colored bangles. He bought her a sari. She feared she'd never wear the sari, although the way the fine cotton slipped like silk through her fingers and shone with an iridescent sheen delighted her. It was orange, a color she avoided. Too strident for the office, too loud for a casual shirt or skirt.

India, she reflected, was turning her taste upside down. As she watched a vendor outside the Golden Temple selling handfuls of yellow flower petals from a great heap, and saw pilgrims choosing orange garlands from her overflowing baskets, it seemed extraordinary that she had ever thought dahlias and marigolds vulgar. They are just wonderful, she thought. They vibrate with color.

Rajiv had not yet allowed Jane to visit the ghats. He wanted her to see them on an auspicious day, when the Ganges would be teeming with pilgrims. But on their fourth morning in Varanasi they rose at 4 a.m. It was cold. Jane wore her cashmere coat over trousers and shirt, and wished she'd bought a woollen blanket like Dharam's, or an all-enveloping shawl, like Rajiv's. They both looked, thought Jane, like something out of the Bible.

Thousands of pilgrims were walking down to the river, carrying tiny candles. It made a stream of stars, winking and jiggling, as the excited crowd hurried to the Ganges, determined to be there in time to perform puja to the rising sun.

Jane was delighted at the lack of solemnity. The crowd chattered, children darted about, hawkers extolled their wares, cows and goats stood their ground as the human stream lapped around them. Lighted street stalls were doing brisk trade in devotional candles, soap, garlands and sweet milky tea.

Dharam's boat was moored at the Dasashwamedh Ghat, and they were on the river while it was still dark.

As Dharam rowed slowly upriver, the dark gave way to a misty dawn, and to sights that Jane knew would be imprinted on her mind forever. If the scene had been directed by Zeffirelli, she thought, he could not have improved it.

Across the river the great orange sun rose slowly and turned the river into a sheet of fire. Thousands of pilgrims stood in the water, facing the sun and chanting Ram Ram.

The mist lent the scene an unearthly quality. The Venice-like vista of grand but crumbling buildings rising from the river, of towers and temples, of steps and terraces, provided a backdrop to the pilgrims' earnest activities. Old men did yoga exercises on the steps; dhobi-wallahs beat clothes on washboards; women, fully dressed, held their jeweled noses and sunk under the water of the Ganges. Bathers poured the holy water over their heads, drank it, soaped their armpits in it and prayed in it. Near-naked skeletal sadhus, covered in ashes, meditated cross-legged on the banks, and milling crowds gathered around holy men to pay for prayers and blessings.

Dharam turned the boat and rowed faster downstream, past where they started, until they came to the burning ghats.

"If you want to see funerals in progress, you need to come later," said Dharam. "It takes hours to get a proper fire going."

He indicated a fire on a burning platform. Jane watched a group of people, presumably the mourners, standing about, talking. One of them fed a couple of logs to the fire. A vendor came past and sold them sticks to clean their teeth with and then another sold them glasses of tea.

Jane was taken aback at the casualness of it all. It is because they have a better attitude to death, she thought. It is just a rite of passage, not the end. But she didn't feel convinced.

"The deceased is a woman," continued Dharam in a matter-of-fact voice. "You can tell because the corpse is wrapped in red silk."

Jane's eyes followed as Dharam indicated a long red bundle lying on the ghat. It was strapped to a wooden stretcher and lay at right angles to the steps, one end toward the river. Jane thought uneasily it might shoot into the river, like a child on a toboggan.

As they rowed back, Dharam said, "Really holy men, and tiny children, are not burned as they don't need the purification of fire. They just go in the river as they are."

"Same with cows," said Rajiv.

He pointed to a line of boats, far out in the middle of the river. Jane looked, shading her eyes from the sun, and saw a large heavy object rolled or tipped into the water. She felt her stomach tighten.

"But what happens to the bodies?"

"They are weighted with stones and the river is very deep. They sink to the bottom and rot."

"And the vultures take care of anything that floats or gets washed up downstream," said Rajiv, pointing to slowly circling birds in the sky and a row of them on a rooftop above the ghat.

Jane swallowed quickly, twice. Neither of the men looked at her, for which she was grateful. She was silent after that. She leaned into Rajiv's shoulder and told herself everything was wonderful and fascinating. But in truth, she was shocked. That people could drink water that others defecated in and threw bodies into disgusted her. Suddenly the foreignness of it all upset her. She found herself longing to lie deep in her own bath at home, with the Brandenburg Concertos and Givenchy bubbles enveloping her in equal measure.

That evening they ate spicy cauliflower fritters and a red kidney bean stew in a café. It was a happy evening. Dharam had even unbent enough to talk to her about the restaurant trade in London, and promised to visit her if he ever got to England.

After supper Dharam went home to get to sleep early, and Rajiv and Jane sat under Dharam's banyan tree and shared a cigarette, rolled by Rajiv and heavily mixed with marijuana.

Jane had smoked a few joints in her life, but always with a degree of nervousness. She hated the thought of losing control. At Oxford she had shared joints with her girlfriends, which seemed less dangerous and more relaxing than doing so with men. And when she and Patrick were first married, they'd sometimes buy a little block of hash at a late-night club, and keep it for Sunday evenings—the one evening they had together because Jane's was closed.

But when Patrick gave up cigarettes, it seemed a bad idea for him to be inhaling the tobacco they mixed with the hash or grass. And smoking the stuff in a pipe was such a performance.

But Jane was now so completely in Rajiv's thrall it did not occur to her to question him. Smoking ganja was, she thought, part of being in India. When she was back in London, she'd resume her City suits and respectability, but while this other life lasted, she'd live it to the full. She lay back on the grass, and looked at the stars through the leaves of the tree. She felt dreamy and sleepy, content right through.

"Rajiv," she said. "Why don't you come back to London with me? You could get a job at the British Museum or School of Oriental and African Studies."

Rajiv didn't answer at once, but Jane was drifting contentedly on a little fantasy of Rajiv making love to her on her Hammersmith carpet, and didn't hurry him.

"Because, my darling independent, rich and successful business lady, I haven't any money."

"But I've got lots."

"You're mad. You cannot keep me like a pet."

At other times Jane would have reacted sharply to the jibe. But she said peaceably, "I don't want to keep you. I don't want to own you at all. I don't want to own anyone ever again. But I could buy you an air ticket—a return one if you like—and if you live with me you won't have any expenses while you look for a job."

Rajiv said nothing, and Jane continued, still gazing at the banyan branches, "You can pay me back if you like. But you want to go to London. And I don't think I can face London in February without you."

"You are crazy. You've only known me for ten days, fifteen if you count the train."

"So? It's now or never, since I'm going back on Saturday. By then you will have known me seventeen days. Is that enough?"

Rajiv didn't answer and Jane's thoughts drifted. She thought idly about Chalkers. She'd faxed them to say she'd be back on Monday, a week later than she'd planned. Somehow it didn't seem to matter, which was odd. Always before, if she'd been due to return to work from a holiday, even on schedule, her mind during the last few days seemed to detach itself from the beach, the luxury, the meals, and start to think about her caseload, sort her files, decide whom she needed to see. Now she could not remember what briefs she was working on, and didn't care. Must be the ganja. Early the next morning, Jane ruined their lovemaking by throwing up. Rajiv was lying, heavy and spent, on top of her, when Jane realized she was going to be sick. She tried, wordlessly because she was clenching her mouth shut, to struggle out from under. Rajiv, thinking she needed air, rose onto his elbows, which now imprisoned her head, and tried to kiss her.

She whipped her head from side to side, her "No, no" trapped in her throat. As Rajiv met her eyes, wide and desperate, her body suddenly heaved and vomit exploded over his neck and shoulder.

"Oh, God," she cried, struggling up. Grabbing the sheet, she ran out of the door to the verandah. Dharam woke to the sound of her retching over the verandah rail.

As soon as it was over, she felt better. But the shame of it immediately gripped her. The first thing she was conscious of was that her back and buttocks were bare—the sheet she'd grabbed only covered her front. And Dharam was coming toward her, calling for Rajiv. Pulling the sheet hastily around her, she ran barefoot across the baked earth to the banyan tree, darkly visible in the dawn light.

She had no plan in mind. Just to get away. Wiping her mouth and eyes on the sheet, she sat down on the grass and put her face between her knees.

Suddenly she laughed. Oh, sweet Jesus, what a way to end a romance! She remembered now that last night when the food came, it was barely warm, and she'd even had a fleeting thought that any bugs in it would be multiplying happily. But Dharam was with them and she didn't want to be rude. She'd said nothing, and the food had tasted fine.

Maybe it was the ganja joints, she thought. Whatever. Anyway, it served her right for telling Chalker and Day she was sick. She started to shiver, and then knew, with a sinking cer-

147

tainty, that she was going to be sick again. But this time she had time to get herself to the ditch beyond the tree, safely out of sight of the bungalow.

When she returned to the house, she was shivering, pale, her forehead sweaty, her stomach sore from unproductive heaving, and her eyes red-veined. Rajiv came to meet her. He was dressed and he smelled of soap.

"Oh, Rajiv, I'm so sorry . . ."

"Darling girl, you couldn't help it."

His arm, comforting and clean smelling, shepherded her up the steps onto the verandah. Dharam was sitting on the charpoy, doing up his sandals. He said, "Bad luck, Jane. Drink plenty of weak tea, and get some rest. See you tonight."

As naturally as if nothing had happened, as if he hadn't woken to the sight of a naked Englishwoman throwing up over his balcony, he waved to them both and set off to his morning meditations. Jane thought with relief, at least I wasn't sick under his banyan tree.

Rajiv told her to take a shower and then to rest on Dharam's charpoy. He would go and fetch a woman to clean up and look after her. Jane did as she was told, like an obedient child. As she sat on the shower stool, the warm soapy water seemed to cleanse her of the whole hideous experience. She washed her hair and scrubbed her teeth and, feeling restored, went into the bedroom to clean up.

Before Rajiv returned, Jane had managed, with repeated rests in which she shivered and sweated and with pauses for painful retching, to wash the sheets and mop the floor. She was hanging the sheets on the clothes-line in the little yard.

He was angry. "Jane, I told you to rest. What do you think you are doing?"

She was hurt that he didn't see she was trying to make amends, but she felt too rotten to argue. On being ordered into Dharam's bed, she accepted its alien smell without protest. She hadn't the strength to demand a clean sheet. She'd caused enough trouble already.

The next three days were hell. An old woman, Mridula, who spoke no English, brought her thin spicy soups that she promptly threw up, and bitter teas which, she assumed, were medicinal. When she wasn't in an exhausted sleep, she was being sick or suffering diarrhea.

She wanted plain bottled water to drink, but both Rajiv and Mridula seemed to think the bitter teas better for her. She forced them down because she knew the risks of dehydration, and she did not dare drink the tap water.

When Rajiv went out to fax Chalker and Day again for her, she felt trapped in India. She wanted Western comforts, a Western doctor. Rajiv promised one if she wasn't better in a day or two. She was too weak to argue.

She hardly saw Rajiv and Dharam, who now shared the bed inside. Dharam went to work as usual, and Rajiv disappeared, she knew not where.

She both wanted Rajiv with her and she did not. She missed him, but she felt ugly and unattractive and she hated him seeing her so. What I really want, she thought, is for him to stroke my forehead and dab cologne on my wrists and tell me that I am a beautiful languishing princess. I want him to tell me Indian tales, and bring me pomegranates. Whereas he thinks the sickroom is women's work, and finds me a real turn-off.

On the fourth day of her illness, Rajiv again left before she woke and did not return all day. Jane was almost recovered, though she still had no appetite. When he appeared, at 7 p.m., she was close to tears.

"Rajiv, I'm going home. Tomorrow."

"You are not well enough for tomorrow. Wednesday, maybe."

Her first leaping thought was joy. Home in sight. Wednesday was the day after tomorrow. But the joy was followed by a pang of misery. Rajiv was sending her away. He didn't love her. For him, she'd been only a pleasant interlude. It must have been just sex. It was love for me, she thought, the tears threatening behind her eyelids.

She turned her head away, and said, "So, that's it, then."

He pulled the cane chair up to the charpoy, sat on it and said, "Do you want it to be?"

She turned to face him. With his thumbs he rubbed out the tears under her eyes. The gesture was too much for her. His tenderness undid her. Weeping in earnest now, her words came out in jerks, "No, I don't. I . . . I love you. But it is obvious . . . you . . . you . . ."

Then suddenly she got it out, all in a rush. "It's obvious you don't love me. You liked me fine when we could fuck all the time, but I ruined it all by getting sick. You've been nowhere near me since I threw up all over you. And who can blame you for that? At least Meera won't defile the marriage bed by vomiting."

She hoped she'd hurt him, and wasn't ready for his reaction. Slipping off the chair, he knelt beside the charpoy and put his hands on each side of her head to turn her face to his.

"Jane. I want to tell you several things. So listen carefully. First, I do love you. I love everything about you. I love your body. To distraction. I love your mind. It's original and bright and unafraid. I love your spirit. *Specially* your spirit—your mix of independence and dependence. Your confidence and lack of it."

Jane stared at him, blank-faced. His gaze, steady and fixed on her face, nonetheless enveloped her, washed over her.

Very slowly and gently he kissed her mouth.

"And I *love* the way you throw up into a bucket."

Jane didn't smile. Her face was immobile, her eyes, open and astonished, on his. He went on. "And the reason I have neglected you is because I have been back to Khajuraho two days running, first to tell my family that I'm going to England with you, and to tell Meera that I'm not going to marry her, and then to collect my luggage, see my boss, sell my worldly goods and generally burn my boats."

He paused, and without unlocking his eyes from hers he put a parcel on her lap.

"And to buy you this."

Jane still did not move.

"Open it."

She did, removing the crumpled brown paper as if in a trance. Inside was a stone statuette, not more than nine inches high. It was a perfect copy of the elephant god Ganesh, his head cocked to the side the better to see the sexual cavorting of his neighbors on the frieze.

"So I hope to hell you haven't changed your mind."

THIRTEEN

Patrick had tried not to let Sandra see how shaken he was by their conversation about Stella. The awful thing was, he'd been more upset by Alastair's revelations than by the staff's fears for the business. All the time he was protesting to Sandra that he *was* concentrating on the business, that he'd been out of the office renegotiating the bank loan, getting estimates for the kitchen refurbishment and even considering other, better, premises, he'd had mental flashes of his Stella with the egomaniac John Reilly—her lips on his designer stubble, his grimy hands in her shining hair.

By the next day, Patrick had decided to say nothing to Stella. He told himself her past life was none of his business. She was young and exuberant, and twenty-four-year-olds had a freer, more honest, approach to sex. And anyway, the chef gossip was probably just that. Foul gossip. All chefs hated restaurant critics. They'd say anything. He would ignore it. Pretend he'd never heard.

Things couldn't go wrong now. His happiness depended on Stella. For the first time since Jane had left six months ago in October, he was happy. Stella made him drunk on water.

Up until that magical afternoon at Claridges, he had been quite unable to banish his wife from his mind. He'd think of her at the most unlikely times: when shaving, he'd be reminded of the way she used to push her face into his when he was newly shaved, nuzzling like a puppy. Or when the phone rang late at night and his heart leapt with unreasonable hope. Or when Benedicat threaded himself through his legs, yowling at her absence. But most of all when he came back late from Jane's and there was no laptop charging in the hall, no briefcase on the floor, no hump in the bed, no smell of her anywhere.

But Stella had melted his unhappiness like morning mist. He was besotted by her. He told himself he was in love with her, but there was also gratitude. He knew his adoration stemmed a little from her magical ability to keep his wife out of his thoughts, to make Jane seem distant and less important, someone from his past. Someone he'd loved, but got over. The relief and freedom was almost a pleasure in itself, like the easing of intense pain. He was proud of the fact that black dog was beaten. That he'd vanquished his wimpish moping and self-pity. That there was life after Jane.

He rang the bell of Stella's mews cottage and waited. Through the door he heard an upstairs door slam, then a thud as she jumped the last few stairs into the tiny hall.

"Hi, sweetheart," she said, flinging the door wide and herself into his arms. She was wearing contact lenses and they emphasized the aquamarine of her eyes. He preferred the glasses. They slightly disguised her blatant beauty, made it less obvious to the world. And the little ritual of easing them from her face before he made love to her had become a potent aphrodisiac. The first act of undressing. But today it was the contacts. Her freckled arms smelled of Badedas, sharp chestnut and pine. She was wearing a ridiculously short khaki skirt, like a skating skirt, and a yellow ribbed top. It was sleeveless, and too skimpy to cover her bra straps. The sight of a thin white ribbon as he lifted her great mass of hair to kiss her neck, made him bite her shoulder instead—not hard, but enough to produce a tiny sound, which could have been protest and could have been pleasure, from her. As the now familiar flood of desire washed into him, he thought, how odd, I used to find visible bra straps a real turn-off.

She lifted her face to his, eyes dreamy and unfocused. She slipped one leg between his and let her body go limp against him, her arms hanging behind her. An offering.

"Hey, hey," he said, holding her away. "Hold your horses. We're going premises hunting, remember?"

The speed with which she dropped the invitation, stepping back and grabbing her handbag and jacket from the hall table, dismayed Patrick. He felt bereft, discarded.

She said, "I can't wait. Patrick, I know this is the right one. It's big enough and the Goldhawk Road is the perfect location. Up and coming, and full of PLUs."

"PLUs?"

"People Like Us, of course. Not out-of-towners, or pompous old farts or working-class crusties."

Patrick frowned, disconcerted. But Stella's great eyes shone with mischief, daring Patrick to reprove her. He didn't. He laughed, shaking his head.

Sitting on the sports car's side, she swung her legs over the car door without bothering to open it and slithered into the passenger seat. She put on her sunglasses and snuggled down into the white leather.

Patrick loved his car. Well, his and Jane's. Or, to be absolutely precise, Jane's, since it was her money that had bought it. She'd seldom driven it though, preferring taxis for the City because of the parking. It was a 1975 white Mercedes 300SL, much cherished and in perfect shape.

As they left Stella's mews and accelerated up Craven Road, he looked at her and thought, she's too beautiful to be real. She's made for the car, like a girl in a commercial. Except in a commercial the model's hair streams back away from her face. Stella's tangled mane was blowing forward over her face, exposing the back of her thin neck.

They drove slowly through West Kensington. Late March was really too cool to have the top down, but it was still and sunny and Stella lay back, looking up at the early leaves of the

154

plane trees and the elegant old houses. She looked happy and excited. Like a kid on an outing, thought Patrick.

He pushed away the thought of her with John Reilly, or some such other loutish lad. Of course she's had lovers. Just look at her. She's irresistible. And she's young and bursting with life.

They joined the Bayswater Road and speeded up along Holland Park Avenue, passing Jane's. Glancing down the side street as they came abreast of the restaurant, Patrick was amused to see Alastair and Sonia outside the kitchen door, having a quick smoke, and Tony and the barman, unaware of the other two around the corner, lighting up outside the front entrance.

"That's what No Smoking does to business," said Patrick. "Stops the workers working for ten minutes every hour."

But Stella hadn't noticed them, and wasn't listening. Indeed, she seemed unaware of Jane's altogether. A tiny flicker of irritation licked his mind, and died.

At the Third Man, the estate agent Mr. Banham was waiting on the doorstep. They parked the car on the yellow lines opposite. Stella said traffic wardens had been specifically excluded from her horoscope for the day, and Patrick wanted to keep an eye on the Mercedes's badge and hubcaps.

The pub smelled awful. Beer, smoke and sweat, all stale. But as they pushed through the double doors, they stopped in amazement.

The pub's frontage had looked wide from the street, but there was no suggestion of its depth. A huge, wide, mahogany bar formed a great oval in the middle of the room, directly under an enormous central skylight. The room was eighty feet deep at least, with high ceilings. Great planks of sun shafted through the dusty air from four sash windows on the street side and from the skylight.

"Amazing. Is it Victorian?" asked Patrick. "What was it built as?"

"A hotel, I think." The agent consulted his papers. "It's Edwardian. Built in 1910. This side was the dining room, and the other was the ballroom. The last owners took out the internal walls. They had it as a Tex-Mex theme pub."

He waved his notes over his head, indicating crude interruptions in the ornate ceiling cornices, both at the sides and at the skylight. No attempt at making good had been made. The ceiling itself was plaster, elaborately patterned, but incomplete and coming down in patches.

"It would cost a fortune to restore," said Patrick. "And it would be a crime to take it all down."

"Oh, but we'd need to anyway," said Stella. "We'd want something modern and cool."

Patrick was momentarily dismayed at her blithe dismissal of such craftsmanship, but said nothing, and Stella continued, "It's perfect, Patrick. Nothing could be more perfect. The light is fantastic. And that's before we get rid of this horrible wallpaper and put in a new skylight." Her eyes were bright and wide as she turned them full voltage on Patrick. "The space just blows your mind. The ceiling must be twenty feet high. The new bar can go just where this old thing is."

She was spinning about, her short skirt swirling, her long legs running around the bar, her face alight.

Mr. Banham said, "There are some rooms upstairs and kitchens and offices downstairs. I'll show you."

Patrick wanted to stay cool and detached, but he was excited too. The place was stunning. A natural for a big brasserie.

They inspected the rooms above. They were large and square with sash windows, solid wooden doors and open fireplaces, most with their original firebacks and tiled surrounds. Patrick ticked the rooms off in his mind. He and Stella could live on the top floor, facing south, away from the main road. The biggest and lightest of the rooms could be their bedroom. It already had its own enormous bathroom with a giant bath complete with claw-and-ball feet and great brass taps. Even a shower and bidet and his-and-her basins wouldn't clutter it. His mind went into a mini-fantasy of Stella in the bath and him on a sofa, feet on a footstool, drink in hand, winding down after the evening service.

The other big room, almost as large, could be a sitting room opening onto the wide roof terrace at the back. That left a room for an open-plan kitchen/dining room, and another for who knows what? Dressing room for Madam? And that was before they touched the front-facing rooms, which could be studies for each of them.

And on the first floor: restaurant offices, sumptuous public loos and staff locker rooms. That still left two or three private dining rooms for the restaurant. And—luxury almost unheard of in the trade—a staff room. Patrick felt giddy at so much choice.

He didn't say anything to Stella. They'd never discussed living together, and Stella, after a few admiring remarks about the blue and green fireplace tiles, and the possibility of a Japanese garden on the terrace, had gone down again to the ground floor. She said she wanted to work out how many covers the restaurant could take.

Patrick toured the basement with Mr. Banham, leaving Stella pacing the ground floor. Her absence allowed Patrick more rational thought, and the excitement produced by the upstairs floors was replaced by disappointment and doubt.

There were reasonable storerooms. The wine cellar was damp, but the wine would not mind that. But the kitchen was horrific. Dark, filthy, damp, unventilated and too small. It would cost a fortune to get it usable. If they knocked together the scullery and three of the storerooms they could get a fair-sized kitchen out of it, but the ceiling would still be too low. They'd have to dig down two or three feet to give decent headroom, put in a damp course, and ventilate the whole basement. And then fit it out to suit the temperamental Alastair. It's not viable, thought Patrick.

When Patrick returned upstairs, Mr. Banham, who had left him in the basement a few minutes before, had gone.

"I told him I couldn't tear myself away and we needed hours

157

more to measure everything, so he agreed to leave me the keys." She held them up, jingling them with glee. "I said we'd return them later."

Patrick shook his head. "Stella, my darling girl. There is no point in measuring anything. You haven't seen the basement. It's a disaster."

"What do you mean?" Stella's voice was sharp.

"Unless I sell Jane's for twice its value, I can't afford this place: £600,000 is top-whack anyway, leaving almost nothing for fixing the place. And down there is hundreds of thousands of pounds' worth of fixing."

Stella stood stock still, her eyes wide. "Oh, Patrick, don't say that. We'll never find something as good as this, I know it. Just look at it, for Chrissake."

She spun round, arms embracing walls, ceiling, bar. "This place is beautiful. There's nothing like it. I don't think £600,000 is a lot for something so unusual."

"I agree. It's great. But it is out of my reach. Stella, it is no go."

Stella's eyes were huge, shiny with desperation or imminent tears.

"Patrick, you can't turn this down. I've seen restaurants that don't have anything like the character of this place go for twice as much. We could have the hottest brasserie in town. It'll make a fortune."

Patrick shook his head, hating crushing her dreams.

She said, "Darling, trust me. I know this is the one. When you are making half a million a year, £600,000 will seem like peanuts."

Patrick said nothing further, but reached out to her, wanting to comfort her. She spun out of his reach, but kept her eyes locked on his.

She said, "Oh, come on, honey. Don't say no. Not yet anyway. At least you could see if they'll take less if the basement is a wreck. At least you can try."

Patrick turned his eyes away, refusing the influence of hers.

"Stella. It's not a matter of trying. It may be the greatest buy ever, if you've got the money. But it's like saying a Rolls Royce is a better buy than a Lada. It might be, but not for the chap who only has money for a Lada."

"Oh, sweetheart, you sound like my father! So middle-aged and cautious. Jeez, at least get an estimate. And how do you know what you'll get for Jane's? You could at least get it valued. And why can't you borrow the money? At least see the bank."

There was an impatience and irritation in her voice that momentarily hardened his resolve, made it easier for him. He thought, poor spoiled kid.

But then, sensing the wrong tack, she came up to him, and took him by the shoulders, her face flushed and pleading, tears welling up.

"It's a chance of a lifetime, Patrick. I know it is. Don't blow it."

He put his arms around her. Weariness and tenderness combined to defeat him. "OK. I'll look into it. But no promises."

She kissed him then. Her mouth felt soft under his, warm and ready. He knew he was being rewarded for compliance, but pushed the thought away as he gave in to the smell, the warmth, the availability of her. The ever-readiness of Stella delighted him. It made him feel terrific—that he had this instant, reliable effect on her. Any time, day or night, that he felt the slightest desire, she was ahead of him, willing, eager, randy as hell. He reached around her, pulling her waist into his body so that her back arched and her heels lifted from the floor.

She was making little, now familiar, moans, trying to say Patrick, Patrick, as he kissed her. He ran his free hand over her bottom. His fingers felt the hem of her short skirt, and then his hand was under the skirt, caressing first one buttock, rapidly moving to the other, then back. He had the clearest picture of her firm round bottom, lace-edged ivory boxer shorts, narrow waist. Jesus, she had a lovely ass.

Only just in control now, he slipped both hands down her waistband over her cool smooth skin and cupped a handful of bum in each hand. With a suddenness that drew a gasp from her, he lifted her bodily off the floor.

"I've never had a woman up against a bar," he said into her hair. "Or on a filthy bar-room floor. Or on top of the bar. Which is it to be? Take your pick."

"The floor," she said.

FOURTEEN

When, months ago, Sally had rung to tell him about Jane and Rajiv, Patrick had been fine about it. No pain. His indifference surprised him. Pleased him too. He was over her, clearly. He was even a little impatient with Sally.

"Why are you telling me this, Sally? Jane is not my business anymore."

"She's still your wife."

"Only technically. We've been apart since October."

"You're not getting divorced?"

"Not yet, but I guess we will. I've been too busy to think about it, and I've heard nothing at all from Jane. Too engrossed with the Indian lover, I guess."

"She'd never have had a lover at all if you'd made any effort to get her back."

"Sally, we've been over this before. It's too late. Forget it." There was a pause, and Patrick was tempted to put the telephone down. But he said, "You are a good soul, Sally, but this is, if I may say so, none of your business."

"It's the business of both of us. You can't pretend you don't still care for Jane. You can't *like* the fact that she's shacked up with some young tourist guide she picked up in India. He hasn't got a job. She's keeping him. It can't be right."

"Sally, Jane is thirty-seven. Old enough to make her own decisions. She decided our marriage was over. It turns out she was right. And as far as I'm concerned, she's welcome to spend her money as she likes."

But afterward, he'd not felt so cool. He did find the news

161

disturbing, but he pushed the matter out of his mind. None of his business. And he had Stella.

And now, seven weeks since Jane's departure, he had Stella and the Third Man. Between them they had completely changed his life. It was now both dizzying and terrifying.

During the day the combination of his new girlfriend and his new business bore him along at breakneck speed. He flew from meeting to meeting: with architects, lawyers, bankers, wine brokers. He ran Jane's with new vigor. He was cheerful and in control, and his snatched hours of love-making with Stella, usually in the early afternoons, were charged, shot-through with happiness.

Alastair and Sandra and the rest of the staff caught his mood of optimism and looked forward to the move to the Goldhawk Road. All the staff were going, and Patrick was busy hiring more people—the new place was three times the size of Jane's.

But at night Patrick slept badly. He'd fall asleep fast enough, exhausted by the day's pace. But within an hour or two he'd be wide awake, a hard fist of anxiety in his guts. At three in the morning he knew for certain he was being a fool. Black thoughts chased each other through his brain: the Third Man was too risky a project; if he didn't get a quick sale for Jane's, the bridging loan could sink him; Alastair was the wrong chef for a busy brasserie, would never handle a brigade of twenty, nor knock out 200 meals in an hour.

But most of all he fretted about Stella. He could not put her previous lovers out of his mind but still he did not tackle her. In the day they were irrelevant, none of his business. But at night he tormented himself with the question: what does she see in me? She could have anyone she liked with one glance from those sea green eyes. In the day he gloried in his fortune. At night he saw himself the middle-aged dupe of a cunning young woman, providing her with a plaything—the Third Man—which would be the ruin of him.

But she was so sublimely happy when she won even the

162

smallest victory that resisting her was impossible. Her eyes would shine, she'd burrow into his arms, kiss his neck and stick her tongue in his ear.

When Stella stayed overnight in the Primrose Hill house, sex, alcohol and exhaustion kept night thoughts at bay. But mostly Stella preferred to sleep in her Paddington cottage. "I need my own space," she'd said.

The trite phrase dismayed Patrick. But he thought he understood: Stella was reluctant to occupy Jane's side of the bed. He'd replied, "At the pub you'll have acres of space. There will be Stella space, Patrick space, and Stella-and-Patrick space."

Stella did not answer, and Patrick did not press it. She was only twenty-four, and he mustn't crowd her. It was the youthfulness and blitheness of her that he so adored. If he pressed her too remorselessly, she might shy away.

But her ability to spend his money like water terrified him. She had insisted on retaining a public relations company on £50,000 a year; she'd hired flavor-of-the-month restaurant designers who, it seemed to him, were bent on designing everything, right down to the door handles in the Gents; and she'd commissioned an astronomically expensive construction of abstract metal and glass from the installation artist Aavee, which was to dominate the restaurant.

Patrick had argued that the money would be better spent on a giant vase filled twice weekly with branches of pussy willow or great long lilies as the season demanded. But Stella had said, "Honey. Trust me. I know about this stuff."

So they had gone to Aavee's studio, converted railway stores overlooking the Stewarts Lane depot in Battersea. The wide north window looked down onto the railway lines, twisting and glinting like silver tagliatelli.

The great barn of a studio had more of an air of an engineering works or car repair shop than of Patrick's idea of an artist's studio. Aavee showed them round, explaining that most of the pieces were models or maquettes of much bigger ones, already completed. Curved strips of metal, mostly stainless steel or polished aluminium, seemed to feature in most of them.

"I can see where you get the sinuous ribbon stuff from," said Stella. "It's the railway tracks, isn't it?"

Aavee was a thickset curly-headed young Irishman with the hardness of a boxer and a dark, pitted face, out of which grew an uneven and sparse red stubble. He smiled to reveal a bright row of small even teeth and a cherubic, almost Toby-jug jollity.

"It is that. They get into most of my work, those tracks. I'd move to a bigger studio if I could find one with a railway junction below. But I can't."

To Patrick the sculptures were incomprehensible, but Stella, to Patrick's astonishment, was on home ground. Looking at a four-foot-high collection of five wavy metal spikes, planted close together, each with a small, slightly different bulbous head containing a light bulb, she exclaimed with pleasure, "I've seen this before. I saw it in the Yorkshire Sculpture Park. And the stems wave, don't they?" She looked at Aavee with that childish excitement that never failed to move Patrick. He felt a twist of jealousy, mixed with pride and admiration.

Aavee said, "They should. But I nicked its motor for something else. But if I shake it, you'll get the idea."

He put his thick boot against the base of the piece and gave it a mighty shove with a powerful leg. The metal stems, which on close examination were made of linked overlapping pieces like the scales of a snake, slid into action, and miraculously swayed and curled about each other, never touching. "It looks better thirty feet high," said Aavee. "It's in a German pine forest now. It's called *Acid Rain*."

Patrick asked, *"Acid Rain?"*

But it was Stella who explained that the work represented both leafless trees and the wind that blew the pollution toward Germany from Britain; that the light bulbs flashed a desperate SOS; that the trees' continuous sinuous dance was intended to seduce the viewer with an exhibition of elegance and beauty

164

while hiding corruption and death. She ended her rather breathless explanation with, "You know, like in Blake's 'O Rose, thou art sick!/The invisible worm,' etc. Leafless trees in winter are beautiful, aren't they? Even dead trees are. But there is another story inside." She stopped and turned to Aavee. "That's right, isn't it?"

"Jesus, I don't know," said Aavee. "That's what the catalog said." Aavee's fat face creased in merriment. "I hate being asked to explain things. But the poncy art galleries say they can't sell the stuff without it, so I make up the meaning when I've finished the work."

Patrick laughed. He liked Aavee. He reminded him of his cheese supplier, who sold wonderful cheese, only matched by the bullshit he talked about widows in Welsh valleys making their grandmothers' recipes, and goats fed on acorns and sorrel to get the right tang to the curd.

But Stella looked dismayed. Patrick put an avuncular arm around her and said, "But I need explaining to. Explain this." He waved an arm at a small plantation of metal daisy-like flowers whose anthers were mobile telephones. Stella replied, somewhat sulkily, that they represented the invasion of country peace by modern technology. She looked at Aavee, expecting him to contradict her, but he grinned his toby-jug grin at her and shrugged.

Patrick could see that some of the things were witty, but he found them either inconsequential or silly. The only exception was a huge reclining metal woman made entirely out of what had made her fat—her lips were hamburgers, her double chins sausages. She was gross, but there was something voluptuous and fascinating about her.

Aavee stood looking at his creation with distaste. He said, "I can't be doing with that fat cow anymore. I'd have her out of here but it'd cost an arm and a leg to shift. I should never have agreed to do it." He explained that it had been made for an American fast-food restaurant chain, and the full-size twenty-

165

foot-high sculpture now reclined outside their Philadelphia offices. "I thought it was good at the time. But it's rubbish."

"No, it's not," said Stella, going up close and running her
fingers lightly down the woman's thighs, strung up like rolls of
beef. "It's good. And full-size it must be awe-inspiring—like the
Botero *Venus* outside Liverpool Street Station."

She turned to Aavee and said, "You just don't like it because
you wouldn't do that figurative stuff now." Aavee shrugged. It
did not interest him.

In the taxi, Stella asked, looking into Patrick's face and holding his hands, "He's good, don't you think? Aren't you pleased
we're commissioning him?"

Patrick lifted her hand and turned it over, kissing the pale
blue veins of her wrist. He replied, "To be truthful, no. I liked
the guy a lot, but the only work I liked was the fat lady, which
had at least some power and beauty about it. Most of the others
were all angular and spiky and somehow soulless. Certainly not
beautiful."

Stella withdrew her hands and said, "Why does art have to
be beautiful? Why can't it be about cruelty, or transience or anything at all?" She looked at him, challenging.

Patrick knew he wasn't going to agree with her, and said,
"Why don't we buy the maquette of the fat lady instead of commissioning something new? She must be six foot long, and if we
put her on a plinth, she'd be big enough, don't you think?"

Stella clicked her tongue in exasperation and said, "Patrick,
don't you understand anything? You can't just buy a sculpture
off the shelf, and plonk it somewhere. It has to be site-specific,
and—"

Patrick interrupted. "Why? If it looks good where you put
it? And since that woman is all about food, and indulgence, it
would have some meaning at the Third Man."

"But Patrick. Sculpture should be artist-centered . . ."

Patrick burst out laughing. "What on earth does that mean?"

Her voice was cold. "It means that it should reflect the artist's conception, his response to the space the work is to be in. It is no longer appropriate to . . ."

"Oh, Stella, darling, you sound like the Arts Council. We are only talking about a centrepiece for a brasserie. And you like the fat lady, you said so. And I like her. At least more than the other stuff. It's worth a try." He reached for her hands again, but she pulled away, sitting stiffly in the corner of the cab.

She said, "Patrick, you cannot go back on your commission to Aavee. It would be unforgivable. And the fat lady is ten years out of date. It will send all the wrong messages. We need a modern installation, not something so obvious and conventional. Don't be so boring."

She said it with a mixture of earnest pleading and conviction. Patrick felt the now familiar sensation of being outpunched by his darling Stella, and said, "OK, darling. You win."

She kissed him then, and Patrick remembered that other taxi ride, that first one when the Stella reign began.

Somewhere between that first day, when he had been in control, master of himself and of her, and now, he'd lost it. When? he wondered.

FIFTEEN

The fat little Italian sat perfectly still in his chair, his hands on his knees, and insisted, "Patrick, the Third Man is not going to sell the sort of wine that Jane's can shift and it just seems a good time for me to move on."

Patrick pushed his draft of the Third Man's wine list across the desk.

"But Silvino," he said, "the new list will be as good as Jane's. The only reason we are selling stock is because I need the capital. We will still be able to get good vintages from the suppliers, and they will let us pay for it as we sell it, and we won't have the cost of carrying it, that's all."

Silvino waved a dismissive hand at Patrick's papers and replied, "Pub customers do not drink first-growth clarets or vintage port. They'll drink nothing but House Chardonnay and mineral water."

"The Third Man won't be a pub any longer. It will be an up-market brasserie, serving Alastair's food and your wine. Like Jane's, but bigger, cheaper and with more buzz. At least give it a try."

Silvino shook his head. "I'm sorry, Patrick. It's no good. I've decided. I must go."

"Have you found another job?"

Silvino smiled. "Not yet. I will do so in the next two weeks, before the move."

Patrick was impressed. It was true good sommeliers were hard to come by, but Silvino was nearly sixty and his slicked-back hair, fat stomach and tiny feet made him look more like a cartoon waiter than a real one. Patrick did not think he'd get a job that easily.

Silvino said, "I will stay to send the wines you are auctioning to Sotheby's and to deliver the rest to the pub."

Patrick said, "Well, thank God for that at least. I couldn't trust anyone else."

Silvino looked pleased at the compliment. "Do not worry. I've started packing up the bins in the cellar and I'll do the upstairs racks after the last service."

"What are you using for wine crates? Shall I ring around the suppliers for you?"

"Threshers down the road gave me thirty-two boxes. If I get another lot from them next week that will be enough for the loose bottles. The rest are in unopened cases."

Patrick stood up and reached over his desk to pat Silvino's shoulder. "You've thought of everything."

Silvino shut the door in his precise way as he left. Oh, well, thought Patrick, I was bound to lose a few of them. And Stella will be pleased. She wants all the staff to be under twenty-five, Australian, with Armani shirts and shaved heads. But where will I get anyone as conscientious as Silvino? The man frets if there is a bottle of Perrier missing.

The next afternoon Silvino put the stock sheets on Patrick's desk. The total value of the wine, in the cellar, in bond and with their suppliers was £84,000 at current prices. Then there was a further £9,000 not yet paid for, and £8,000 of beers, sherry and port, spirits and minerals.

Patrick spent an unhappy two hours steeling himself to part with £70,000 worth of it. He would also return the unpaid-for wines to Corney and Barrow and run the spirit stocks down as much as possible. The Third Man would have to run on "just-in-time" stocking principles.

He marked up the list. Thank God for Silvino, who was sparing him a lot of the agony. Almost every case reminded him of some Burgundy cellar, some terrace overlooking sunlit vines, some friend in the wine trade, some tense auction, some memorable meal. Who would have thought selling booze could be such an emotional business?

"Hello, Patrick. It's me."

Patrick's stomach gave a lurch. He had not spoken to Jane since she'd gone to India, six months ago.

"Hi, Jane."

"Are you all right? I heard you were selling Jane's." She sounded, he thought, very bright.

"Yes."

He didn't elaborate and she dashed on.

"Can I have Benedicat back?"

Patrick said, "Benny? Yes, of course, but why? What's changed?"

"I just think it's not fair to leave my cat with you forever and I'm less frazzled now, and would like him. Is that OK? Or do you want to keep him?"

"Darling Jane, I am not going to get into a custody battle about a cat. Especially one who peed on my shoes for weeks after you left."

She laughed. Neither said anything, and then they both spoke at once. Jane said, "Do you want to meet? I have to tell you . . ." and Patrick said, "Shall we have dinner at the restaurant? It will be closed in two weeks, and . . ."

They both laughed again and Jane said, rather hesitantly, "Fine. Yes. Fine."

Patrick said quickly, "I'll bring Benny to your flat. It's in Hammersmith, isn't it? Then we can go to Jane's."

"No, no. Don't do that." Jane seemed flustered. "I'll collect him."

Patrick said, "Jane, it's OK. I know about the Indian boyfriend. Sally told me."

Jane said, "It isn't that. Or rather it is and it isn't. It's true I don't want you to meet Rajiv. I don't know why. It's sort of separate. I can't explain."

Patrick said, "OK. I understand. I'm not too keen on you meeting Stella either. You know about Stella?"

"Yes, Sally . . . And then I saw a picture in the *Standard*."

Patrick winced. He'd been mortified at the picture, over an item about restaurateurs and chefs being the new fashion leaders, usurping the style-obsessed designers and self-obsessed pop stars. But the Third Man had got a mention and Stella said that every column inch was worth thousands. It was what you paid the PR people for. Don't knock it, she'd said.

Jane said she'd collect the cat on Saturday morning and they agreed to make a date for dinner then.

Saturday morning was glorious, clear-skied and warm. Jane had trouble convincing the taxi driver he would be able to turn around at the end of the little cul-de-sac. She wanted him to wait. She hadn't seen Patrick since October and she thought she might need a quick getaway. The driver advanced with reluctance down the narrow lane. Jane peered out at the climbing white rose cascading over the wall from their—or rather Patrick's—garden. She'd forgotten that rose. Climbing iceberg, almost thornless, with blowsy extravagant swathes of flowers that went on, as the catalogues say, until the first frosts. Oh, I'd love to have a garden again, thought Jane.

At the end of the lane was a small courtyard, with more roses, bright red this time, hanging in trusses around the cottage doors.

Nostalgia (or was it sadness, or what?) assailed her. Nothing had changed. She felt she could just let herself into No. 4, scoop up Benny, who always ran to the door at the sound of her key, and walk through to the little garden behind. She imagined Patrick sitting at the garden table, writing wine notes, a few open bottles and glasses before him.

Patrick opened the door. He didn't kiss her, but ushered her in, as if she was a guest. Well, I am a guest, she thought. Benny oiled the awkwardness of greeting by curling himself once around Jane's legs, then, before she could pick him up, jumping to chair, table, bookcase. He stepped loftily along the bookshelves out of her reach. She watched him with remembered pleasure, then looked slowly around the room, absorbing the familiarity of it.

"Oh, Patrick, you've let my oleander die." She fingered the withered leaves. Some fell to the floor.

"Yes. The pot plant in the office died too."

Jane crouched down to pick up the fallen leaves, tucking them into the pot. She pushed her fingers into the dry soil.

"You only needed to water them."

Patrick noticed how thin Jane's neck and shoulders were. She'd lost weight. It did not suit her.

"I did. I think I drowned them. Still, I tell myself this one looks very sculptural there against the light. What do you think?"

"I think it looks like a dead oleander. But it's my fault, I should have taken it with me." She smiled at him, rueful.

"You didn't take anything except your clothes. Do you want anything?"

"No, not yet." She hesitated. "Why? Do you want to get rid of my stuff?"

"No. Or rather, yes. I'm going to live over the new restaurant, so if you want anything, I can get the movers to deliver to you while they are at it."

Up to now Jane had barely looked at him, her gaze directed at the cat, the oleander, the big studio room. Now she swung to him, alarmed.

"You're not leaving this house? Oh, Patrick."

"Well, yes, I am."

"Oh, God. Patrick, you can't . . ." Jane stopped. There was a tiny pause in which Patrick noticed for the first time that Jane had wrinkles around her eyes. Pain does that, he thought.

172

She went on, rushing at the thought, "Do you want a divorce? Should we be seeing lawyers? I suppose . . ."

"I expect so. But you're the lawyer. You handle it. I don't want to get into a wrangle."

Jane thought, he does want a divorce. Oh, God, he's going to marry Stella. She blurted the question, full on, "Are you going to marry her?"

"No. She's too young to marry anyone." That means he wants to, thought Jane. And she's not a child. She's a top columnist. He just means she's young compared to me.

She wrenched her mind to the practical. She said, "Once we let lawyers in, they'll ruin everything between us. And some things are still OK?" She looked up at him, eyes troubled, asking agreement.

He saw she was biting the inside of her cheek, a trick she'd used since childhood to fight off crying. Touched, he said, "Sure, Jane. I don't see why we need lawyers at all. But it's been nine months. We should move on. You just draw up whatever needs to be drawn up and I'll agree." He put a hand on her arm. "I don't want half your worldly wealth, I promise."

She said nothing, but her eyes were wide, dismayed. He added, "And you don't want half my debts, I'm sure." He smiled at her, trying to lighten her mood.

She turned away abruptly. "Can I make us some coffee?" She walked fast into the kitchen.

Patrick looked after her, but did not follow at once. He thought she'd recover her composure and reemerge. He heard the kettle boil and switch itself off. And then, through the french window, he saw her stepping out of the kitchen door into the garden. She walked the few paces to the wall and stood under the white shower of roses, looking up. From where he was sitting he could not see her head at all. Head in a cloud of roses, he thought.

He made two mugs of coffee and followed her into the garden. He sat at the garden table and said, "Coffee up."

173

She sat down opposite him and said, "I'm sorry. I didn't know I'd be so affected. But I love this garden so, and seeing the house, and Benny, and you. And then hearing you are leaving. I hadn't thought of that. So silly. I'm a fool."

Patrick put his hand over her forearm, leaned forward to look into her face and said, "You did leave it all, Jane. You left the house, the garden, the cat, me. Did you think we would all just stay as you left us, in case you came back in a hundred years to kiss us all back to life?"

Jane looked at him steadily and he watched her eyes filling with tears. As they spilled onto her cheeks she smeared them with the back of her hand and said with something between a snort and a gulp, "I suppose I did. How childish."

Patrick did not ask if she wanted to come back. He could not risk a yes. Stella had changed everything. But he felt a mixture of sadness and satisfaction. The boyfriend could not be worth much if seeing her ex-husband threw her so.

How selfish we all are, he thought. She wants me on ice, in case one day she needs me and I want her boyfriend to turn out a no-hoper. He said, "Do you want a drink? You look as if you could do with one."

"No, I'm fine. But thanks." Then she said, "Have you got the cat basket?"

"Cat basket? Good lord. No. Never seen one. Did we have one? Can't he go in a wine box? I've got plenty of those."

Jane went to the little cupboard under the stairs and sure enough, there was the cat basket, where it had lived for years.

Benedicat, sensing imminent imprisonment, took his time to be caught, but gave up when he found the cat-flap to the garden closed. Disdainfully, he stood perfectly still at the kitchen door and Jane lifted him into the basket while Patrick held it.

As he handed her the basket, he bent to kiss her cheek.

"How about our dinner then?"

"I'll call you."

But she didn't. She sent him a fax:

Sorry, Patrick. Don't think I can face Jane's. Might embarrass us both. Drink a toast from me by way of obsequies. I'll always be proud of having had a restaurant named after me. J.

The last night at Jane's, a Saturday, was hard work. Stella was out working, reviewing a new restaurant on the South Bank. Most of Jane's customers were long-time faithfuls who obviously regarded the event as more of a wake than a night out. Patrick chatted to them all, handing them leaflets about the Third Man, but he knew they thought big brasseries too noisy and the Gold-hawk Road uncharted and dangerous territory. They all said they would try it, but Patrick knew few would.

After the service, the staff had their "thank-you" dinner. Alastair had roasted a large leg of lamb which he served with potatoes and frozen peas. He'd also fried great baskets of had-dock in batter with deep-fried potato skins. Patrick marveled at their appetites: even the most talented cooks often lived on beer and cigarettes, eschewing the gastronomic wonders they pro-duced for the customers. Sometimes they bought McDonald's. But if you gave them fish and chips or Sunday lunch (or both, as tonight) they could put away more than his old army trainees. Two crates of Beck's and one of Budweiser disappeared in an hour.

After that, getting everyone to do the pack-up for the re-moval men was hard work. No one wanted to wash down the storerooms and fridges when they were emptied or hoover the packing-straw shreds off the restaurant carpets. But Patrick was determined that prospective buyers of the premises should find things shipshape.

They finished the job at 4 a.m. and most were too tired for any sentiment beyond a desire for home and bed. Patrick set the alarm and closed Jane's elegant front doors for the last time and drove back to Primrose Hill, too tired to care that Stella had not, as arranged, come on to Jane's after her dinner.

Next day, Patrick, Silvino and two of the kitchen porters

loaded sixty cases of wine onto a rented truck. Patrick was tired and Silvino's efficiency was a blessing. He made sure the wine for the pub went onto the truck last, so that he could drop it off before heading for the lock-up. Patrick put his arm around the little Italian.

"Are you sure you can manage on your own? Shall I come with you?" he asked.

"Thanks, boss, but I'll be fine. There are only a few cases for the pub and everything else stays on the truck until tomorrow. I will deliver to Sotheby's and Corney and Barrow in the morning, then return the truck."

"OK, if you're sure. But for God's sake, drive carefully. This thing is enormous."

Silvino climbed into the truck, the steering-wheel creasing his fat belly as he eased himself behind it. His small polished shoes looked out of place on the huge pedals. He adjusted the rectangle of rear-view mirror on the door-frame, and said, "See you tomorrow. When I'm done I'll come to the Third Man with the pub keys. And you can give me my wages and a written reference about my talent for selling the most expensive bottles."

"It's a deal. I'll give you a drink too."

On Monday after lunch Patrick went down to the cellar of the Third Man to check how Silvino had stacked the wine. The cellar was empty.

Poor Silvino, he thought. Probably had trouble with that truck. We should have spent the money on a proper removal firm.

He rang Silvino's number. A message in his wife's voice told him there was no one home. He rang the van-hire company. The truck had not yet been returned and they had heard nothing from Silvino.

Patrick frowned. What could have happened? He drove fast to Jane's to check the answer phone. As he listened to goodwill messages from a couple of customers and a worried one from a supplier, his mind raced. If something has happened, why hasn't Silvino telephoned?

There was no message from Silvino. He rang Sotheby's. They had had no delivery. Oh, God, he thought, I don't want to think what I'm thinking. He rang Corney and Barrow, but he knew the answer before he heard it: no delivery.

He sat at his old roll-top desk and took deep breaths, trying to stem the rising panic. Then an appalling thought, an unthinkable thought, entered his mind. No, it couldn't be. Silvino would not.

But the thought would not go away and, hands shaking, he rang WineStore, the bonded warehouse where most of his best wines, probably £50,000 of them, were stored.

"Can I speak to David?"

It took forever for David to come on the line.

"Hello, Patrick. No hitches I hope?"

"What do you mean?"

"With the collection this morning. Silvino got it all to Sotheby's OK?"

Patrick could not speak. The telephone was slimy with his sweat, and he transferred it to his other hand, wiping his palm on his thigh.

David said, "Patrick, are you there? Is something wrong?"

"I think Silvino has just stolen a hundred grand's worth of my wine."

"*What?*"

"He's filched the lot."

"Oh, my God. Patrick. Silvino would never . . . He said *you* were selling it because you needed the money for capital investment. Isn't that true?"

"I was going to sell it, but in bond. I was going to leave it with you."

"Patrick. This is terrible. I believed him of course. We've dealt with Silvino for years . . ."

Patrick said, "Oh, Jesus, I can't believe . . ." And then a sudden hope surfaced. "David, you hadn't the authority to let the wine go. It was in bond. Duty hasn't been paid. Silvino could not get it out without paying—"

"Patrick, all the papers were in order. Silvino signed them. The duty has been paid. I'll check."

There was the click of the telephone, then silence as David went to get the papers. Before he returned, Patrick knew what he was going to say. Silvino had paid the duty from Jane's wine account, on which he had signing powers.

David picked up the telephone and said, "He used Switch. Jane's wine account, I'm afraid. The money is already in the coffers of Customs and Excise. I'm so sorry, Patrick."

Patrick said nothing. His brain would not work. He heard the removal men ringing Jane's doorbell. I hope they're careful with this desk, he thought. With an effort he pulled his attention back to David.

"Patrick, call the police."

SIXTEEN

Jane had left work early and was feeling good. For once the summer air in London was breezy and warm. There was none of the customary haze of pollution, and Jane came home feeling good. She dumped the M & S bag and the dry-cleaning on the pine table in the kitchen, took a bottle of Sauvignon Blanc out of the fridge, picked up two glasses and a corkscrew and went in search of Rajiv.

She found him on the sitting-room sofa, wearing head-phones and listening to a CD. The remains of a take-away were on the floor beside him. He didn't hear her come in.

She stood in front of him and waved. There was no reaction. His eyes were closed and he looked far away, drifting.

She put the wine and glasses down on the coffee table and turned off the CD player. His eyes shot open. His expression jumped from bewilderment, to anger, to resignation. He pulled the headset off, but left it around his neck. Jane thought, he'd rather I wasn't here.

She kissed him and said, "What were you listening to?" But she knew the answer.

"Ravi Shankar." His voice was flat.

Jane was determined to maintain her mood. She put the glasses and corkscrew down on the table and put her thumbs into imaginary waistcoat pockets as she exaggerated the plummy tones of Giles Charteris, Managing Partner at Chalker and Day: " 'My dear Jane, it gives me great pleasure to tell you that your annual bonus will be fifty percent up on last year and is a just reflection of the contribution that your excellent work, notably in the Portuguese tanker tax fraud case, has made to the fortunes of the firm.' "

Rajiv said, "Congratulations," but without enthusiasm.

Jane was hurt, and said, "You're in a lousy mood."

Rajiv said, "I agree. I am. But so would you be if your Indian accent prevented you getting even an interview."

"Rajiv, you do not have an Indian accent."

She sat down on the edge of the sofa, but he stood up, answering without looking at her. "Then how come I never get past the telephone application stage?"

Jane felt rebuffed, but she said without heat, "Because, I suppose, there are thousands of applicants, as well or better qualified. There are no jobs for historians, that's all." Jane stood too now, and hurried on, in an effort to lift his spirits. "Look, I think earning a bonus of £130,000 deserves a celebration. Let's call Sriram and Gopal and go out to dinner. Somewhere special. Like the Red Fort, or the Bombay Brasserie."

"It doesn't have to be Indian," said Rajiv.

"I know it doesn't. I just thought you'd prefer it. Shall we go to Coast? Or to Bibendum?"

"Let's go to the River Room at the Savoy. Or some other stuffy hotel dining room. None of your fancy friends are likely to go there and I won't have to be introduced and explained away."

Jane said, anger beginning to show, "Rajiv, what's that supposed to mean? I do not 'explain you away.' What do you want me to say?"

"I don't want to be introduced at all. How do you think I feel, standing there while your mates look admiringly at you because you've dared to bring home a bit of exotica?"

Jane knew she'd been patient long enough, and she burst out, "Rajiv, what the hell is this? What are you trying to do?"

Rajiv turned away, his lean profile hard, the mouth a tight line. She thought he was going to walk out, but he turned and mimicked a high Belgravia voice, " 'And what do you do, Mr. Ku-

mar?' Those patronizing snobs are quite right to pity me trailing along in your wake. Watching you pick up the tab, buy the tickets, pay the taxis."

Jane felt the hot blood of anger flush her cheeks. "What the hell do you want me to do, Rajiv? Would you like to handle the money? You're welcome. Would you like me to give you an allowance? You're welcome. But don't bite the hand that bloody feeds you."

Realizing she'd gone too far, she said, more calmly, "I can't help it if I've got money and you haven't." He didn't answer, but walked to the window and looked out. The movement was insulting and immediately she was angry again. She shouted, "I come home pleased as punch because I've had a good day and am met by all this temperament and garbage. It is too much."

She bent down and scooped up the polystyrene container with a half-eaten samosa and a plastic fork in it, and went on in a reckless stream, "You sit about eating cheap take-aways and listening to that bloody Indian music all day and then wonder that you don't get taken on by SOAS as Sanskrit professor." For an instant she was tempted to throw the take-away at him, but she turned and dumped it in the waste-paper basket.

Then she picked up the wine, corkscrew and one glass and walked out. As she went she said, no longer shouting but her voice hard as steel, "I'm going to change. Then I'm going out to dinner. You can come if you like, or not."

The neck of the bottle clattered against the wine glass as she poured. She put it down on the dressing-table with a shaking hand. Then, holding her glass untasted, steadying it with two hands, she sat for perhaps five minutes, her face frozen.

Slowly the tight ball of anger softened, dissipated. She thought, poor Rajiv. Of course he can't stand it. He comes from a proud race, full of patriarchs and subjugated women. Believing in equality doesn't guarantee you'll like it.

I should not have waved my bonus in his face, when he can't get a job at all. The more she thought about it, the more insensitive she realized she'd been. Rajiv did not sit about. He'd spent the whole spring and summer trying to get a job and had been rewarded only with the official status of "long-term unemployed," accorded him after six months of out-of-work probation. Of course he was down.

She remembered his account of the Job Centre and interminable Job Club sessions. He found them so insulting. A twenty-year-old female case officer, with half Rajiv's education, had taken care to tell him that one of her other "clients," a Nigerian professor of geography, had accepted a job in the pot-wash of a hotel kitchen.

She wished he would just forget about claiming benefit. She could easily support him, but he refused. Jane both admired his determination to live on the dole and was irritated by it.

But what really upset her, she knew, was the way the balance of the relationship had changed. In India he'd been the master and she'd preferred it. Why could neither of them handle her being the one in control? So much for women's liberation, she thought. Most of us are pining for the shackles.

When they had first arrived in England, Jane had tried to slide Rajiv into her old London life. But it was not a success. Rajiv had as little interest in theater and ballet as Jane had in Indian music. Indeed her interest in all things Indian seemed to disappear as she set her foot on British soil. My Indian exposure has proved as meaningless as bringing back rose-petal jam from Turkey or jasmine tea from Hong Kong, she thought. They lose their appeal at Heathrow airport. Her passionate pursuit of Indian culture while she was in India now seemed to her a bit like an infection, something she had contracted badly, but had recovered from completely.

She remembered the evening she'd bought tickets to see *Sleeping Beauty,* with Sylvie Guillem as the Princess Aurora. Jane found her wonderful, dancing with astonishing flash and grace, and the production magical. But Rajiv was not impressed. "It's so boring. Like a school concert. One after another the fairies all

182

trip on, do a little number and trip off again," he said. "I've seen pantos with more tension."

Jane bit back a sharp answer. But she was put out. The tickets had cost a fortune, the audience had given Guillem a standing ovation, and Rajiv, who had never been to Covent Garden before, chose to pour scorn.

Thinking back, Jane thought that evening had been a turning point. Up until then, about a month after their return from India, Rajiv had been happy to go to restaurants or wine bars with Jane's friends, but he increasingly refused to contribute to the conversation and Jane felt his silence lying there, obvious and insulting—a constant reproach. Once the subject of India or his hopes for a job were exhausted, the others gave up on him. Jane was embarrassed that so much of their conversation seemed to be either about Patrick, or Jane's restaurant or about things that did not interest Rajiv.

It began to dawn on her that not much interested him outside Indian culture, history and themselves. His English schooling, which had made him so acceptable to her in India, seemed to fade to nothing in London. He was entirely Indian, not cosmopolitan as she'd thought. He seldom bothered with the newspaper, did not read any politics and, apart from Sriram and Gopal, he had no friends.

They stopped going to the theater or private views. They went to the cinema or to a museum, where there was no chance of running into her friends. He liked the Japanese netsuke in the V & A and they visited the Chinese exhibition in the British Museum. At such times something of their old teacher-pupil relationship would return and Rajiv, enthusiastic and knowledgeable, would talk of warriors or craftsmen, of myth and magic and Jane would be happy. But the mood generally lasted only as long as the outing. Back at the flat, Rajiv would sink into the sofa and Indian music and Jane would make supper, then return to her briefcase.

Jane was blowing her hair dry at the dressing-table when

Rajiv came in and put his arms around her shoulders. Looking at him in the mirror she turned off the drier and said, "I'm so sorry, darling. Telling you about the bonus was crass. And I should never . . ."

"Forget it. I am far more to blame than you. I am a whinging bastard." He kissed her hair. It was hot from the drier. She turned around and reached up to pull his face down to hers. As always, his kiss woke her desire, and she said, "We needn't go out at all. We could . . ."

"No, we couldn't." He disentangled her arms, stood up and said, "If you'd brought the other glass, I could have had a drink and watched you dress. But since I have to choose . . ." He grinned at her, picked up the wine bottle and walked back to the sitting room.

She watched him go, feeling drained and cheated. How could he so arrogantly assume that a pat on the head made things right again?

Sriram and Gopal lived in Hampstead, in a mews house. Rajiv had known them ever since he'd arrived as a little boy with his family from Uganda. Gopal had arranged for the Kumars to stay, illegally but perfectly comfortably, in a warehouse until Rajiv's father found a job and a flat. Sriram and Gopal were younger then and not yet wealthy. It was not until the eighties that a taste for the Orient and a consumer boom had combined to make them seriously rich.

In recent months, Jane had realized that this eccentric homosexual couple were the only friends that Rajiv and she both liked. Tonight they had agreed to have a drink at the house before going to a new Thai restaurant in Hampstead village. Jane rang the bell and they listened to its brassy tinkle through the door, then the shuffle of slippered feet on polished floors. Gopal opened the door and threw his arms wide in greeting.

"Oh, my friends, we are so delighted you telephoned. We were about to be doomed to another episode of *The Bill* and now

184

we are saved. Come in, come in. Sriram is just dithering between his old brocade jacket and his new satin one. The man is such a poofter." He threw back his sleek head to display an impressive scattering of gold teeth and laughed. Jane and Rajiv laughed too, partly at Gopal's childish enjoyment of his own jokes, partly in pleasure at seeing him.

They followed his waddling gait into what he insisted on calling their withdrawing room. European and Oriental paintings and carvings covered every inch of wall and every shelf or table. Chinese jade vied for surface space with Fabergé flowers and Indian brass. Not for the first time, Jane concluded that the only thing that drew this lot together was shiny color. It was like being in a magpie's nest.

Gopal poured Dom Perignon into Venetian glasses of a lurid pink, encrusted with gold. Then, having examined Jane's earrings, her shoes and her clothes in great detail, he chided her for wearing a Nicole Farhi jacket with Gap trousers.

"My dear girl," he said. "You owe it to the economy not to shop at Gap. The only way for the UK to make headway is to have a consumer-led spending spree. So no more spending £50 when £500 will do."

Jane had at first been surprised at her liking for Gopal. He was so excessive. He wore more rings on his fingers than Jane possessed. And his taste, however expensive, was excruciating. There was hardly an object in the room that Jane would have bought, even if she could have afforded it. Sriram had told her once that the secret of their import business was that he knew what was really good and Gopal knew what would sell. But Jane was as fond of the laughable Gopal as of the elegant Sriram.

Sriram came in and indeed was wearing a brocade jacket. Jane looked at it in fascination. It was fine Indian silk with a repeated pattern of two lovers standing in front of a cow. The cow's horns and hooves were gold and so was the lady's sari. Behind the lovers was a stylized tree, a silver moon and golden sun. It was certainly shiny and colorful, but it was exquisite.

185

Sriram was twenty years older than Gopal, in his seventies, gray, lean and distinguished. He wore his finery with nonchalance and dignity. Jane wondered how someone as cultured and stylish as Sriram could live with Gopal's indiscriminate taste. But she knew Sriram had been with Gopal for thirty years. Passion had been replaced by indulgent affection, but there was a solidity and depth to the relationship that Jane envied.

As soon as the champagne was poured and the ritual of greeting was done, Sriram said in his impeccable, old-fashioned English, "Rajiv, you will excuse me while I lead your lovely lady into the garden. You and Gopal are not gardeners, but Jane and I share the addiction and I want to show her *Fremontedendron californicum*."

He took Jane's arm and led her through the french windows. They followed the path around to the south of the house and stood in front of a tall tree, trained flat against the house. It was covered in yellow flowers, most of them dead and the rest bedraggled.

"It's almost over of course, but those two will not know that and I wanted you to myself."

Jane smiled, pleased.

"Why?"

"So I could ask you if I can help. Rajiv is making you unhappy. Shall I send him home? Give him a job?"

Jane laughed. "Oh, Sriram, if it was that simple!"

"It is that simple. If it is more complicated, then you are making it more complicated."

Sriram broke a small branch off a bushy gray-leaved plant— a santolina, thought Jane absently—and used it to brush autumn leaves and London dust off the terrace wall. They sat down and Jane looked at Sriram in the half-light of dusk and longed to put her cheek against that elegant brocade chest and close her eyes. She was tired, tired to her bones.

She said, "It is such a strain. I'm not good at it."

"At what?"

"At love."

Sriram looked at her quietly, then said, "Love is not meant to be a strain."

Jane returned his gaze but her eyes were anguished. She said, "He is a scholar. In India he's respected. Here the Job Centre tells him to wash dishes. He misses the color, the sun, the smell of India. And then I earn so much money. It's hard for him."

"And you. Is it hard for you?"

"Only because he doesn't like me leading. Or paying for things. Oh, Sriram, it's so boring. So predictable. If I was a man and he was a woman, there would be no problem at all." Jane speeded up as her protest turned into a speech. "A woman would change countries, put up with English skies, think nothing of being supported, make friends of her man's friends, rejoice when he gets a pay raise, be thrilled at the prospect of a holiday in Normandy or of a trip to New York. But with us all these things are Big Issues. I have to be so bloody tactful. She stopped, depressed by the truth. "It is very tiring."

Sriram asked, "Is he regretting Meera?"

Jane shook her head. "I don't think so. Meera is going to marry a lawyer. Rajiv says he's dull and worthy and they are perfect for each other. But his parents have not really forgiven him, though they write to him. They won't answer my letters at all."

"That doesn't matter. If you love Rajiv, and he loves you, then causing some unhappiness is the price you have to pay. The Kumars will come round. Blood is thicker than water and all that. But if Rajiv's misery with himself puts the light out in you, it's time for goodbye." He stood up, saying, "It's getting too dark to see. Let's go in."

As he ushered her through the door, he said, "Give it some thought. I'll help him stay, or help him go, but you need to know what you want."

After her conversation with Sriram, Jane felt inexplicably ener-
gized and positive. She decided Rajiv needed cheering up. She
would have a dinner party. Her excuse would be their birthdays,
only two weeks apart. Her thirty-seventh, which she had intended not to celebrate at all, and his thirty-first. She would have
it on Rajiv's, a Saturday.

She invited the Applebys, whom she'd not seen since they'd
parted at the Delhi Oberoi, her sister-in-law Sally and brother
Tom, and Sriram and Gopal. She didn't tell Rajiv. She decided
a surprise party would be more fun. But in truth she knew she
wasn't telling him because she feared he'd quench it. Or put such
a damper on it that it would be a failure.

Somehow this was a test, a test for them both. She would
bust a gut to make the evening a success. Everything would be
as Rajiv would want it. And he had to be pleased. He had to
return to her. She had to know that underneath the weight of
his joblessness, the passion and excitement of Khajuraho or the
loving intimacy of Varanasi, were there, still alive, needing only
nourishment.

Gopal and Sriram colluded to get Rajiv out of the flat. They
asked him to lunch and then to see a matinee of *Macbeth* in Hindi
at the Tara Arts Theater in Wandsworth. They said they needed
someone with an English education to explain Shakespeare to
them. Jane said she had to work on a case and couldn't go.

The minute Rajiv was out of the flat she flew around like a
dervish. She removed the table lamps, photographs, Mediterra-
nean pottery and Staffordshire dogs and piled them in the spare
room wardrobe. She cleared the fridge of all except milk and
stashed it full of champagne and white wine.

Her taxi arrived as she pushed the last Provençal cushions
under the spare bed. She directed it to Moyses Stevens, who
charged her £6 for a handful of white freesias, then to Nicky
Clarke's.

Nicky delegated her hair to a minion. Perhaps, mused Jane, twining freesias into piled-up hair was beneath him. Or maybe, as she came so rarely now, she no longer had the right to the boss. At Rajiv's request she had not cut her hair since they'd met and it was now long enough to put up.

Nicky looked quizzically at her as she was leaving and said, "What's all this then? Fifties fancy dress?"

She laughed and replied, "Pretty nearly." But the jibe gave her a pang of unease. Was she making an utter fool of herself?

Party Props Ltd arrived fifteen minutes after she got back and within an hour the sitting room was transformed. Soft Indian drapes of rich dark colors and arched mirrors with scalloped frames covered the walls. Brass candelabra and a mass of tiny floating candles provided light, at once festive and romantic. Tiny mosaic elephants shared space with bright flowers and inlaid ceramic bowls containing sweet-smelling oils. The dining table was covered in a deep purple silk shot with gold and decorated with Indian statuettes of the dancing Shiva. Fresh flower petals and sequins were strewn artfully among the enamelled plates and colored glass.

Jane fetched her little statue of Ganesh from the bedroom and put it at Rajiv's place at the head of the table.

Jane was as excited as a child and when the Bombay Brasserie arrived with four chafing dishes of different sorts of curry and a dozen side dishes and desserts, she was happier than at any time since they had come back from India.

Leaving the waiter from the Brasserie to finish his preparations and make himself a cup of tea, she went to change.

Knowing she was being both silly and romantic, she ran a deep bath, tipped a heavy splash of jasmine-scented bath oil into it and, her hair and freesias protected by a gauzy scarf, sank carefully into it. Taking her time, she shaved her legs, her armpits and what the magazines called her bikini line.

This is an age-old business, she thought. Preparing for the master's pleasure. I should be dipping in asses' milk. As she heaved herself out of the bath she smiled, a little nervous, at her clouded mirror image and thought, well, he'd better bloody well take the bait. Any sulks and it's curtains for us.

It took her another half hour to make her face up like an Indian dancer's, with exaggerated eyes outlined in black, highly colored cheeks and full red mouth. She was careful not to overdo it. She wanted to look different and exotic but not, she thought, like a whore.

She slipped the intricate silver and topaz earrings into her ears and they dangled almost to her shoulders. She stuck a red glass talik on her forehead. Then she painted her toenails and fingernails orangey-pink and stuck tiny flower transfers on each nail.

Then she dressed herself in her orange sari and every bangle she possessed—electric-hued ones from Varanasi being lent a bit of class by an assortment of silver, gilt and horn ones collected over the years.

She wasn't sure she'd mastered the sari, though it felt secure enough. She was dithering about drawing the end over her head as a veil when the doorbell rang. Deciding against it, she threw the end over her left shoulder, pushed her feet into her sandals and went toward the door. She felt like a million dollars.

SEVENTEEN

When Rajiv arrived with Sriram and Gopal, the Applebys and Sally and Tom were already there, and Jane was still feeling wonderful. The Applebys were every bit as nice as she'd remembered, and Lucy's genuine pleasure and excitement at Jane's Indian sari and piled-up hair made up for her brother's greeting: "Heavens, Jane. If I'd known it was fancy dress, I'd have come as a golliwog too."

Sally, who disapproved of Rajiv, was nonetheless behaving in a proprietorial way about him, as she had met him since they'd returned from India and the Applebys hadn't. When Rajiv entered the room, she was saying, "He's highly educated, you know. And very high caste. A Sanskrit scholar. I expect he will get a professorship at SOAS."

"SOAS?" asked Lucy.

"School of Oriental and African Studies. Either that or something at the British Library."

Jane couldn't tell if Rajiv had heard or not. He stood stock-still at the door, his face blank.

Tom said, "Surprise! Surprise!" and then broke into a half-hearted "Happy Birthday to You," but gave it up when no one joined in.

Sriram came smoothly to the rescue. Leaving Rajiv rooted to the spot, with Jane on her way to him, he advanced into the room and introduced himself and Gopal. Gopal kissed Lucy's and Sally's hands, bowed to their husbands and, ignoring the look of distaste on Tom's face, spun around on his small shiny feet and fluttered his hands at the décor.

191

"Oh, Jane, what complete perfection! I love it. You should keep it all like this forever. And, darling, you look quite delicious in that sari!"

He bent both wrists in the exaggerated manner of the stage queen, and flapped across to the waiter who had appeared with a tray of champagne.

Rajiv came to life, and looked at Jane, smiling.

"You do look amazing," he said. "But I don't think I'll forgive you for this."

Jane felt the heady mix of relief and pleasure.

"Come," she said, kissing his cheek. "Meet my brother, Tom. He's so right wing he makes Mrs. Thatcher look like a bleeding heart. And of course you know Sally. And the Applebys, whose fault it is that we ever ventured off that Indian train. If they'd not aided and abetted me, we'd never have jumped ship."

John shook Rajiv's hand and said, teasingly, "And Jane would not have got a taste for independence and tracked you down."

"I did not!" protested Jane. "I had no idea he was in Khajuraho."

" 'The lady doth protest too much'," said Lucy, laughing.

Jane had a fleeting thought—Is it true? Did I follow him?—followed by a mental shrug. Who cares? I love him.

For the next two hours the evening had a dream-like quality for Jane. She felt she was in an exotic play. Sriram and Gopal, as usual, were dressed in exquisitely tailored Nehru jackets, the waiter looked like something out of the British Raj with a wide red sash and cummerbund over his white jacket. And she was undoubtedly the star. She knew she looked beautiful and exotic, she was confident, competent and in control. Feeling Rajiv's eyes on her, she looked at him over the brass thali laden with small enamelled bowls, the flowers and the scattering of candles. Reading the admiration and desire in his look, her body responded with the obedience of a puppet on a string: her heart thumped her ribs, and for a split second she closed her eyes in longing.

She opened them to read his message. Me too, it said.

"Do you know," Jane said as the waiter offered her the rogan josh for the second time. "When I had dinner at Rajiv's parents' house in Khajuraho, and I was stuffed to my ears with his mother's cooking, he decided to give me a lesson in eating Indian style with the fingers. We had to eat the whole meal over again." She looked affectionately at Rajiv, half her mind on how wonderful he looked by candlelight, his topaz eyes darkened to black, his high white collar framing his lean, almost arrogant, face.

"Good lord, Rajiv, do you chaps still eat with your fingers out there?" It was Tom of course.

" 'Fraid so," said Rajiv, imitating Tom's plummy tones to perfection. "Years of British rule utterly failed to civilize us." He paused minutely, then added, "Out there, old chap."

The irony was lost on Tom. "Oh, I don't know. We managed to teach you to beat us at cricket. And we left you with a bloody good civil service. Though that has all gone to pot since."

Jane said quickly, "Why should you think knives and forks are more civilized anyway? Eating with your fingers is hygienic, it's easy, and there is no washing up."

Tom said, leaning back in his chair, his words close to a drawl, "It's hardly hygienic. But then I suppose Asians are used to it. Must have guts like girders." Then, vaguely aware that he was in trouble, he said, "Of course I knew the masses ate with their fingers. Nothing else to eat with, poor things. But proper people, middle-class people, they could afford knives and forks, you'd think."

"Tom," said Sally, "do shut up. There's a dear." She spoke to her Member of Parliament husband with the firmness she used when her daughters found television more appealing than mucking out their ponies. Tom smiled and shrugged, dismissing any thought that he might have given offense, and continued to rock his chair on its back legs.

Sriram turned to Lucy to ask if she'd done any painting in

193

Rajasthan, and John effectively steered Tom into the safer waters of party politics.

Jane looked at Rajiv, but the ribbon of intimacy was cut. He did not meet her eye, and the open loving expression had been replaced with that veiled look so familiar to her in the past months. The closed, passive mixture of stoicism and indifference that had seemed to her so unwarranted. Now she understood. If her own brother, who presumably had *her* interests, if not Rajiv's, at heart, could display such naked prejudice, what hope was there for her lover in England?

The talk drifted over her while she sat silent. At first she felt nothing other than creeping despair. But rising anger pushed misery aside. She knew she'd had a lot to drink, she knew she was overwrought and emotional. But it was almost a relief to have Tom to blame. She'd been shouldering the guilt for Rajiv's woes for months.

Her crass, overbearing, fascist bloody brother had managed, in a single sentence, to put her and Rajiv back into the maw of unhappiness this carefully planned evening had so nearly lifted them out of. And what about Sriram and Gopal? How could Tom so easily assume superiority? She blushed for Tom, her cheeks hot with shame and fury.

Jane watched Rajiv put down his kulfi spoon and excuse himself politely to Lucy and Sally on either side of him. He rose from the table, and walked past her toward the bedroom. He did not give her a glance.

It was too much. Half an hour ago, Rajiv had looked at her with love and desire. Suddenly exhaustion, rage and disappointment combined and she burst out, "Tom, you absolute bastard. What the fuck do you think you were doing? How dare you insult Sriram and Gopal and Rajiv? Don't you know I love Rajiv?"

"My dear little sis. Calm down. Your Omar Sharif surely has a sense of humor, doesn't he? What have I done?"

Jane jumped up, her face aflame, eyes narrowed with fury. She was shouting, and close to tears.

"What have you done? What you always do. What you've done all my life. Belittle what I have. Denigrate what I love. And Omar Sharif is Egyptian not Indian, but you wouldn't know that since you believe all wogs begin at Calais—"

Tom interrupted, "Woah, woah, woman. I wouldn't go that far. And I am sure your friends can take a joke?" He turned to Sriram for support, but Jane could not stop now. She was sobbing and yelling at the same time.

"You've lived your whole bloody life in the same self-satisfied club: Eton, Oxford, the City, the Athenaeum, the Conservative Party. The kind of place that allows ignorant pompous fools like you to think that the only thing a woman would see in a foreigner is Omar Sharif eyes."

She threw her napkin down, and ran, gulping and distraught, from the room. But when she reached the bedroom door she rushed past it into the spare room. She did not want to see Rajiv. She could not explain or apologize for Tom. Or comfort Rajiv. Or even be comforted by him.

She was conscious of a certain pleasure in the total abandonment to weeping. She had not cried, face down on a bed, since she was a child. But she could not stop and she did not want to. She pressed her hot face into the pillow, which was cool and fresh-smelling and which muffled the noise she was making. I'm thirty-seven, she thought, and I want my daddy. Or Patrick. I want someone who *loves* me. Except that Patrick no longer does, and Daddy is dead. Self-pity renewed her tears.

Presently she sat up, and saw with odd satisfaction that the pillow was streaked with make-up—black mascara, purple eyeshadow and reddish streaks of lipstick or rouge. Rising, she looked at her reflection in the dressing-table mirror. I look like a prostitute in a B movie, she thought. Her mouth was swollen and her eyes red. Her face was blotchy and raw, and her hair was coming adrift. The freesias, still attached, but hanging drunkenly, gave her a tragi-comic air.

She sat on the dressing-table stool, squirted some face-cream on a wad of cotton wool, and started to wipe her face. She heard the door open, and braced herself for Sally's sensible encouragement or Lucy's rueful humor, but it was Rajiv. He knelt beside her, his face only slightly lower than hers, and said, "Let me."

One by one he used the balls of cotton wool, charged with cream, to clean her face. She watched him as he did it. His expression was serious, tender, and he did it skillfully. It was therapy for her soul as well as her swollen face. The cold cream was heaven on her hot cheeks, and he was close enough for her to smell his aftershave, fresh and familiar. She looked at herself in the mirror, and knew she had never looked uglier. She shut her eyes, not caring that he should see her like this, hoping he'd keep it up forever.

"There," he said, kissing first one eye, then the other. "You are not as glamorous as at dinner, but just as desirable." He kissed her mouth. "Have you ever seen *The Discreet Charm of the Bourgeoisie?*"

She looked blank.

"The film."

"No," she said. "I've never seen it." Her voice was thick with crying and she looked as solemn as a child.

"There's a wonderful bit when the hosts leave their guests in the house and sneak out of the back door for a bonk in the bushes."

He paused, then said, "It's a great movie." His fingers started to unwind her sari.

When they reappeared, their guests had left the table and were sitting in the living room.

Sriram said, "I ruled that Gopal and I are old enough friends of Rajiv, and the others are old enough friends of you, Jane, for

us to consume your drink in your absence. We did debate politely leaving, but decided that would make you feel bad."

"Oh, Sriram, thank God for you," said Jane. "Of course you
were right. And I'm sorry. We are both sorry."

Tom stood up and kissed his sister. "I don't know what I
did, but Sally says it is all my fault. I apologize."

Jane smiled her acceptance, thinking how miraculous sex
was. It made you feel you could forgive the world.

They all left a quarter of an hour later. Jane and Rajiv went
to bed, leaving the waiter to clear up and let himself out. Jane,
emotionally exhausted and replete with sex, lay warm in Rajiv's
arms, his body curled around her, his breath on her neck, and
slept blissfully, deeply, like a child.

When she woke next morning, he was gone.

A month later Jane was still liable to tears if Sally or Lucy, who
had both been wonderful, talked about Rajiv. She wanted to talk
about him, but it was dangerous territory. The knowledge of
irreparable loss could suddenly undo her.

She could not forgive him for such betrayal. To steal away
after such tenderness, such transcending love, was cruelty beyond belief. All that day, Sunday, she'd roamed the flat in her
dressing-gown, reading and rereading his note—left, she
thought bitterly, in time-honored fashion on the mantelpiece.

It was an unsigned folded page, with the words:

*It won't work, my darling. I am too chauvinist, too Indian,
for a life in your shadow. My churlishness is dousing you. It
doesn't mean I do not love you. I do.*

At first her feeling of ill-use, her anger at his abandonment
masked a worse kind of anguish. Over and over she tore at him
in her heart. Why couldn't he be happy? Why could he not
spend his time on research in the British Museum? Why did he

need a paid job to be a scholar? Why could he not be grown up enough and civilized enough to rise above the fact that she earned the money?

But then, anger and indignation exhausted, she started to claw at herself. How could she have been so self-absorbed, so indifferent to his feelings? Why had she not realized how unhappy he was? Worst of all, why had she not stopped him going? She realized now that she had heard Rajiv moving around, packing, early that fateful morning. Half-asleep, deep in her own selfish cocoon of catlike semi-sleep, languorous after the emotion and sex of the evening, she'd thought nothing of it.

That she had been so blind to his misery and unaware of his leaving seemed to her a crime for which the only consolation was the rightness of the punishment. She deserved to lose what she had failed to treasure.

She wanted him back with desperate, raw longing.

She told herself that if only he would return she would be happy, loving, uncritical and they would live on his terms. She wanted to write to him, to beg him to come back.

But Sally and Lucy would not let her. Lucy would let her weep herself dry, patiently waiting for her sense of humor to reassert itself and for her to say, "Sorry, Luce. What an idiot I am. And of course it would never work." Sally's technique was different, and tougher. She would not let Jane get away with a rose-colored view of her love affair. She would briskly remind Jane how irritated she'd been with Rajiv, tell her to brace up and face the fact that it was over, and that writing to Rajiv would cruelly prolong the death-throes of a great, but now gone, passion.

There was real consolation in the friendship of the two women. She had never had close women friends, and now she wondered how she'd managed without them. Their matter-of-fact loyalty, their acceptance of her in her unravelled state comforted her. And she knew they were right. After a month of daily—it seemed hourly—struggles with herself not to write to

Rajiv, not to catch a plane for India, not to think about him, she surfaced into a kind of life.

She worked eleven- or twelve-hour days. She worked on into the evening, sometimes past midnight. She ate Müller Rice and yogurts at her desk. Came home, washed toast and Marmite down with whiskey, then fell into bed and slept. After an hour she'd wake, swallow two Temazepam and sleep unmoving until the alarm dragged her, foggy and heavy-faced, into the world.

Then one morning, standing with her forehead against the wall-tiles of the shower, the luke-warm water drenching her back to life, she admitted to herself that Rajiv had been right to go. She had seen him, under the chill skies of an English winter, lose his authority, his confidence and his humor. He was not the man she'd fallen in love with in Khajuraho. Only when they were alone, isolated from reminders of his joblessness, away from her friends, had they regained some of that pervading contentment of the early days of Varanasi. She had been bluffing herself that all was well, or would be well, because they could always swim back to love and intimacy on a wave of sex. But the gap between them had widened remorselessly.

Sally and Lucy, in their different ways, had helped to put Jane together again, but it was Sriram who made her see the thing in some sort of perspective. He'd come round, unannounced, one crisp October Sunday, bringing dry-fried spicy potatoes and chicken with coriander in plastic boxes. They ate in the little conservatory—really just a covered-in balcony, but with enough space for a few pots and two chairs.

It was the first proper meal Jane had had in ten days. Unexpectedly, she found the food tasted delicious. She ate fast, trying to hide her hunger. She felt the warmth of the autumn sun slanting through the blinds.

"This is really nice," she said, surprise in her voice. Then, looking around at the leggy geraniums and the spent lilies, their leaves hanging exhausted and yellowing over the sides of the pots, she said, "Look at those pots. Poor things. I haven't gone

199

near them since Rajiv left. If the cleaner didn't water them, they'd be dead."

Sriram smiled. "It does seem a bit unfair to make your plants pay for Rajiv's disaffection."

"That is precisely what is so hard to bear," she said. "That all my old pleasures, gardening, going to the movies, even reading, have gone just because he's gone. I've been thinking of selling the Normandy farmhouse. I never go there. How can he have so ruined my life? All of it. Every inch of it. Not just the loving-him bit."

Sriram said, the harshness of his words softened by his non-accusatory tone, "Jane, it is time to stop blaming Rajiv for being unable to make the leap to the West. Could you have lived in Rajiv's world? It never even occurred to you to give up your job and live in India as Rajiv's wife, did it? He may have failed to adapt. But at least he tried."

EIGHTEEN

"That Stella of yours is well named, Patrick," said George, *Tatler* food critic and inveterate gossip. "Look at her. She's sparking away like a whole galaxy."

Patrick looked across at the bar, where Stella was center stage. Her courtiers, Patrick noticed with a now-familiar clutch of jealousy, were exclusively young men with very long or very short hair. None of them was older than thirty. Patrick did not know any of them, but he knew they were chefs because they had excruciating dress sense. All loud jackets in imitation Armani, sneakers with suits and faces that looked as if they never saw the sun or a healthy meal. And they were drunk already.

Patrick, going behind the bar to give the overworked barman a hand opening the champagne, said, *sotto voce,* "Stella, can you circulate a bit? Go charm your press colleagues."

Stella turned her full attention to him, big eyes working their reliable magic. "Oh, hullo, sweetheart. Isn't this great? It's a brilliant party, and I know we've got a wow on our hands." She turned to the muscular young man next to her. "Don't you love it, Brian?" Her brown bare arm reached out and half caressed, half lassoed Brian's neck. Brian, concentrating on staying upright, didn't notice. Anger that this young pup should ignore Stella's attentions, and jealousy that Stella should bestow them, assailed Patrick.

Stella shook Brian's shoulder with, Patrick thought, too much affection, and said, "Brian, I'm talking to you. Isn't this a great restaurant?"

"Yeah. Great." It was a mumble more than a reply. Then,

201

seeing the bottle of champagne in Patrick's hand, he pushed his glass at Patrick's chest, saying, "Thanks mate." Patrick obediently filled the glass.

Patrick said, "Darling, come here a sec." He moved along the bar, away from the group of chefs. Stella ducked under the bar-flap and followed him.

"Stella, I really do want you to work the room. Go chat up some of the press."

"Oh, Patrick, relax. Enjoy the party. The critics won't review the food tonight. It's only a stand-up schmooze."

"I know," replied Patrick, keeping the irritation out of his voice, "but the gossip columnists will carry something. And they've still got to be buttered up. You should know that. You've been at the receiving end of enough of it."

"Maybe. But they don't want brown-nosing from me. They all hate me."

"Nonsense. Why should they?" Patrick was trying to ignore the use of "brown-nosing." He thought the expression disgusting. But Stella reacted badly to lessons in behavior.

"Because I'm American. Because I've got the best job in this room. Because I'm paid more than any of them—other than the TV people. Because I write better copy than they do. Because I'm half their average age." She grinned that perfect teeth-and-gums smile of hers, eyes alight with devilment, and said, "Besides, I'm prettier than those bloated old has-beens."

Patrick, won over, laughed. "OK, but will you at least talk to the fat-cat customers? I can't bear you to spend the whole evening with those kitchen louts. Why did you invite them anyway? They aren't going to get us any business. And they're drinking us dry."

Stella pouted, blew him an exaggerated kiss and said, "Jealousy, jealousy." She swung away to talk to Lord Churley, a young peer who had managed to stay landed and rich, and Jason Andrews, football star. The two youngest, richest, best-looking and most famous men in the room, thought Patrick. Well, it's my own fault. No fool like an old fool.

A week later Stella had been proved right. The Third Man was the hottest ticket in town. The place was packed. Jonty, the pony-tailed manager that Stella had poached from Quaglino's, was, thought Patrick, the perfect proof that power corrupts. Jonty was never rude. Indeed he was courtesy personified. But customers did not argue with him. If you were on Jonty's "A" list you could somehow get a table whenever you wanted one. If you weren't, you could book three weeks out, but nothing would get you a window seat or the see-and-be-seen tables near the bar. Patrick, who, up till now, had always been his own restaurant manager, watched in amazement as £20 notes crossed palms, and how the young, beautiful and famous were always seated in a cluster where they could feel they were among their own—the London glitterati.

He did not interfere, except to say, "Jonty, I hope all those bribes are finding their way into the waiters' tronc."

"But of course," said Jonty, with an ironic click of the heels.

Why don't I believe him? thought Patrick.

The insurance company had refused to pay up on the stolen wine. They were perfectly within their rights: inside jobs were not covered. The police said they were still hopeful of tracing the wine. But Patrick suspected they'd lost interest since their theory that Patrick had masterminded the scam had collapsed. The aggressive young Detective Sergeant had only backed off when Patrick produced the insurance documents proving that Silvino's involvement invalidated any claim.

Juggling the Third Man's finances took most of Patrick's time. For the first time in his life he was doing what Jonty considered routine, but he thought tacky: he was hanging on to bills as long as he could, and only paying them when his suppliers were screaming. Conversely, he was on the telephone dunning customers the minute their bills were due. He'd had more meetings with his bank manager in the last three months than in all his time with Jane's. And the irony was that the whole world, unable to get a table while reading rave reviews and gossip column snippets, thought he was minting money.

But the truth was that the combination of initial overspend, bridging loan, Stella's extravagance, Silvino's thieving, and his failure to get a top price for Jane's meant that the interest on his astronomical bank loan was eating up every penny of profit they made. They were not losing money, but it was terrifying. The takings were enormous, but the outgoings matched them. He knew Alastair was not controlling the food costs rigorously enough. At Jane's he had ordered fresh *porcini* or *fraises de bois* as the fancy took him, and, up to a point, Patrick had been able to price the dishes to match. But a barn-like pub could not charge Michelin-star prices.

Also, they were still expensively hiring and firing. Patrick had hoped by now to have a stable staff, the incompetent weeded out, the experienced happy and earning well. But experienced old stagers did not fit Stella's image. Indeed she objected if he hired anyone much over twenty-five, and he'd ended up leaving the staffing to Jonty. Jonty did not bother with references. He believed in the two-week trial. Which meant an unacceptable level of staff pilfering, expensive agency fees for temps, and on-going advertising costs.

Patrick felt increasingly out of his depth.

But Stella was in her element. The Third Man had developed a club-like atmosphere combined with high style and fashion. It was busier at 11 p.m. than at 8, and Stella now wanted late night live music, so far resisted by Patrick. Most evenings Stella appeared in the restaurant bar after dining elsewhere, and joined the fashionable mix of media types, chefs who had escaped their kitchens earlier, and young actors and dancers who came on after the theater. Patrick joined them sometimes, but always found the experience bitter-sweet.

He'd look at Stella, happy, excited and beautiful, and marvel that she was his. But it hurt that these days it was this crowd rather than him that set her sparking. He loved to see her happy, but sometimes he suspected he had little to do with her happiness.

He tried not to mind as she gave away his champagne and used his taxi account to send her friends home when they were too drunk to drive. Such mean considerations disappeared when, tiddly and loving, she hung on him as they went upstairs at the end of the evening. In the abandon and dizzy satisfaction of loving her, he'd throw off the threads of doubt that gathered during the evening, and think himself a jealous fool.

But very often, Stella's fizz would fade as the last friend left, and she'd say, "Darling, do you mind? I must go home. I need to crash."

He always kissed her and said, "Of course," but he wished she wanted to crash beside him. It wasn't something they could discuss. Stella would resent the suggestion that love meant more than sex and a good time. He could hear her voice, rising in irritation: "Oh, Patrick, don't be so bloody deep. I just want to sleep, that's all. And I sleep better on my own."

One warm evening Patrick and Stella were sitting in the Japanese garden on the terrace of Patrick's flat above the Third Man. It was a rare night off for Patrick, and for once Stella did not have a restaurant to review or a party to go to. They'd eaten sausages and mash sent up from the restaurant kitchen, and drunk a bottle and a half of South African Roodeberg. Patrick felt relaxed and expansive, and briefly free of the anxieties of the Third Man's balance sheet.

Patrick loved this terrace. He'd tried to resist Stella's determination to hire her friend Yoshi to design it. Yoshi was used to designing for mega-millionaires. But now Patrick liked the cool spareness of it with its raked gravel circle, sculptural boulders, stone-lined pool, minimal greenery and no flowers. At night, lit with concealed up-lighters, it had the dramatic look of a stage set. He found the controlled order peaceful, and there was satisfaction in the thought that it was not Jane's sort of garden. Jane liked blurred edges, tumbling extravagance and soft colors.

Patrick said, "Stella, you are a clever woman. This terrace is a work of art, and I even admit the flat is wonderful. But they both lack one thing, and that's you."

Stella started to shake her head, but Patrick forestalled her objections with, "It's daft us both having such expensive houses. Give up the mews and move in. At least we'd see a bit more of each other if we woke up in the same house." He leaned forward, his elbows on the little table, fixing her gaze with his.

Some sort of old-fashioned notion of honor prevented him saying, though he'd thought it often enough, that Stella should not have so blithely, and expensively, taken over the furnishing and decoration of flat and terrace if she had no intention of sharing them with him.

Stella, leaning over the little table to kiss him, said, "Oh, Patrick, not again. Get off my case, will you? I'm twenty-five. I'm not ready for that sort of commitment. I love you, but I need my space. You understand, don't you?"

She looked so anxious and adorable that Patrick gave up. He even let her get away with that done-to-death phrase. What did it matter if she talked in clichés? She was right. He was pompous and old-fashioned and (another Stella phrase) he cramped her style. He knew he wasn't going to win the argument. So he smiled at her, leaned back in his chair and said, "OK, sweetheart. I'll back off."

Then to change the subject before he started to feel the pain of rejection, Patrick said the first thing that came into his head, which was, "I'm not happy with Jonty. Are you?"

Stella's eyes opened wide. She said, "Jonty? He's great. What's the matter with him?"

"I sometimes think he's on something. He can be such a charmer, and then such a bastard."

Stella said, her voice defensive, "Well, I expect he snorts a line of coke sometimes. They all do. But he's doing a great job running the restaurant."

Patrick felt a flicker of worry at her easy acceptance of drugs. God, I'm too old for her, he thought. But he ignored it and said, "I'm just not sure he's right for us."

Stella flicked her head, impatient. "Of course he is. Christ, Patrick, he's the best in the business. He's doing a great job. You must have noticed. For the first time in your life you're running one of the hottest joints in town."

Patrick ignored this. It wasn't true. Jane's had been the rave of London once, but that was irrelevant. He said, keeping his voice steady and reasonable, "I don't think I trust him. He's efficient, I grant you, but he's not straight with the customers and he bullies the staff."

Stella ran one hand through her thick hair, exasperated. "Oh, Patrick. Get a life. If you want a successful restaurant, one that makes money, you've got to be tough. You should know that—you were in the army."

"Yes, but, at the risk of being pompous, I believe in the *best* of the army—the training, the feeling of a joint enterprise. Corny old-fashioned loyalty, I suppose. But I don't buy the bad side of the army—the bullying, the hierarchy, the 'ours not to question why, ours but to do and die.' All that is bunk, and that's the bit that Jonty goes for."

"So what's the problem? He's filling the restaurant. The customers are leaving satisfied. The staff are getting great tips. Everyone is happy."

Patrick raised a hand in protest. "Not everyone. I had a letter from an old couple up from Dorset to celebrate the wife's seventieth birthday. They had saved up for the trip. They'd read about us in the *Telegraph*. They booked weeks ago, and they were kept waiting half an hour at the bar, then given a noisy table by the kitchen doors—they'd asked for a quiet one—and were shooed out again to the bar for coffee so we could resell the table. And we forgot to make them a birthday cake."

"What did Jonty say?"

"He said something like, 'Yeah, well, those geriatric grockles give the place the wrong image. If they hadn't brought our letter confirming their booking, I'd have denied all knowledge of it and tipped the old buggers out.' "

Stella laughed, then, seeing Patrick's disapproval, said, "Well, he's right about the wrong image. No one wants to eat in a restaurant full of senior citizens."

Patrick frowned. It distressed him to hear Stella being so heartless. He knew it was an act, but he hated it. But he also knew Stella was right about the image. Customers seemed to mind more who sat at the next table than what was on their plates. He was remembering her column damning Jane's because it had gray-suited businessmen for customers.

Stella went on, "What did Jonty say about the cake? Why didn't they get it?"

"He admitted we screwed up. Forgot it. But the thing is, Jonty didn't care. As far as he was concerned it was a good thing. As he put it, 'Waiters singing "Happy Birthday" to octogenarians may go down a bundle in the Sunset Home, but it's a downer in a decent restaurant.' "

Stella laughed, then said, "Oh, Patrick, don't look like that. Of course I'm sorry for them. And of course Jonty is tough. But he is funny. And he's right too. You hate 'Happy Birthday' as much as he does."

It was true. In the heyday of Jane's, he'd never allowed birthday cakes, singing or even parties of more than six. But those were the pre-recession days, when exclusive customers paid fancy prices for civilized quiet and exquisite food. He thought, but didn't say, that Jonty would be delighted to provide a birthday cake, and even sing "Happy Birthday" himself, provided the customer was young and wearing the right labels.

NINETEEN

Jane accepted a glass of champagne and leaned back in her seat, feeling a small thrill as she watched the numbers on the bulkhead mounting to Mach 1. In the last two years she had traveled a lot, and generally traveled first class. But this was her first flight on Concorde, and she was pleased with herself.

She felt she deserved it. She'd just pulled off a deal that would mean a Panamanian shipping company paying her client millions in compensation for non-performance. They'd failed to deliver eight tankers of crude to Rotterdam by the due date, and the subsequent shift in oil prices had nearly cost her client his company. But, she thought immodestly, he's now going to be rich rather than bankrupt. I'm sure he's grateful enough to buy me a Concorde ticket home.

Her fellow passengers, she noticed, were too rich and world-weary even to glance at their gift-packs of soft gray leather folders containing Concorde writing paper, or to watch the plane's progress toward the sound barrier. They were almost all businessmen, working or dozing.

She pulled out the thick fax she'd received just before leaving the Plaza Athenee. The top sheet was a handwritten page from her senior partner:

My dear Jane,
I do congratulate you. You are a marvel. How do you do it?
You must have charmed the socks off the opposition. That is

three in a row. Adrienne has attached Number Four. If you
pull that off too, I'll do my best over that equity partnership.
Giles.

Jane felt elation and irritation in quick succession. Her first
thought was, bingo. Equity partnership. Then she thought, patronizing sod. He thinks I waggle my hips or flutter my eye-
lashes to make my case. And how typical to attach his support
to one more blockbuster success. It's not enough that I pull in
the business. I have to win too.

She looked at the next page. It was a note from Adrienne,
the partnership manager. Adrienne wasn't a lawyer, but she was
a first-class business manager, and Jane liked her.

Wow. Terrific work. No one else could have done it. The attached
needs your touch. And the client will walk if we don't win.
Adrienne.
P.S. Don't forget the bacon.

Jane smiled. She hadn't forgotten the bacon. Every time she
went to New York she came back with as many packs of Balducci's Double Smoked as she could stuff into her bag. Ever since
she'd given one to Adrienne, she'd had to buy for her too. But
she didn't mind. She loved Balducci's with its atmosphere of an
Italian market, with its mountains of cheese and vegetables,
pasta and chocolates. She liked the way that in the middle of an
already over-crowded shop, they'd set up a coffee stall, and half
the population of So-Ho seemed to congregate between the meat
counter and the artichokes. Patrick would love it, she thought,
but Mr. Neem, the famous Environmental Health Officer, certainly would not.

Realizing she was deliberately avoiding what the rest of the
fax might hold, she yanked her mind away from Balducci's and
looked at the papers.

She was familiar with the case because it had been around

a long time. It concerned a container ship, owned by Chalkers' American client, the Delaware Cargo Company. The ship had been lost off the coast of Brazil, and the British insurers suspected scuttling and would not pay up.

Delaware Cargo's underwater investigations had revealed a possible design fault, a charge the Japanese shipbuilders and their insurers were resisting with energy.

There were half a dozen international law firms involved, and Chalkers had sent in one of their biggest guns. But he was in hospital with chronic emphysema and had now decided to retire. The client had been patient, then impatient, and was now irritated beyond measure. The insurers had so far failed to meet a penny of their claim, and the case was coming to court in three weeks' time.

Jane knew it would mean working flat out. And, since the client was in America, she'd have to be at the office half the night, most nights. Then the hearing could take weeks, if not months.

And Jane was a little miffed. When this case had first arisen, she'd argued that as the firm's marine insurance specialist she should have been given the job. But she'd been considered too new and too young.

Now they were in a hole and they wanted her to get them out. And if she fell in, they'd be able to say, "Ah, well. Shouldn't have sent a girl in to do a man's job."

But as Jane read on, she felt the familiar thrill of the chase. She began to make sense of the story, to test possible approaches. Thank God they'd had the sense to brief Sidney Hawthorne, QC. He was the best.

As The Delaware Cargo Company v. Wessex Marine Insurance progressed, Jane found she could survive on four hours' sleep a night. Must be the adrenalin, she thought. She was having a great time, and (though she never said so to her client) she thought the defendants were beginning to crack: as new evidence of dodgy design emerged, Jane could feel them wavering, tempted to switch horses: if they accepted the design-fault theory, they could pay up and go for the shipbuilders and *their* insurers.

She had two junior solicitors working with her: a young man just out of law school, and Sarah, a quiet, clever Scot, destined, Jane hoped, to be Chalkers' next female partner. It was a good team: no office politics; no grouching at the hours; all the tension coming from the need to work fast and flawlessly.

One morning, coming back to the office from a meeting at the Heathrow Airport Conference Centre (her client was on a stop-over to The Hague) she stopped her taxi in Grosvenor Street and walked the short distance to Black's.

"Can I help?" The immaculate mouth smiled a professional smile, belied by indifferent eyes. Jane sighed. The woman was on commission, and was determined to make a sale.

"Yes, I hope so. I'm looking for a light wool trouser suit. Something I can wear to travel in, or work in. And then I want a long skirt to wear with the same jacket and a different shirt for the evening or next day."

"I have just the very thing for you. Isn't this too lovely?" She pulled out a silk palazzo suit, printed with swirly ice-cream colors.

"It is, but I'm looking for something for the day. In wool. A business trouser suit with a skirt as well."

The saleswoman swiftly hung up the silk pajamas and extracted a shiny purple-brown trouser suit with heavy gold buttons.

"Ah. Well now, this is *the* season's color. Plum. We have it in taupe too. They both go perfectly with your eyes."

Good God, thought Jane, what can she mean? That my eyes are muddy brown or that the bags under them are plum-colored?

"But it's silk, isn't it?"

"Yes, indeed. The finest corded silk. By Azagury. It keeps its shape beautifully. You could wear it anywhere. For dinner. For the theater. To a wedding." The saleswoman stroked the fabric with pride.

"But I want something to wear to the office, and on an airplane, and to a business breakfast."

"Ah," the woman replied, once more swapping offerings. "Then I have the very thing for you. Jil Sander. She is the choice of all my business ladies. So practical. So smart. What about this town coat? The tiny hound's-tooth check is the very latest thing. And there's a short skirt. So elegant. And if you like this crêpe shirt, I can offer you a ten percent reduction on the coat."

"Stop. Stop," said Jane, smiling, but feeling bullied. "I don't want a coat, or a short skirt. I'm after jacket, trousers and long skirt that go together. I've only got fifteen minutes to do this, and I must stick to what I came in for."

"I understand absolutely." The saleswoman walked briskly to another rail, and flicked through the hangers at speed. "There is a very nice linen suit in the sale. An absolute bargain. I'm not sure if we have your size, but we have a tailoring service, and we could take in the trousers." She pulled out a suit.

Jane looked at the heliotrope linen jacket and trousers the woman held out, and felt completely outclassed. She said with as much firmness as she could muster, "But we are going into winter. I was thinking of wool."

"Oh, but these suits are beautifully lined. And linen is warm too, you know. Natural fabrics are cool in summer and cozy in winter. And you could wear one of these fleecy little bodies underneath. And with a silk shirt . . ."

"I don't want linen, I'm afraid. It crumples so."

"Ah, but they are such *noble* crumples. You can tell the real thing at a glance. All my ladies love the way linen is so obviously linen."

Jane thought, this is crazy. Why can't I stand up to this woman? She said, "But I need something that won't need ironing in every hotel I end up in."

"But that is nothing, madam. All the hotels provide a valet service. And a quick press on the wrong side with a steam iron, and *voilà*!"

Jane was becoming desperate. "Look, let's forget the linen. I really don't want crumples, even noble ones."

But the saleswoman knew her trade and she was too much for Jane. In the end she sold her the Jil Sander short coat and skirt, and even the crêpe shirt. Once Jane had agreed to try them on, she knew she'd lost the battle. The coat hung beautifully, to four inches above the hem of the skirt, which was well above her knee. They made her legs look very long, like a gawky model's, and she ended up buying a pair of Robert Clergerie shoes too, with a strap across the instep that accentuated the youthful awkward look.

She signed her Amex slip quickly, before she could change her mind, saying to herself that time was money and she needed to buy something, today.

But in the taxi she pulled out her mobile telephone and rang Lucy.

"Lucy, when will you next be in town?"

"Next week. I'm coming up to see the Lucian Freud exhibition. Why? Can we have lunch? We could go picture gazing together."

"No chance, damn it. I'm in the middle of a case that's taking all my time. And I've just blown a fortune in Black's because I haven't time to shop sensibly. So I've had a brainwave. You love shopping. Why don't you just shop for me? Would you? I could pay you a sodding great commission, and it would still be cheaper than going to Black's or Wardrobe."

"Sure. I'd love it. Spending other people's money is the best. But you can't be that busy. What about late-night shopping?"

"I am that busy. Most nights I don't get my head down till one or two a.m., and then I'm back in the office by seven. It's the only time I can get any thinking or writing done, when my client in San Francisco is mercifully asleep."

"But how do you eat?"

"Sandwich man comes around with goodies at lunchtime. Delivered pizza at night."

"You must be fat as butter."

Jane looked down at her slim legs, elegantly clad in navy Lycra stockings, and said, "I've *lost* weight. Not sleeping must be good for the figure."

Lucy said, "And what about the two-hour visits to the crimper?"

"I've had Nicky chop my hair off like a boy's so I can wash it in the shower and let it dry in the taxi." She ran her hand up the back of her head from nape to crown. It felt like a brush. "I've discovered that if you cut out your friends, eating, drinking and shopping, you can do an awful lot of work."

"Jane, I hope you're joking. Aren't you having any social life at all?"

"Nope. Or rather, hardly. I saw Sriram and Gopal last weekend. They came around on Sunday morning to entice me into the park to see the autumn leaves. But I talked them out of that— it would have taken too long and I had so much to do. We had breakfast. I love them both. And guess what?"

"What?"

"Rajiv's married Meera."

"He hasn't!"

"Yup. She ditched her lawyer fiancé for him. And Rajiv's working at the Delhi National Museum."

"Rajiv married! Good Lord. Do you mind?"

"I didn't feel a thing."

There was a brief pause. Lucy was thinking that Jane sounded unnaturally bright. And Jane was thinking that it was the whitest of lies. She hadn't felt much at the time. But it had taken two pills to get her to sleep that night.

"Jane, you are nuts. What happened to your theory that the long hours men work are mostly to avoid putting out the rubbish or bathing the kids. *Not necessary*, you said. Or that men get promoted for taking eleven hours a day to do what women do better in eight?"

Jane laughed, relieved to have finished with Rajiv-talk.

"OK, OK. So I've joined the Boys' Club. You cannot be an international solicitor and work Nine to Five. And another shaming admission. I'm loving it. Honestly, Luce, I'm having a great time."

"So, OK. I'm to be your designer-buyer. Suits me. What am I buying? Not Janet Reger and slippery nighties then?"

Jane smiled. "Absolutely not. These days it is M & S boys department pajamas, and very nice they are too. What I'm after is a wool suit, with a long skirt and trousers. And a couple of tops that will go with it. No power shoulder-pads, no synthetics, no bows at the neck and no scratchy stiff stuff."

"You're on. John will be delighted. I'll get my retail therapy without damaging his bank balance."

Giles Charteris looked over his bifocals at the nineteen City-suited men standing, drink in hand, in the Chalkers' boardroom. With the back of his elegant fingers he flicked imaginary dust from his pin-striped trouser leg, and said, "As of course you know, we are here to celebrate Jane's acceptance of our offer to allow her to buy into the partnership. This is a momentous event in Chalkers' hundred-year history, and one I confess I did not think I would see in my lifetime—we now have our first female senior partner. May I ask her fellow equity partners to welcome our newest shareholder, and say that we hope to keep her here at Chalker and Day a very long time."

Everyone clapped. They seem genuinely pleased, thought Jane, thanking them and smiling. I wish Dad could see me now. She felt wonderful. Like school prize day. Everyone beaming approval and pleasure.

Someone said, "Here's to making you rich, Jane."

"She's more likely to make us rich. At the rate she's going she'll overtake you as highest earner any day now, Giles." Simon was the youngest of the partners, and he grinned at Jane. "Welcome aboard, Jane."

"You must be the most eligible bachelor-girl in town," said the elderly Duncan. Jane was too happy and excited to upbraid him. Bachelor-girl indeed.

"Hardly! I'm not divorced yet. And I think I just signed up to forgo all my social life forever, isn't that right?"

Delaware Cargo v. Wessex Marine had come out right. The insurance company had agreed "an undisclosed sum" (actually the full claim and costs) four days into the case. Sidney had, in his careful, intellectual, undramatic way, revealed enough of their hand for the other side to greatly fear the rest.

They would pay up in full, and immediately start proceedings against both the ship's builders and their designers, both of whom looked like defending the action tooth and nail. Wessex Marine had now become a Chalker client themselves, insisting that Jane represent them. Chalkers could look forward to many years of highly satisfactory billings, and Jane to more nights in an airplane than in her bed.

But she was happy. She'd had to sell the Normandy farmhouse and raid her savings to buy into the partnership, which had cost her £150,000. She wasn't surprised at the price. The firm had an impeccable reputation and a rock solid international clientele. It was a good investment.

She'd thought that parting with La Prairie would have been a wrench, but it had in fact been a relief. Somehow the pleasure had gone out of the place since she'd split up with Patrick. It was so steeped in memories of salami and olives on the rosemary-scented terrace and sex after lunch in the cool shuttered bedroom, that going there on her own—which she had attempted a couple of times—made her lonely and thoughtful. It seemed to reproach her with memories of a more balanced life, when she had time to listen to music and sit on the kitchen table and talk while Patrick cooked.

Besides, it had become one more thing she did not have time

to attend to. And she'd got a good price for it, more than twice what she'd spent. She had bought it at the bottom of recession, had stripped out the Formica kitchen, built-in cupboards and fitted carpets, and restored the old stone walls, tiled floors, huge open fireplace and exposed roof beams. The buyer, a film-maker, had bought the lot, right down to the terracotta bread pot and the thick linen sheets.

As she climbed into her taxi, clutching the extravagant bunch of lilies her partners had presented her with, she thought, from now on I'm going to do what I do best. I'm no good at marriage, I'm no good at love affairs, but I'm a bloody good lawyer. Watch this space, Dad.

TWENTY

Inside the small first-class compartment it was warm and cozy, and faintly festive. Passengers helped each other fit awkward-shaped parcels from Hamleys toy shop behind seats, or struggle out of snow-dusted coats in a way they would not do except on Christmas Eve. When the train stopped at Oxford, they smiled at each other as the automatic doors opened to admit wafts of "Good King Wenceslas" from the platform.

"Excuse me. Is anyone sitting here?" A young man, good-looking in a floppy-haired upper-middle-class way, stood swaying over Jane.

Jane wondered if the slight slurring of his s's was upper-crust affectation or drink. She jumped up and scooped the bunch of mistletoe from the seat next to her.

"I'm so sorry. I'd forgotten I'd put it there."

She managed, with the young man's help, to rearrange the coats and bags on the overhead shelf to accommodate the mistletoe without losing too many of the nacreous-green berries.

Collapsing into the now clear seat, the young man put back his head and closed his eyes. His mouth fell slightly open, like a sleeping child's. Drink, Jane decided, as the not unpleasant whiff of alcohol reached her. Poor boy is plastered. She studied him with interest, confident that he was too drunk to wake and resent her gaze. He was beautiful, in an old-fashioned English way, like Rupert Brooke. Clean blond hair covered a smooth forehead, his nose was finely sculpted, his skin translucent and pale, his mouth full and curly.

"Anything from the trolley?" The steward put his head in the door.

The young man opened his eyes, and said, "Um, yes. Certainly. Got any champagne?"

"No, sir. White wine."

"OK. Thanks."

"Anyone else? Sandwiches, coffee?"

"I'll have white wine too," said Jane, leaning forward to get the man's attention.

"Sorry, madam. That was the last one. Red?"

She settled back in her seat thinking, damn. "No, thanks. I'm fine. It doesn't matter."

The young man immediately said, "Oh, but it does. Hey, that's not right. You have this. I'll have red. I don't mind. As long as it's alcoholic, who cares about the color?" He grinned cheerfully, and held out his glass, full but as yet undrunk, and the rest of the little bottle to Jane.

Jane protested, but he insisted, "Go on. It's Christmas. Let me buy you a drink."

Compromise was reached, Jane accepting the white and buying him the red. Jane went back to gazing into the blackness outside, exhaustion ebbing into pleasant tiredness as she drank the wine and let her mind lap around the coming fortnight. Christmas at the Applebys' would be restorative. She had worked so hard these past months, and though there had been satisfaction in the work, and a kind of glory in being so good at it, she had a subterranean feeling that there should be more to her life than law books and meetings. She told herself she was just dog-tired. What she needed was a week or two of country air, no expectation that she would get up for breakfast, and a bit of pampering to set her up for more of Chalker and Day. With luck they'd have crisp winter weather and she'd get a ride or two on one of the Applebys' horses.

And this Christmas would be family-free. Last year she had spent Christmas with Tom and Sally, and it had been hell. She'd left Patrick only two months before and her mother, also staying for Christmas, had championed Patrick's cause until Jane had cracked and shouted at her. She shied off the memory, still able to reawaken guilt and anger. But now she was over Patrick—and Rajiv—and a week with John and Lucy would be good. She closed her eyes and enjoyed the gentle shaking and rhythmic rattle of the train.

"Carrying mistletoe to the country. Isn't that coals to Newcastle?"

His head thrown back, slumped in his big overcoat, her neighbor was looking up at the luggage rack.

Jane returned his smile and said, "I guess it is. But it was going for half price on Paddington station and I can never resist a bargain. Do you think my hosts will have trees full of it?"

"No idea. I'm a country lad who can't tell an oak from an ash."

"Are you going home for Christmas?"

"I am, but it's the first time I've left London or Oxford for weeks. No wine bars in Little Tew, that's the problem."

Her friendliness, the wine and the fuggy comfort of the train, had a confessional effect on her new acquaintance. He told her his name was Matthew, he was a history student at New College, but had done almost no work and was in danger of being sent down. He was also in debt. He was going home for Christmas, and to face his father.

"It's so boring and predictable, isn't it? Like a Victorian melodrama. Young rake turns his old father's gray head grayer."

He laughed, but Jane thought, poor lad, he's whistling to keep his courage up. It is all drink and bravado. Why was he telling a total stranger about his student loan, his inability to get up in the morning to go to lectures or to go to bed at night? About his girlfriend falling for his tutor? He was witty and self-deprecating, but Jane suspected he was more sensitive and less cynical than he wanted to appear.

221

When the guard announced their arrival at Banbury, neither of them was ready for it, and Jane jumped up.

"Oh God, I get off here." Grabbing her coat, she shrugged into it.

"Me too. Here, let me." He reached up over Jane and gripped the mistletoe. The train driver applied the brakes and Jane, losing balance, lurched against him.

"Oops, sorry. And thanks," she said, reaching up to relieve him of the bundle.

Holding it over her head in one hand, and steadying her with the other, he leaned down and kissed her, smack on the mouth.

For a second Jane stood stock still. Then she opened her mouth to protest, and heard him say, "Happy Christmas." Then he grabbed her suitcase and said, "Is this yours? I'll take it."

Jane followed him off the train, still speechless. At the station entrance, he turned and handed her the case.

"Look, I'm sorry I kissed you. I shouldn't have. But with the mistletoe and all, it seemed too good to miss. And I only managed it because I'm so pissed. Normally I wouldn't have the courage to speak to anyone half so beautiful. Goodbye."

He waved, and grinned, and weaved off down the road.

It was years since Jane had been on a horse. But the gentle nicker of the chestnut mare as they approached her loosebox filled her with familiar excitement. Jane slipped the snaffle into the pony's mouth and the headpiece over her ears with well-remembered ease. Holding the flap of saddle up with her forehead so she could see to tighten the girth, she breathed in the warm smell of leather and horse and shut her eyes with pleasure. A New Year's Day ride in bright sunshine and cold air would be wonderful.

As a child she had longed with pain and passion for a pony. But they had no stable in the orchard/paddock, and livery at the riding school was too expensive. Her father had tried to compensate her with a donkey, which resolutely refused to be trained, though Jane had spent hours, days, with stick and carrot. But Thomas the Tank Engine had triumphed, gaining the role of family pet with no duties other than to look decorative and be patted. And Jane had settled for Saturday mornings at the riding school and summer camp with the Pony Club.

As the little mare skittered along sideways tossing her head, twelve-year-old Nathaniel said, "You ride OK. Mum's useless." He sounded sulky. His head was down, the brim of his riding hat obscuring his eyes, and Jane couldn't see his expression.

But, pleased to have wrung approval from him, she said, "Thanks. So do you. You look as if you were born in a saddle."

"I like riding, and horses. David says it's wet. He only likes jumping and galloping. He says he'd rather have a motor bike."

Jane smiled and said, "Well, I'm glad he didn't want to ride Cherry today, because I get the chance."

Nat went on, morosely, "David never rides. If I want him to come with me he makes me catch Cherry for him, and tack her up and everything. And feed her after, all the boring stuff."

Jane said, "She's lovely. Aren't you, Cherry?" She patted the mare's shoulder. Cherry stopped prancing, and consented to walk in a straight line. "Good Cherry."

Nat said, "Mum wants to sell her. She's too frisky for her. She's scared of falling off. And Dad's too heavy. She says it's a waste with David hardly ever riding. Dad says when we go to boarding school in September we should sell them both."

"Will you go to boarding school?"

"I suppose so."

"Do you want to?"

"No." Jane looked at the boy's face. He was scowling. "David does. He loves school. I like it at home."

"Well, maybe he can and you needn't."

"I shouldn't think so." Nat was unravelling a thong of plaited rein, sulkily tugging at it. "We're twins. And everybody always expects twins to do the same things."

Jane said, "Don't pull your reins to bits, Nat." She leaned

over and touched his shoulder. "Cheer up. Maybe it will turn out right."

They emerged from the wood into a field that stretched to the horizon with a wide bridle path running along the top of it. The minute they were through the gate, Cherry resumed her sideways skittering, desperate to be off. Jane said, "I gather this is where you boys go like the clappers. Cherry can't wait."

Nathaniel grinned, all traces of his former moodiness gone. He said, "Shall we race to the end?" And he was off, his fat black cob sending a shower of mud over Cherry and Jane as he went from a standstill to a gallop.

Jane held Cherry back with difficulty and made her canter well to the left of Nat to avoid more splattering, then let her go, leaning low over her neck and whispering, "C'mon girl, bet you can't catch them." Cherry leapt like a bolt from a crossbow.

It was exhilarating. Breathtaking. The pony galloped so eagerly, and the sense of freedom and danger, the pounding speed were fantastic. She caught a glimpse of Nat's excited face turned to look at her, eyes shining, cheeks flushed, mouth open, and she thought, that's exactly how I feel. Reckless and happy.

But she had forgotten how fit you need to be to gallop two miles, and after a few minutes she was aware that her knees were going like pistons, pumping back and forth so fast she could not grip hard enough to keep them steady. With her lungs hurting with every gasp, she decided to let Nat be the victor. Sitting back a bit, and using her legs for leverage, she tried to pull Cherry up. But Cherry's response was to arch her neck, tuck her nose into her chest and keep going.

Jane struggled with her. Sitting back in the saddle, she remonstrated with the mare. "Woah, woah, old girl, we have to stop before I fall off from exhaustion." Cherry slowed to a canter, then shifted to a trot, albeit a head-tossing, fidgeting one. Jane relaxed the reins, leaning down to pat her, her cheek on the mare's neck.

At that moment a partridge burst from the grass at her feet.

Cherry reared, her neck hitting Jane hard in the face. Then she shied, leaping off the path. She wheeled around full circle, and took off after Nat and the black cob. Jane, still on top, had lost one stirrup, and was clinging to the mare's neck. Then she fell, with one foot still in the stirrup, and still clutching the reins. She was off the horse, and being dragged.

Her mind shouted, "Don't let go the reins. Don't let go." But she had to. Once Cherry's head was free she bucked and kicked, desperate to rid herself from the still-attached Jane. Jane felt her body arching backward; her feet, freed, rising in the air; her shoulders thudding into the ground.

She thought, oh, God, I don't want to die without Patrick.

By the time Nathaniel, white faced and leading Cherry, returned, Jane was in agony.

"I think I've broken my leg." She tried to smile, but tears were running down her face and it looked more like a grimace. "You'll have to go and get your dad with the Suzuki."

Nathaniel flung himself off his horse and said, "But I can't leave you here. You're crying. And you're shivering."

It was true. She hugged her arms tight to her to stop them shaking, and tried to reassure him. "Nat, I'm OK. I'm cold, that's all. And I'm blubbing out of relief that you came back to save me. But I can't move my leg. Can you go back on your own and fetch your mum or dad?"

Cherry, calm now, consented to be held by Jane, and began nosing the winter grass at the edge of the path.

Nat took his waxed jacket off and draped it around her shoulders. "I'm OK," he said. "I've got a jersey."

"Nat. You are a wonderful lad. Don't gallop and break your neck now. Just make sure your dad comes fast, and brings a heap of painkillers and a half-jack of whiskey with him." She was trying to joke, but she was talking through clenched teeth.

Nathaniel replied, with the solemnity of a boy scout, "I promise." And he swung his leg over the cob's saddle and dug in his heels.

Jane's leg wasn't broken, but the tendons and muscles were so badly torn it might as well have been. John and Lucy had driven the Suzuki over a planted field of winter wheat to get to her, mercifully unseen by the farmer, who, John feared, would take a shotgun to his tires without waiting to ask questions.

Lucy had helped him lift Jane into the passenger seat and they'd taken her straight to the district hospital. Within thirty minutes she had been X-rayed, strapped up, dosed full of painkillers, and was in bed with a cup of tea.

"Do you want me to ring Sally? Or your mum?" asked Lucy.

Jane shook her head. She looked around the ward, the walls and ceilings pathetically dotted with Christmas decorations. She felt a wave of overwhelming self-pity, and her eyes filled with tears. She wanted Patrick.

"Jane, Jane, it's OK. You're safe now. It's the shock," said Lucy.

No, it's not, thought Jane. I'm crying because I'm so feeble. How can I want my ex-husband running to my bedside? She willed herself not to ask Lucy to call him.

Next morning Jane was discharged and went back to the Applebys' with orders to stay more or less put, with her leg up, for three weeks. Her protests were overruled by John and Lucy. Since she wasn't in the middle of a court case, she could work by fax and e-mail, and that was that.

The large downstairs study became her bedroom since it obviated hobbling up and down the stairs and had the further advantage of a desk with a fax, a telephone and a socket for her laptop. John packed up his Hornby trains and track to make room for a bed, a sacrifice forced on him by Lucy. "You bought that set years ago. Allegedly for the boys. It should never have been set up here at all." She carried it through to the playroom.

The Applebys' life gradually seduced Jane. She didn't appear for breakfast, but the smell of frying bacon or burning toast generally woke her. Once school started she'd lie listening to shouts about lost football socks, and to slamming doors and yelled goodbyes until the crunch of tires on the gravel outside meant John and the boys were finally off.

Then Lucy would appear with a tray of coffee, and sit on her bed while they drank it. Lucy would help her bathe and dress and leave her to her own devices for the morning.

Lucy had brought in a garden lounger, and Jane spent the morning with her computer or her papers on her lap, legs outstretched. It was extraordinarily peaceful. Hardly like work at all. Lucy disappeared into her garden studio to paint, but would sometimes appear with more coffee, or a sketch she was pleased with, and at lunchtime the women would have soup or toasted cheese together.

Lucy fetched the boys at 3 p.m., which meant leaving the house at 2:40. It impressed Jane that Lucy, who was sufficiently scatty to go shopping in her painting apron, or get absorbed in drawing and forget about lunch, was never a second late for the boys. And if some other mum was due to drop them back, Lucy would have one eye on the clock until she heard the front door. Then her face would smooth out with relief and love as they came through the door.

One morning both women were in Jane's room, Jane on the lounger with her legs up, Lucy sitting cross-legged on Jane's bed, Jane's duvet tucked around her feet. The coffee tray was on the floor between them.

Lucy said, "I don't want the boys to go to boarding school," she said. "For entirely selfish reasons. I like them about. I didn't have them for the benefit of some matron."

"You'll have them at weekends, won't you?"

Lucy shook her head, her eyes unhappy. "Not at Eton. They hardly ever let them out. And boarding-school inhibitions will envelop them and there'll be no more climbing into our bed when they wake, nor anymore hugs and kisses for Mum." She smiled, trying to make light of it.

Jane leaned sideways to pour herself another cup. She lifted the cafetière questioningly toward Lucy, who shook her head.

Jane asked, "David wants to go, doesn't he?"

"Can't wait. But poor Nat. And poor us." She shook her head slowly, smiling, despairing.

Jane said, "Won't John agree to split them up? Nat could stay at home and go to a day school?"

"He says that Nat might come to resent missing out on Eton. That his brother went and he didn't. Especially if David does well and Nat doesn't." She shrugged, weary of the argument, resigned. Then she suddenly rallied and said, with force, "But I think it's because John went to Eton and loved it. Captain of cricket, wonderful housemaster who shared his obsession with trains, member of that silly club, Toff or whatever. You know— whose members wear fancy waistcoats."

Jane laughed. "Pop. Not Toff. My brother went to Eton and hated it. Though to hear him now, you'd think he'd been in paradise."

Lucy said, hugging the duvet around her knees, "Of course they still have to pass Common Entrance. But they are both bright, so I expect they will." She sounded so gloomy Jane smiled. There cannot be many mothers dreading their sons doing well in exams, she thought. Lucy went on, "They've been offered places in John's old house if they do OK." She picked at the piping around the edge of the duvet, and Jane was reminded of her son picking his reins apart in the same unhappy way when discussing the same unhappy subject. Lucy was not finished. She said, "Surely there is something wrong about an all-male, ninety percent adolescent society of over-privileged, very clever people?"

"It's certainly good training for a life in the mostly male, over-privileged legal profession, or the City. Chalkers is stuffed with Old Etonians."

Lucy was revolving the arguments, gone over a hundred times, in her head. "Of course John is right that it's a terrible waste—to be clever enough to get the offer of a place, and then turn it down." She was pensive for a second then said, "The truth is that I simply do not know if it is the right thing for Nat. I can't objectively consider his needs without my own getting in the way."

"I would let Nat decide," said Jane. "He's very sensible, and it's his life."

The two women had fallen easily back into the intimacy they'd had after Rajiv's departure. In one of what Jane referred to as their "dorm talks," she told Lucy that, at thirty-seven, she didn't think she was properly grown up. How else to explain the all-encompassing love of Rajiv, extraordinary despair at his leaving, and then her even more extraordinary recovery. They also talked about her ambivalent attitude to Patrick, that she both missed him and didn't. That she'd been unable to stay with him, and yet hated to think of him with the young and captivating Stella. That she wanted to get to the top of the City solicitor tree, but she dreaded going back to the office. That the thought of children scared her, yet made her sentimental and broody.

"When I see you sewing name-tapes on football jerseys, I should thank my stars I don't have children. But what I feel is envy."

Lucy said, "It's generations of programming and it's in your genes. The mothering type."

"Do you think so? Patrick used to say I'd be a good mother, but until very recently—until it's safely too late, I guess—I've not wanted kids at all. I've always thought I was the career-woman type."

"Why can't you be both? One only has to see you with Nat

to see you'd be a good mum. You enjoy the company of children—look at the hours you spend playing Monopoly with ours."

"I'm so competitive I'd play Monopoly with anyone. And I can't be both lawyer and mother. The lawyer bit's all right, but I'm thirty-seven. And lover-less." She said it cheerfully, and before Lucy could say, as John had, that she had lots of breeding time ahead of her, she went on, "But I must get over this mawkish interest in infants. It's all those nappy commercials with adorable babies in them. I can barely pass a pram. I'll end up snatching one."

"Rather make one. At least it will grow up intelligent and good-looking."

"Depends who the dad is." Jane wondered whether Lucy was imagining a brown Rajiv baby, or a pale Patrick one. She thought she wouldn't really mind. A Petri dish or test tube would do.

But then there was a pause, and Lucy said, suddenly serious, "I think you want Patrick back. What I don't know is why. Is it because you want to trounce Stella? Or because you want emotional security? Or so you can pretend Rajiv never happened?"

Jane didn't reply. Her throat tightened and she shook her head, almost imperceptibly. She swallowed and said, more firmly than she'd meant to, "No. That's nonsense. I've grafted for this partnership, I'm damn good at it, and I do not need Patrick, or kids. I've just got to get a grip, that's all."

Lucy didn't press it. She said, "Don't pick at it. It will resolve itself. You'll see."

After a fortnight, and newly bandaged, Jane was given permission to hobble about on crutches.

John suggested she visit his office "to see how the country cousins in the legal profession live.' Lucy dropped her at the door at 5 p.m., and John helped her up the narrow stairs to the offices of "Appleby and Atherson, Solicitors." The suite of rooms had been knocked together from the first floors of three high-street houses, over a row of shops. But if the houses from the outside had an air of Dickensian fustiness, the partnership's offices sent a message of up-to-the-minute modernity.

"Wow, John. This makes Chalkers look positively nineteenth century," said Jane, looking at the reception area's spare white walls, pale gray modern furniture, small abstract sculptures in perspex boxes held just off one wall, a huge streaky orange and red painting of Lucy's on another.

"This is Lucy's doing," said John. "She says the unexpected is what excites people, and clients would expect us to have leather-bound books and manila folders tied up with red tape everywhere. So we have to file everything in matching deep blue files and keep the law books out of sight."

"But it's amazing. More like an ad agency than a law firm." She examined one of the perspex sculptures and said, "It looks like a ginseng root, or some creature. What is it?"

"God knows. Ask Lucy. I leave art and aesthetics to her. But it's a nice office to work in."

John's guided tour took her through the building, and, sure enough, she saw only deep blue files and ivory partnership paper (with deep blue letterhead). Even the paper-clips were deep blue.

They ended up, drink in hand, in John's office, with two of his partners. The third, Peggy Pearce, apologized. "I'd love to stay, but I've got two under five, and the baby-sitter gets restive." She bumped carrier bags, handbag and briefcase against the door frame as she backed out.

"What a jolly woman," said Jane, thinking that her bottle green trousers and Aran jumper would not have gone down too well at Chalkers.

"She's also a damn good solicitor. Does most of our family stuff," said Roger Atherson, a balding merry-faced man of perhaps fifty.

Jane asked, "But don't you find this emphasis on design distracting? Seeing you have the right paper-clips is a bit silly, isn't it?"

"I suppose it could be," said John. "But just because we are lawyers doesn't mean we all have to have hunting prints or portraits of long-gone lawyers on the walls. But the décor is incidental really. What's nice about this practice is that we are friends. It's enjoyable, most of the time."

On the way home, his eyes on the road, John said, "Jane, why not join us? We need another partner."

Jane looked at him in astonishment. "Are you serious?"

"Yes, I am. The four of us are really stretched, and we've been talking of taking on someone else. You'd be perfect, though you'd earn a whole heap less than you do now, and you'd have to do general corporate law. Not too many shipping companies in Banbury."

Jane leaned over and kissed his cheek. "Oh, John, you are a real friend, and I'm really touched. But it's crazy."

"Maybe. But think about it."

TWENTY-ONE

Patrick Chambers is having a tough week. His fashionable eaterie, the Third Man, fave watering hole of media-trendies, is being taken to court by its sacked manager, Jonty Stevens, for breach of contract. On top of that, his head chef, the renowned Alastair McKinlock, is leaving for the bright lights of television. And I'm told the debt-burdened pub-cum-brasserie has never fully recovered from the theft of its uninsured wine cellar and the extravagant refurbishment masterminded by Stella Richmond, restaurant hackette and Patrick's chef-crazy girlfriend. Will she be next to desert the sinking ship? Or is she dining late most nights at Franco's because she admires his food?

Patrick stood between the breakfast table and the sink and read the paragraph for the third time. He dropped the paper on the table and sat down heavily. Elbows on the table, he shoved all his fingers into his hair and pressed his forehead hard between his palms. He closed his eyes and for a moment let the pain of it drench him. Then he stood up, picked up the paper and walked through to his office. He dialed Stella's mews house. No answer. He dialed again, but after three rings he put back the handset.

He didn't want to think at all, and for a moment was tempted not to, but then started to arrange his thoughts in tidy good order.

Stella was not at home. Relentless, his mind clicked up the evidence: it was 7 a.m.; she was sleeping elsewhere; she had only slept here two nights this week; she was sleeping with someone; she had written about Franco's twice recently; she was sleeping with Franco.

Patrick wrenched his mind off Stella: the *Dispatch* diarist could not have got the breach of contract story from official sources. The case was not yet listed. It was unlikely that Jonty would have told him; he was officially on holiday—in fact under suspension—and was in Amsterdam. Apart from Sandra, none of his staff knew. Stella must have leaked it.

Alastair's television offer had only been confirmed on Monday and he had come to discuss it with Patrick at once. Patrick had advised him to take it—they both knew he wasn't happy at the Third Man, and telly would make him famous, and bankable, and backable. They'd agreed to keep it quiet until they'd replaced him. But he had told Stella.

Only he and Stella (and Sandra of course) knew how finely balanced the Third Man's finances were. Everyone else, seeing the packed tables, and knowing nothing of their borrowings, thought they were minting money.

There was no escaping it. His beloved Stella had just blown him out of the water.

What he wanted to do was get in his car and search for Stella in the hopes of venting his anger or soothing his hurt. He wanted to shake her and shout at her. And he wanted her to tell him it was all a mistake—she'd got drunk and blabbed, she didn't realize, she hadn't meant to. She wasn't sleeping with Franco. He wanted her to weep so he could forgive her.

But the soldier in him swept Stella out of his thoughts. He had to rally the troops. Every one of them, except Sandra, reported either to Jonty or to Alastair. The loss of their superiors, and the hint of bankruptcy, would have every one of them scanning the *Dispatch* for jobs tonight and every rival restaurant after them with offers. He'd need to ring all his major suppliers and tell them the bankruptcy rumor was unfounded. Not that they'd believe him. He might have to pay on delivery or pro forma, and that *could* bankrupt him. He must talk to his bank manager. And get a response ready for the inevitable press calls.

He rang Sandra at home, and caught her as she was putting on her coat.

"Sandra. I need a staff meeting at 10 a.m. Both shifts. It is important everyone possible is there."

"Patrick. Why? We're not going under?"

"No. Absolutely not. It's fine. But read the Diary in the *Dispatch*. They've got wind of Alastair and Jonty leaving, and of our finances. We've got to knock it on the head. I must rush. See you later."

He went down the stairs, let himself into the restaurant, and walked through the dining room. It smelled fusty with last night's smoke, booze and food. He flipped the ventilation and heating switches to override the program that normally turned them on at 11 a.m. when the lay-up started. He needed the room habitable for the meeting. He walked through to the still-room and turned on the espresso machine.

Then he went up to Sandra's office, booted up her computer and tapped at the keys while it chittered into life, and finally came up with a screenful of suppliers' names and telephone numbers. He printed out the list, and took it through to his office. It was still only 7:35 a.m., but both his fishmongers, the two butchers and three veg suppliers were all wholesalers, and they would be halfway through their day. He'd do them first, and tackle the laundry, wine merchants, stationers and equipment people when *their* day started. He wanted to be finished by 9:30, so he could think through what he'd say to the staff at 10.

At 9:15, Sandra put her head around the door and said, "I've got Stella on the other line. Shall I put her through?"

Patrick hesitated, but only for a second.

"No. Could you find out where she'll be at eleven-thirty? I'll be through by then."

Jane sat at her desk looking dispiritedly at the three neat, but high, piles of paper on it, reluctant to jump in. Her leg, declared by the hospital to be healed, ached dully and she stood up to ease it. She walked stiffly to the window and thought she'd like a cigarette. It was nearly a year since she'd given up and her continued cravings for a fag irritated her. She walked briskly back to the desk, making an effort not to limp, and sat down.

The telephone buzzed and her secretary said, "Sally Finlay says she must speak to you. It's urgent."

"OK." Jane picked up the receiver, slightly uneasy. Sally never telephoned her at work.

"Sally?"

"Jane. Have you seen the *Dispatch*?"

"No. Why?"

"The Diary. I'll read it to you."

As she listened, Jane's hand flew to her mouth and her eyes widened in distress. When Sally was through, Jane groaned. "Oh, no. Oh, God. My poor Patrick." Then she said, "But Sally, why are you telling me this? I'm not with Patrick anymore."

"You're still married to him, you know. The poor sod is completely fixated with that American bimbo, and now it looks, thank God, as if she's off. I just thought you should know. I'll fax the article to you."

"No, Sally, don't do that," Jane said hastily, thinking of the secretaries in the fax room giggling over Patrick's problems. "I'll buy a copy."

"OK. But Jane, this is a good moment to do something about him." Jane felt the old irritation at Sally's bossiness, and shifted the telephone to her other ear.

She said, "But it's none of my business. And I don't want it to be."

"Nonsense, Jane. I know, and you know, that you still care about Patrick. He's in trouble, and you should be there. That's all."

Six months ago Jane would have erupted. But now irritation was replaced by a sort of weary admiration for her sister-in-law.

"Oh, Sally, darling. Get off my back. I've had quite enough of the Patrick supporters' club. But I will ring him. Maybe I can help on the money side."

"That would be a start," said Sally.

As always, Jane found that there was truth in Sally's forthright analysis. She did still care for Patrick. Indeed she knew she still loved him. What kind of love? was the only question.

Reading the *Dispatch* piece upset her. She was conscious that, if true, Stella was doing no more than she had done: leaving Patrick. But she wanted to believe they were different, that Stella was no good. And she was appalled at the financial news. Like the rest of the world, she'd believed that a restaurant turning over millions must make money.

She had in fact been rather pleased with herself for not resenting Patrick's success with the Third Man. Though there was some residual nostalgia about the original Jane's, she knew that its mediocre performance could not be lifted, and she was glad for him when he'd grabbed his chance and got out. And she was genuinely delighted that he was proving, as she thought, that he could rake in the money every bit as well as she had. Sometimes she'd even thought that if he'd had the Third Man when they were together, the tensions that led to her leaving might not have arisen.

She could not get the piece out of her head. She found herself mentally arguing with the *Dispatch* writer, asking if he enjoyed kicking people when they were down. And she thought with distaste that Patrick was embroiled in the very world he had seemed, before, so confidently apart from—the world of opportunistic staff taking good employers to court, of dishonest friends ripping you off, of the tawdry London world of backbiting critics, TV egomania and fashionable unprincipled people.

Three days later she booked a table for lunch at the Third Man. She took Sriram with her, partly because she didn't want Patrick to find her alone and feel obliged to look after her, and partly because she wanted advice. She had been turning over the idea of somehow helping Patrick financially, but she knew he'd never accept her money. Maybe Sriram would think of some impersonal way of her investing in the Third Man that Patrick would accept.

Sriram was astonished at the size and modernity of the place. But Jane was dismayed. It was just like all the other wide-open, expensively lit restaurants. It did not seem to reflect Patrick's personality at all. She would have expected Patrick to have kept some of the old pub's 1900s feel, for there to be some warm character to it, some good pictures, some flowers. But it was all stainless steel, chrome, glass and pale wood floors. She could not fault it, but it made her feel tired. Formula design, she thought. And then, what a spoilt cow I am. Only someone as blasé and overpaid as me could possibly not like this place. I'm just determined not to be impressed by Stella's work, I guess.

They had an excellent lunch, without any sign of Patrick.

"This is Alastair's cooking, I'd swear," said Jane. "This way of rolling up salmon is his trade mark." She looked down at the salmon steaks, neatly boned and rolled into perfect noisettes held in place by a circle of salmon skin, the grill marks glistening under the thin shine of dill and parsley butter. "Either he's learned to delegate, which he certainly could never do at Jane's, or he's not gone yet."

When Sriram was eating a marmalade tart with a fine crackly top, achieved, Jane knew, with a blow-torch, and Jane was on her second double espresso, a voice with a hint of aggressiveness said, "You're Patrick's wife, aren't you?" It was Stella, in tight black leather trousers and a short matching jacket. Jean-Paul Gaultier, thought Jane inconsequentially, noticing the gold chains and tiny gold knives and forks sewn on the pockets.

Jane's heart sank. She'd hoped Stella had gone off with Franco.

"Yes, I am. You must be Stella. Please. Join us. This is Sriram Mahanta."

"OK. Thanks," said Stella, sitting down on a chair produced by a nervous waitress.

"A double espresso and a vodka," Stella said without looking at the waitress, who said, "Certainly, madam," and set off at speed.

"Is Patrick about?" asked Jane. "I didn't want to warn him I was coming in case he thought he should be polite to me, but I'm not trying to sneak in like a spy. I just thought it was time I visited the Third Man. You don't mind do you?" Jane smiled at Stella, making an effort to be open and friendly.

"No, why should I?"

"No reason," said Jane quickly, then asked again about Patrick.

"I've no idea where he is," said Stella. "I'm not his mother."

I will not rise, thought Jane. If she wants to be rude, fine. She said nothing.

Sriram came to the rescue. He said, "Tell me about that thing in the middle, Stella."

He was looking across the tables at the Aavee installation, which dominated the space between the windows and the bar. Stainless-steel rods and laser lights twirled slowly inside a 10-foot-high cylindrical pod of clear Perspex, apparently balanced on a deep blue acrylic pyramid, itself on a raised podium of stainless steel. From one of the rods hung a pair of industrial black rubber gloves. They dipped and rose slowly as the sculpture went round.

"I suppose you hate it?" said Stella, leaning back and tapping her cigarette over the ashtray.

"No. I am merely puzzled, and seek enlightenment." He spoke quietly and without irony.

Stella didn't answer but her manner softened and she swung around to look at the hypnotically revolving rods and gloves.

Sriram continued his charm offensive. "I'm told you were responsible for the decor?" He waited for Stella's response but she just stared back at him, looking sulky and beautiful, thought Jane. Sriram went on, "It is obviously very successful. I congratulate you. But I do not understand these things. Explain to me what that is all about. Is it art, or a joke?"

Flattered into relaxing, Stella said, "Both, I guess. It's called *Marigold*, because of the rubber gloves, which represent the endless washing-up in a restaurant. Also, the laser beams go from cool colors to hot ones as the noise level goes up, and the gloves move faster. That's because the dishwashing gets more frantic and the kitchen gets hotter the busier the restaurant is. It's hooked up to a computer."

Sriram, amused but baffled, shook his head. "But who is *Marigold*?"

"Oh, dear Sriram," said Jane. "You're like that judge who asked 'Who are the Beatles?' Marigolds are the most famous, if not the only, make of rubber gloves. But then you'll never have touched such things."

"You are right of course. I know nothing of rubber gloves. Or of modern art. But if the customers like them, why not? What does something like that cost?"

"Twenty K," said Stella.

"Good lord," said Jane, looking with disbelief at the sculpture. "Twenty thousand pounds?"

Stella said, somewhat tartly, "If you want quality, you have to pay for it. If we'd got Damien Hirst, it would have been ten times that."

"I'm not sure a Hirst cow in a tank of formaldehyde would be good for beef sales." Jane was trying to lighten the mood, but Stella did not return her smile.

At that moment Patrick appeared, and Jane had a few seconds after catching sight of him weaving through the tables in his practiced way, and while he was kissing Stella, to get her face in order—welcoming, friendly, but relaxed. She could do nothing about the lurch and clutch of her heart.

Patrick slid onto the bench next to Jane, and kissed her cheek.

"I wondered when my woes would bring you to pat my hand."

Jane's immediate thought was that he was using some new aftershave. But his lips on her cheek felt just the same. She said, "I admit to worrying, yes. But I had been promising myself a look at the restaurant for months. It is amazing. Congratulations to you both." She included Stella in her smile.

Patrick said, "Don't look at me. The décor is all Stella's doing."

Stella said, "To listen to your ex, you'd think I was determined to ruin him." Her voice was flat, petulant.

Patrick reached across the table to touch Stella's hand, but she withdrew it. He pulled back his own as his mouth tightened. He said, trying to joke, "The truth is, Jane, Stella and I have the reverse partnership to the one you and I had. I used to spend your money, so it is probably only fair that Stella now spends mine. The trouble is she spends the bank's too."

"Oh, don't start that again, Patrick," said Stella. She slid her bottom forward on the chair, leaned back and signaled to a passing waiter. "Another vodka, please."

Even spoilt and scowling, she was very lovely. Her mouth, in a down-turned pout, was full and very red, yet seemed to have no lipstick on it. She pushed her spectacles onto the top of her head, struggling a bit with them because her hair was too thick and full and tangled to slide them up. She had to take them off and thrust the earpieces into her hair. She looked across the table at Patrick, her aquamarine eyes wide and defiant.

Jane watched this exchange and felt she understood. She saw how captivating Stella was, and she saw how trapped and beaten Patrick was. He looked wearier than she'd ever seen him. His

241

skin was pale, with dark patches under his eyes. He needed a haircut, some sun on his face, a holiday. Or just a good night's sleep. Suddenly Jane felt a small trickle of anger that Stella should be so beautiful and so oblivious of Patrick's suffering.

They talked around the edges of things for ten minutes or so, and then Stella left. She suddenly stood up, saying, "I've got work to do. Thanks for the coffee. And the vodkas. Patrick doesn't approve of freebies for friends, so he'll probably charge you for them." She gave a casual wave to include them all and was gone. No kiss for Patrick. No See you later. Nothing.

Some love affair, thought Jane, longing to put out a hand and comfort Patrick, who was sitting, smiling but stiff, beside her.

Sriram finished his coffee, then said, "Jane, I must go. Thank you for an excellent lunch. And Patrick, it was a pleasure to meet you. And congratulations. Look, I'll leave you. You must have plenty of catching up to do."

When he'd gone, Patrick said, his voice dropping into a deeper, more relaxed tone, "I've been trying to work it out. That cannot be the Indian lover. Too old, though I must say very handsome. And anyway I know he's left."

"Not only left, but married his childhood sweetheart." Jane looked up, rueful.

Patrick returned her gaze, his eyes sympathetic, and said, "That's hard. I'm sorry."

"It's OK, funnily enough. Hurt like hell at the time. But I really think it was right for him. Even for me." She did not look at him, but concentrated on stirring her coffee, quite unnecessarily, since she did not take sugar.

At four o'clock Jane and Patrick were still sitting in the now almost empty restaurant and Jane had a good idea of Patrick's financial predicament. In essence the combination of the loss of the wine, the borrowings on the building, the astronomical wage bill, and Alastair's lack of control of kitchen costs was going to sink him. Patrick would have to sell more than half of the equity to pay back the loans. It would mean working for someone else, but there was no other way out.

Jane said, knowing the answer, "Why can't I buy the equity?" She leaned forward and fixed her eyes on Patrick's, willing him to hear her out. "You shouldn't let some boring male pride prevent you taking up a decent business offer. I could buy whatever shares you want to sell and then you can buy me out again gradually. It would be purely business."

Patrick put his hand over her wrist and said, "Jane, darling. The answer is *no*. You are the most generous creature God ever put on earth, but you are also the very last person I would let bail me out, boring male pride or not. It's no go."

She knew he meant it, and they moved onto Alastair's new job. Patrick said, "The truth is I encouraged him because it is an elegant way out for both of us. He is a wonderful cook, but he's no bloody good at cost control. At Jane's it did not matter, partly because we were posh, but mostly because it was small enough for me to keep his nose to the gross profit. But the head chef of a place this size and this busy has to be more cost controller than cook." Patrick's gaze circled the room. Without pleasure, thought Jane.

"What about the manager? Jonty, is it? Is he really taking you to court?"

"He is. He can't get me on unfair dismissal because he's been with us less than two years, so he's claiming breach of contract. He might well win too, because how can I prove that he had his hand in the waiters' tronc? The waiters are not going to stand up and be counted." Patrick's tone was expressionless. The bounce has gone out of him, thought Jane.

"Why not, if he's cheating them?"

"Because they don't want the taxman to get wind of any tronc at all. Service is included and they are meant to declare any *petit tronc* they get on top. In a restaurant like this that's not to be sniffed at. And anyway his contract doesn't say he must put his tips into the pool."

"But that can't be all? Fiddling tips?"

"No, of course not." Patrick frowned into his coffee cup. "The truth is he is not a nice guy. He's a bully. His idea of staff motivation is a kick up the backside. And since it works up to a point, I probably have a pretty weak case."

Jane looked at her ex-husband squarely and said, "I agree. And, if you want the advice of a lawyer, albeit not an employment one, you should settle."

"I agree, but I can't afford to. His lawyers are going for £65,000. A full year's wages, plus tips."

Jane knew it was useless to renew her offer of help. Patrick's matter-of-fact resignation distressed her.

He broke the silence, saying, "OK, that's me. Now for the Jane update. Tell me." Jane could see him doing his familiar trick of shaking off gloom and being cheerful. "Things must be good. You look the picture of success. And Sally tells me you have been holidaying in the Shires."

She told him about her equity partnership, her falling off Cherry (omitting her childish need for his presence) and subsequent sojourn in the country. As she talked, she ran her fingers absent-mindedly up and down the water tumbler and Patrick noticed that she wasn't wearing nail polish. She always used to wear it, he thought, even if it was the see-through stuff.

She told him of John's offer, and that she might just take it. He looked up, astonished.

"I don't believe it. You'll never leave Chalkers. Especially now you've made it to the top. It's what you always wanted."

She laughed. "I know. It's not logical. Typical female inconsistency, you'll say." Then, more seriously, she went on, "But now I've finally got there, I feel flat. It isn't any different from before, except I now have even more meetings to go to. Not interesting ones about cases. Ridiculous ones about the cost of photocopying paper and whether we should have a Mission Statement, and whether the turnover growth is half a percent below plan."

"But, darling, you must expect that. You're now responsible for the partnership's business, not just for your own work." The "darling" had slipped out, a relic from the past. Patrick wondered for a second if she'd react but she appeared not to have noticed. Perhaps everyone called her darling. He concentrated on what he was meant to be saying, and continued, "Don't you quite enjoy that? The business side?" He signaled for more coffee. Jane deliberately did not look at her watch. She didn't want to go.

She replied, "No, I find it boring. And I'm not good at it. I just want to agree to everything so I can get back to my desk. I *resent* partnership meetings. And Giles is *so* pompous and slow." She was silent for a moment, and he waited for her. "But it's not just that. I don't know. I'm not even enjoying the work as much as I used to. So much of it is just helping the big guys get one over each other, or more often, over the little guys. Sometimes I want to shout at clients, 'Why don't you just go away and run an honest business, and stop running in here looking for tax loopholes or ways to stop your rivals trading, or inventing sky-high damages for nonexistent infringements of something or other.' "

She was obviously not through yet, and Patrick waited while she considered the question and swiveled her silver bracelet—one he'd given her, he remembered, on a holiday in Corfu—around and around her wrist. Finally she shrugged, and looking up with a lame smile, said, "And I just so loved being with Lucy and John. I started reading Thackeray and Trollope again. And riding—though that ended in tears."

"You could go back to riding in Richmond Park. You used to go, what, twice a week, when we were first married." Jane had a sudden picture of them both rising at 5 a.m., she pulling on her jodhpurs as he blundered into the kitchen to make coffee before setting off for New Covent Garden or the meat market. She remembered the exhilaration of cantering through the park on a sturdy little polo pony, the beauty of the morning light, the spotted deer in the trees.

I'm remembering happiness, she thought, and found herself saying, "We were happy then, weren't we?" She hadn't meant to sound wistful.

"We were."

Suddenly she asked, "Are you happy now? I mean with Stella? I know the business is giving you grief."

"Frankly, no."

"Why not? She's stunning."

"Isn't she?" Patrick looked proud. And pleased that Jane should recognize Stella's beauty. But then his face took on some of that battered look she'd noticed when he arrived. He shook his head. "Trouble is, I'm too old and restrictive for her. I don't believe in free spirits, going with the flow, personal space and all that crap."

"Oh, dear," said Jane, feeling for him. But she also felt a small involuntary bubble of pleasure.

Once again Patrick determinedly swung the conversation back to Jane, saying, "I just can't see you in the country." He smiled at her as one might at a child who says she is going to be a princess when she grows up. "A weekend cottage with a pony maybe, but living out of London? What about the cultural high life? The exhibitions, restaurants, theaters? What about designer clothes and Nicky Clarke hairdos?"

He was ribbing her. She didn't mind. In fact she liked it.

"Banbury isn't the Outer Hebrides. And anyway I've given most of that up."

"You can't have. Look at you. If that's not designer gear and Nicky Clarke then I'm no judge of these things." He waved a hand at her light gray jacket, with one large silver button just visible at the bottom of the deep collarless V of the neckline. The V was filled in with a soft-pink silk shirt, its feminine color countermanded by its mannish collar and gray spotted tie.

She smiled, pleased. "You *are* no judge of these things. The hair gets washed in the shower. Though I confess to still getting it cropped at vast expense. And this jacket was bought for me by Lucy at Next, and the tie comes from Paddington Station's Tie Rack."

"I'm impressed. And what about the twice monthly theaters and monthly operas?" Patrick leaned back, feeling more relaxed than he had in weeks.

"I stopped going when Rajiv was here. He hated what he called trailing in my wake, and he hated me paying."

"Poor guy." Patrick grinned, teasing. "I know how he feels."

But Jane took him seriously and, leaning forward, she reached for his arm: "Oh, Patrick. Don't say that. One of the things that was so wonderful about you is you did *not* have any of those boring male hang-ups. You never minded my making more than you, did you? Sally swears you did, but I refuse to believe it."

He put his hand over hers on his arm and said, "No, I never minded your being rich, and independent, and the best at what you did. I just wanted you to spend it differently, I suppose. On, let's say, a pub in the country, a nice big farmhouse behind it and four children's school fees." He smiled broadly at her, then stood up, saying, "They'll be wanting to lay up. Darling Jane. Be happy. It was lovely to see you."

It was only when she was in the taxi that she realized he'd not given her a bill. No wonder he was going broke, she thought. She shut her eyes. She was tired to the bone, but curiously happy.

TWENTY-TWO

Stella's voice rose. "Patrick, I'm not going to total the thing. I've never trashed a car yet."

"I'm sorry, sweetheart," said Patrick, "but it's Jane's car, not mine. I'd feel tacky lending it to you without her knowing."

Stella put her glass down with a little bang, the vodka splashing up the ice-cubes.

"So I'm tacky then? Not squeaky-clean like your precious Jane?" Her eyes flashed at him, accusing.

Patrick sighed. "No. I did not say that. I said *I'd* feel tacky if I lent you Jane's car."

Stella swung around the kitchen table to come up close to Patrick. He thought how lovely she looked, like a pre-Raphaelite angel, all orange hair and flushed skin. But her beauty did not stir him. She said, "I don't understand you. Why don't you give that damn gas-guzzler back to her and buy a decent car that you won't be a wimp about me driving? It's ridiculous hanging on to your ex's old heap."

Patrick was stung by both her tone and her dismissal of his beloved car. As he turned away, walking to the door, he said, "Stella, if you want a car, buy a car."

Stella at once ran after him, face alight, arms open. "Oh, Patrick. Do you mean it? Really? You darling . . ."

"Woah, Stella." He turned, forestalling her hug. His voice was dry. "I didn't say I would buy you a car. I said, 'Buy a car.' '

Stella froze, arms still aloft. Then she dropped them to her sides and said, her voice soft, eyes pleading, "Oh. I'm sorry, honey. I thought for a moment . . . But sure, I understand."

248

Oh, God, thought Patrick, is she 100 percent manipulative or 100 percent spoilt? Or both? He knew his role was now to give in as he'd done more times than he could count. But he felt too old, too weary, too detached. Besides, he couldn't afford to buy her a car. He turned away again and walked out of the flat and down to his office.

He sat at his desk feeling beleaguered. The business was trading well, but interest payments took most of the profit, and credit card commissions took the rest. Who am I working for here, he thought?

And things with Stella were not wonderful. She'd sworn there was nothing between her and Franco, and he believed her. Franco seemed even less her type than he was. But he didn't totally trust her. She hated to be questioned about her movements and he'd learned that a simple enquiry about her day could get a sharp "What's this? The inquisition?" or a bored "Nothing mind-blowing" as she picked up a magazine or turned on the TV.

Twenty minutes later he heard the diesel put-put of a black cab below his window. He swiveled his chair and looked down to see Stella reaching for the cab door. As she opened it, she turned to look up at his window, but she didn't wave. She ducked her head and climbed in. She was wearing the pale velvet designer dungarees she'd worn the day they'd met, but with a black polo-neck, black boots and a kookie black hat without a crown. He could see her bright hair, smooth over the crown and exploding each side of the hat brim.

Since my restaurant taxi account receives such faithful patronage, he thought, I wonder why she wanted the car.

Stella didn't reappear at all that evening and Patrick was vaguely anxious. Maybe he'd been too hard on her. He wished he was rich enough to indulge her, keep her happy and loving and smiling. But he knew it wasn't just money.

At 9:30 the next morning he walked the two blocks to the side street of garages where he kept the car. Hiring a lock-up was expensive, but it preserved his hubcaps. He lifted the up-

and-over door and then stood stock still, registering the empty space. His first thought was that the car had been stolen. Then the truth whammed in and a sudden torrent of anger filled him. Stella had taken his car. Last night. The taxi had been a blind.

He strode back to the Third Man and mounted the stairs two at a time. He opened the kitchen corner cupboard and checked the line of keys hanging on the rack. The spare keys for the garage and the Mercedes were missing.

Grim-faced, he dialed Stella's mews cottage, but only got her blithe machine message. "I'm out. If it's fun, please call again. If it's not, give me a break."

He knew she was seldom in the office before lunch, but he tried her private line at the *Dispatch*.

After three rings a male voice with an Australian accent answered. "Features. Food and Drink."

Patrick asked for Stella. There was a short pause, then: "Stella doesn't work here anymore. Can I help?"

Patrick frowned, mystified. "What do you mean she doesn't work there? She's the restaurant critic."

"*Was*, mate. As of today, I'm the restaurant writer. Phil Hanborough. Can I do anything? . . . Are you there? Hullo?"

"Er . . . Yes. Sorry. Look. Are you sure? She didn't say anything to me . . . Can you tell me when she left?"

"Yeah, 'bout an hour ago."

"Do you know why?"

"You a friend of hers? You'd better ask her, mate."

Patrick put the telephone down with the unreal sensation that he was in a play, and the silly conversation he'd just had was fiction. He shook his head as though to clear it. Stella had nicked his car, left her job and disappeared. Bit like Silvino.

He was no longer angry. Just weary. And puzzled. He wondered if he should report the missing car to the police, but decided to give it till the evening.

He cancelled his appointment with the crockery importer in Wimbledon, and spent the morning in the office. He found he was curiously unworried. She'll turn up, he thought.

250

She did, at 11:30. She was still wearing the dungarees, but had shed the hat. She was unmade-up and pale, her hair looked unbrushed. She closed the office door behind her and slumped into the chair opposite his desk.

"I expect you know I took the car?" She spoke dully, looking at the window behind Patrick's head.

"I do."

Her eyes flickered to his, tinged with hope. "Don't you mind?" she asked.

"Yes, I mind."

Stella put her head down on the desk, cradled by her arms. Patrick could not see if she was crying, or pretending to or trying to. God, he thought, what a cynic this woman has turned me into. He reached over and put a hand on her shoulder. She looked up briefly. The tears were real.

Her voice came muffled through her arms, and in jerks. "You are going to be seriously pissed off with me."

"I am already. So try me." Patrick's voice was kind, but he wasn't as moved by her tears as he usually was. I'm immunized, he thought, looking at the untidy mass of hair.

Stella said, "I've dented the rear wing, and the badge was stolen."

Patrick said nothing. The car could be fixed. He didn't mind the damage to it as much as that she'd taken it.

Stella straightened up, and looked directly at Patrick. "And I've been sleeping with Oberon, Franco's chef."

Patrick absorbed this information in silence, waiting for the expected shaft of pain. But what he felt was a kind of subdued sadness.

She said, "But it's over now."

Patrick stood up and looked out of the window, seeing nothing. Finally, he said, "Why is it over now? Who is next on the list?" Then he thought it was a petty remark, and pointless. He knew, with sudden certainty, that he and Stella were over. What did it matter if there was yet another stubble-faced youth waiting in line?

251

She said, "There's no one. Only you. I had to tell you." She looked so solemn and waif-like it would move a hangman to tears, thought Patrick. But I'm all out of tears.

He said, "Why? You've managed not to tell me up till now. And it's been weeks, if not months. Hasn't it?"

"Oh, Patrick, you don't understand. I didn't mean . . ." She stopped, feeling his lack of sympathy. "OK. The fact is that you would have known pretty soon anyway. Half of Fleet Street know by now. Some thing's happened. And now I've been sacked, and it turns out Oberon can't take the heat and he's dumped me. And I don't know what I'm going to do." She dropped her head into her arms again. This time Patrick knew her sobs were genuine.

He came around to her side of the desk and said to her rounded, heaving back, "Stella, I don't understand a word you are saying. But I do know one thing. And that is that you and I are finally washed up."

Stella lifted her head, her eyes wide and tear-filled, the skin around them reddening. She shook her head, denying it, but he wouldn't let her speak.

He went on, "It's as much my fault as yours. We come from different planets, you and I. But I can't stand the heat of the kitchen either." He opened the door to Sandra's office, and said, "Sandra, could you get Stella a taxi? 'As directed.' She'll tell the driver."

At 1 p.m. Sandra came to find Patrick in the restaurant. She found him talking to the barman and drew him a little way down the bar. Patrick could tell by her expression of matronly concern that more bad news was coming his way. He said, "What is it, Sandra? More suppliers screaming for payment?"

"No. I'm sorry to catch you down here, but the *Standard* are telephoning every ten minutes. They've got a story about Stella being sacked from the *Dispatch*, and they want a comment from you."

Patrick smiled cheerfully at her. The *Standard* was the least

252

of his problems. He said, "Well, they can't have it. Just keep saying no comment, no comment. It's tough to keep up, but if you say it ten times, they will give up, I promise."

The late edition of the paper had the story, and it explained a lot.

CELEBRITY SEX ROMP LEADS TO SACK

Stella, the *Dispatch*'s star food-critic, is tonight out of her highly paid job, after being summarily dismissed for using the editor's office for sexual frolics. She and trendy TV chef Oberon (presenter of the Caribbean Cooking series *Oberon's Magic*) were discovered cavorting naked on editor Robert McFisk's sofa in the small hours of this morning.

A *Dispatch* spokesperson said, "I can confirm that Ms Richmond's contract has been terminated for gross misconduct. The company will be taking no further action."

Stella, speaking from her fashionable mews cottage, said, "I guess Robert McFisk has never had an illicit **** on someone else's sofa, or he wouldn't be sacking the most read restaurant critic in the country. It's a seriously bad move for the paper. But it might be a great career move for me. Who knows? I'm open to offers."

Oberon's employer at Franco's, where the Caribbean-born cook is also head chef, said, "Oberon is back in the kitchen, and he's cooking, albeit with a hangover. He regrets an evening of madness with Stella Richmond, and has nothing further to add."

The red-headed bar babe has had her arm through that of restaurateur and wine buff Patrick Chambers for several months, and lives, at least some of the time, in his penthouse over his restaurant, the Third Man, in Hammersmith. Mr. Chambers was unavailable for comment.

Patrick's first reaction was a kind of cringing mortification. Stella's infidelity was bad enough. To have it broadcast in "sex scandal" format shriveled his spirit. And they'd got his name in there, and as the duped lover. So much for no comment. Also he was embarrassed at the word "penthouse." But then he told himself nothing was staler than yesterday's newspaper. It was vanity to mind.

He read the piece again, and this time felt a mixture of admiration for Stella's gutsy riposte and distaste for the tone of it. He flung the paper into the wastepaper basket as the telephone rang.

"That Patrick?" The voice was deep and Caribbean.

"Yes, Patrick Chambers here."

"I'm Oberon. You'll have read 'bout me and Stella in the *Standard*."

"Yes."

"Man, I just wanted to say I'm real sorry. For the business with Stella. That is some dangerous lady. But you know that yourself, right?"

Patrick smiled in spite of himself. He said, "I certainly do."

"Well, that's not the reason I'm callin'. The reason is I want to pay to fix up yo' car. It was me driving it, and we were high on stuff, an' shit-full of booze. Should never have been behind the wheel. Tha's all."

"*You* were driving it?"

"Fraid so. I thought it was Stella's, till I hit a bollard. Then she told me."

Patrick thought for a minute, realizing that if he had to sign a claim now, he'd have to say that Oberon had been driving and had been drunk. Which would invalidate it. He said, "OK. I see. Thanks. I'll send the bill to you then. It's one wing and the badge. Although my insurance will cover the badge, I guess. Do you want to see an estimate?"

"No, man. Jus' send it. I'll pay it. The badge too. I owe you."

Patrick warmed to the man. He asked, "Tell me one thing. Why were you in the *Dispatch* office? Why not at Stella's house? Why live so dangerously?"

"That lady likes danger, I reckon," Oberon answered. "We went to some restaurant miles into Essex—that's why she wanted your car—and then we stopped at Canary Wharf to pick up some stuff she'd left at the office. I wanted to see inside a newspaper office. And then, on her desk, was a bottle of vintage port from some sucker wants a good write-up. So we drank it on the editor's sofa. Bad idea."

"I'll say," said Patrick. But as he put the telephone down, he had a wry, twisted thought: maybe it's not all bad.

TWENTY-THREE

"You cannot do this to Chalkers. You owe us some loyalty, Jane. We have gone to enormous lengths to accommodate you." Giles Charteris spoke through a rigid face.

Jane looked at her senior partner across his large leather-topped mahogany desk, legal books in glass cases behind him, half-moon spectacles in one hand. He looks as if he's sitting for his boardroom portrait, she thought.

"Oh, Giles. Don't be silly. You haven't had to accommodate me at all. You let me buy in because you needed me. And you are cross now because you still do."

"You are the first female equity partner this firm has ever had, and I went out on a limb for you."

He sounded almost querulous, and for a second Jane felt sorry for him. He probably thinks finally withdrawing his objections to me *was* going out on a limb. But she said, "Oh, that's rubbish, Giles. You did no such thing. You made me an equity partner because it was in the firm's interest to do so."

Giles changed tack. "But it is preposterous to quit after two months. Surely you see that." He put on his glasses, dropping his chin so he could see over the top of them.

"Five."

"All right, five months. What is that in the history of a firm that has been here since 1900? I would have thought that counted for something. That we were prepared to break with tradition . . ."

Jane began to feel the old irritation blossoming in her gut, but she kept her voice devoid of it. She said, "Giles, do calm

256

down. Chalkers must have been about the last firm of solicitors in England to let women in. It was about bloody time. But all that is irrelevant. You can take in another woman if equal opportunities have suddenly got to you after a hundred years."

"I should think it extremely unlikely that we'll ever risk another one after the way you are behaving. You should at least be concerned about the sisterhood or whatever you feminists call each other, shouldn't you?"

Jane burst out laughing, and replied, "If you mean the women lawyers here, I doubt if the sisterhood will mind. If Chalkers don't promote the women lawyers, they'll go somewhere that will. It's nice of you to be concerned for them, but I think they'll forgive me not being the perfect role-model."

"I've never heard of anything like it. A partner selling out after five months. It is absolute betrayal."

Jane said peaceably, "Giles, would you be in such a paddy if you had another marine specialist up your sleeve?"

Giles opened his mouth to protest, but Jane raised her hand to stop him and continued, "Don't worry. Rhetorical question. Look, this is getting us nowhere. I'll give your secretary the paperwork, and you can decide who buys me out."

She stood up, picking up her handbag from the floor and the folder in front of her. Then she paused and said, "I am sorry, Giles. I've had a lot of good experience here, and I've enjoyed it. Thank you for that."

She went out quickly, before Giles's middle-class good manners forced him to be polite, or his natural instincts forced him to be rude.

Things moved fast after that. She handed over her cases to her partners or juniors, and left Chalkers at the end of March. There were no official farewells, but she bought her team a few bottles of bubbly in a City wine bar, and they all promised each other, with emphasis born of doubt, that they would keep in touch.

She bought a new car, a boring Subaru with a hatchback,

good for the garden center, wet wellies and maybe, someday, humping hay bales and pony nuts.

She took a month off to find somewhere to live, and ended by renting a pretty stone-tiled cottage on the edge of Long Compton, a fifteen minute drive from Banbury, and ten minutes from Lucy and John. It had a paddock and a derelict garden, and a big kitchen that doubled as dining room.

She put the Hammersmith flat up for sale, and got the asking price from the first couple who looked at it. Tom, convinced his sister was hopeless with money, advised reneging on the sale and raising the price—if it sold that fast the price was obviously too low. But Jane said she'd agreed the deal and she liked the purchasers. And she wanted to get on with the revolution in her life.

The first night she slept in the cottage, she put out her bedside light feeling pleased with herself. The quiet of the country was thick around her, but friendly. Once she was disturbed by Benedicat, yowling at his unfamiliar surroundings, and once by an owl hooting, and at first light she woke to a burst of birdsong. Shuffling pleasurably into her duvet, she drifted back to sleep, thinking what an inept name "dawn chorus" was: more like the cacophony of an orchestra tuning up.

By mid afternoon she had put everything in its place except the books. She was standing amid piles of them, roughly sorted into subject matter or author, when the back doorbell buzzed.

Puzzled, she went through to the kitchen. Only Lucy and John knew her well enough to come to the back door, and they were not due until tomorrow, when they were coming to lunch.

She opened the door to find young Nathaniel there, looking anxious.

"Hullo, Nat. How nice to see you. How did you find me?"

"Mum told me."

"Well, come on in, you can help me make serious decisions about which books to junk, and which to keep."

"I . . . I can't come in . . ." He had been standing to the side

258

of the door, with his hands behind his back. Now he stepped aside and lifted his hand, to show that he was holding the reins of a bridle. Jane stepped out of the door and followed his gaze. Cherry was contentedly eating the hedge.

"Heavens, Nat. Don't let her eat that. It's probably poisonous."

"No, it's not. It's hawthorn."

He sounded cross, and Jane said, "What's up, Nat? You look worried."

"No, I'm not. Well, yes, I suppose I am. Mum would be livid if she knew I'd come to you, but you see I thought you could keep Cherry and Holly in your paddock, and look after them for us, and then Mum wouldn't have to worry, and we could go riding together in the evenings." He stopped suddenly and Jane opened her mouth to intervene, but he restarted in a rush. "David never rides Cherry, and you like her, and we can't separate her from Holly, and in the autumn David's going to Eton. And then Dad will say we have to sell . . ."

"Nat, Nat, stop. Let's put Cherry in the paddock, and then you can come in and have a Coke and we'll discuss it."

They had to tie the paddock gate shut with a piece of rope, but the fences seemed pony-proof. They improvised a water bucket with Jane's Habitat bread bin.

"She'll kick it over and dent it," said Nat.

"That's OK. I never liked it anyway."

Nat gave Jane a look of pure idolatry.

Within a month Jane had changed her life. She worked at Appleby and Atherson's, with interest and satisfaction, from nine to five, and brought very little work home with her. She spent hours prising lumps of Cotswold stone out of what would one day be the herbaceous border, and clearing the pony shed of old bath tubs and rusting corrugated iron. She found the unthinking labor of such activities satisfying, and she'd fall into bath and bed with the uncomplicated content of physical exhaustion.

She agreed to have her name added to the church flower rota. She wasn't sure she believed in God, but it seemed churlish to refuse, and anyway she liked doing flowers. Where the flowers were to come from when it was her turn was another thing. God will have to put up with cow parsley and buttercups, she thought. She joined the Ramblers' Association with the vague plan, so far unrealized, that she might join them for walks and make local friends.

As the evenings got longer, Nat came riding with her after school. With a bit of help from Jane, and a lot from his mother, he'd escaped the threat of boarding-school, and he was a different boy. His happiness was infectious, and Jane felt almost as young and bold as he was as they galloped flat out through muddy lanes and hurtled over logs and fences.

But mostly Jane rode alone, getting up at first light to crunch across the frosted paddock and catch Cherry. She would put a pair of secateurs in her pocket and come back with an armful of pussy willow, or the still sticky buds of chestnut, or just-bursting blackthorn blossom and stick them in the bread bin—which had survived its short duty as horse bucket and now did service as flower vase—in the sitting room.

At first Cherry didn't care for branches tickling her neck and sides, but she got used to it and soon gave up fretting in favor of walking out eagerly, good as gold. Jane found being alone on horseback in the chill mornings exhilarating, and also deeply satisfying. The early sunlight washed the soft Cotswold stone of walls and houses and highlighted the even lines of frost along ridge and furrow. It was beautiful.

If Cherry's behavior permitted it, Jane would allow her mind to freewheel, to dwell on her Indian adventure, on her marriage to Patrick, her half-formed hopes for the future. Indulgent self-absorption, her father would have said. She remembered sitting on the roof terrace of Amber Fort in Rajasthan, looking down on the floating garden, and thinking how peaceful life must have been for women who knew their place in society, who had been brought up to be wives and lovers. Maybe, she thought, happiness consists of deciding where one's rightful place is, and going for it. I think my rightful place might be here, in the country, with a country practice, an Aga in the kitchen, and a vegetable plot to keep me busy.

But her mental picture was not of herself hoeing the carrots or picking slugs off the spinach leaves. It was of a hammock under the apple tree in the overgrown orchard, with a baby lying in it, kicking its fat legs in the air, confident in the soppy devotion of Patrick on one side and herself on the other.

Jane marveled at her emotional turn around. Rajiv in India had been intoxicating, irresistible. But the sober reality of London had destroyed him like sun dispersing mist. She missed the passion and the sex, but she did not want her Indian lover back.

Until she'd fallen off Cherry, and had needed Patrick like a child at boarding school needs its mother, she had told herself that any desire for Patrick was simple affection, or dog-in-the-manger jealousy of Stella.

But now she realized that what she had been doing over the last few months was turning herself into the woman Patrick had, she suspected, always wanted. She had given up the high-powered job, the international traveling, the French farmhouse. She'd given up London and her old haunts of theaters, exhibitions, restaurants.

But more than Patrick, she wanted a baby. She told herself it was neurotic. But the ache, the sickness, the yearning for a child would not go away. Or not for long.

She made another date with Sriram, and this time they met in the Hampstead house. While he leaned against the carved mantelpiece, elegant as ever, Gopal fluttered about, fussing like a mother hen. As Jane sat down on the brocaded French sofa, he said, "Jane, what on earth have you done to your hair? It looks as if it's been cut by the village barber. Has it?"

Jane, defensive, answered, "Well, yes, in fact it has. Except she's a barberess. And comes to your house for £15."

Gopal walked behind the sofa in his quick, waddling gait. He took a few strands of Jane's hair in his beringed fingers and dropped them with disdain, saying, "And it looks it. Before you go home today, you had better go to your London hairdresser and see if he can do anything with it."

Twisting her head as she followed Gopal's petulant progress to the marble-topped console on which stood an ice-bucket and glasses, Jane said, "Sorry, Gopal, but I would not dare. First of all you don't walk into Nicky Clarke's without an appointment, and anyway I'd get ticked off worse by him than by you for village barbering."

"And you'd deserve it." He poured champagne into gilt-stemmed champagne saucers, elaborately engraved. He brought one to Jane, saying, "Sriram disapproves of these glasses. But you will accept one, dear Jane, I am sure."

"I'd love one," she said, reaching for it. "My wine-buff husband would disapprove too, but I'd drink champagne out of a teacup." It occurred to her that in London she'd drunk champagne all the time, at Jane's, with Patrick, in the City. She doubted if she'd had a glass since she'd left Chalkers. She said, "Champagne is a real treat these days. And the charm of £200 haircuts has lately lost its appeal. I seem to need that kind of money just to keep the ponies fed. And to buy compost and topsoil and sharp sand for the jungle that passes as my garden."

"Good God, Jane, what on earth is sharp sand?" Gopal took a step back, his face a comic mixture of confusion and disgust.

Jane laughed. "Grit to make the soil drain. You must come and see my gardening works. I'm very proud of them. You will be impressed."

"No, he won't," said Sriram. He looked with affection at Gopal. "Gopal is allergic to the country. Full of mud and things that bite. But I will come. Is it to be colorful cottagey, or Gertrude Jekyll color coded?"

"I don't know yet. Right now it is thistle and nettles and

couch grass. I've started a death-by-weedkiller program to the outrage of young Nat, Lucy's son, who thinks I'm personally polluting the whole Thames Valley water table."

Gopal brought them a large baroque silver tray of smoked salmon and brown bread, arranged with skill and style: the salmon in soft translucent waves on one side of the dish, the bread, a mixture of pale rye and seeded granary, cut in medium-thick even slices and buttered to the edges, perfectly marshalled in overlapping curves, on the other. In the middle were two limes, cut in half, and a small silver peppermill.

Jane's mouth watered. She was suddenly ravenous.

Gopal left them to return to the office. He wanted to look at a new consignment of carpets, he said. "I'll pick out a little one for your little cottage, Jane."

"It had better have a little price then. I'm no longer the millionaire high-flyer, you know."

When he'd gone, Sriram sat beside Jane on the sofa with the smoked salmon on the black marble coffee table in front of them. Jane said, folding a slice of salmon into a sandwich of rye, "I'll never understand Gopal. He so loves fancy things, and yet when he serves food, it is so simple and straightforward and delicious. You would think his nature would demand radishes carved into roses and cucumber twists all over the place."

"Yes, it's odd. Gopal has the taste of a magpie, but the taste buds of a gourmet."

Jane laughed and said, "You won't let him buy me a carpet, will you?"

"Don't worry. I'll choose it."

When they'd finished the smoked salmon and drunk a bottle of Montagny, Sriram came to the point.

"I've had my agent look into the possibility of your bailing out Patrick, and you could certainly do it, but not without his knowing."

"Why not?"

"Because he owes the bank over half a million pounds and

it's the interest on that that's eating up his profits. He is looking for someone to buy half the business, so he can pay back the bank. He would not agree to that someone being you, would he?"

"No." Jane shook her head with finality. "But why can't I hide behind someone else, some supposed keen backer of restaurants?"

"Because Patrick is not a fool. He is going to want to know someone very well before he parts with any shares. He needs to trust his partner."

Jane was silent for a minute or two, her brow furrowed. Then she asked, "Patrick didn't give Stella any stake in the Third Man?"

"No, which is just as well if they've now split up. He seems to have given her *carte blanche* to spend his money, but has never given her any shares. One hundred percent of the Third Man is owned by Patrick, which currently means one hundred percent of the debts of an over-borrowed business."

"Poor Patrick. Sriram, there's got to be some way I can help, surely?" She looked into Sriram's face, her eyes earnest.

"Well, there is of course," said Sriram, leaning back, and crossing his long legs.

"How then?"

"Do you think Patrick would sell out completely, for, say, a million?"

"Of course he would! Didn't you see how ill and trapped he looked? But I haven't got a million."

"Ah, but I have. We could do it together." He smiled at her, his eyes crinkling into folds at the edges.

Jane's eyes were wide. "But Sriram, you don't want to run a restaurant. And nor do I, for God's sake."

Sriram stood up to get a cigar from the sideboard. He raised his eyes in enquiry, offering Jane one. She shook her head, impatient at the interruption.

Sriram said, "But Gopal does. Gopal is overexcited by the whole project. He wants to make it into the first Balti house with Thai and Chinese touches."

"*What*! I don't believe it."

"It's true. And you know Gopal has an unerring instinct for what the public wants. He has two Balti houses in Birmingham, you know. They make a lot of money."

"Gopal? A restaurateur?" She said, for the second time, "I don't believe it."

"Ah, I assure you, my dear Jane. Gopal may look like something out of a pantomime, but under that gaudy waistcoat beats a most businesslike heart."

"But who would run it? I can't see Gopal . . ."

"Oh, he has more relatives in the restaurant business than a dog has fleas. He'll staff it in no time."

Patrick was intrigued by the fat shiny Mr. Gopal Patel. His rings flashed as he talked, and he laughed a lot. His small fast steps gave him a floating gait, and he seemed to swirl around the brasserie as if on a magic carpet. He exclaimed with unaffected pleasure at the gleaming modern kitchens and unabashed horror at the Aavee sculpture.

"I hope that is not included in the price," he said, waving a merry hand at it.

"I haven't said I'll sell at all yet."

"But I do hope you will. I do hope so. You will not regret it. I am sure."

When Gopal had gone, Patrick retreated to his office and stood looking out on the Goldhawk Road, feeling oddly detached. He had said he needed to do some sums, speak to his accountant, consider the offer.

But he knew that he was going to accept it. He had known for weeks now that he'd have to sell at least half the business, which would mean having a partner interfering, or an investor breathing down his neck. At least this way he could get right out and start again. Clean. Without a partner. Without a backer. Without complications. Without Stella.

He tasted this thought, mouthing it tentatively. And found a mixture of sadness and relief.

Then he thought, and without Jane. He had a sudden return of his old dream of a country pub and a brood of children.

No chance of that, he told himself briskly. But you could have the country pub. Get away from the Jontys of this world snorting coke in the staff room, punters claiming to have booked tables when they haven't, ad agencies not paying their bills for six months, Hammersmith residents complaining at the late-night noise. You could have what you've always wanted. A straightforward neighborhood pub and restaurant, for local likeable people, who pay their bills on the night, behave like human beings and want simple food and sound wine.

"Yes," he said aloud, punching his right fist into his left palm. "Yes."

TWENTY-FOUR

Jane clicked her In Box. Rajiv to Jane, it said. The e-mail fluttered into existence. It read:

> Ha! Bet you never thought I could track you down in deepest Oxfordshire. Chalkers gave me your e-mail address. Jane, I don't want to rekindle old passions, or disturb any liaisons/ love affairs or marriages, but I can't be in London and not see you. I'm arriving on Tuesday, and staying 'til Friday, trying to prize some documents out of the British Museum for a Sanskrit exhibition in Delhi. Will be at the Hotel Russell. Free Weds or Thurs evening. Rajiv.

Jane looked at her computer screen, and found herself smiling. She was surprised at how carefree she felt. Her heart did not race. She did not feel sick. She just felt glad. It would be good to see Rajiv.

But she was nervous when she arrived at Wagamama. She had thought the choice of restaurant curious. Jane had never been there before and she felt too old to be in a queue of young students and tourists. She also felt faint irritation that she should have to stand in the street, letting the queue to the basement shuffle past her, because Rajiv had not arrived.

Then suddenly he was there, a loose arm around her neck, his cheek against hers in a hug. Oh, my God, she thought, he smells just the same. He was just as she remembered, but with the confidence and calm of the Indian Rajiv, not the depressed, gray, London Rajiv. Aquiline and tall, with his curious deep-set topaz eyes, he looked into her face, studying it with earnest care. He was wearing light trousers, a thin cotton shirt and soft leather shoes. He carried a slim leather bag on a long thin strap.

"Rajiv. Only you could look macho with a handbag."

"And only you could look so different and yet so wonderful. What have you done to yourself?"

"Do I look different? Must be the country life. I spend more time on a pony than I do on an airplane these days." She dismissed the compliment lightly, but she was glad he still found her attractive. His clean, familiar smell had triggered a wash of warm desire in her.

They joined the line and shuffled slowly down the stairs, their shoulders rubbing the once white walls, adding to the band of gray. It took twenty minutes before they were in the restaurant, seated side by side between total strangers. Roast duck, chopped through the bones into mouthful-sized chunks, emerald green spring onions and noodles, slithery and soft, steamed in large white bowls before them.

By then Jane was feeling relaxed and happy. "Rajiv, why are we in a fast-food noodle joint? I know you're an impoverished academic, but paper place-mats and bottled beer! Or do you want to be rid of me in thirty minutes?"

"Two reasons. First, the food's good." He poked his chopsticks into her bowl, expertly lifting a piece of glistening duck between them and deftly dipping it into the tiny saucer of soy. He put it into her mouth. "Isn't it?" She opened her mouth and took the duck. It was delicious, tender and succulent. She didn't know if Rajiv was flirting as well as feeding, if he felt what she felt.

She said, "And?"

"Second reason. I chose this place so that if you took one look at your erstwhile lover and wanted to flee, you could. But it's obvious I didn't have to worry. You're well and truly over me, aren't you?" He asked the question directly, neither demanding flattery nor expecting denial.

"Yes, I am. At first I couldn't forgive you, but in the end I had to admit you were right. And I'm glad now."

They ordered Stella Artois. Jane had hardly drunk beer since the Kingfishers in India. But tonight it felt right.

They talked with animation and real pleasure. Rajiv told her about his life: the flat in New Delhi; Meera, cheerful, undemanding, and attentive; the baby they were expecting; his and Meera's parents, who would spoil the child like a god; his job in Delhi, his prospects of being Curator of Manuscripts.

"But are you happy? Really happy?"

"Yes. I am doing work that is important, and I have a good life. Yes, I would say I'm happy. And you?"

"I'm certainly happier than I was at Chalkers. But I think that is just as much because I'm not dog-tired and oppressed by the work in my briefcase as anything. But no, I am not completely perfectly happy."

"What would make you 'completely, perfectly happy'?"

Jane sipped her beer, considering whether to tell him the truth. "A baby, I think. That is very unfeminist and boring of me, isn't it?"

"No, it's very feminine and understandable. Though dangerous."

"Dangerous? Why dangerous?"

"People love their children so much, and forever. It overtakes the love of wife or husband. I can feel it already, and our child is still only a kicking lump in Meera's belly. But it's a one-sided business. Children love their parents only as long as they're needed. Then, for the children, it's duty, not love."

Jane knew it was probably true. But it wasn't a message she wanted to hear.

When they emerged the air was soft and warm, more like summer than spring, and they wandered through the Bloomsbury streets, looking in art and music shop windows. They stopped outside an antiquarian bookshop, and peered at the texts and books in the window.

Suddenly Jane said, "Actually, I want a man too. I miss the sex."

Rajiv put his hands on her shoulders and turned her to face him.

"Is that an invitation?"

"It could be."

"Without morning-after regrets?"

"Do you mean am I still in love with you? I told you, no."

Rajiv said nothing and they walked on. But he stopped again almost immediately. He put both his arms right around her neck, holding her with her face pressed into his shoulder. She breathed in, her eyes shut, memories of Varanasi and Khajuraho flooding into her head, making her knees weak as water.

"Trouble is, darling Jane, I am still half in love with you. And I can't afford to fall right in again. It's too soon. You are still too much in the warp and weft of me."

Jane's first thought was, he's right, it would be the same for me. Then immediately it was overridden by a stronger thought: Oh, God, I don't care. I just want him to make love to me again. But what she actually said was: "Warp and weft. What an old-fashioned, very English phrase." Her voice was unusually low, but steady.

Rajiv unwound his arms, putting a little safe distance between them.

She said, "You are right. It's just that celibacy doesn't suit me really. It's very withering. And it's months since you left."

They walked on, the danger past. He said, "You mean there has been no one, not even a flirtation?"

"No, unless you count being kissed by a slightly drunk student in a train. Funny thing is, I've thought of that kiss a lot. He was a divine-looking boy."

Jane told him about her Christmas Eve encounter with the student Matthew, and Rajiv said, "You should take a younger lover. It would be wonderful for him, and you are made for love."

•   •   •

A month later, on a warm sunny day in May, Jane got out of her car in Blockley, and walked up to the little group of ramblers, feeling awkward. They were all in their fifties and sixties, and looked, Jane thought, as if they were setting off for the Himalayas. They wore anoraks, woolly hats and sturdy leather hiking boots. They carried merry-colored backpacks and some had stout sticks. They were in a loose huddle, oblivious of her approach, and she was tempted to get back into her car and go.

But she advanced, and spoke to the back of a bottle-green waxed jacket.

"Excuse me. Are you the Ramblers?"

The jacket spun around to reveal an open front with checked shirt, and above it, a smiling, lined face half obscured by a full gray beard and spectacles. "Spot on. We are. Are you joining us?"

"Well, yes, I hope to. I rang the organizer. Jean Letts? Is she here?"

"Not yet. But she's coming, we hope. She's leading the walk, so she'd better." He laughed, a picture of bonhomie.

At that moment a Volkswagen Beetle drove up, with three people in it. The curly-haired driver, a woman of fifty or so, sprang out, calling cheerfully, "Sorry we're late. Matt's fault. He wouldn't get out of bed."

Striding forward, she put out her hand and said, "You must be Jane Chambers. How nice to have you with us."

She looked anxiously at Jane's feet. "Have you brought any walking boots?"

"No, should I have?" Jane was bare-headed, and wore sneakers, T-shirt and shorts. She had a jumper tied around her waist, but carried nothing. "I thought I'd wear sneakers, it's such a nice day."

A male voice called from the Volkswagen, "Sneakers are fine. Mother bangs on about the Ramblers' rules, but take no notice." Jane turned to see a young man untangling his leg from a dangling seatbelt as he emerged from the rear seat of the car.

Shaking his foot clear (sneaker-clad, she noticed) he slammed the car door and turned round. For a moment she was confused. She knew this boy. Then she remembered, and felt the blood mount to her face. It was her Christmas Eve train companion.

Mrs. Letts, not waiting for her son, who was now rooting around in the car boot, led them off at a brisk pace, up the steep rough path into open fields above the village. Jane followed, wondering if Matthew had recognized her.

He caught them up after ten minutes or so, and fitted his stride to Jane's.

"I hadn't put you down as a rambler," he said.

"Nor I you," she replied.

"Oh, I come occasionally to humor my mum. She's the local Queen Bee Rambler. She thinks I'm a complete layabout, and she's mostly right. So when I need Brownie points, I come on a walk. Finding you here is a real bonus." He smiled at her with open pleasure.

"Why do you need Brownie points?" asked Jane. "Still in debt, or still failing to do any work?" She knew she should disapprove of Matthew. He was so obviously feckless, and so sure of his charm. But he *was* charming.

"Both, I guess. But mostly because yesterday I borrowed her car and left it with the seat pushed back, the radio tuned to a rock station, and with two empty Coke cans, but no petrol, in it. There was a bit of tension."

She laughed. "I bet." She trailed her hand through the feathery tops of a patch of cow parsley and felt distinctly cheerful.

They walked on in silence for a while, Jane beginning to see the point of strong shoes and long trousers, or at least thick socks. The path, uneven and stony, weaved its way through nettles and brambles. The walkers with sticks imperiously swatted

272

the nettles, or trampled them confidently underfoot. Jane, with her bare legs, had to pick her way with care.

When she had recognized Matthew, she'd thought he'd be embarrassed. After all, the last time they had met, he'd been drunk and amorous. But he was as breezy sober as he was drunk, and she was enjoying herself. When they came to a marshy patch that the seasoned ramblers splashed through in their water proof boots, he said, "I'll give you a piggy back." Turning his back to her, he bent his knees. "Jump on."

"But you've only got sneakers on yourself."

"I know. But I am macho man, and you are the damsel in distress, so jump up."

She looked ahead at the other walkers. Hoping none of them would turn around and see her, she put her hands onto his shoulders and jumped onto his back. Hooking his arms under her thighs he splashed through the soggy ground. When they were over the marshy patch, he ran on, bouncing her up and down as he might a child.

"Put me down, you idiot."

He obeyed, but said, "Maybe rambling's worth getting up for, after all."

By the end of the walk, Jane was pretty sure she was going to sleep with Matthew. As she lowered her body into her bath, and let the pine-scented water soothe her nettle-stung legs and tired feet, she was mentally justifying a break-out, considering, with pleasurable anticipation, the possibilities of ditching the conventional moral code of her upbringing.

She'd only ever had two lovers, Patrick and Rajiv, and she'd never before thought it possible for her to go in for uncommitted sex, just for the joy of it.

But Rajiv had said she was made for love, and it was true. She did find the celibate life unsatisfying, and she felt mature and confident enough for a carefree affair. An affair of the body, not the heart, she thought. Even a one-night stand if it came to that. Why not? She could not spend her life waiting for Mr. Right to turn up or for Patrick to come back.

But it wasn't a one-night stand. They first made love the following Saturday. Matthew had come, as promised, to help her dig her truckloads of compost, sand and topsoil into the clods of sticky Cotswold clay that her garden seemed to consist of. Jane had hired a mini-digger, and Matthew spent the morning operating it. At first he had enjoyed it, feeling her eyes on his bare chest and arms as he maneuverd the bucket to mix everything together, and then dug it into the cleared patches of garden that were to be the flowerbeds. But when she stopped watching, and disappeared into the paddock, it began to bore him. By one o'clock he felt ill done by.

Jane heard the machine stop, and then he was standing at the pony shed door, watching her applying creosote to the wooden manger.

"God, that stinks. What are you doing?" She looked up to see his lean outline against the light. She could not see his face, but he sounded cross.

She replied, "Trying to prevent Cherry eating her food trough. She chews worse than a puppy." She put the brush back in the pot and said, "Shall we have some lunch?"

It was a perfect day, with the leaves fully out but with the freshness of early summer. They sat on a rug in the orchard and had pizza and Pilsner Urquell. The combined effects of beer, warm sun and the closeness of Matthew made sex inevitable. When he twisted his long body around so he could lie with his head in her lap, it seemed the most natural thing in the world to bend her face over his and kiss him.

"Are you still sulking?" she said, then silenced his answer with her mouth, soft and half open, on his. Of course his arms came up around her head and pulled her down to him.

She didn't resist. Even when he turned his back to her, fiddling with a condom, and she had a moment for second thoughts. What she actually thought was: so he knew we'd do this too. Or maybe he always carries condoms in his pocket. Maybe all young men do. She had no idea how Matthew lived his life. She knew nothing of the world of a twenty-something student. And the truth was, she wasn't all that interested. She was, she admitted, after his body.

She knelt behind him and kissed his bare shoulders. He smelled healthy and slightly sweaty. She ran her lips down his spine, tiny exact kisses. She gently bit his neck, teasing, wanting to make him mad for her.

"Stop," he said. "Or I'll come before I've got this fucking thing on." His voice was lust-deep.

He was too quick. Eager, desperate, but with no thought for her. The urgency of his desire aroused her, but then it was all over.

They were still half dressed, his jeans around his ankles, her shorts and knickers off, but T-shirt intact. Pulling on her clothes, she looked at him, lying face-down on the rug, and said to his naked bottom, "How about we continue this indoors? What will my new neighbors think if they look over the fence?"

Later, when she was almost dressed and he was still sprawled on her bed, he asked, "You don't really care about the neighbors, do you?"

"Well, yes, I do." She spoke lightly, almost absently. "And so should you." She had one foot up on a chair, tying a double bow with her sneaker laces. As she answered, she swapped feet and jerked the laces of the second one tight, then tied them too. Matthew could not secure her gaze.

He said, "Why? I'm not ashamed of what we just did. Are you?"

Jane straightened up and crossed to the dressing-table. Running her brush through her hair, she answered, "No. But I'm not keen to get a reputation for cradle snatching. And you don't want to have to explain this little older-woman liaison to your parents or friends, do you?"

"I wouldn't care. I'm in love with you."

She dropped the brush back on the dressing-table and walked to the bed. She kissed his head, then rubbed his hair. "No, you aren't. But lust will do."

He twisted his head out of her reach and said, "Don't patronize me."

"Am I patronizing you? Poor Matt. I shall try not to. But do you think you could get that lovely bod of yours out of my bed and onto that expensive digger? It's costing a hundred pounds for the day, and so far it's not exactly earning its keep."

Matthew sprang out of bed, angry. "OK, OK. I get it. I'm to be workhorse or stud as her ladyship pleases. Fine." He pulled on his jeans, and set off barefoot into the garden. Jane, half sorry and half amused, picked up his sneakers and followed him.

"Here," she said, putting the shoes into the digger. "You'll need these or the pedals will hurt your feet. And I like your feet just the way they are." She kissed her fingers and laid them on his toes, first one foot, then the other.

His face, at first wooden, softened. She went on, "In India, you know, touching the feet is a sign of respect and submission."

TWENTY-FIVE

Matthew stayed on with Jane. His parents thought he had returned to Oxford, but he said term was almost over, and what the hell?

Jane went to work on Monday, and came home to find Matthew playing house, with the table laid and supper on the go. He had been shopping and they had Safeway's chicken Kiev, followed by some sort of butterscotch whip out of a packet. Upstairs she found a poem on her pillow:

> I'm swimming in your body
> Drowning, dying, falling
> Who says that sex is not love?
> That love is higher things?
> Sex with you is higher things.

The next day he made lasagne. It was a disaster—greasy, gray and undercooked—but Jane, not wanting to hurt him, ate it.

Another poem on the pillow:

> Jane. How can such a plain
> Name carry such magic?
> Who'd have guessed that inside
> that little word lives a world
> of heady wonder, drunken joy,
> and love, oh love.

Jane kept the poems. No one had written poetry to her before. She knew they were awful poems. But she was moved.

But by Wednesday, Jane wanted Matthew gone. The sex was good, and getting better, but she didn't want him about all the time. She couldn't live on student food, and his clothes were everywhere. And he liked the radio on full blast, tuned to some mindless station with a thrumming beat which made everything sound the same.

Perhaps sensing his shaky hold on anything more than her body, he made great efforts to please her, and spent his days working in the garden. Both the flower-beds were now weed free and dug to a fine tilth, and every nettle, dock and thistle in the paddock and orchard was sprayed.

On the fourth evening they went to the village pub. Jane felt Matthew's adoration must be obvious to everyone, and she found his spaniel-like gaze more irritating than flattering. She wanted to tell him to pull himself together. But once home, when he could barely let her through the door before his hands were all over her, up her skirt, down her front, his mouth demanding hers, she dissolved, and they made love for hours. First in the kitchen, half on her pine table, then more slowly in the living room, and once more when she woke him in the night.

But she had a bad conscience about him. That was the truth. She felt she'd seduced him out of caprice, and now, less than a week later, the boy was in love with her, or thought he was. She knew she was using him, for sex of course, but also to make her feel young and desirable and carefree; to keep loneliness at bay; to stop her thinking about babies; or Patrick; to stop her thinking at all.

She made up her mind to tell him to go back to Oxford or home to his parents, and to forget her. But she put off the moment. Anywhere near the bedroom was impossible: then she wanted him as much as he wanted her. And at all other times she was either irritated by him, when dismissing him would seem heartless, or sorry for him, when she couldn't do it. She told herself that she'd do it at the weekend, when there was more time for the inevitable *Sturm und Drang*.

On Thursday, at work, she had a telephone call from Patrick.

Her first jumping thought was that he must know about Matthew. Then, almost worse, that he'd guessed her part in buying the Third Man off him. Her mind raced as she framed answers to both accusations.

"Guess what?" he said. "I've bought a pub in your part of the world."

"What?" Relief flooded through her. She took a deep breath. "Good Lord. Where? What's it called?"

"It's in Stow on the Wold. And it's called the Farmer's Arms. Do you know it?"

Jane was so relieved not to be found out, she could not marshal her mind. She repeated, "The Farmer's Arms. Stow on the Wold." Then, pulling herself together, she said, "How wonderful, Patrick. And no, I don't know it. Tell me."

"It needs some fixing, but for once I can afford it. You know I sold the Third Man to some Indians? I got a good price too."

Jane felt another wave of anxiety. She did not want to lie to him, and she did not want to discuss the Third Man. She said nothing, and Patrick went on, "They've already turned it into a sort of up-market Balti house. It's doing good business. It's called East in the West."

"Yes, I know."

"Well, they paid up immediately, and I found this place, and here I am."

"Are you there now? In Stow?" The thought of him twenty miles away made her feel faint.

"Yes. Which is why I'm ringing. I thought you could give me supper?"

"Supper?" She knew she must sound like an idiot, but she could not give him supper. Matthew was there.

279

"Yes, supper. You could show me the cottage. And the pony. Sally told me you had a pony."

"Yes, I have. There are two of them. Cherry and Holly. Or, rather, they are not mine. I've borrowed them. They really belong to a friend. Or the sons of . . . Oh, never mind." She was gabbling. With an effort she pulled her mind to the essentials. "But look, I don't want you to see the cottage yet. It's not ready. Can't you give me supper in your new pub?"

Her mind was racing. At least if she met him in Stow, there was no chance of Matthew seeing them. But what would she tell Matthew? Patrick's voice penetrated her panic. "No, it's a building site. But we could go to the Brimstone and Treacle. I've no idea if it's any good but I should check out the opposition."

"OK. Lovely. What time?" The relief was intense. She thought, it's eighteen months since I left, yet anyone would think I was still married to him.

She put the handset down. Her hands were clammy with fright.

As she let herself into the cottage, she called out, "Matthew, are you there?" There was no reply, and for a second the hope that he was out cheered her. But when she saw the kitchen table set for two, with a bunch of buttercups in a glass jug in the middle of it, her heart sank. He must be upstairs.

She had telephoned him from the office, saying she had to meet a client for dinner. She resented lying to him (why could she not just tell him she was meeting her ex-husband?). But she had taken the easy way out, saving her energies for dinner with Patrick. She had intended to go straight from the office to Stow, and so avoid more lies and a possible scene. But then the desire to change into something nice, and her irritation with herself for being feeble, decided her on going home.

Matthew was lying on top of her white quilted bedspread, watching a video. He had not taken off his shoes and she could see a dusty smudge on the quilt. He'd brought the video recorder from the sitting room and it now occupied most of her dressing-table. Irritation doused her guilt. His large sprawling presence in her pretty bedroom offended her. Why couldn't he watch television in the sitting room?

He barely looked up in response to her "Hi, Matt." So. He was angry. Tough. She would not rise. She went through to the bathroom, pushed the bath plug into the hole with an angry shove, and turned both taps on full blast.

She went back into the bedroom and started flipping through the hangers in the wardrobe, looking for something re-laxed but flattering, like her old Jean Muir bottle green trousers and top. The long jacket, almost like a cardigan, with narrow wrists and raglan sleeves was country-casual and yet stylish. She'd wear an ivory shirt and her amber beads, and tan jodhpur boots.

She couldn't find the suit. Matt had drawn the curtains to better watch the telly, and there was too little light to distinguish dark green from black or navy. Exasperated, she swung around from the cupboard, strode to the door and punched on the ceiling light.

Looking up for the first time, Matt protested. "What's got into you?"

"I can't see, that's what. Why can't you watch it in the sitting room?"

"I prefer it here. The telly has a better picture." His eyes were back on the screen. It was a football movie and the sound of chanting crowds swelled so Jane had to raise her voice to be heard.

"Well, that's tough, but I'd like the use of my bedroom." She knew she sounded stuffy but did not care. She pulled the curtain cords with a rough jerk and bright summer light flooded the room.

Matthew looked at her, offended. He said, "OK. OK. Cool it, Jane. I'm going." He swung off the bed and made for the door.

Jane yanked the video lead out of the television. The screen

281

flashed and died, and the noise stopped in mid-crescendo. She called to Matthew's back, her voice hard, without affection, "Matt. Take the video, will you? I need the space on the dressing-table."

Matthew obeyed, but petulantly. As he lifted the machine, a trailing lead caught a bottle of cleansing milk and sent it, lid off and spilling, onto the carpet.

"Oh, *Matt!*" Jane cried, exasperated. Then as Matt made to put the machine down on the bed to free his hands to help, she said, "Oh, just *go*, Matt. Go. I'll clear it up." She bent down and scooped up the trailing lead and plug, and put them on top of the video, shoving the plug roughly between the machine and Matthew's chest. He hesitated, and she said again, "Matthew. Please *go*."

She turned away from him and grabbed a handful of tissues from the box on the dressing-table and crouched to mop up the cream, already soaking into the pale blue carpet. Damn. She picked up the bottle, found its cap, wiped them both and re-stored them, reunited, to the dressing-table. Then she went back to her hunt for the Jean Muir.

She had just found it when she heard Matthew shouting from downstairs. There was a note of triumph in his voice.

"Jane. Turn the bath off. It's coming through the ceiling."

TWENTY-SIX

Seeing Patrick so happy was a revelation. She hadn't seen him since that day in February in the Third Man, when his eyes had been dull with strain. Tonight, sitting in the corner of the Brimstone and Treacle, he looked younger and fitter than he had for years. They slipped into closeness, catching up on months of separation as if they were swapping notes on a day, or a week, apart.

Jane was surprised when Patrick brought up the subject of Stella. Patrick was not of the talk-it-through school. He thought there was something self-indulgent and mawkish about analyzing emotions. He belonged, thought Jane, to the onward-and-upward, get-a-grip school. Nevertheless, he now said, "The truth is, Jane, Stella had me completely enslaved. And yet when she finally blew it, I think the relief was greater than the pain." He smiled at her, shaking his head at his own folly, relieved at a dangerous crossing successfully navigated.

"Blew it?"

"Didn't you know? She was two-timing. I found out." Patrick was smiling, but Jane felt a rush of sympathy.

"So *was* she having an affair with Franco? The *Dispatch* said . . ."

Patrick shook his head, smiling. "No, but close. Franco's head chef. You know, the black guy, Oberon."

Jane frowned, and said, "Never met him. Doesn't sound very Italian."

"He's from Barbados. Looks like a body-builder. He's only twenty-two or so. But he's hot stuff. Alastair said Stella's affair with me was an aberration. So I guess she returned to type: good-looking young chefs with working-class credentials."

Patrick told Jane about the romp on the editor's sofa, and Stella's subsequent sacking. He told the story lightly, but Jane did not think it was funny. She asked, "And she's living with him now?"

"No." His smile was wry. "I don't think the macho chef-star was quite up to Stella full-time."

"Chef-star? I've never even heard of him."

"That's because you are a country mouse, out of the jetstream of who is in and who is out."

It's true, thought Jane, not minding. She used to take some secret pride in knowing who was up-and-coming in most things: in art, or film or food. Now she was barely interested. Was that the country, or middle age? Either way, she could bear it.

Patrick started to top up her glass from the bottle of Sauvignon Blanc, but she covered it with her hand, saying, "Better not. I'm so excited at seeing you I'm likely to throw it back like water. And we haven't got to supper yet."

Patrick returned to the subject of Oberon.

"He's got a TV series about Afro-Caribbean food. *Oberon's Magic.* Franco's furious because he thought it would be great PR for his restaurant, but had no idea Oberon was going to go all ethnic and soul-food. Now people come in demanding black-eyed peas and grits."

"Poor Franco." Jane laughed, remembering Franco's stagy Italian accent masking his East London upbringing, his snatches of Verdi, his bravura performance with the pepper mill, his pretense that his mama made the pasta in the basement.

Jane watched Patrick twirl his glass as only wine buffs did, by putting two fingers onto the base, one each side of the stem, and swirling the glass without lifting it from the table. She'd completely forgotten he did that. He'd said it was to keep his fingerprints off the bowl of the glass. But he always did it, even when he wasn't tasting.

284

He said, musing, "Poor Stella. She does so badly want to travel first class. I'm amazed she stuck me as long as she did." He said it tolerantly, even affectionately, and both tolerance and affection got to Jane.

She burst out, "Oh rot, Patrick! Poor Stella my foot. She's a selfish gold-digger, and presumably left when the gold ran out."

For a second Jane regretted this, fearing she'd hurt him. But he laughed.

"Oh, Jane, how sweetly loyal. But I don't think Stella's much to blame. I never really met the specification. Stella is made for a good time. And I turned out altogether too middle-aged."

Jane frowned. Those words again. Middle aged. The idea was ridiculous. Neither she nor Patrick was remotely middle-aged. She changed the subject, saying, "I'm starving. Can we eat?"

Patrick fetched a menu from the bar. "Not much competition here," he said, passing her the fake leather folder which held both menu and wine list. "Though the wine isn't bad."

Jane studied the menu. It was of the gammon-with-pineapple and Black-Forest-gateau persuasion. Much of it was deep-fried. Which was, Patrick said, a sure sign that it came in ready-made and frozen.

Jane read the description of steak au poivre aloud: "Best Aberdeen Angus sirloin, char-grilled to your liking and served with Chef's special sauce of French brandy, Jersey double cream, Moutarde de Meaux and fresh green peppercorns. Served with salad garnish, a selection of seasonal vegetables, and your choice of baked jacket potato with soured cream and chives, or home-fried chips."

Jane shuddered. "Could we have the steak without the sauce, do you think?" she asked.

"We could try."

The waitress, a bored young woman with silver fingernails and black lipstick, had trouble understanding.

"No sauce?"

Patrick nodded, but she wasn't looking at him. So he said, clearly, "That's right. Just plain grilled."

"Well done, medium or rare?"

"Rare."

"That's one without sauce and one rare," she said, writing on her order pad.

"No. Two without sauce and both rare." He spoke pleasantly, but slowly, as to a dim child.

Making alterations on her pad, she said, "Two steaks. Rare. No sauce." Then, without looking up, she said, "Chips or jacket?"

"Neither," said Patrick. "No potatoes, no vegetables and no garnish, but could we have a green salad on the side?"

"Two mixed salads on the side." She scribbled again.

"No. Two green salads."

"It's called mixed salad."

Feeling that if the girl would only look at him, he could make her understand, Patrick said, "Look, all we want is two steaks, grilled, rare, and two salads made of only lettuce. Do you think you could persuade the chef to do that?"

"Don't think so. The meat always comes with stuff on the plate. And the salad is already mixed together. Comes in bags."

"Well, could you try? And could we have a bottle of the Figeac?"

She looked blank. He translated: "A bottle of Number 11."

When the steaks arrived, the oval plates were brimming with chips, and the steaks were almost invisible under a pile of shredded lettuce, spring onion curls, and tomatoes cut into crowns. Two oval plates heaped with more shredded lettuce, watercress, chopped red cabbage, potato salad, sliced tomato and coleslaw followed. Patrick was about to remonstrate, but Jane said, "Forget it. Life's too short."

Patrick asked the waitress for two empty plates, a request she managed with indifference.

They tipped the chips onto one plate and the "salad garnish" onto the other, and tried the steaks. They were overcooked to a uniform gray, tough and dry.

Patrick signaled for the waitress, who came over, her hands in her apron pocket, her eyes aimlessly roving the room.

An upward jerk of her chin signaled her readiness to hear what he had to say.

Patrick tipped his steak so she could see its gray interior. "I'm afraid the steaks are overcooked. We asked for rare."

The waitress took her pencil out of her mouth and replied with a shrug, "I know. I don't know why he makes us ask how you like it cooked, because they always come like that. It's microwaving them first that does it."

"What? He microwaves the steaks? I don't believe it!" exclaimed Jane.

Defensive, the waitress said, "Well, we have to thaw them first or they'd be frozen in the middle."

Both Jane and Patrick burst out laughing, and Patrick said, "Look, you just take away all this"—he waved his hand over the plates of steak, salad and "garnish"—"and we'll just keep the chips." He looked at Jane, and added, "Unless you want your salad, darling?"

Jane was pleased about the "darling." She wondered if he'd realized he'd said it. She answered, "No. The dressing's horrible. All vinegar and sugar." She grinned across the table at him. "I think we may live to be glad we got the chips in spite of diligent efforts not to."

Jane, in spite of the dire food and depressing waitress, was feeling wonderful. The tensions of Matthew were far away, and Patrick was again so himself, so apparently unscathed by the misfortunes of the past two years, that she felt nothing but goodwill to the world. She'd have liked them to stay as they were forever, picking chips out of the dish and eating them in their fingers, elbows on the table.

The chips weren't bad. The chef—if there was such a thing as a chef in this place—at least knew how to lower precooked frozen chips into hot clean fat. They were crisp on the outside, squashy in the middle, dry and hot.

She thought how curious it was that eating chips with Patrick in a seedy pub should give her so much pleasure: sprinkling salt over the communal pile of chips; matching him chip for chip as their hands took turns at the plate; watching him dispatching them, two bites per chip.

She was very hungry, and the chips tasted delicious, every bit as delicious as a fancy meal could have tasted. And there was also something mellow and companionable about the process.

They ordered another portion of chips, and followed that with ice cream with hot chocolate sauce, which Patrick decreed the safest option on the menu. Their waitress elicited no surprise or curiosity at their meal, and only came to life when Patrick paid the bill in full and added a 15 percent tip.

For the first time she looked him in the eye. She said, "Don't you want to complain about the steaks?"

Patrick, amused, replied, "We already did. We sent them back, remember?"

"But I mean about the bill? We have to put every thing on and hope the customer will pay, even if they don't eat it, but if you complain I have to tell the boss and he might take it off."

"Well, no. You see I paid the lot in order to *avoid* having to meet the boss."

As they walked across the square, Jane said, "Well, so much for gastronomy. I haven't enjoyed a meal so much in years."

"Nor I," agreed Patrick. "It would have been cheap at twice the price."

The Farmer's Arms was a typical Cotswold stone building, with a gloomy public bar and a marginally posher one facing the street, a big "function room" at the back and a small walled garden behind. They picked their way through builders' rubble, Patrick explaining his plans for knocking the ground floor into a first-class bar-restaurant.

They went upstairs to the flat, and Jane felt a pang of nostalgia and affection at the familiar sight of Patrick's orderly life. There was almost no food in the kitchen, just a packet of coffee beans, a block of butter and some milk in the fridge, a jar of Oxford marmalade in the cupboard and a loaf of granary bread in the bread bin. Everything was neat and clean and where it should be. Patrick produced a bottle of The Macallan and they sat at the kitchen table. They resumed their conversation, talking as they had not done for years, about everything and anything.

"Alastair is rejoining me. Coming to work here. And Sandra."

"Really?" Jane thought how typical it was of Patrick to command the loyalty of the troops, even across a couple of counties.

"Mm. Sandra's husband is retired now and they fancy the country life. Also the Indians who bought the Third Man have dozens of relatives who are all bookkeepers and she thinks nepotism will win out sooner or later."

Jane opened her mouth to defend Gopal, then shut it quickly. She said, "And Alastair? I thought he was going to be a telly star too?"

Patrick shook his head. "He hates it. Says it's ninety percent hanging about and ten percent cooking, and they keep badgering him to go over the top—to say 'Yummy, yummy!' and 'Glorious, mate!' "

Jane shook her head, disbelief and sympathy mixed. Patrick said, "They wanted him to wear a chef's toque covered in bananas and grapes, but he stuck to his old skullcap. He can't wait till it's over. Which is in two weeks."

"But do you think he'll like the sleepy Cotswolds? Won't he miss the late-night drinking with the lads?"

"I guess he's growing up. He's a father now, and thinks the country would be good for the bairn. But mostly he's coming because I'm giving him a piece of the action. He'll be a partner."

"Oh, Patrick. That's marvelous. I hope he's pleased."

Patrick said, a little wryly, "Let's hope it will make him more interested in keeping the food costs down." Then he added, "Actually, he'll be fine. He learned a lot at the Third Man. I think this operation will be perfect for him. Posh enough to charge reasonable prices. Big enough for us to make money."

Jane learned more of Patrick's fortunes. Jonty had dropped his claim against Patrick for sacking him. He'd been arrrested on a drugs charge and would be lucky to get away with being done for possession. Patrick said, "Apparently he had enough heroin wraps in his flat to supply half Hammersmith."

Jane said, "What the hell is a heroin wrap?"

"Heroin cigarette. He'd gone from snorting coke to smoking heroin. Drugs are so cheap now it seems everyone under thirty is stuffed full of them every weekend. Makes one feel very old."

Jane shuddered, feeling glad for the first time in her life to be over thirty.

"Tell me something jollier," she said.

"Well, my jolliest news is that I've got back three quarters of the wine Silvino nicked."

"I don't believe it!" Jane jerked back in her chair, delighted, and spilled a splash of whiskey on the table. Patrick leaned forward and used the side of his hand to rub the drops into the pine surface. Jane watched his hand, so familiar and yet curiously new to her eyes, as he did it.

Patrick explained that the police had, by a complete stroke of luck, stumbled on his stock in a warehouse in Essex. Silvino had apparently done a deal with a known villain, and when the excise police had followed a van from Dover, they'd found the place stacked floor to ceiling with beer and wine smuggled in from France, plus the haul from Jane's.

Patrick said, "The joke was the crooks could not shift the really good stuff, the vintage port and the top growths—too risky, too traceable. So what I got back, which was only a third of the load, was worth two thirds of the money. They'd flogged the rest to pubs, according to the cops. I think they'd have preferred a truckload of Californian plonk."

Patrick leaned back, beaming at her. Jane thought, I hope

that smile is as much on my account as that of the regained wine.

"But that's marvelous, Patrick!"

"Isn't it?" He grinned at her. "A few first growths will provide a bit of classy decoration for the Farmer's Arms wine list. But I guess I'll have to sell most of it. Depends on what fixing the place costs."

He looks so open and relaxed, really happy, thought Jane. She asked, "What happened to Silvino? Did they catch him?"

"They did. Sad really. He'd fled to Orvieto, his home town, the fool. He must have made very little, and is now in jail, awaiting trial."

Patrick stood up and went to fill the water jug. He poured half an inch of whiskey into both their glasses and added the same amount of water, holding the glasses up to the light to judge the strength. Jane watched him, remembering with affection his insistence that 50/50 with tepid tap-water was the only way to drink malt whiskey.

The talk moved to Jane's new job, her addiction to early morning rides on Cherry, her plans to find a house to buy. As she talked, Jane wanted Patrick to understand what made her tick now, how different she felt about all sorts of things: how she was, so far unsuccessfully, teaching herself to make bread, how doing the church flowers, which she thought would be a joke at first and then a bore, pleased her. How she could peaceably pass a damp afternoon on her knees, weeding.

He watched her with a mixture of admiration and disbelief. In many ways she looked younger than before—less sophisticated, more open, less brittle. She had changed. And yet she hadn't.

"Why do you want to buy a house? What's wrong with the cottage?" he asked.

"I've only got it for two years. I'd like to be putting so much money and time into my own garden, not someone else's." But her unvoiced answer was: it's too small for children.

At 2:30 she stood up to go to the bathroom, and realized she was drunk. By walking quickly she managed not to stagger or lurch. For some reason it was important that she maintain her independence, and the air, at least, of sobriety. In the bathroom she looked into Patrick's small wooden shaving mirror and her face looked back at her, solemn, large-eyed, a little flushed, but, she thought, looking good.

She drank a mug of water in an attempt to dilute the alcohol, and splashed her face with cold water. Then she turned to find a towel. There wasn't one, so she buried her face in Patrick's toweling dressing-gown, hanging from a hook behind the door. It smelled of Patrick. Clean and wholesome, but definitely of him. She stood there, her forehead against the door, just breathing in. It was bliss. She wanted great lungfuls of the familiar, reassuring, faintly (but only faintly) erotic smell of Patrick.

A knock on the door, and Patrick's voice. "Jane, are you OK?"

She opened the door and said, "I'm fine. But you haven't got a towel so I used your dressing-gown. It smells nice." She gave him a wide happy smile and walked past him, saying, "Do you know it is two-thirty? I must go."

As Patrick leaned through her car window to kiss her good-bye, he said, "Jane, that is the happiest evening I've spent for a very long time."

"I know. Me too." The familiar smell of him, the dressing-gown smell of him but multiplied, triggered, for the first time that evening, the desire to touch him, to put her arms around his neck and respond to his brotherly kiss with ardour. But she didn't.

TWENTY-SEVEN

Jane turned off the main road down the hill to Broadwell. She knew she was well over the alcohol limit and shouldn't be driving. So she avoided the main roads and drove gently through the shallow ford in Broadwell. She rolled down the window and felt the cool night air on her face. She was half excited, half content. It was, she knew, partly to do with the coffee and the whiskey, but the phrase "sunlit uplands" blew into her head. Am I through the woods, and onto the sunlit uplands? Or was it just this country life? Where else could you drive through a stream with timeless Cotswold houses around a village green?

She took a great lungful of air, smelling mostly of newly cut grass and faintly of manure. She felt she was inhaling happiness.

Even giving Matthew his cards no longer seemed a problem. It would be grim, but it had to be done. If she was to have a lover, she needed a grown-up. Someone like Patrick. No, not like Patrick. Patrick.

Then suddenly she said aloud to herself, "What an idiot you are. Why don't you stop pussy-footing about and get him back? It is what you want, isn't it?"

She stopped the car at the top of a hill beyond the sleeping village of Barton on the Heath and got out. She sat on the warm bonnet. She needed to think this through before she got home.

It had taken her less than a week to decide that casual sex with a lusty young man was an empty business. Rajiv was wrong. Even the kind of transporting sex she'd had with him wasn't enough. What I want, she said, is so trite I've been refusing to admit it for years: I want a husband—my husband;

I want love and companionship and security; I want a baby, his baby; I want a house in the country, and I want a career—but not an all-consuming one; I want some balance in my life; I want time to ride Cherry, to garden, to learn to cook, to read the Barchester novels; to talk.

Jane sat on the cooling car bonnet for twenty minutes, thinking hard. And she made up her mind to end it with Matthew in the morning. Then she would ask Patrick to come back to her. The thought that he might reject her was terrible to her, and she pushed the possibility away. She was sure that he still loved her. And would forgive her—would understand the longing she'd had for something else, for something new and dangerous. He'd been through the Stella experience. He must understand.

But she would not tell him about Matthew. It was too shaming. One day, maybe, when it could be dismissed as the peccadillo of a lonely woman, she might tell him. But not now.

And the other thing she could not tell him was about her shares in the Third Man. Tomorrow she would ring Sriram and see if he would buy them, or find a buyer for them.

She got back into the car with her action-list clear in her lawyer's mind. First Matthew. Then Sriram. Then Patrick.

Matthew pushed aside the bowl and plate in front of him. Jane watched him lower his tousled head onto his arms. Sleepy and cross, he demanded, "Why this sudden insistence on breakfast? Last night you weren't too keen on dinner, I seem to recall."

"I know, Matt. I'm really sorry about that, but . . ."

He looked up, feeling his advantage. "I stayed up till two waiting for you. If I'm knackered now and don't want breakfast, that's why."

The whine in his voice helped Jane harden her resolve. She said, quite gently, "Matt, stop grumbling. I have to talk to you and you have to listen. Have some cereal. Or at least some coffee. We can talk over breakfast."

A flicker of anxiety crossed his face, and Jane felt for him. He was unshaven and rumpled and looked very young. She wanted to touch his hair, but didn't. She had to stay outside the range of his sexual pull.

He said, "If you want to talk, fine, go for it. I just don't want breakfast, that's all."

His sulkiness made it easier for her. She flicked the switch of the coffee-grinder and used the racket of grinding beans to give her time to steady her thoughts. When the noise stopped, she said, "Matt. I want you to leave today. I've made a mistake. And it's over."

Matthew, his face expressionless, stared at her.

She abandoned the attempt at normality, and put down the beaker of ground coffee. She said, speaking slowly, "The truth is this. Last night I had dinner with my ex-husband. And I realized I am still in love with him. I want to go back to him."

Matthew shook his head, as though to clear it, and swallowed. "But you were at the office last night, right? You said . . ."

"I know. I lied. I met Patrick. And that made me certain that you and I are a mistake."

Matthew jumped up and, leaning over the table, his hands gripping the edges of it, said, "That's not true. You and I are great together. You love me . . ."

Jane faced him across the table. She said, "I don't, Matt. I love sex with you. But the truth is that I seduced you because you've got a great body, and you are young and charming, and I was flattered at your attention. But I don't love you." She reached across the table, trying to take his hand.

He took a step back. "*You* seduced *me*?" He was shouting now.

Jane realized this was too much for his pride, and recanted. "Oh, Matt. I don't know. We both found each other attractive. But it isn't love, you know."

Matt pumped both hands down in furious denial. "Jesus,

295

how can you *say* that? What do you know about how I feel?"

"We have nothing in common, Matt. Think about it for one minute. And you'll see it is not love."

"It is. It is." His voice was strangled now.

Jane went on, feeling like an executioner, "You don't love me anymore than I love you, Matt. It's lust."

"You haven't seemed so disparaging about lust over the last few days."

She ignored the bitterness of his tone and answered, "I know. Sex with you is wonderful. You've made me feel so great, so young and desirable. But you see, I can't sleep with you if I'm to go back to Patrick. And that is what I want to do."

He said nothing. He stood there looking dazed, marooned in disbelief and misery.

"So you have to leave, Matt. Today. Before I come back from the office."

He straightened up, started to say something, and then swung out of the room and up the stairs, two at a time. She heard the bedroom door bang.

Jane poured herself a cup of coffee. She had to use both hands to keep the pot steady enough for the coffee to go into the cup.

She heard him banging cupboard doors upstairs and thought with relief that he was going to leave at once. If he did that, there would be less chance of a rearguard action. She didn't think she'd be able to go through another scene this evening.

She put the coffee cup into the sink and turned to clear the table. As she did so, she heard the front door ring. She walked through the house and swung open the door.

Patrick was standing on the step, almost hidden by an armful of peonies.

He held them out to her, but she didn't take them.

"Let's start again, Jane."

She did not hear what he said. All she could think of was Matt. Matt upstairs.

White with fear, she opened her mouth, but nothing came out. He went on, "I couldn't sleep at all last night. Darling, I love you as much now as I did the day we married. More. Much more. I spent all last evening gabbling away to try to hide the joy, the real unspeakable joy, of being with you again. How could we have allowed ourselves to get so far apart, when being together makes us so happy? You were happy last night, weren't you?"

"Patrick, I can't . . . Look, you can't come in." She stepped out onto the step, trying to push him away and close the front door behind her.

He didn't hear her and seemed oblivious of her panic. He said, speaking fast and happily, "I got up at six and picked these, whatever they are. My predecessors must have been nuts about them. The garden is full of them. I'd have come over then, but thought I'd frighten you banging on the door so early."

Jane now put both hands on Patrick's arms, each side of the peonies and said, "Patrick. Please, I can't explain. But I will. But please. You can't come in yet."

"Oh, darling Jane. I am not prepared to wait until you've had the Designer's Guild turn the cottage into something out of *House and Garden*. I love you, don't you understand, and we can't both stand here forever. These bloody flowers weigh a ton. So stop trying to shut the door and let me in." And he stepped past her into the house.

Jane, living a nightmare, followed him. He went by instinct into the kitchen, and dumped the peonies in the sink. There was no sound from upstairs.

A tiny flicker of hope that she might just get him out of the house without him finding out about Matthew died as she realized he was looking at the table. It was unmistakably laid for two. His eyes met hers, and there was a plea in them. He was asking her to tell him that it was nothing. That her breakfast companion was Sally, or Lucy, or her mother.

Her expression, dismay, fear, guilt, gave him his answer, but just to confirm it, Matthew banged downstairs and into the kitchen. He was still wearing Jane's kimono, one that Patrick had given her on their first anniversary.

Jane, desperate for salvage, said, "Matthew, this is my husband, Patrick, who I was telling you about this morning. I want to go back—"

Matthew interrupted, "And I am her young stud. All services performed to order. Pleased to meet you."

Patrick walked out, shutting the front door carefully behind him.

TWENTY-EIGHT

Patrick would not return her calls, but at lunchtime sent her a fax at her office:

> *I apologize for making a complete ass of myself. Too much malt whiskey and no sleep leads to foolish ideas. See you around. Patrick.*

Jane felt her stomach contract with anguish. But after an hour, hope, small at first but growing, began to fill some of the spaces not occupied by misery and fear. Looking as dispassionately as she could at the evidence, she thought it might yet go her way.

Matthew, having triumphed in his brief moment of cruelty, had burst into tears. Jane was at first too wretched herself, and too angry with him, to pay much heed. But she'd ended by trying to comfort him, and eventually he had dressed, and left.

But her real source of optimism was that she now knew that Patrick still loved her. And she also now knew that she loved him. As soon as she got to the office she faxed the Farmer's Arms, not caring if the builders read it.

> *Patrick. It has taken me nearly 2 years to realize that I left the man I love, and who was offering me everything I want: love, children, and ever after. Last night I resolved to clean up my life, then try to woo you back. You arrived during the clean up. Please come back.*

All day she expected him to ring, but he didn't. She stayed at her desk through lunchtime and delayed leaving the office until 6:30, then drove home, cowed by the thought of the coming weekend, alone.

Once home, she occupied her mind with clearing away the last vestiges of Matthew. Upstairs she binned a pair of split sneakers and a squashed toothpaste tube. She made the bed, changing the fitted sheet and duvet cover, all four pillowslips and the bathroom towels. At her dressing-table she picked up a can of Matt's Lynx deodorant and dropped it in the waste basket. As she did so her eye caught the slips of paper tucked under her hair drier. Matthew's poems.

She picked them up with the intention of binning them, then hesitated. She read them both through, then pushed them quickly into the box of Indian bangles she'd bought in Varanasi. Tucked down the back of the box was the handmade postcard of the orange-legged bird, the child's drawing she'd bought in Chittorgarh. She stood for a moment, thinking how she'd vowed never to forget Princess Padmini's palace. But now her whole Indian adventure seemed far away. She shook her head, a little sadly, and bent to open the bottom drawer of the dressing-table. She pulled out the orange sari. It was folded, but the slithery cotton came undone as she lifted it, and she draped it over her shoulder, feeling its cool sheen brush her cheek. She picked up the little statue of Ganesh, which had cast its sardonic eye on all her dressing-table titivations since she'd brought it back from India. She carried it and the bangle box to the chest on the landing.

As she knelt by the chest, refolding the sari and finding room among the family memorabilia of her school reports, her mother's wedding veil and Tom's first booties, she thought, why do I want to keep these things if I want to clear the way for an assault on Patrick?

Because I would not have missed either love affair, that's why, she thought. I'm glad they happened. And a grown woman is bound to have a few secrets. Such as that I own shares in a Balti house that used to be the Third Man. She'd spoken to Sriram, and he'd said he'd find her a buyer among his or Gopal's many relatives, but it would take a month or two. For the moment, she was still part-owner of East in the West.

The thought made her slightly uneasy, and she went back to sorting the chest. She picked out a book, thinking books should be on bookshelves, then remembered why she'd thought it important to safeguard: it was a copy of Browning's poems inscribed to her mother from her father. She opened it and read, in his familiar sloping hand: "Grow old along with me, the best is yet to be." It felt like an omen. Oh, I hope so, she said to herself. I do hope so.

Jane went downstairs. A copy of *Private Eye* and the video of *Fever Pitch* were all the evidence of Matt in the sitting room. She chucked both.

In the kitchen she threw away the rest of the packet of butterscotch whip and a packet of cheap frozen pizzas. By 8:30 she had nothing to do, and the temptation to ring the Farmer's Arms was too much for her.

She felt physically sick as the steady rings stretched to ten, eleven, twelve. No reply. And Patrick had not set the answering machine. She felt almost relieved. Though she wanted Patrick back so badly, she felt too overwrought for anymore scenes. She put the telephone down.

She could not concentrate on the television or on her book—*Ayala's Angel*, a Trollope she had found unputdownable before.

She was very tired. She'd not got to bed till 3:30, and the day had been emotionally exhausting. But she knew she would not sleep.

She wasn't hungry, and she was still too hung-over from the night before to want a drink. What she felt like, she thought, was a tray of tea and a lump of good bread. But the only bread was a half-packet of white sliced—the kind that Matthew liked and she could only stand toasted.

301

She would make some bread. And while it was in the oven, she'd have a bath and get ready for bed. Then she'd carry the tray up to her solitary cot with the nice clean sheets and pig out on newly baked bread. The thought cheered her. It was something to do. It would stop her thinking.

To date, her efforts at bread-making had not been a triumph. She'd started with a packet pizza-dough mix, and though the pizza base had turned out more tough than crisp, she'd enjoyed the process. Her next attempt was wholemeal bread with stoneground flour and that had been horrible: doughy with an unpleasant bitter flavor, and so heavy it would have held a swing-door open. Even Cherry would not eat it: Jane ground it to crumbs in the liquidizer, and the pony nuzzled the bucket and blew through her nostrils, but ate none of it. It ended on the compost heap.

For Attempt Three she would try the recipe in a dog-eared little book called *Use Your Loaf*. She'd bought it for 50p from the secondhand rack outside the Oxfam shop. She got it down and opened it at "Baking Bread." She read:

Any fool can make bread. It is easier, and much more pleasant, than most of the duties of the housewife, like making beds, mending socks, or washing nappies.

She followed the instructions: mixing white bread flour, salt and instant yeast (the booklet, published in 1975, assumed fresh yeast, but the lad in the supermarket had looked at her in disbelief) in one bowl, and warm water, beaten egg and melted butter in another.

Most recipes will tell you to add the liquid to the dry ingredients. But it is easier the other way round. Just toss in handfuls of flour until the mixture is too stiff to stir. Then tip it out onto a floured surface and knead it, adding more flour if it sticks.

302

Jane soon discovered that if she interlocked her fingers, and rubbed them together, the sticky dough worked itself into little rolls and flakes and fell off her fingers—like "washing" your hands in dry sand when gardening.

The secret of kneading is to do it with a will. Punch it, pull it, push it, lambast it, stretch it, throw it, slap it, do whatever you like. But the idea is to work it, not play with it.

Jane started awkwardly, pummeling the dough with more aggression than skill. The exertion did not stop her mind churning. As she pulled and punched, she thought how crass, how stupid, how blind she'd been. How badly she had behaved to everyone. She had left Patrick for no good reason. She had made Rajiv leave his fiancée and come to London, where he was miserable. She had abandoned Chalkers just when they'd finally given her an equity partnership. She'd seduced and used poor Matthew, and hurt him.

Her face set with effort and unhappiness, she twisted and thumped the dough. She imagined hitting a punch bag in a gym would feel like this. She had the idea that the dough had somehow to be beaten into shape, mangled into submission, and she mauled it as she might an enemy. She felt a drop of water land with a tiny splash on the back of her hand. She was crying, and kneading her tears into the dough.

But gradually she got the hang of it and her expression softened as the effort tired her and she was gentled by the steady rhythm of her kneading. She began to regard the dough with more friendliness: as a partner in this process.

After a few minutes she stopped, went through to the sitting room and started the CD player. Beethoven's Pastoral. That would do. She didn't want to change the CD with floury fingers. She turned up the volume so she could hear it in the kitchen and went back to her kneading.

As the music swelled and swooped, Jane kneaded the

dough. She was into the rhythm of it and felt she could go on forever.

She was enjoying the steady cycle of push, gather up, turn, and push again. She allowed the regular movements, and the soft and satisfying feel of the dough to soothe her. She found herself thinking that she would survive without Patrick, and she felt a flicker of pride: she was going to be all right, Patrick or no Patrick.

Yet she knew if she lost him now it would be the tragedy of her life. But she thought he would come back. And if he did, this time she'd stick to him for good. Patrick might not be the lover that Rajiv was, or as adoring as young Matthew, but he was worth a dozen of either of them. He was humorous and hardworking, strong and grown-up. He was incapable of mean-mindedness. He was completely without vanity. He was logical and intelligent but never boring. She shook her head in tired disbelief, marveling that she could ever have left him.

She thought, I really do love him and, what's more, I know that I love him. As much, she thought, as my mother loved Dad. Or he loved her. A love for life.

She remembered something she had not thought of for years: the words of a letter her father had written to her mother. She could remember every word, as though she had learned them, like a poem. She had found the note when helping her mother clear her father's sickroom after his death, and the depth of her father's emotion had amazed her. He was not a demonstrative man, and she had not realized that he loved her mother so. More than that, she had not thought that he might love her mother more than he loved her. It had hurt.

The note was in the book her mother had been reading aloud to him. It had been written on the eve of the operation which had removed half his gut, and left him with a colostomy bag, an operation he feared he might not survive.

My darling,
You know, and I know, what you have meant to me. First

there was you, and still there is you and steady for 40 years
you have been my blessing, my gift, my pride, my love, my
life. Thank you, my dearest heart. First and most for you. Then
for dear confident gallant Tom, and for lovable, sweet, clever
Jane, but beyond and above everything in my life, thank you
for you.

She realized now, and for the first time, how very like her
father Patrick was: the same loyalty, the same lack of ego, the
same pride in her, the same high standards. The same deep, but
seldom voiced, emotion. Why had she never seen it before?
Maybe, she thought, I tried to leave him because I did not want
to be married to my father.

Or could not live up to a marriage like my parents'. The
perfect marriage. Where the couple count more than the kids.

Maybe it wasn't quite so bloody perfect, she thought. Who
knows what shadowy unexpressed aches lie in other people's
hearts? And anyway, who says there is only one model of a
happy marriage?

Then she shrugged, thinking, stuff the psychobabble. I want
to be married to Patrick, whoever he's like, for whatever kind of
marriage.

When you are hot and sweaty and the dough is elastic, cool
and silky, it's kneaded.

She felt the ball of dough with the back of her wrist. It was
cool. She grabbed one end of it and held it up, wobbling her
hand back and forth. The dough stretched down, reaching for
the table, dangling and elastic.

Dump the dough back in its bowl, and cover with a damp
floured cloth. If planning on baking it soon, leave it somewhere
cozy to rise—in the airing cupboard, next to the Aga, near

the boiler. If you want to go to bed, put it in a refrigerator
overnight, and plan on hot fresh rolls for breakfast.

All at once, and unexpectedly, Jane was utterly exhausted.
She couldn't face anymore bread-making, or even clearing up.
She put the dough in the bowl, decided that a Safeway bag
would do instead of a floured cloth, took a shelf out of the fridge
to make room, and put the bowl into the fridge.

She went like a zombie through the house, forcing herself to
do the essentials: putting a protesting Benny into the kitchen,
locking the back door, turning off the CD player. She was too
tired to make the promised tray of tea and blundered upstairs,
her legs leaden. She pulled off her clothes, flinging them on a
chair, and crawled, unwashed and teeth unbrushed, between the
sheets. She put her face against the cool pillow and shut her eyes.
At once she felt the blissful slide into certain sleep.

She woke early, sunlight in her eyes. She sat up, confused. She
had not closed the curtains the night before. She'd been, she
remembered, blind with exhaustion. She fumbled for her watch.
Six-thirty. She wriggled into the dark of the bed and tried to go
back to sleep. She must not think. She must not remember that
Patrick had not telephoned all yesterday. And had not returned
her calls. She must not think of him at all. She'd go back to sleep.

But she couldn't. She would ring Patrick. Too early. She
would get up and go for a ride. It was Saturday, so if she waited
till nine or so, maybe Nat would come with her. Or she could
go to the garden center and spend her way to cheerfulness.

She remembered her father's maddening habit of quoting
Kipling at her when she was sulky:

> The cure for this ill
> Is not to sit still
> Or frowst with a book by the fire,
> But to take a large hoe,

And a shovel also,
And dig till you gently perspire.

OK. So she would dig. She'd make a start on the asparagus
bed, double-digging a trench. Or, maybe she would tackle the
ivy under the yew hedge. She'd paint all the leaves with Tum-
bleweed. Killing things will probably cheer me up, she thought
with savagery.

She washed her hair under the shower, and, longing for a
cup of tea, looked around for her kimono. Then she remembered
that in the great post-Matthew clearup (was that only last night?)
she'd put it in the washing-machine with the towels. She pulled
on a long yellow T-shirt, pushed her feet into espadrilles, and
went down to the kitchen. She opened the fridge for the milk
and saw the Safeway bag over the bowl of dough. She took it
out and lifted off the bag. Inside was a perfect puffed-up ball of
dough, grown to twice its size, and filling the bowl. It smelled
delicious, yeasty and fresh. She pressed it with her knuckles and
that section of the dough collapsed, misshapen.

Why not? she thought. Hot fresh rolls for breakfast, the recipe had said.

While the tea brewed she walked quickly around the house,
opening the sitting room curtains, collecting the milk from the
front step. Being normal. Being alone and independent. She fed
Benny, then drank her tea leaning against the Aga.

She kneaded the dough again as instructed, and divided it
into three. She loved the smooth and tender feel of it. She shaped
two of the lumps into loaves, putting one into her only bread tin
and the other on a baking sheet. Then she rolled the third piece of
dough into eight more or less even balls. She hoped they would
not take long to rise. She was starving.

It was a glorious day. The early sun shone on Benny's coat,
which crackled with static as she stroked him. She wandered
around the garden, her cat in her arms, longing with a physical
aching for Patrick, and yet thinking how basically resilient she

was. She was unhappy, but she would be fine. Life would go on. It was good to be able to wander around like this, half-dressed, with no one's needs to consider. She liked her work, she loved the country. She had great friends in the Applebys. She would learn to cook. It was OK. She was OK. Only, only, if Patrick would return, she would love him so.

She walked around the side of the cottage to the front, to see if the newspaper had arrived. As she glanced down the lane, her heart leapt. She stopped dead. Patrick's car, her old 300SL, was parked outside her gate.

There was no one in the car. She looked about wildly, and there, sitting on her doorstep, beside another giant-size bunch of peonies, was Patrick. He looked steadily at her, then picked up the flowers and sloped to his feet. He said, "Take two. Action." He held them out to her, and continued, "Jane Chambers, love of my life and wife of my bosom, could we start again, do you think?"

She said nothing, just stood there, legs weak as water.

He said, "I'd have come back at once, but I went straight to London, and only saw your fax at midnight. I've been up picking these things since dawn again."

She ran at him then, letting the cat go, her arms rising, out and up. He just had time to drop the peonies as she rocketed into his chest. She felt the roughness of his jacket against her cheek, and her throat hurt. She took a shuddering breath which turned into a stifled sob.

Holding her very tight, he said, "Your hair's wet, and you smell of shampoo."

She was trying to say something, but he could not hear. He held her away so he could see her face.

"What did you say, my darling?"

"I said, 'There can't be anymore peonies in that garden.'" They both looked down at the flowers, lying scattered around their feet and over the steps.

"Is that what they are? Peonies? No, I've had the lot. But I won't need anymore, will I?"

She shook her head, and again said something he could not catch.

"Say it again." His arms seemed to wrap her up completely. She was aware of her nakedness under her T-shirt, and she wondered if he could feel that too. But mostly what she felt was safe. Safe at last. Home.

She said, "I'm making bread rolls for breakfast." She was crying and smiling, proud of the fact. "Can you believe it?"